BUSINESSW

They're usu...
or pla...
Now, they and th... g...eous grooms-to-be
are about to take centre stage!

Prepare to be dazzled by exotic destinations
and wedding bells in:

A WEDDING AT LEOPARD TREE LODGE
by Liz Fielding

THREE TIMES A BRIDESMAID...
by Nicola Marsh

He got out first, offered her his hand as if she was visiting royalty, and walked her across to a point where there was a clear view of the mighty Zambezi, pouring into the gorge in a dizzying rush.

Everywhere was overgrown with ferns and tropical plants, dripping with moisture in the steamy atmosphere.

'Will you kiss me, Gideon?'

Would he kiss her?

Did she have any idea what she was asking?

Would he kiss her? In a heartbeat.

Should he?

'Be still,' he said. Then again as, startled, she looked up at him and he captured her face between his hands, lowered his lips to hers. 'Be still…'

A WEDDING AT LEOPARD TREE LODGE

BY
LIZ FIELDING

First published in Great Britain 2010
Harlequin Mills & Boon Limited,
Eton House, 18-24 Paradise Road, Richmond, Surrey TW9 1SR

© Liz Fielding 2010

ISBN: 978 0 263 87667 3

Harlequin Mills & Boon policy is to use papers that are natural, renewable and recyclable products and made from wood grown in sustainable forests. The logging and manufacturing process conform to the legal environmental regulations of the country of origin.

Printed and bound in Spain
by Litografia Rosés, S.A., Barcelona

Liz Fielding was born with itchy feet. She made it to Zambia before her twenty-first birthday and, gathering her own special hero and a couple of children on the way, lived in Botswana, Kenya and Bahrain—with pauses for sightseeing pretty much everywhere in between. She finally came to a full stop in a tiny Welsh village cradled by misty hills, and these days mostly leaves her pen to do the travelling. When she's not sorting out the lives and loves of her characters she potters in the garden, reads her favourite authors, and spends a lot of time wondering 'What if…?' For news of upcoming books—and to sign up for her occasional newsletter—visit Liz's website at www.lizfielding.com

CHAPTER ONE

Destination weddings offer up a host of opportunities for a ceremony with a differ-ence…

—*The Perfect Wedding* by Serafina March

'WHERE?'

Josie Fowler wasn't sure which stunned her most. The location of the wedding which, despite endless media speculation, had been the best kept secret of the year, or the fact that Marji Hayes, editor of *Celebrity* magazine, was sharing it with her.

'Botswana,' Marji repeated, practically whis-pering, as if afraid that her line might be bugged. If it was, whispering wouldn't help. 'I called Sylvie. I had hoped…' Her voice trailed off.

'Yes?' Josie prompted as she used one finger to tap 'Botswana' into the search engine of her computer. Silly question. She knew exactly what Marji had hoped. That the aristocratic Sylvie Duchamps Smith would rush to pick up the pieces of the most talked about wedding of the year. Sylvie, however, was too busy enjoying her new baby daughter to pull Marji's wedding irons out of the fire.

'I realise that she's still officially on maternity leave, but I had hoped that for something this big…'

Josie waited, well aware that not even a royal wedding would have tempted Sylvie away from her new husband, her new baby. Trying to contain a frisson of excitement as she realised what this call actually meant.

'When I called, she explained that she's made you her partner. That weddings are now solely your responsibility.' She couldn't quite keep the disbelief out of her voice.

Marji was not alone in that. There had been an absolute forest of raised eyebrows in the business when Sylvie had employed a girl she'd found working in a hotel scullery as her assistant.

They'd got over it. After all, she was just a gofer. Someone to run around, do the dirty work. And she'd proved herself, become accepted as a capable coordinator, someone who could be relied on, who didn't flap in a crisis. A couple of bigger events organisers had even tried to tempt her away from Sylvie with more money, a fancy title.

But clearly the idea of her delivering a design from start to finish was going to take some swallowing.

She'd warned Sylvie how it would be and she'd been right. She'd been a partner for three months now and while they had plenty of work to keep them busy, all of it pre-dated her partnership.

'You're very young for such responsibility, Josie,' Marji suggested, with just enough suggestion of laughter to let her know that she wasn't supposed to take offence. 'So very…eccentric in your appearance.'

She didn't deny it. She was twenty-five. Young in years to be a partner in an events company but as old as the hills in other ways. And if her clothes, the purple streaks in her lion's mane hair, were not conventional, they were as much a part of her image as Sylvie's classic suits and pearls.

'Sylvie was nineteen when she launched SDS Events,' she reminded Marji. Alone, with no money, nowhere to live. All she'd known was how to throw a damn good party.

Despite their very different backgrounds, they'd had that nothingness in common and Sylvie had given her a chance when most people would have taken one look and taken a step back. Two steps if they'd known what Sylvie knew about her.

But they had worked well together. Sylvie had wooed clients with her aristocratic background, her elegance, while she was the tough working class girl who knew how to get things done on the ground. An asset who could cope with difficult locations, drunken guests—and staff; capable of stopping a potential fight with a look. And in the process she'd absorbed Sylvie's sense of style almost by osmosis. On the outside she might still look like the girl Sylvie had, against all the odds, given a chance. But she'd grabbed that opportunity with all her heart, studied design, business, marketing, and on the inside she was a different woman.

'And if I changed my appearance no one would recognise me,' she added, and earned herself another of those patronising little laughs.

'Well, yes.' Then, 'Of course there's no design involved in this job. All that was done weeks ago and at this late stage…'

In other words it was a skivvy job and no one with a 'name' was prepared to take it on. The wretched woman couldn't have tried any harder to make her feel like the scrapings at the bottom of the barrel and Josie had to fight the urge to tell her to take her wedding and stick it.

Catching her lower lip between her teeth, she took a deep breath; she still had quite a way to go to attain Sylvie's style and grace, but this was too important to mess up.

With this wedding under her belt—even in the skivvy role—she could paint herself purple to match her hair and clients would still be scrambling to book her to plan their weddings.

Not as a stand-in for Sylvie, but for herself.

But she'd had enough with the I-really-wish-I-didn't-have-to-do-this delaying tactics.

'Can we get on, Marji? I have a client appointment in ten minutes,' she said and Emma, her newly appointed assistant, who was busy filling in details on one of the event plans that lined the walls of her small office, glanced up in surprise, as well she might since her diary was empty.

'Of course.' Then, 'I'm sure I don't have to impress upon you the need for the utmost confidentiality,' she said, making it absolutely clear in her lemon-sucking voice that she did.

Not true.

Josie had seen the build-up to the wedding of Tal Newman, one of the world's most highly paid footballers, to Crystal Blaize. The ferocious bidding war against all-comers had cost *Celebrity* a fortune—money that the couple were using to set up a charitable trust—and the magazine was milking it for all it was worth. Hyping up the secrecy of the location was all part of that. It also helped keep rival publications from planting someone on the inside to deliver the skinny on who behaved badly and grab illicit photos so that they could run spoilers.

If she let slip the location, SDS might as well shut up shop.

'My lips are sealed,' she said. 'I'm not even sure where Botswana is,' she lied. According to the screen in front of her, it was a 'tranquil' and 'peaceful' landlocked country in southern Africa.

Marji clucked at her ignorance. 'It's a very now destination, Josie.'

'Is it? That information seems to have passed me by.' But then she didn't spend her life obsessing over the latest fads of celebrities.

'And Crystal is such an animal-lover.'

Animals? In Africa?

'So that would be… Elephants? Lions?' No, smaller… 'Monkeys?'

'All of those, of course. But the real stars will be the leopards.'

Even with his underdeveloped human sense of smell, Gideon McGrath knew Leopard Tree Lodge was close long before the four-by-four pulled into the compound. There was a sweet, fresh green scent from the grass that reached out across the sparse bush that drew the animals from across the Kalahari, especially now as they neared the end of the dry season.

Once his pace had quickened too, his heart beating with excitement as he came to the river-bank that he had claimed as his own.

The driver who'd picked him up from the airstrip pulled into the shaded yard and he sat for a moment, gathering himself for the effort of moving.

'*Dumela, Rra!* It is good to see you!'

'Francis!'

He clasped the hand of the man who emerged from the shadows to greet him with a broad smile of welcome.

'It has been a very long time, *Rra*, but we always hoped you'd come…' His smile quickly became concern. 'You are hurt?'

'It's nothing,' he said, catching his breath as he climbed down. 'I'm a bit stiff, that's all. Too many days travelling. How is your family?' he asked, not wanting to think about the tight, agonising pain in his lower back. Or its cause.

'They are good. If you have time, they will be pleased to see you.'

'I have some books for your children,' Gideon said, turning to take his bag from the back seat.

He spent half his life on the move and travelled light but, as he tried to lift it, it felt like lead.

'Leopards?' Josie repeated. 'Aren't they incredibly dangerous?'

'Oh, these are just cubs. A local man has raised a couple of orphans and he's bringing them along on the day. All you'll have to do is tie ribbons around their necks.'

'Oh, well, that's all right then.' Maybe. She had a cat and even when Cleo was a kitten her claws were needle-sharp...

'The wedding is going to be held at Leopard Tree Lodge, you see?' Marji told her. 'It's a fabulous game-viewing lodge. Utter luxury in the wilderness. To be honest, I totally envy you the opportunity to spend time there.'

'Well, golly,' she said, as if she, too, couldn't believe her luck.

'You won't even have to leave your private deck to view the big game. None of that racketing about in a four-wheel drive getting covered in dust. You can simply sit in your own private plunge pool and watch elephants cavorting below you in an oxbow lake while you sip a glass of chilled bubbly.'

'Well, that's a relief,' Josie replied wryly, recognising a quote from a tourist brochure when she heard one. Marji might believe that she was offering her a luxury, all expenses paid holiday; she knew that once on site she wouldn't have a minute to spare to draw breath, let alone dally in a plunge pool admiring the view.

Relaxation in the run-up to a wedding was the sole privilege of the bride and good luck to her. Although, with half a dozen issues of *Celebrity* to fill with pictures, even she wasn't going to have a lot of down time before, or during, the big day.

For the person charged with the responsibility of ensuring that everything ran smoothly it was going to be a very hard day at the office, although in this instance it wouldn't be her own calm, ordered space, where everything she needed was no more than a phone call away.

As she knew from experience, even the best organised weddings had the potential for last minute disasters and in the wilds of Botswana there would be none of the backup services she was usually able to call on in an emergency.

And it would take more than a look to stop a leopard disturbing the party. Even a baby leopard.

'There's nothing like being covered in dust to put a crimp in your day,' she added as, with the 'where' dealt with, she confronted a rather more pressing problem.

Unless the word 'wilderness' was simply travel brochure hyperbole—and the reference to elephants sloshing about in the river at her feet suggested otherwise—there wasn't going to be an international airport handy.

'How is everyone going to get there?'

'We've booked an air charter company to handle all the local transport,' Marji assured her. 'You don't have to worry about that—'

'I worry about everything, Marji.' Including the proximity of elephants. And the damage potential of a pair of overexcited leopard cubs. 'It's why SDS weddings run so smoothly.'

'Well, quite. If Sylvie's company wasn't so highly thought of we wouldn't be having this conversation.' She paused, her train of thought disrupted. 'Where was I?'

'Transport?' Josie prompted, doing her best to keep a lid on her rising irritation.

'Oh, yes. Serafina was due to fly out first thing tomorrow. You heard what happened?'

The official version was that Serafina March, society wedding 'designer'—nothing as common as 'planner' for her—and self-proclaimed 'wedding queen' who had been given the awesome responsibility of planning this event, had been struck down by a virus.

Insider gossip had it that Crystal had thrown a strop, declaring that she'd rather get married in a sack at the local register office than put up with another moment with 'that snooty cow' looking down her nose at her.

Having been looked down on by Serafina herself on more than one occasion, Josie knew exactly how she felt.

'How is Serafina?'

'Recovering. It's just a shame she can't be there, especially when she's put her heart and soul into this wedding.' Then, having got that off her chest, she proceeded briskly, 'The bride's party will be flying out the following day but Tal has a number of official engagements in the capital so he and Crystal won't arrive until the next evening. Plenty of time for you to run through everything before they arrive so that you can iron out any last minute snags.'

'Since there's so little to do, maybe I could leave it until the day after tomorrow?' Josie suggested, unable to help herself.

'Better safe than sorry. This is going to be a fairly intimate wedding. Leopard Tree Lodge is a small and exclusive safari camp, however, so we've chartered a river boat to accommodate the overflow.'

Wilderness, water and wild animals—three things guaranteed to send shivers down the spine of the average event planner. And there was also the word 'camp'—not exactly reassuring.

No matter how 'luxurious' the brochure declared it to be, a tent was still a tent.

When she didn't rush to exclaim with excitement, gush at the honour being bestowed on her, Marji said, 'All the hard work has been done, Josie.'

All the interesting work.

The planning. The design. Choosing food, music, clothes, colour scheme, flowers. The shopping trips with a bride whose credit never ran out.

'You just need me to ensure that everything runs smoothly,' Josie said.

'Uh-oh!' Emma's eyebrows hit her hairline as she picked up on the edge she hadn't been able to keep out of her voice, but being patronised by Marji Hayes really was more than flesh and blood could stand.

'Absolutely. Serafina's organised everything down to the last detail.' The wretched woman had a skin as thick as a rhinoceros. It would take more than an 'edge'; it would take a damn great axe to make an impression. 'I just need someone to ensure her design is carried through. Check that all her wonderful detail is in place so that our photographers can get great shots for the series of features we have planned. Exactly what you'd do for Sylvie.'

'And ensure that the bride and groom have their perfect day?' she offered, unable to stop herself from reminding Marji that this was about more than a skirmish in her circulation war with the growing number of lifestyle magazines on the market.

'What? Oh, yes,' she said dismissively. Then, 'We're running out of time on this, Josie. I'll email the flight details and courier the files over to your office. You can read them on the plane.'

It was the opportunity of a lifetime but she'd been insulted, subtly and not so subtly, so many times in the last ten minutes that she refused to do what was expected and simply roll over.

'To be honest,' she said, her voice growing softer as her fingers did to her hair what she wanted to do to Marji, 'with so little to do, I don't understand why you need me at all. Surely one of your own staff could handle it?' She didn't wait for an answer but added, 'Better still, why don't you go yourself? Once you've dealt with all those little details you'll be able to chill out in that plunge pool.'

With luck, a leopard would mistake her for lunch.

'Oh, don't tempt me,' Marji replied with one of her trilling little laughs that never failed to set Josie's teeth on edge. 'I'd give my eye teeth to go, but I have a magazine to run. Besides, I believe these things are best left to the professionals.'

Professionals who didn't patronise the bride…

'I've promised Crystal the wedding of her dreams, Josie.'

Her dreams? Maybe.

It had no doubt started out that way, but Josie wondered how Crystal was feeling about it now. Giddy with excitement, thrilled to be marrying the man she loved in the biggest, most lavish ceremony she, or rather Serafina March, could imagine?

Or was she frazzled with nerves and desperately wishing she and Tal had run away to Las Vegas to say their vows in private?

Most brides went through that at some point in the run-up to their wedding, usually when they were driven to distraction by family interference. Few of them had to cope with the additional strain of a media circus on their back.

'We can't let her down,' Marji persisted, anxious as she sensed her lack of enthusiasm. 'To be honest, she's somewhat fragile. Last minute nerves. I don't have to tell you how important this is and I believe that Crystal would be comfortable with you.'

Oh, right. Now they were both being patronised. Tarred with the same 'not one of us' brush, and for a moment she was tempted to tell Marji exactly what she could do with her wedding and to hell with the consequences.

Instead, she said, 'You'll run a piece in the

next issue of the magazine mentioning that I'm taking over?'

'It's Serafina's design,' she protested.

'Of course. Let's hope she's fit enough to travel tomorrow—'

'But we will be happy to add our thanks to you for stepping in at the last moment, Josie,' she added hurriedly.

It was a non-committal promise at best and she recognised as much, but everyone would know, which was all that mattered. And in the end this wasn't about her, or Marji, or even the wedding queen herself.

If Sylvie had taught her anything, it was that no bride, especially a bride whose wedding was going to be featured in full colour for all the world to see, should be left without someone who was totally, one hundred per cent, there for her on the big day. Josie let out a long, slow breath.

'Courier the files to my office, Marji. I'll email you a contract.'

Her hand was shaking as she replaced the receiver and looked up. 'Email a standard contract to Marji Hayes at *Celebrity*, Emma.'

'*Celebrity!*'

'Standard hourly rate, with a minimum of sixty hours, plus travel time,' she continued, with every outward appearance of calm. 'All expenses to their account. We've picked up the Tal Newman/Crystal Blaize wedding.'

As Emma tossed notebook and pen in the air, whooping with excitement, her irritation at Marji's attitude quite suddenly melted away.

'Where?' she demanded. 'Where is it?'

'I could tell you,' she replied, a broad grin spreading across her face. 'But then I'd have to kill you.'

'Dumela, Rra. O tsogile?'

'Dumela, Francis. *Ke tsogile.'*

Gideon McGrath replied to the greeting on automatic. He'd risen. Whether he'd risen well was another matter.

This visit to Leopard Tree Lodge had taken him well out of his way, a day and night stolen from a packed schedule that had already taken him to a Red Sea diving resort, then on down the Gulf to check on the progress of the new dhow he'd commissioned for coastal cruising from the traditional boat-builders in Ramal Hamrah.

While he was there, he'd joined one of the desert safaris he'd set up in partnership with Sheikh Zahir, spending the night with travellers who wanted a true desert experience rather than the belly-dancer-and-dune-surfing breaks on offer elsewhere.

He was usually renewed by the experience

but when he'd woken on a cold desert morning, faced with yet another airport, the endless security checks and long waits, he'd wondered why anyone would do this for pleasure.

For a man whose life was totally invested in the travel business, who'd made a fortune from selling excitement, adventure, the dream of Shangri-La to people who wanted the real thing, it was a bad feeling.

A bad feeling that had seemed to settle low in his back with a non-specific ache that he couldn't seem to shake off. One that had been creeping up on him almost unnoticed for the best part of a year.

Ever since he'd decided to sell Leopard Tree Lodge.

Connie, his doctor, having X-rayed him up hill and down dale, had ruled out any physical reason.

'What's bothering you, Gideon?' she asked when he returned for the results.

'Nothing,' he lied. 'I'm on top of the world.'

It was true. He'd just closed the deal on a ranch in Patagonia that was going to be his next big venture. She shook her head as he told her about it, offered her a holiday riding with the gauchos.

'You're the one who needs a holiday, Gideon. You're running on empty.'

Empty?

'You need to slow down. Get a life.'

'I've got all the life I can handle. Just fix me up with another of those muscle relaxing injections for now,' he said. 'I've got a plane to catch.'

She sighed. 'It's a temporary measure, Gideon. Sooner or later you're going to have to stop running and face whatever is causing this or your back will make the decision for you. At least take a break.'

'I've got it sorted.'

Maybe a night spent wrapped in a cloak on the desert sand hadn't been his best idea, he'd decided as he'd set out for the airport and the pain had returned with a vengeance. Now, after half a dozen meetings and four more flights, the light aircraft had touched down on the dirt airstrip he'd carved out of the bush with such a light heart just over ten years ago.

It had been a struggle to climb out of the aircraft, almost as if his body was refusing to do what his brain was telling it.

His mistake had been to try.

The minute he'd realised he was in trouble, he should have told the pilot to fly him straight back to Gabarone, where a doctor who didn't know him would have patched him up without question so that he could fly on to South America.

Stupidly, he'd believed a handful of painkillers, a hot shower and a night in a good bed would sort him out. Now he was at the mercy of the medic he retained for his staff and guests and who, having conferred with his own doctor in London, had resolutely refused to give him the get-out-of-jail-free injection.

All he'd got was a load of New Age claptrap about his body demanding that he become still, that he needed to relax so that it could heal itself. That it would let him know when it was ready to move on.

With no estimate of how long that might be.

Connie had put it rather more bluntly with her '…stop running'.

Well, that was why he was here. To stop running. He'd had offers for the Lodge in the past—offers that his board had urged him to take so that they could invest in newer, growing markets. He'd resisted the pressure. It had been his first capital investment. A symbol. An ever-lasting ache…

'Are there any messages, Francis?' he asked.

'Just one, *Rra*.' He set down the breakfast tray on the low table beside him, took a folded sheet of paper from his pocket and, with his left hand supporting his right wrist, he offered it to him with traditional politeness. 'It is a reply from your office.' Before he could read it, he said, 'It says that Mr Matt Benson has flown to Argentina in your place so you have no need to worry. Just do exactly what the doctor has told you and rest.' He beamed happily. 'It says that you must take as long as you need.'

Gideon bit back an expletive. Francis didn't understand. No one understood.

Matt was a good man but he hadn't spent every minute of the last fifteen years building a global empire out of the untapped market for challenging, high risk adventure holidays for the active and daring of all ages.

Developing small, exclusive retreats off the beaten track that offered privacy, luxury, the unusual for those who could afford to pay for it.

Matt, like all his staff, was keen, dedicated, but at the end of the day he went home to his real life. His wife. His children. His dog.

There was nothing for him to go home for.

For him, this company, the empire he'd built from the ruins of the failing family business, was all he had. It was his life.

'Can I get you anything else, *Rra?*'

'Out of here?' he said as he followed the path of a small aircraft that was banking over the river, watched it turn and head south. It had been a mistake to come here and he wanted to be on board that plane. Moving.

The thought intensified the pain in his lower back.

After a second night, fuming at the inactivity,

he'd swallowed enough painkillers to get him to the shower, determined to leave even if he had to crawl on his hands and knees to Reception and summon the local air taxi to pick him up.

He'd made it as far as the steps down to the tree bridge. Francis, arriving with an early morning tray, had found him hanging onto the guard rail, on his feet but unable to move up or down.

Given the choice of being taken by helicopter to the local hospital for bed rest, or remaining in the comfort and shade at Leopard Tree Lodge where he was at least notionally in control, had been a no-brainer.

Maybe the quack was right. He had been pushing it very hard for the last couple of years. He could spare a couple of days.

'Is that someone arriving or leaving?' he asked.

'Arriving,' Francis said, clearly relieved to change the subject. 'It is the wedding lady. She will be your neighbour. She is from London, too, *Rra*. Maybe you will know her?'

'Maybe,' he agreed. Francis came from a very small town where he knew everyone and Gideon had long ago learned that it was pointless trying to explain how many people lived in London. Then, 'Wedding lady?' He frowned. 'What wedding?'

'It is a great secret but Mr Tal Newman, the world's greatest footballer, is marrying his beautiful girlfriend, Miss Crystal Blaize, here at Leopard Tree Lodge, *Rra*. Many famous people are coming. The pictures are going to be in a magazine.'

As shock overcame inertia and he peeled himself off the lounger, pain scythed through him, taking his breath away. Francis made an anxious move to help him but he waved him away as he fell back. That was a mistake too, but whether the word that finally escaped him as he collapsed against the backrest was in response to the pain or a comment on whoever had permitted this travesty of everything his company stood for was a moot point.

'Shall I pour your tea, *Rra?*' Francis asked anxiously.

'I wanted coffee,' he snapped.

'The doctor said that you must not have…'

'I know what he said!'

No caffeine, no stress.

Pity he wasn't here right now.

He encouraged his staff to think laterally when it came to promoting his resorts but the Lodge was supposed to be a haven of peace and tranquillity for those who could afford to enjoy the wilderness experience in comfort.

The very last thing his guests would expect, or want, was the jamboree of a celebrity wedding scaring away the wildlife.

The last thing he wanted. Not here…

If that damn quack could see just how much stress even the thought of a wedding was causing him he'd ban that too, but having prescribed total rest and restricted his diet to the bland and boring he'd retired to the safety of Maun.

'Tell David that I want to see him.'

'Yes, *Rra*.'

'And see if you can find me a newspaper.' He was going out of his mind with boredom.

'The latest edition of the *Mmegi* should have arrived on the plane. I will go and fetch it for you.'

He'd been hoping for an abandoned copy of the *Financial Times* brought by a visitor, but that had probably been banned too and while it was possible that by this evening he would be desperate enough for anything, he hadn't got to that point yet.

'There's no hurry.'

CHAPTER TWO

Luxurious surroundings will add to the bride and groom's enjoyment of their special day.

—*The Perfect Wedding* by Serafina
March

JOSIE, despite her many misgivings, was impressed.

Leopard Tree Lodge had been all but invisible from the air as the small aircraft had circled over the river, skimming the trees to announce their arrival.

And the dirt runway on which they'd landed, leaving a plume of dust behind them, hadn't exactly inspired confidence either. By the time they'd taxied to a halt, however, a muscular four-wheel drive was waiting to pick up both her and the cartons of wedding paraphernalia she'd brought with her. 'Just a few extras…'

Marji had assured her. All the linens and paper goods had been sent on by Serafina before she had been taken ill.

The manager was waiting to greet her at the impressive main building. Circular, thatched, open-sided, it contained a lounge with a central fireplace that overlooked the river on one side. On the other, a lavish buffet where guests— kitted uniformly in safari gear and hung with cameras—helped themselves to breakfast that they carried out onto a shady, flower-decked terrace set above a swimming pool.

'David Kebalakile, Miss Fowler. Welcome to Leopard Tree Lodge. I hope you had a good journey.'

'Yes, thank you, Mr Kebalakile.'

It had felt endless, and she was exhausted, but she'd arrived in one piece. In her book that was as good as twenty-four hours and three planes, the last with only four seats and one engine, was going to get.

'David, please. Let's get these boxes into the office,' he said, summoning a couple of staff members to deal with all the excess baggage that Marji had dumped on her, 'and then I'll show you to your tree house.'

Tree house?

Was that better than a tent? Or worse?

If you fell out of a tent at least you were at

ground level, she thought, trying not to look down as she followed him across a sturdy timber walkway that wound through the trees a good ten feet from the ground.

Worse…

'We've never held a wedding at the Lodge before,' he said, 'so this is a very special new venture for us. And we're all very excited at the prospect of meeting Tal Newman. We love our football in Botswana.'

Oh, terrific.

This wasn't the slick and well practised routine for the staff that it would have been in most places and, as if that wasn't bad enough, it was the groom, rather than the bride, who was going to be the centre of attention.

The fact that the colour scheme for the wedding had been taken from the orange and pale blue strip of his football club should have warned her.

Presumably Crystal was used to it, but this was her big day and Josie vowed she'd be the star of this particular show even if it killed her.

'Here we are,' David said, stopping at a set of steps that led to a deck built among the tree tops, inviting her to go ahead of him.

Wow.

Double wow.

The deck was perched high above the

promised oxbow lake but the only thing her sub-
stantial tree house—with its thatched roof and
wide double doors—had in common with the
tent she'd been dreading were canvas sidings
which, as David enthusiastically demonstrated,
could be looped up so that you could lie in the
huge, romantically gauze-draped four-poster
bed and watch the sun rising. If you were into
that sort of thing.

'Early mornings and evenings are the best
times to watch the animals,' he said. 'They come
to drink then, although there's usually something to see whatever time of day or night it is.'
He crossed the deck and looked down. 'There
are still a few elephants, a family of warthogs.'

He turned, clearly expecting her to join him
and exclaim with delight.

'How lovely,' she said, doing her best to be enthusiastic when all she really wanted to look at
was the plumbing.

'There are always birds. They are…' He
stopped. 'I'm sorry. You've had a long journey
and you must be very tired.'

It seemed that she was going to have to work
on that one.

'I'll be fine when I've had a wake-up shower,'
she assured him. 'Something to eat.'

'Of course. I do hope you will find time to go
out in a canoe, though. Or on one of our guided

bush walks?' He just couldn't keep his enthusiasm in check.

'I hope so, too,' she said politely. Not.

She was a city girl. Dressing up in a silly hat and a jacket with every spare inch covered with pockets to go toddling off into the bush, where goodness knew what creepy-crawlies were lurking held absolutely no appeal.

'Right, well, breakfast is being served in the dining area at the moment, or I can have something brought to you on a tray if you prefer? Our visitors usually choose to relax, soak up the peace, after such a long journey.'

'A tray would be perfect, thank you.'

The peace would have to wait. She needed to take a close look at the facilities, see how they measured up to the plans in the file and check that everything on Serafina's very long list of linens and accessories of every kind had arrived safely. But not before she'd sluiced twenty-four hours of travel out of her hair.

'Just coffee and toast,' she said, 'and then, if you could spare me some time, I'd like to take a look around. Familiarise myself with the layout.'

'Of course. I'm at your command. Come to the desk when you're ready and if I'm not in my office someone will find me. In the meantime, just ring if you need anything.'

The minute he was gone, she took a closer look at her surroundings.

So far, they'd done more than live up to Marji's billing. The bed was a huge wooden-framed super king with two individual mattresses, presumably for comfort in the heat. It still left plenty of room for a sofa, coffee tables and the desk on which she laid her briefcase beside a folder that no doubt contained all the details of what was on offer.

Those bush walks and canoe trips.

No, thanks.

Outside, there was the promised plunge pool with a couple of sturdy wooden deck loungers and a small thatched gazebo shading a day bed big enough for two. Somewhere to lie down when the excitement got too much? Or maybe make your own excitement when the peace needed shaking up—that was if you had someone to get excited with.

The final touch was a second shower that was open to the sky.

'Oh, very "you Tarzan, me Jane",' she muttered.

To the front there were a couple of director's chairs where you could sit and gaze across the oxbow lagoon where the family of elephants had the same idea about taking a shower.

All she needed now was the bubbly, she thought,

smiling as a very small elephant rolled in the mud, while the adults used their trunks to fling water over their backs. Kids. They were all the same…

Looking around, she could see why *Celebrity* was so keen. People were crazy about animals and the photographs were going to be amazing. But, while the place had 'honeymoon' stamped all over it, she wasn't so sure about the wedding.

It had required three aircraft to get her here and the possibilities for disaster were legion.

She shook her head, stretched out cramped limbs in the early morning sunshine. She'd worry about that when it happened and, after one last look around, took herself inside to shower away the effects of the endless journey, choosing the exquisitely fitted bathroom over the temptations of the louche outdoor shower.

She was here to work, not play.

Ten minutes later, having pampered herself with the delicious toiletries that matched the 'luxury' label, she wrapped herself in a snowy bathrobe and went in search of a hairdryer.

Searching through cupboards and drawers, all she found was a small torch. Not much use. But, while she had been in the bathroom, her breakfast tray had arrived and she gave up the search in favour of a caffeine fix. Not that David had taken her 'just coffee and toast' seriously.

In an effort to impress, or maybe understanding what she needed better than she did herself, he had added freshly squeezed orange juice, a dish of sliced fresh fruit, most of which she didn't recognise, and a blueberry muffin, still warm from the oven.

She carried the tray out onto the deck, drank the juice, buttered a piece of toast, then poured a cup of coffee and stood it on the rail while she ruffled her fingers through her hair, enjoying the rare pleasure of drying it in the sun.

It was her short punk hairstyle as much as her background that had so scandalised people like Marji Hayes when Sylvie had first given her a job.

Young, unsure of herself, she'd used her hair, the eighteen-hole Doc Martens, scary make-up and nose stud as armour. A 'don't mess with me' message when she was faced with the kind of hotels and wedding locations where she'd normally be only allowed in the back door.

As she'd gained confidence and people had got to know her, she'd learned that a smile got her further than a scowl, but by then the look had become part of her image. As Sylvie had pointed out, it was original. People knew her and if she'd switched to something more conventional she'd have had to start all over again.

Admittedly the hair was a little longer these days, an expensively maintained mane rather than sharp spikes, the nose stud a tiny amethyst, and her safety pin earrings bore the name Zandra Rhodes, who was to punk style what Coco Chanel had been to business chic. And her make-up, while still individual, still her, was no longer applied in a manner to scare the horses.

But while she could manage with a brush and some gel to kill the natural curl and hold up her hair, the bride, bridesmaids and any number of celebrities, male and female, would be up the oxbow lagoon without a paddle unless they had the full complement of driers, straighteners and every other gadget dear to the crimper's heart.

Something to check with David, because if it wasn't just an oversight in her room they'd have to be flown in and she fetched her laptop from her briefcase and added it to her 'to do' list.

She'd barely started before she got a 'battery low' warning.

Her search for a point into which she could plug it to recharge proved equally fruitless and that sent her in search of a telephone so that she could ring the desk and enquire how on earth she was supposed to work without an electrical connection.

But, while David had urged her to 'ring', she couldn't find a telephone either. And, ominously, when she took out her mobile to try that, there was no signal.

Which was when she took a closer look at her

room and finally got it. Fooled by the efficient plumbing and hot water, she had assumed that the fat white candles sitting in glass holders were all part of the romance of the wilderness. On closer inspection, she realised that they were the only light source and that the torch might prove very useful after all.

Wilderness. Animals. Peace. Silence. Back to nature.

This was hubris, she thought.

She had taken considerable pleasure in the fact that Marji Hayes had, through gritted teeth, been forced to come to her for help.

This was her punishment.

There had been no warning about the lack of these basic facilities in the planning notes and she had no doubt that Marji was equally in the dark, but she wasn't about to gloat about the great Serafina March having overlooked something so basic. She, after all, was the poor sap who'd have to deal with it and, digging out the pre-computer age backup—a notebook and pen—she settled herself in the sun and began to make a list of problems.

Candlelight was the very least of them. Communication was going to be her biggest nightmare, she decided as she reached for the second slice of toast—there was nothing like anxiety to induce an attack of the munchies. As she groped for it there was a swish, a shriek and, before she could react, the plate had crashed to the deck.

She responded with the kind of girly shriek that she'd have mocked in anyone else before she saw the small black-faced monkey swing onto the branch above her.

'Damn cheek!' she declared as it sat there stuffing pieces of toast into its mouth. Then, as her heart returned to something like its normal rate, she reached for a sustaining swig of coffee. Which was when she discovered that it wasn't just the monkey who had designs on her breakfast.

'Is that coffee you're drinking?'

Letting out the second startled expletive in as many minutes as she spilled hot coffee on her foot, she spun to her left, where the neighbouring tree house was half hidden in the thickly cloaked branches.

'It was,' she muttered, mopping her foot with the edge of her robe.

'Sorry. I didn't mean to startle you.'

The man's voice was low, gravelly and rippled over her skin like a draught, setting up goose bumps.

'Who are you?' she demanded, peering through the leaves. 'Where are you?'

'Lower.'

She'd been peering across the gap between them at head height, expecting to see him leaning against the rail, looking out across the water to the reed-filled river beyond, doing his David Attenborough thing.

Dropping her gaze, she could just make out the body belonging to the voice stretched out on one of those low deck loungers.

She could only see tantalising bits of him. A long, sinewy bare foot, the edge of khaki shorts where they lay against a powerful thigh, thick dark hair, long enough to be stirred by a breeze coming off the river. And then, as the leaves stirred, parted for a moment, a pair of eyes that were focused on her so intently that for a moment she was thrown on the defensive. Ambushed by the fear waiting just beneath the surface to catch her off guard. The dread that one day someone would see through the carefully constructed shell of punk chic and recognise her for what she really was.

Not just a skivvy masquerading as a wedding planner but someone no one would let inside their fancy hotel, anywhere near their wedding, if they could see inside her head.

'Coffee?' he prompted.

She swallowed. Let out a slow careful breath.

Stupid…

No one knew, only Sylvie, and she would never tell. It was simply lack of sleep doing things to her head and, gathering herself, she managed to raise her cup in an ironic salute.

'Yes, thanks.'

Without warning, his mouth widened in a smile that provoked an altogether different sensation. One which overrode the panicky fear that one day she'd be found out and sent a delicious ripple of warmth seeping through her limbs. A lust at first sight recognition that even at this distance set alarm bells ringing.

Definitely her cue to go inside, get dressed, get to work. She had no time to waste talking to a man who thought that all he had to do was smile to get her attention.

Even if it was true.

She didn't do holiday flirtations. Didn't do flirtations of any description.

'Hold on,' he called as she turned away, completely oblivious to, or maybe choosing to ignore her 'not interested' response to whatever he was offering. Which was about the same as any man with time on his hands and nothing but birds to look at. 'Won't you spare a cup for a man in distress?'

'Distress?'

He didn't sound distressed. Or look it. On the contrary, he had the appearance of a man totally in control of his world. Used to getting what he wanted. She met them every day. Wealthy, powerful men who paid for the weddings and parties that SDS Events organised. The kind of men who were used to the very best and demanded nothing less.

She groaned at falling for such an obvious ploy. It wouldn't have happened if she'd had more than catnaps for the last twenty-four hours. But who could sleep on a plane?

'The kitchen sent me some kind of ghastly herbal tea,' he said, taking full advantage of her fatal hesitation.

'There's nothing wrong with herbal tea,' she replied. 'On the contrary. Camomile is excellent for the nerves. I thoroughly recommend it.'

She kept a supply in the office for distraught brides and their mothers. For herself when faced with the likes of Marji Hayes. Men who got under her skin with nothing more than a smile.

There was a pack in the bridal emergency kit she carried with her whenever she was working and she'd have one now but for the fact that if she were any calmer, she'd be asleep.

'I'd be happy to swap,' he offered.

Despite her determination not to be drawn into conversation, she laughed, as no doubt she was meant to.

'No, you're all right,' she said. 'I'm good.'

Then, refusing to allow a man to unsettle her with no more than a look—she was, she reminded herself, now a partner in a prestigious event company—she surrendered.

After all, she had a pot full of good coffee that she wasn't going to drink. And unless he was part of the wedding party—and, as far as she knew, no one was arriving until tomorrow—he'd be gone by morning.

'But if you're desperate you're welcome to come over and help yourself.'

'Ah, there's the rub,' he said before she could take another step towards the safety of the interior, leaving him to take it or leave it while she got on with the job she'd come here to do. 'The mind is willing enough, but the back just isn't listening. I'd crawl over there on hot coals for a decent cup of coffee if it were physically possible, but as it is I'm at your mercy.'

'You're hurt?' Stupid question. If he couldn't make the short distance from his deck to hers there had to something seriously wrong. She would have rung for room service if there had been a bell. Since that option was denied her, she stuck her notebook in the pocket of her robe, picked up the coffee pot and said, 'Hang on, I'll be right there.'

His tree house was at the end of the bridge, the furthest from the main building. The one which, according to the plan she'd been given, had been allocated to Crystal and Tal as their bridal suite.

Definitely leaving tomorrow, then.

There was a handbell at the foot of the steps and she jangled it, called, 'Hello,' as she stepped up onto his deck.

Then, as she turned the corner and took the full impact of the man stretched out on the lounger—with not the slightest sign of injury to keep him there—she came to an abrupt halt.

Even from a distance it had been obvious that he was dangerously good-looking. Up close, he looked simply dangerous.

He had a weathered tan, the kind that couldn't be replicated in a salon and never entirely faded, even in the dead of winter. And the strength of his chin was emphasized by a 'shadow' that had passed the designer stubble stage and was heading into beard territory.

She'd already experienced the smile from twenty metres but he wasn't smiling now. On the contrary, his was a blatantly calculating look that took in every inch of her. From her damp hair, purple-streaked and standing on end where she'd been finger-drying it, her face bereft of anything but a hefty dose of moisturiser, to her bare feet, with a knowingness that warned her he was aware that she was naked beneath the robe.

Worse, the seductive curve of his lower lip sparked a heat deep within her and she knew that he was far more deadly than any of the wild animals that were the main attraction at Leopard Tree Lodge.

At least to any woman who didn't have her heart firmly padlocked to her chest.

Resisting the urge to pull the robe closer about her and tighten the belt, betraying the effect he had on her, she walked swiftly across the deck and placed the coffee pot on the table beside him.

'Emergency coffee delivery,' she said, with every intention of turning around and leaving him to it.

Gideon had watched her walk towards him.

Until ten minutes ago, he would have sworn he wasn't in the mood for company, particularly not the company of a woman high on getting her man to sign up for life—or at least until she was ready to settle for half his worldly goods. But then the tantalising scent of coffee had wafted towards him.

Even then he might have resisted if he hadn't seen this extraordinary woman sitting on the deck, raking her fingers through her hair in the early morning sun.

If he had given the matter a second's thought, he would have assumed anyone called Crystal to be one of those pneumatic blondes cloned to decorate the arms of men who were more interested in shape than substance when it came to women.

Not that he was immune. Shape did it for him every time.

But she wasn't blonde. There was nothing obvious or predictable about her. Her hair was dramatically black and tipped with purple and her strong features were only prevented from overwhelming her face by a pair of large dark eyes. And while her shape was blurred by the bulky robe she was wearing, she was certainly on the skinny side; there were no artificially enhanced curves hidden even in that abundance of white towelling.

In fact she was so very far from what he would have expected that his interest had been unexpectedly aroused. Rather more than his interest if he was honest; a sure sign that his brain was under-occupied but it certainly took his mind off his back.

An effect that was amplified as she stepped up onto his deck and paused there for a moment.

Straight from the shower, her face bare of make-up, her hair a damp halo that hadn't seen a comb, without sexy clothes or high heels, it had to be the fact that she was naked under that robe that momentarily squeezed the breath from his chest as she'd walked towards him.

'You're an angel, Miss Blaize,' he said, collecting himself.

'Not even close,' she replied.

She'd worked hard to scrub the inner city from her voice, he judged, but it was still just discernible to someone with an ear for it.

'On either count,' she added. 'I'm sorry to disappoint, but I'm plain Josie Fowler.'

She wasn't the bride?

Nor was she exactly plain but what his mother would have described as 'striking'. And up close he could see that those dark eyes were a deep shade of violet that exactly matched the highlights in her hair, the colour she'd painted both finger and toenails.

'Who said I was disappointed, plain Josie Fowler?' he said, ignoring the little leap of gratification that she wasn't Crystal Blaize. It was her coffee he wanted, not her. 'I asked if you'd share your coffee and here you are. That makes you an angel in my eyes.'

'You're easily satisfied…?'

On the contrary. According to more than one woman of his acquaintance, he was impossible to please—or maybe just impossible—but right now any company would be welcome. Even a big-eyed scarecrow with purple hair.

'Gideon McGrath,' he said in answer to the unvoiced question. Offering her his hand.

She hesitated for the barest moment before she stepped close enough to take it, but her hand matched her features. It was slightly too large for true femininity, leaving him with the feeling that her body hadn't quite grown to match her extremities. But her grip was firm enough to convince him that, apart from the contact lenses—no one had eyes that colour—its owner was the real thing.

'Forgive me for not getting up, but if I tried you'd have to pick me up off the deck.'

'In that case, please don't bother. One of us with a bad back is quite enough. Enjoy your coffee,' she said, taking a clear step back.

'Would you mind pouring it for me? It's a bit of a stretch,' he lied. But he didn't want her to go.

'Bad luck,' she said, turning to the tray and bending to fill his cup. 'Especially when you're on holiday.' Then, glancing back at him, 'What on earth made you think I was Crystal Blaize?'

Her hair, drying quickly as the sun rose, began to settle in soft tendrils around her face. And he caught the gleam of a tiny purple stud in her nose.

Who was she? What was she? Part of the media circus surrounding the coming wedding?

'One of the staff called you the "the wedding lady"?' he replied, pitching his answer as a question.

'Oh, right. Milk, sugar?' she asked, but not bothering to explain. Then, looking over the tray, 'Actually, that would be just milk or milk. There doesn't appear to be any sugar.' She sighed as she straightened. 'I was assured that this place was the last word in luxury and to be sure it looks beautiful…'

'But?'

'There's no power point or hairdryer in my room, no sugar on your tray and no telephone to call the desk and tell them about it, despite the fact that David told me to ring for anything I needed. I can't even get a signal on my mobile phone.'

'You won't. The whole point of Leopard Tree Lodge is to get away from the intrusion of modern life, not bring it with you,' he said, totally ignoring the fact that he'd been fuming about the same thing just minutes before.

Well, obviously not the hairdryer. But he could surely do with a phone signal right now, if only to reassure himself that this was a one-off. That someone in marketing hadn't decided that weddings were the way to go.

Since he was the one who'd laid out the ground rules before a single stone had been laid or piece of timber cut, however, he could hardly complain.

But it occurred to him that if 'plain Josie Fowler' was with the wedding party, she would be given free run of the communications facilities and, if he played his cards right, she'd be good for a lot more than coffee.

'The electricity to heat the water is supplied by solar energy,' he explained, 'but it doesn't run to electrical appliances.'

'Once I'd clocked the candles, I managed to work that out for myself,' she replied. 'The escape from reality thing. Unfortunately, I'm here to work. If I was mad enough to come here for a holiday I'd probably feel quite differently.'

Clearly that prospect was as unlikely as a cold day in hell.

'You don't like it?'

'I'd like it better if it was beside a quiet bay, with a soft white beach and the kind of sea rich people pay to swim in.'

'This is supposed to be a work-free zone,' he pointed out, more than a touch irritated by her lack of enthusiasm. He put all his heart and a lot more into building his hotels, his resorts, some of them in exactly the kind of location she described.

But this had been his first. He loved it and hated it in equal measure, but he had the right.

'For others, maybe,' she retaliated, putting her hand to the small of her back and stretching out her spine, 'but for the next few days it's going to be twenty-four/seven for me.'

'Sore back?' he asked.

'Just a bit. Is it catching?' she asked with a wry smile.

'Not as far as I know.'

Maybe.

Her back hadn't seized up—yet—but just how many of his guests arrived feeling as if they were screwed up into knots? Zahir had built a very profitable spa on the coast at Nadira, where most of his travellers chose to spend a couple of days after the rigours of the desert. Would that work here, too? Massage, pampering treatments, something totally back to nature…

There was plenty to keep the dedicated naturalist happy. Canoe trips, bush walks, birdwatching, but big game viewing was the big attraction and that was primarily a dawn and dusk event.

Not that he was interested, but it would be useful to mention the possibilities for expansion when it came to negotiations with potential buyers.

'So, tell me, what's the deal with the herbal tea and no sugar?' she asked.

'It's a mystery,' he lied. 'Unless the ants have got into the stores.'

'Ants?'

'Big ones.' He held thumb and forefinger apart to demonstrate just how big.

Her eyes widened a fraction. 'You're kidding?'

He said nothing. There were ants that big but the storeroom had been designed and constructed to keep them out.

She had, however, been rather dismissive of

Leopard Tree Lodge. Worse, she was on a mission to disrupt it.

Protecting the unspoilt places where he built his resorts from pollution of every kind—including noise—had been high on his agenda from the outset. And, in his admittedly limited experience, weddings tended to be very noisy affairs.

Unfortunately, *Celebrity* would have a contract and wouldn't hesitate to sue him and his company for every lost penny if he messed with their big day. And that would be small beer compared to compensation for distress to the bride, the groom, their families, the bridesmaids…

He was stuck with the wedding, so tormenting the woman he now realised was the wedding planner was about as good as it was going to get.

CHAPTER THREE

A wedding is a day to spend with friends…
—*The Perfect Wedding* by Serafina
March

THE WEDDING PLANNER, however, refused to fulfil the role assigned.

There was no girly squeal at the thought of giant ants munching their way through the sugar supply. No repeat of the shriek provoked by the raid on her breakfast by a thieving monkey.

She merely shook her head, as if he'd done no more than confirm her worst fears, took a small black notebook out of her robe pocket, wrote something in it and then returned it to her pocket before turning back to the tray.

'There's a little pot of honey, here,' she said, picking it up and showing it to him. 'According to my partner, it actually tastes better in coffee as well as being healthier than refined sugar.'

'That'll be fine. I don't want milk.' He watched her open the pot, then said, 'Partner?'

From the way Francis had spoken, he'd assumed she was on her own. He hadn't noticed anyone with her, but he hadn't been interested enough to look until the scent of coffee had reached him.

'Is he with you?'

'She.' She stirred a spoonful of honey into his coffee. Then, realising what kind of partner he meant, she added, 'Sylvie's my business partner. And no. She's got a project of her own keeping her busy right now.'

The thought widened her mouth into a smile that momentarily lit up her face, transforming the 'striking' into something else. Not beauty—her features were not classically proportioned. It was nothing he could put a name to. He only knew that he wanted to see it again.

'Not that she'd have come with me even if she was free. Weddings are my department.' Then, as if aware that she hadn't made it clear, 'I'm an events planner.'

'I'd just about worked that out. It was just that when Francis said you were the "wedding lady" I assumed that you were the bride.'

'Not in this life,' she said matter-of-factly as she handed him the cup. 'My role is simply to deliver the wedding on time, on budget, with no hitches. Will that do?' she asked as he sipped it and, when he smiled, made another move to go.

'Stay. Sit down,' he said with a gesture at the lounger beside him.

'Do you always issue invitations as an order?' she asked, ignoring the invitation.

'On the contrary, I always issue orders as an invitation.' Then, before she could walk away— he couldn't remember the last time he'd had to work this hard to keep a woman's attention; when he'd wanted to—he said, 'Simply?'

'Sorry?'

'You think delivering a wedding here will be simple?'

That earned him a smile of his own. A slightly wry one, admittedly, with one corner of her mouth doing all the work and drawing attention to soft, full lips.

'Weddings are never simple,' she said, perching on the edge of the lounger rather than stretching out beside him as he'd hoped. Keen to be off and conquering worlds. No prizes for guessing who that reminded him of. 'Certainly not this one.'

'But you're the wedding lady,' he reminded her. 'It was your bright idea to have the wedding here.'

'You don't approve the choice of location?' she asked, her head tilting to one side. Interested rather than offended.

He shrugged without thinking and as he caught his breath she moved swiftly to steady the cup with one hand, placing her other on his shoulder.

'Are you all right?' she said.

No. Actually, far from all right.

As she'd leaned forward her robe had gaped to offer him a tantalising glimpse of the delights it was supposed to conceal. Her breasts were not large, but they were smooth, invitingly creamy and, without doubt, all her own and he was getting an overload of stimulation. Pain and pleasure in equal measure.

'A noisy celebrity wedding doesn't seem to fit the setting,' he said and, doing his best to ignore both, especially the warmth of her palm spreading through him, he looked up.

Her face was close enough to see the fine down that covered her fair, smooth skin. Genuine concern in those extraordinary eyes. But what held his attention was a faint white scar that ran along the edge of her jaw. It would, under normal circumstances, have been covered by make-up, but Josie had come on her errand of mercy without stopping to apply the mask that women used to conceal their true selves from the outside world.

No make-up. No designer clothes.

It left her more naked than if she'd stripped off her robe and he had to clench his hand to stop himself from reaching out, tracing the line of it from just beneath her ear to her chin as if he could somehow erase it, erase the memory of the pain it must have caused her, with his thumb.

'What about the other guests who are here to watch the wildlife?' he demanded, rather more sharply than he'd intended as he sought to distance himself. 'Don't they get any consideration?'

'There won't be any,' she said, removing her hand as she sat back, distancing herself. Leaving a cold spot where it had been.

'Exactly my point.'

'No, I meant that there won't be any other guests, Gideon. We've taken over the entire resort for the wedding so we won't be disturbing anyone.'

'Apart from the animals. Every room?'

'And the rest. We've got a river boat coming to take the overflow.'

'Well, I hate to be the one to say "I told you so", but here comes your first complication. I'm not going anywhere.'

'Then you're going to have to bivouac in the bush because you're certainly not staying here,' she replied.

He didn't bother to argue with her. She'd find out just how immovable he could be soon enough.

'Did you get a good discount for block booking?' he asked.

'What?' She shook her head. 'There's nothing discount about this wedding but, since I wasn't part of the negotiations, I couldn't say what financial arrangements were made with the owners. I was brought in at the last minute when the original wedding planner had to pull out. Not that it's any of your business,' she added.

'If it had been your call?' he pressed. 'Would you have chosen Leopard Tree Lodge?'

'The venue is the bride's decision,' she replied. Then, with the smallest of shrugs, 'I might have tried to talk her out of it. Not that the location isn't breathtaking,' she assured him. 'The drama of flying in over the desert and then suddenly seeing the green of the Okavango delta spread out below you, the gleam of water amongst the reeds. The river…'

She was going through the motions, he realised. Talking to him, but her brain was somewhere else. No doubt working out the implications of a cuckoo in the nest.

'The photographs are going to be breathtaking,' she said, making an effort. 'Any special deal that *Celebrity* managed to hammer out of the company that owns this place is going to be cheap in return for the PR hit. Six weeks of wall-to-wall coverage in the biggest lifestyle magazine in the UK. Well, five. The first week is devoted to the hen weekend.'

Undoubtedly. A full house as well as a ton of publicity. Whoever it was on his staff who'd negotiated this deal had done a very good job. The fact that he or she hadn't brought it to his attention in the hope of earning a bonus suggested that they knew what his reaction would have been.

Not that they had to. His role was research and development, not the day-to-day running of things. No doubt they were simply waiting for the jump in demand to prove their point for him. And earn them a bonus.

Smart thinking. It was just what he'd have done in their position.

'If the setting is so great, what's your problem with it?' he asked.

It was one thing for him to hate the idea. Quite another for someone to tell him that it was all wrong for her big fancy media event.

'In my experience there's more than enough capacity for disaster when it comes to something in which such strong emotions are invested, without transporting bride, groom, a hundred plus guests, photographers, a journalist, hair and make-up artists, not to mention all their kit and caboodle six thousand miles via three separate aircraft. One of them so small that it'll need a separate trip just for the wedding dress.'

'You're exaggerating.'

'Probably,' she admitted. 'But not by much.'

'No. And that's another problem,' he said, seizing the opening she'd given him. 'It's a gift to the green lobby. They'll use the high profile of the event to get their own free PR ride over the carbon footprint involved in transporting everyone halfway round the world just so that two people can say "I do".'

'You think they should have chosen the village church?'

'Why not?'

'Good question,' she said. 'So, tell me, Gideon McGrath, how did you get here? By hot-air balloon?'

For a man who probably flew more miles in a year than most people did in a lifetime that sounded very appealing and he told her so.

'Unfortunately, there is no way of making a balloon take you where you want to go.'

'Maybe the trick is to want to go where the balloon takes you,' she replied.

'That's a bit too philosophical for me.'

'Really? Well, you can stop worrying. Tal Newman's PR people have anticipated the negative reaction and he's going to offset the air travel involved by planting a sizeable forest.'

'Where?' he asked, his interest instantly piqued. A lot of his clients offset their travel, but maybe he could make it easy for them by offering it as part of the package. Do more. Put something back, perhaps. Something meaningful…

'The forest?' She shook her head. 'Sorry, that information is embargoed until the day before the wedding.'

'In other words, you don't know.'

'No idea,' she admitted. 'Everything about this wedding is on a "need to know" basis. Not that you could call anyone and tell them.' She thought about that and added, 'You know it's possible that the lack of communication may be one of the reasons *Celebrity* seized on this location. Without a signal, there's no chance of the guests, or staff, sending illicit photographs to rival magazines and newspapers via their mobile phones so that they can run spoilers.'

'I thought you said the location was the bride's call?'

'It is for my brides but this isn't just a wedding, it's a media event. Of course Crystal apparently loves animals so it fits the image.'

He snorted derisively.

'Any animals she sees here are going to be wild and dangerous—especially the furry ones. She'd have done better getting married in a petting zoo.'

'You might say that,' she replied with a dead-straight face. 'I couldn't possibly comment.'

Then she took out her notebook and jotted something down. 'But thanks for the idea.'

He laughed, jerking the pain in his back into life.

Josie's hand twitched as if to reach out again, but she closed it tight about her pen and he told himself that he was glad. He preferred his relationships physical, uncomplicated. That way, everyone knew where they were. The minute emotions, caring got involved, they became dangerous. Impossible to control. With limitless possibilities for pain.

'You don't believe in any of this, do you?' he said, guarding himself against regret. 'You provide the flowers and frills and fireworks but underneath you're a cynic.'

'The flowers and frills,' she replied, 'but it was stipulated by the resort that there should be no fireworks.'

'Well, that's a relief. You never know which way a startled elephant will run.'

'That's an image I could have done without,' she said. 'But, since you won't be here, there's no need to concern yourself. How was the coffee?'

Gideon looked at his empty cup. 'Do you know, I was so absorbed by all this wedding talk that I scarcely noticed.' Holding it out for a refill, he said, 'I'll concentrate this time.'

Josie replenished it without a word, then

leaned forward to stir in another spoonful of honey.

'Enough?' she asked, raising long, naturally dark lashes to look questioningly at him.

'Perfect,' he said as he was offered a second glimpse of her entrancing cleavage. A second close-up of that faint scar.

Was it a childhood fall? A car accident? He tried to imagine what might have caused such an injury.

'So, what have you actually done to your back?' she asked, distracting him. 'Did you get into a tussle with a runaway elephant? Wrestle an alligator? Total a four-by-four chasing a rhino?'

'Actually, since we're in Africa, that would be a crocodile,' he pointed out, sipping more slowly at the second cup. Savouring it. Making it last. He didn't want her to rush off. 'The creatures you should never smile at.'

'Sorry?'

'It's a song. *Never smile at a crocodile…*' As he sang the words, he felt the tug of the past. Where the hell had that come from?

'*Peter Pan,*' she said. 'Forgive me, but I wouldn't have taken you for a fan.'

He shrugged without thinking, but this time it didn't catch him so viciously. Maybe the doc was right. He just needed to relax. Spend some time talking about nothing much, to someone who didn't want something from him.

Apart from his room.

Obviously a woman at the top of her field in the events industry—and she had to be good or she wouldn't be in charge of Tal Newman's high profile wedding—would have that kind of easy ability to talk to anyone, put them at their ease. He'd only been talking to her for a few minutes and already he'd had two good ideas.

Even so.

Most women he met had an agenda. Hers was to evict him and while, just an hour ago, he would have been her willing accomplice, just the thought of getting on a plane tightened the pain.

She might not be a babe, nothing like the women he dated when he could spare the time. Who never lasted more than a month or two, because he never could spare the time, refused to take the risk…

What mattered was that she had access to coffee, the little pleasures that made the wheels of life turn without squeaking, and she would have that vital contact with the outside world.

The fact that she was capable of stringing an intelligent sentence together and making him laugh—well, smile, anyway; laughing, as he'd discovered, was a very bad idea— was pure bonus.

'My father was into amateur dramatics,' he told her. 'He put on a show for the local kids every Christmas.'

'Oh, right.' For just a moment she seemed to freeze, then she pasted on a smile that even on so short an acquaintance he knew wasn't the real thing. 'Well, that must have been fun. Were you Peter?' She paused. 'Or were you Captain Hook?'

Something about the way she said that suggested she thought Hook was more his thing.

'My father played Hook. I didn't get involved.' One fantasist in the family was more than enough.

She lifted her eyebrows a fraction, but kept whatever she was thinking to herself and said, 'So? Despite the paternal advice, did you smile at one?'

'Nothing that exciting. Damn thing just seized up on me. I was planning to leave yesterday, but apparently I'm stuck here until it unseizes itself,' he said, firing a shot across her assumption that he would be leaving any time soon.

'That must hurt,' she said, her forehead puckering in a little frown. 'Have you seen a doctor?'

Good question.

She was going to be responsible for the health and safety of a hundred plus people. If anyone hurt themselves—and weddings were notoriously rowdy affairs—she needed to know there was help at hand.

Or maybe she was finally getting it. What his

immovability meant in terms of her 'block booking'.

'There's a doctor in Maun. He flew up yesterday, spoke to my doctor in London and then ordered complete rest. According to him, this little episode is my body telling me to be still.' He made little quote marks with his fingers around the 'be still'. He wouldn't want her, or anyone else, thinking he said things like that.

'It's psychological?'

Something about the way she said that, no particular shock or surprise, suggested that it wasn't the first time she'd encountered the condition.

'That's what they're implying.'

'My stepfather suffered from the same thing,' she said. 'His back seized up every time someone suggested he get a job.'

She said it with a brisk, throwaway carelessness that declared to the world that having a layabout for a stepfather mattered not one jot. But her words betrayed a world of hurt. And went a long way to explaining that very firm assertion—strange for a woman whose life revolved around it—that marriage wasn't for her.

'I didn't mean to imply that that's your problem,' she added with a sudden rush that—however unlikely that seemed—might have been embarrassment.

'I promise you that it's not,' he assured her. 'On the contrary. It's made worse by the fact that I'm out of touch with my office. That I'm stuck here when I should be several thousand miles away negotiating a vital contract.'

Discovering that the marketing team he'd entrusted with selling his hard won dream appeared to have lost the plot and being unable to do a damn thing about it.

'I'm beginning to understand how that feels.' She was still leaning forward, an elbow on her knee, chin propped on her hand, regarding him with that steady violet gaze. 'The being out of touch thing. I usually spend the twenty-four hours before a big event with my phone glued to my ear, although who I'd call if I had a last minute emergency here heaven alone knows.'

'Necessity does tend to be the mother of invention when you're this far from civilisation,' he agreed.

'Even in the middle of civilisation when you're in the events business. Clearly, this is going to be an interesting few days.' Then, looking at him as if he was number one on her list of problems, 'Would a massage help?'

'Are you offering?' he asked.

Josie had thought it was quiet here, but she was wrong.

There was no traffic, no shouting or sirens—the constant background to daily life in London—but it wasn't silent. The air was positively vibrating with energy; the high-pitched hum of insects, bird calls, odd sounds she couldn't identify, and she was suddenly overwhelmed with a longing to lie back, soak it all up, let the sun heat her to the bone.

The shriek of a bird, or maybe a monkey, snapped her out of her reverie and she realised, somewhat belatedly, that Gideon McGrath's dark eyes were focused not on her face, but lower down.

Typical man…

'All I'm offering is coffee,' she said crisply, rising to her feet, tightening her belt.

'Pity,' he replied with a slow, mesmerising smile. It was like watching a car roll towards you in slow motion; one minute you were safe, the next…

'Shall I leave the pot?' she asked.

'Better take it with you, or the room service staff will get their knickers in a twist hunting for it.'

'It's not a problem,' she said abruptly. Calling herself all kinds of a fool for allowing herself to be drawn in by a smile, a pair of dark eyes. He might be confined to a deck lounger, but he was still capable of inflicting terminal damage and she wished she'd stuck with her initial response which had been to ignore him. 'I'll let them know where it is.'

'Don't bother about it. Really. You've got more than enough on your plate.'

'It's no trouble,' she assured him, backing towards the exit. 'I'll be visiting the kitchen anyway.' She had to talk through the catering arrangements for the pre-wedding dinner with the chef. 'I can mention the mistake with the herbal tea while I'm there if you like.'

'No. Don't do that, Josie.'

Something about his persistence warned her that she was missing something and she stopped.

'It wasn't a mistake,' he said. 'The tea.'

'I'm sorry, I don't understand…' Then, quite suddenly, she did. 'Oh, right. I get it.' She stepped forward and snatched up the coffee pot, brandishing it at him accusingly. 'This is a banned substance, isn't it?'

'You've got me,' he admitted, his smile turning to a wince as he shrugged without thinking and she had to fight the urge to go to him yet again, do something to ease the pain.

'I believe I'm the one who's been had.' And, before he could deny it, she said, 'You've made me an accessory to caffeine abuse in direct contravention of doctor's orders and—' as he opened his mouth to protest '—don't even think about apologising. I can tell that you're not in the least bit sorry.'

'Actually, I wasn't going to apologise. I was going to thank you. Everyone keeps telling me that I should listen to my body. Its demands for caffeine were getting so loud that I'm surprised the entire camp couldn't hear it.'

'Not the entire camp,' she replied. 'Just me.'

'You were very kind and I took shameless advantage of you,' he said with every appearance of sincerity. She wasn't taken in.

'I was an idiot,' she said, holding up her hand, palm towards him as if holding him off, despite the fact that moving was clearly the last thing on his mind.

'Not an idiot.'

'No? So tell me about the sugar?'

'You didn't give me sugar,' he pointed out.

'I would have done if you'd…' She stopped, furious with herself.

'The honey was inspired,' he assured her. 'Tell your partner that I'm converted.'

'So what else is banned?' she demanded, refusing to be placated.

'White bread, red meat, salt, animal fats.'

Gideon knew the list by heart. His doctor had been trotting it out for years at the annual check-ups provided for all staff. Annual check-ups which the firm's insurance company insisted should include him, despite his protestations that it was totally unnecessary. Now she'd got him captive, she was taking full advantage of the situation.

'All the usual suspects, in other words.'

'Along with the advice to walk to work…' as if he had time '…and take regular holidays.'

He spent half his life at holiday resorts, for heaven's sake; why would he want to go to one for fun?

And of course there was the big one. Get married.

According to actuarial statistics, married men lived longer. But then that doctor was a woman, so she would say that. He wasn't going to.

'The holiday part doesn't appear to be working,' Josie pointed out.

'Nor does the diet. My life has been reduced to steamed fish, nut cutlets and oatmeal,' he complained. And there wasn't a damn thing he could do about it. Unless, of course, he could convince Josie to take pity on him.

She'd been quick with a tender hand and he was sure that if he'd asked she'd have gone and fetched sugar for him from her own tray. If he'd done that she'd be really mad at him.

She might even have indulged his massage fantasy if she hadn't caught him with his eyes rather lower than they should have been.

'I take it that I can cross ants off the list of things I have to worry about,' she said without the least sign of sympathy.

Okay, so she was too mad to indulge him now, but it wouldn't last. She laughed too easily to hold a grudge.

'If I say yes, will you have lunch with me?' he asked.

'So that you can help yourself to forbidden treats from my tray?'

'Me? I'm helpless. Of course, if you forced them on me there isn't a thing I could do to stop you.'

'You can relax,' she replied, but her lusciously wide mouth tightened at the corners as she fought to stop it responding to his outrageous cheek with a grin. 'I wouldn't dream of it.'

'I'd make it worth your while,' he promised.

'Give it up, Gideon. I can't be bribed.'

Of course she could. Everyone could be bribed. You just had to find out what they wanted most in the world. Preferably before they knew they wanted it.

'You're going to need a friendly ear in which to pour your frustrations before this wedding is over.' That he would be the major cause of those frustrations didn't preclude him from offering comfort. 'A shoulder to cry on when everything falls apart.'

'All I need from you is your room,' she

replied. 'Besides, you're supposed to be on a low stress regime.'

'It would be your stress, not mine,' he pointed out.

'Yes, well, thanks for the offer,' she said, losing the battle with the smile and trying very hard not to laugh. 'I appreciate your concern, but SDS Events do not plan weddings that fall apart—'

'You didn't plan this one.'

'—and you won't be here long enough to provide the necessary shoulder for tears or any other purpose.'

'I'll be here until my back says otherwise.' And, quite unexpectedly, he didn't find that nearly as infuriating as he had just half an hour earlier.

'Your back doesn't have a say in the matter. I hate to add to your stress, but unless you intend playing gooseberry to the bride and groom you would be well advised to make other arrangements.'

'Are you telling me that this is going to be the bridal suite?'

'Twenty-four hours from now, you won't be able to move in here for flowers,' she assured him, so seriously that he laughed.

It hurt like hell but he didn't care. He was throwing a spanner in the wedding works and he didn't have to lift a finger—let alone a telephone—to do it.

'I'm glad that amuses you, Mr McGrath. They do say that laughter is very healing, which, since you have to be out of here by first thing tomorrow, is just as well. Maybe you should try the plunge pool,' she suggested. 'It will take the weight off your muscles. Ease the pain.'

'I'm willing to give it go,' he assured her. 'But I'll need a hand.'

'No problem. I'd be happy to give you a push.'

'But will you stick around to help me out?'

'Sorry, I have a full day ahead of me. Enjoy the herbal tea and nut cutlets.'

'You're full of excellent ideas, Josie. You just don't follow through.'

'Don't test me,' she warned.

She turned with a splendid swish of her robe, giving him an unintentional glimpse of thigh.

'I'll give you one thing,' he called after her.

'Your bed?'

'Communication.'

She stopped and, when she turned back to face him, he said, 'If you'll make a call for me.'

'You want me to call your wife and tell her you're catching the next plane home?'

'There's no one waiting for that call, Josie.' No one to rush back to. 'I want you to ring my office. Give me your notebook and I'll write down the number.'

She came closer, drawn by the temptation,

took the notebook from her pocket and handed it to him with her pen. It was the kind of notebook he favoured himself, with a pocket at the back for receipts and an elastic band to hold it together. He slipped the band and it fell open at the bookmarked page where she'd started writing a list.

Hairdryers?
Ring???
Phone?
Florist
Caterer
Confectioner

He smiled and beside 'Ring' he jotted down a number.

'Call Cara,' he said, handing it back to her. 'She's my PA.'

'And say what?'

'Just ask her what the hell is going on in Marketing.'

'What the hell is going on in Marketing,' she repeated, then shook her head. 'I can see why you're stressed. You're on holiday. Let it go, Gideon.'

'Holidays are my work, which is why I know that David has a satellite telephone and Internet access. He keeps it a dark secret from the guests, but I'm sure he'll make an exception in your case.'

'You—' She let slip a word that was surely banned from the wedding planners' handbook. 'Had again.'

'You're going to need me on your side, Josie.'

'I need you gone!'

He left her with the last word and his reward was a view of an unexpectedly sexy rear as she walked away. A pair of slender ankles. He was already looking forward to making his acquaintance with the legs that connected them.

'I don't suppose you've got a London newspaper to spare for a man dying of boredom?' he called after her.

'Never touch them,' her disembodied voice replied from the bridge. 'Far too stressful.'

'Liar,' he called back as he tugged on the bell pull that Francis had extended from its place by the bed so that it was within reach of the lounger.

He really should have explained what David had meant when he'd told her to 'ring'. Actually, David should have told her himself, but maybe he'd been distracted.

She was a seriously distracting woman.

'Don't forget lunch.'

CHAPTER FOUR

A stylish wedding often owes more to natural elements than the designer's art…
—*The Perfect Wedding* by Serafina
March

JOSIE was trying very hard not to grin as she walked back through the trees to her own deck and, once safely out of reach of those dangerous eyes, a mouth that teased without conscience, she swiftly recovered her senses.

Gideon McGrath might be in pain but it hadn't stopped him flirting outrageously with her. Not that she was fooled into thinking it was personal, despite the way he'd peered down her robe until she'd realised what he was doing and moved.

All he was interested in was her coffee. In having her run his errands.

'One o'clock…' His voice reached her through the branches.

And her lunch, damn it!

She was sorely tempted to stand by the rail and eat that luscious blueberry muffin, very slowly, just to torment him.

Perhaps it was just as well that the monkeys had taken advantage of her absence to clear her tray. Upsetting the milk, scattering the little packets of sugar, leaving nothing but crumbs that were being cleaned up by a bird with dark, glossy green plumage who gave her a look with its beady eyes as if daring her to do anything about it.

She wouldn't want the man to get the impression that she gave that much of a damn and, quite deliberately turning her back towards him, she looked up at a monkey chittering at her from a nearby branch. He turned on the charm with a smile, an outstretched hand, the moment he'd snagged her attention, hoping for more little treats.

It had to be a male.

'You've cleaned me out,' she said. 'Try next door.'

She was treated to a bare-toothed grin before the little monkey swung effortlessly away into the trees, putting on a dazzling acrobatic show just for her.

'Show off,' she called after him. But the fact that she was smiling served as a reminder, should she need it, of just how dangerous that kind of self-serving charm could be. How easy it was to be fooled, sucked in.

She took a slow breath, then turned her face up to the sun, absorbing for a moment the heat, the scent of warm earth, the exotic high-pitched hum of the cicadas.

Five years ago she had been peeling vegetables and washing up in a hotel kitchen; the only job she could get.

Today, *Celebrity* magazine was paying for her to stay in one of the most exclusive safari lodges in Africa. Paying her to ensure that the year's most expensive wedding went without a hitch. And, with her name attached to this event, she would be one of the 'chosen', accepted in her own right; finally able to justify Sylvie's faith in her.

Gideon McGrath could flirt all he wanted. It would take more than his devastating smile to distract her from her purpose.

She swiftly unpacked, hung up her clothes, then waxed up her hair before dressing for work. At home she would have worn layers of black net, Lycra and jersey; the black tights, T-shirt, a sleeveless belted slipover that came to her thighs, the purple DMs that had become her trademark uniform.

On her first foray into a 'destination' wedding,

on the island of St Lucia, she'd shed the neck-to-toe cover-up in favour of black shorts, tank top and a pair of strappy purple sandals.

The misery of sunburn, and ploughing through soft sand in open-toes, had taught her a sharp, painful lesson and she hadn't made the same mistake again. Instead, she'd invested in a hot weather uniform consisting of a black long-sleeved linen shirt and a short skirt pulled together with a purple leather belt. Despite the heat, she'd stuck with black tights, which she'd also learned from experience, protected her legs from the nasty biting, stinging things that seemed to thrive in hot climates. As did her boots.

She took a folder from her briefcase that contained the overall plan for the wedding as envisaged by her predecessor, the latest guest list Marji had emailed to her—she'd need to check it against the rooms allocated by David—and her own lists of everything that needed to be double and triple-checked on site.

Marji had also sent her the latest edition of *Celebrity* with Crystal's sweetheart face and baby-blue eyes smiling out of the cover. The first of half a dozen issues that would be dedicated to the wedding.

She glanced in the direction of Gideon's tree house. It wasn't the requested newspaper—far from it—but it did contain a dozen pages of the bride on her hen party weekend at a luxury spa. Impossibly glamorous girls poolside in barely-there swimsuits, partying till all hours in gowns cut to reveal more than they concealed would do a lot more to take his mind off his back than the latest FTSE index.

It was just the thing for a man suffering from stress overload.

Then she felt guilty for mocking him. Okay, so he'd taken shameless advantage of her, but it had to be miserable having your back seize up when you were on holiday in a place that had been designed to wipe out all traces of the twenty-first century. No television or radio to distract you. No way to phone home.

If he was as incapable of moving as he said he was. He looked fit enough—more than fit. Not bulky gym muscle, but the lean, sinewy lifestyle fitness of a walker, a climber even.

That first sight of him had practically taken her breath away.

Not just his buff body and powerful legs, but the thick dark hair and sexy stubble. Eyes from which lines fanned out in a way that suggested he spent a lot of time in the sun.

Eyes that unnerved her. Seemed to rob her of self-will. She'd been on the point of leaving him more than once and yet she'd stayed.

She dismissed the thought. It had been a long trip and she never had been able to sleep on a plane. She was simply tired.

The only thing that bothered her about Gideon McGrath was that he was here. Immovably so, according to him, and she could see how impossible it would be for him to climb aboard the tiny four-seater plane that had brought her here.

But there had to be a way. If it had been a life-threatening illness, a broken leg, they would have to get him out somehow.

She'd ask David about that.

The entire complex would very shortly be full to bursting with the wedding party, photographers, hairdressers and make-up artists for the feature on the build-up to the wedding, the setting, and no one was immune from an accident, falling ill.

She needed to know what the emergency arrangements were.

Meanwhile, whatever he came up with, they were going to need Gideon McGrath's goodwill and co-operation and she regretted dropping yesterday's newspaper in the rubbish bag before she'd left the flight from London. Getting him out of Tal and Crystal's bridal suite was her number one priority and, for that, she needed to keep him sweet. Even if it did mean hand-feeding him from her lunch tray.

She put on her sunglasses and, shouldering her bag, she headed back across the bridge. Trying very hard not to think about slipping morsels of tempting food into his mouth. Giving him a massage. Helping him into the plunge pool.

She jangled the bell to warn him of her arrival, then stepped up onto his deck.

He hadn't moved, but was lying back, eyes closed and, not eager to disturb him, she tiptoed across to the table.

'Admit it, Josie, you just can't keep away,' he said as she put the magazine down.

She jumped, her heart jolting against her breast as if she'd been caught doing something wrong and that made her mad.

'I'm on an errand of mercy,' she said, then jumped again when he opened his eyes. He did a good job of hiding his reaction to her changed appearance. Was doubtless a good poker player.

But, for a woman who knew what to look for, the mental flinch that was usually accompanied by a short scatological four-letter word was unmistakable.

He had enough control to keep that to himself, too—which was impressive; there was simply a pause so brief as to be almost unnoticeable unless you were waiting for it, before he said, 'So? Have you changed your mind about the massage?'

And it was her turn to catch her breath, catch the word that very nearly slipped loose. Was it that obvious what she'd been thinking? Had he been able to read her mind as easily as she'd read his?

It wasn't such a stretch, she realised.

He must know how important it was to her that he move and she let it out again, very slowly.

'Sorry. It was your mental well-being I was concerned about. I didn't have a newspaper,' she said, 'but I did have this in my bag.'

He took one glance at the magazine she was offering him and then looked up at her. 'You've got to be kidding?'

'It's the latest issue.' She angled it so that he could see Crystal on the cover. 'At least you won't mistake me for the bride again.'

'I always did think you were an unlikely candidate,' he admitted, taking it from her and glancing at the photograph of the bikini-clad Crystal. 'She is exactly what I expected, whereas you are…'

He paused, whether out of concern for her feelings or because he was lost for words she didn't know. Unlikely on both counts, she'd have thought.

'Whereas I am what?' she enquired.

'I'm not sure,' he replied. 'Give me time and I'll work it out.'

'There's no rush,' she said, taking a step back.

'You've got until ten o'clock tomorrow morning. And in the meantime you can get to know Crystal.'

'Why would I want to do that?'

She shrugged. 'You tell me. You're the one who wants to share her room.'

Deciding that now might be a good moment to depart, she took another step back.

'Wait!'

And, even after all these years, her survival instinct was so deeply ingrained to respond instantly to an order and she stopped and turned without thinking.

'Josie?'

It had taken no more than a heartbeat for her to realise what she'd done, spin on her heel and walk away.

'I'm busy,' she said and kept going.

'I know, but I was hoping, since you're so concerned about my mental welfare, that you might fetch a notebook and pen from my laptop bag?'

Gideon had framed it as a question, not an order and she put out her hand to grasp the handrail as the black thoughts swirling in her brain began to subside and she realised that his 'wait!' had been an urgent appeal rather than the leap-to-it order barked at someone who had no choice but obey.

She took a moment while her heart rate slowed to catch her breath, gather herself, before turning slowly to face him.

'Do correct me if I'm mistaken,' she said, 'but I'd have said they were on the doctor's forbidden list.'

'At the top,' he admitted, the slight frown at her strange reaction softening into a rerun of that car-crash smile.

'Well, there you are. I've done more than enough damage for one day—'

'No. It's important. I've had a couple of ideas and if I don't make some notes while they're fresh in my mind, I'm just going to lie here and…well…stress. You wouldn't want that on your conscience, would you?'

'You are a shameless piece of work, Gideon McGrath,' she told him, the irresistible smile doing nothing good for her pulse rate.

'In my place, you'd do the same.'

Undoubtedly.

And, since they both knew that right now her prime motivation was keeping him stress-free, he had her. Again.

It took a moment for her eyes to adjust to the dim interior, but at first glance his room appeared to be identical to her own. It certainly wasn't any larger or fancier, so presumably Serafina had chosen it as the bridal suite purely because of its isolation at the furthest point from the main building.

Tomorrow it would be decked with flowers.

There would be fresh fruit, champagne, every-thing laid on for the stars of the show.

For the moment, however, it was bare of anything that would give a clue to the character of its occupant. There was nothing lying on the bedside table. No book. No photograph. Nothing to offer any clues as to who he was. What he was. He'd said travel was his business, but that could mean anything. He could work for one of the travel companies, checking out hotels. A travel writer, even.

No laptop bag, either.

'I can't see it,' she called.

'Try the wardrobe.'

She opened a door. A well-worn carry-on leather grip was his only luggage and, apart from a cream linen suit, his clothes were the comfort-able basics of a man who had his life pared to the bone and travelled light.

His laptop bag was on a high shelf—put there out of reach of temptation by his doctor?

'Got it!'

She took it down, unzipped the side pocket, but there were no files, no loose paperwork. Obviously it wasn't just his wardrobe that was pared to the bone. The man didn't believe in clutter. Not that she'd been planning to snoop, but a letterhead would have given her a clue about what he did.

'Forget the notebook, just bring the bag,' he called impatiently.

All he carried was a small plain black notebook held together by an elastic band, an array of pens and the same state-of-the-art iPhone that she used and a small but seriously expensive digital camera.

She extracted the notebook, selected a pen, then zipped the bag shut and lifted it back into place.

'I thought I asked you to bring the bag,' he said when she handed them to him.

'You did, but I thought I'd give you an incentive to get back on your feet.'

His eyes narrowed and he took them on a slow, thoughtful tour of her body. It was as if he were going through an empty house switching on the lights. Thighs, abdomen, breasts leaping to life as his eyes lighted on each in turn. Lingered.

Switching on the heating.

Then he met her eyes head-on with a gaze that was direct, unambiguous and said, 'If you're in the incentive business, Josie, you could do a lot better than that.'

She'd had her share of utterly outrageous propositions from men since she'd been in the events business, most of which had, admittedly, been fuelled by alcohol and, as such, not to be taken seriously, even if the men involved had been capable of carrying them through.

They were all part of the job and she'd never had any problem dealing with them so the heat searing her cheeks now had to be caused by the sun. It was rising by the minute and the temperature was going up with it.

'Lunch?' he prompted.

'What?'

'As an incentive?'

Another wave of heat swept over her cheeks as he laughed at her confusion. Furious with herself—she did not blush—she replaced her dark glasses and managed a brisk, 'Enjoy the magazine, Mr McGrath.'

'I don't think so,' he said, holding it out to her. 'Give it to Alesia.'

'Alesia?'

'The receptionist. The girls on the staff will get a lot more enjoyment than I will, catching up with the inside gossip on the wedding.'

'Are you quite sure?' Something about him just brought out the worst in her. The reckless… 'You have no idea what you're missing.'

'You can tell me all about it over lunch.'

The man was incorrigible, a shocking tease, but undoubtedly right. And thoughtful, too. Who would have imagined it?

Taking the magazine from him, she said, 'So, what would you like?' His slate-grey eyes flickered dangerously, but she didn't fall for it again.

'For lunch? Why don't you surprise me?' he said after the briefest hesitation.

'I thought I already had,' she replied, mentally chalking one up to herself. 'Don't overdo it with that heavy pen,' she warned. 'I need you fit and on your feet, ready to fly out of here tomorrow.'

'Don't hold your breath,' he advised.

'So that would be a light chicken soup for lunch…' she murmured as she walked away. 'Or a little lightly poached white fish.'

'Chilli.'

Nothing wrong with his hearing, then.

'Or a very rare steak.'

'Maybe just a nourishing posset…'

A posset? Gideon frowned. What the heck was a posset? It sounded like something you'd give a sick kid…

Oh, right.

Very funny.

And she'd also managed to get in the last word again, he realised as the sound of her humming a familiar tune faded into the distance.

Never smile at a crocodile…

He grinned. Any crocodile who came face to face with her would turn tail and run, but plain Josie Fowler didn't frighten him. She could strut all she wanted in those boots but she'd made the fatal error of letting him see beneath the mask.

He knew that without wax her spiky purple-tipped hair curled softly against her neck, her cheeks. That her eyes needed no enhancement and, beneath the unnatural pallor of her make-up, her complexion had a translucent glow.

But, more important than the surface image, he'd recognised an odd defensiveness, a vulnerability that no one who saw her now, head high, ready with a snappy retort, would begin to suspect.

She'd had the last word, but he had the advantage.

Josie hummed the silly song as she walked along the bridge to the central building, well pleased to have got in the last word. It would serve Gideon McGrath right if she delivered up some bland invalid dish.

Probably not a posset, though.

She didn't want to risk the cream and eggs giving him a heart attack, although actually, come to think of it…

'Behave yourself, Josie,' she muttered as she stepped out of the sun and into the cool reception area and got an odd look from a sensibly dressed middle-aged woman who was wearing a wide-brimmed hat and carrying binoculars.

Although, on consideration, that probably had less to do with the fact that she was talking to herself than the way she looked.

In London she didn't seem that out of place. Here…

'Hello, Miss Fowler.' The receptionist greeted her with a wide smile. 'Have you settled in?'

'Yes, thanks. You're Alesia?'

'Yes?'

'Then this is for you,' she said, handing over the magazine.

The woman's eyes lit up as she saw the cover. 'It's Crystal Blaize,' she breathed. 'She is so beautiful. Thank you so much.'

'Don't thank me, thank Mr McGrath. He said you would like it.'

'Gideon? He thought of me, even when he is in so much pain? He is always so kind.'

Gideon? If she was on first name terms with him, he must be a regular visitor, which went some way towards explaining his almost pro-prietorial attitude to the place. The fact that he seemed almost…well…at home here, despite the lack of any personal touches in his room.

'Have you met her?' Alesia asked.

'Who? Oh, Crystal. Yes.' Briefly. She'd insisted on a meeting before she'd left, wanting to be sure that Crystal was happy with the arrangements. Happy with her. 'She's very sweet.'

And so desperately grateful to have someone who didn't terrify the wits out of her to hold her hand on her big day that Josie had dismissed the gossips' version of Serafina's departure as utter nonsense.

Apparently Marji, with more of a heart than she'd given her credit for, had taken pity on her.

Or maybe she just wanted to be sure that the bride didn't turn tail and run.

'Is Mr Kebalakile in his office?' she asked.

'Yes, Miss Fowler. He said to go straight through.'

'Come in, come in, Miss Fowler,' David said, rising to his feet as she tapped on the open door. 'Are you settled in? You've had breakfast?'

'It's Josie,' she said. 'And yes, thank you. It was perfect.' What she'd had of it. But it had gone down well with the monkey. 'I do, however, have a few problems with the accommodation. Only,' she hastened to add when his face fell, 'because I'm here on business rather than attempting to get away from it all.'

'You mean the lack of communications?'

'Since you bring it up, yes. How, for instance, am I expected to ring for service without a telephone?'

'You don't need a telephone, there's a bell pull by the bed.' He mimed the tugging action. 'It's all explained in the information folder left in the room.'

That would be the one she hadn't got around to reading.

'It's low-tech, but it's low maintenance too. It's just a question of renewing the cords when some creature decides to chew through them. And it works even when it rains.'

'It doesn't reach to the *Celebrity* offices, though.'

He grinned, presumably thinking she was joking.

'David, I'm serious. I understand you have a satellite link for the telephone and Internet?'

'Sorry. I was just imagining how much cord…' He shook his head. 'You're quite right. We have excellent communication links which are reliable for almost one hundred per cent of the time.'

Almost? She didn't ask. She had enough to worry about without going to meet trouble halfway.

'They are, of course, yours to command.'

Of course they were. She wasn't a guest. She was a collaborator on a wedding that was going to make this the most talked about place in the world by next week. Gideon must have realised that, even if she was too slow-witted to work it out for herself. She'd have to take it slowly today so that her brain could keep up, or she was going to do something really stupid.

'I've had a desk brought in here for you,' he said, indicating the small table in the corner. 'I'm out and about a lot so you'll have the office to yourself most of the time but just say if you need some privacy.' He produced a key. 'The office is locked when I'm not here, so you'll need this.'

She'd have willingly sat on his lap if it gave her access to the Net, but it was clear that this wedding was a very big deal for Leopard Tree Lodge.

It might be a venue for the seriously rich—who might, like Gideon, disapprove of their retreat being contaminated by mere celebrities—but everyone was feeling the pinch right now.

'Thank you, David. We'll be working together on this so it makes perfect sense to share an office.' With that sorted, she moved on. 'Next problem. Can you tell with what the situation is with Mr McGrath?'

'You've met Gideon?' He seemed surprised.

'Briefly,' she admitted.

'Well, that's excellent. I'm sure the company did him good.'

'I sincerely hope so. Since he's occupying the bridal suite?' she added.

'Ah. Yes. I was going to—'

'As you know, the photographer will be arriving first thing tomorrow in order to set everything up for a photo shoot and then cover Crystal and Tal's arrival,' she continued, firmly cutting off what she suspected would be an attempt to persuade her to switch rooms. Gideon might be a valued guest but, while she was sympathetic, her responsibility was to her client. 'Presumably you have some way of evacuating casualties?'

'There is a helicopter ambulance,' he admitted, 'and Gideon has been offered a bed in the local hospital.' She let out the metaphorical breath she'd been holding ever since she'd realised she had a problem. 'However, as his condition requires rest and relaxation rather than medical intervention, he chose to remain where he is.'

'Who wouldn't? But—'

'Our own doctor consulted with his doctor in London and they both agreed that would be much the best thing.'

'But not essential?' she pressed.

'Not essential,' he admitted. 'But, since Gideon owns Leopard Tree Lodge—' He raised his hands in a gesture that suggested there wasn't a thing he could do.

Josie stared at him.

He owned Leopard Tree Lodge?

'I didn't know,' she said faintly. 'He didn't mention it.'

'He probably thought you knew. He owns many hotels and resorts these days, but this was his first and he oversaw every phase of the building.'

Oh…sugar. Proprietorial was right. But surely…

'If he owns this place,' she persisted, grasping at the positive in that, 'he must know that the room is taken. That every room is taken. Why it's absolutely essential that he moves.'

Except that he hadn't.

On the contrary, he had maintained that a noisy celebrity wedding was utterly out of place in this setting, which suggested that not only didn't he understand, he didn't approve.

'He didn't know about the wedding, did he?' she demanded.

'I couldn't say, but obviously Gideon doesn't have anything to do with the day-to-day running of the business. Hotel bookings are handled by a separate agency. Gideon's primary role is looking for new sites, developing new resorts, new experiences.'

'So why is he here?' she asked. A reasonable question. This was an established resort.

'His spirit needs healing. Where else would he go?'

His spirit?

Obviously he meant the man was stressed…

'Would you like to get in touch with your office now?' he asked, making it clear that he had nothing more to say on the matter.

She considered challenging him, but what

would be the point? David wasn't going to load his boss onto a helicopter and ship him out.

She'd have to talk to Gideon herself over lunch, make him see reason.

He might not like the idea of a celebrity wedding disturbing the wildlife, but as a successful businessman he had to realise how much he had to gain from the publicity.

So that would be chilli…

'I'm sure you would like to let them know you've arrived safely,' David urged, doing his best to make up for his lack of help over the cuckoo sitting in her bridal nest. 'My computer is at your disposal.'

'Yes. Thank you.'

'If I could just ask you not to mention the facility to any of the wedding guests? If word gets out, neither of us will be able to move for people wanting to "just check their email". People think they want to get away from it all, but…' He shrugged.

'Point taken,' she said. 'And I'll try not to get under your feet more than I have to. In fact, if you could point me in the direction of a socket where I could recharge my net book I'll be able to do some work in my room.' Then, as he took it from her, 'What do you do when the sun isn't shining? You do have some kind of backup?' she asked, suddenly envisaging a whole new crop of problems. 'For fridges, freezers?'

'We use gas for those.'

'Sorry?'

'It's old technology. Gideon considered using paraffin but gas meets all our needs.'

'So do you use gas for cooking too?'

'In the kitchen. We also have traditional wood-fired stoves in the compound which we use for bread and roasts.'

'Fascinating. Well, I'll try not to be too much of a burden on your system, but I would like to check my email for any updates from *Celebrity*. The guest list seems to change on the hour.' She might get lucky and discover someone had cancelled. 'And I need to telephone my office to warn them that I don't have a signal here.'

'Please, help yourself,' David replied, leaving her to it. 'I'll be outside when you're ready to be shown around.'

CHAPTER FIVE

From the original and chic to quirky and fun,
add a highly individual touch to your reception. Use your imagination and follow the
theme of the wedding for your inspiration…
—*The Perfect Wedding* by Serafina
March

JOSIE downloaded the latest changes to the guest list from Marji onto a memory stick and sent it to print while she called her office.

'No mobile signal? Ohmigod, how will the celebs survive?' Emma giggled. 'Better watch out for texting withdrawal symptoms—the twitching fingers, that desperate blank stare of the message deprived— and be ready to provide counselling.'

'Very funny. Just get in touch with Marji and warn her that there are no power points in the rooms, will you. The hairdresser and guests will need to bring battery or gas operated dryers and straighteners.'

While she had the phone in her hand, she double-checked delivery details with the florists, caterers, confectioners. That left Cara, Gideon's PA, and she dialled the number with crossed fingers. With luck, the answer would be sufficiently compelling to get him on her side…

'Cara March…'

March? As in Serafina…

'Miss March, Josie Fowler. Gideon McGrath asked me to call you.'

'Gideon? Oh, poor guy. How is he?'

In pain. Irritable. About to fire your sorry ass…

'Concerned. He wants to know—and I'm quoting here—what the hell is going on in Marketing.'

'Marketing?'

'I get the feeling that he's not entirely happy about having the Tal Newman wedding at Leopard Tree Lodge.'

'Oh, good grief, is that this week?' she squeaked.

'I'm afraid so.'

'Damn! And bother Gideon for taking a sentimental side trip down memory lane this week. If he'd just stuck to his schedule, gone straight to Patagonia as he was supposed to, he'd never have known about it.'

Sentimental? Gideon?

'You don't think he would have noticed six weeks of articles in *Celebrity*?' Josie enquired, wondering why his staff had conspired to keep this from him.

'Oh, please. Can you imagine Gideon reading *Celebrity*? Besides, he's far too busy hunting down the next challenge to notice things like that. He never changes his schedule, takes a day off...'

'No?'

'Look, tell him it's nothing to do with Marketing, will you. Aunt Serafina called in at the office to drop something off for my mother absolutely yonks ago. She asked me for a brochure and, like an idiot, I gave her one. I had no idea she was looking for somewhere unusual, somewhere off the beaten track for the Newman wedding. And I'm here to testify that she doesn't understand the word "no".'

'Oh.'

'You're the woman who *Celebrity* sent in my aunt's place, aren't you?' she asked.

'Yes. How is she?'

'Spitting pips, to be honest, but that's not your fault. She can be a little overwhelming if you're not used to her.'

'So I've heard. Her design is amazing, though. Tell her I'll do my best to deliver.'

'Actually, I won't, if you don't mind. Just the

sound of your name is likely to send her off on one. But you can tell Gideon that I'm entirely to blame and he can fire me the minute he gets back if it will make him feel any better.'

'He won't, will he?'

Anyone with Serafina March for an aunt deserved all the sympathy they could get.

'Probably not. Josie…about Gideon. Since he's there, see if you can persuade him to stay for a while. We've all been concerned about him. He really does need a break.'

'You just wish he'd chosen somewhere else.'

'I have the feeling that Leopard Tree Lodge might have chosen him,' she said.

Terrific. Now she was involved in the conspiracy to keep him here. She picked up the printout of the latest guest list, praying for an outbreak of something contagious amongst the guests.

'All sorted?' David asked as she joined him in the lounge.

'Not exactly,' she said, skimming through Marji's updates. No one had cried off. On the contrary. 'We're going to have to find another room.'

'How's it going?'

Gideon McGrath, cool and relaxed as he lay in the shade, removed his sunglasses as Francis set down the lunch tray beside him, giving Josie the kind of glance that made her feel even more hot and frazzled than she already was.

'How's your back?' she shot right back at him. She was in no mood to take prisoners.

'It's early days.' Then, once Francis had gone, 'The coffee helped, though.'

'I'm glad to hear it,' she replied, helping herself to a glass of water from a Thermos jug. 'And what's on that tray had better finish the job.'

'You're just teasing me with false hope.'

'It's chilli,' she said, in no mood for teasing him or anyone else. 'Why didn't you tell me you own this place?'

'Does it matter?'

He said it lightly enough, but there was a challenge in those dark eyes that suggested it did.

'It does when the manager feels he can't ask you to leave, despite the fact that the room has been bought and paid for by a bona fide guest,' she replied.

'None of my resort managers would expect a sick guest to leave. You, I take it,' he said, 'have no such inhibitions.'

'Too right. Although, since we both now know that you're not a guest, you'd better enjoy that chilli while you can.'

'That sounds like a threat.'

'I don't make threats. I make promises.

Unless you make your own arrangements to leave, I'll be ordering up an air ambulance to take you out of here first thing in the morning. You'd better decide where you want it to take you.'

'Ambulances only have one destination,' he pointed out. 'They're not a taxi service.'

'Right. Well, that's an additional incentive because I'm betting they don't have an la carte menu at the local hospital,' she replied, refusing to think what that would be like.

He was successful, wealthy. Hospital would be a very different experience for him, she told herself, blocking out the memory of her mother shrinking away to nothing in a bare room.

Gideon McGrath would be in a private suite with the best of everything. Maybe. Would the local hospital have private suites?

'Is that really chilli?' he asked gently, as if he genuinely sympathised with her dilemma. And, just like that, all the hard-faced determination leached out of her and she knew that she couldn't do it.

'I wanted you in a good mood,' she admitted. 'I even phoned your PA and gave her your message.'

'What did she say?'

'The exact word was unrepeatable,' she replied. 'Have you never heard of Serafina March?'

'March? That's Cara's name. Is she a relative?'

'Her aunt. She's the queen of the designer wedding. She wrote *The Perfect Wedding*, the definitive book on the subject.'

'I take it there is some reason for you telling me this.'

'You can relax, Gideon. This hasn't got anything to do with your marketing department thinking up new ways to drum up business. Serafina visited her niece in the office and saw some photographs of this place. Quiet, off the beaten track, just what she was looking for.'

'Why didn't someone just say no?'

'Apparently she is unfamiliar with the word. Cara offered to take the blame, fall on her sword if it will help.'

'Only because she knows she's indispensable.'

She'd said that too, but Josie didn't tell him that. Instead, she swallowed a mouthful of water, then, hot, tired, she pushed her glasses onto the top of her head, tilted it back and poured the rest of it over her face, shivering as the icy water trickled down her throat, between her breasts. Then she poured herself another glass before turning to find Gideon staring at her.

'Did you want some water?' she offered.

'Er… I'll pass, thanks.'

She glanced at the glass in her hand and then

at him. 'No…' Then, despite everything, she laughed. 'You really shouldn't put ideas like that into my head. Not after the morning I've had.'

'Pass me the chilli and take the weight off your feet,' he said. 'My shoulder is at your disposal.'

It was a very fine shoulder. More than broad enough for a woman to lay her head against while she sobbed her heart out. Not that she was about to do that.

'You already said,' she reminded him, uncovering the chilli and passing it to him, along with a fork. 'But if your shoulder was truly mine I'd have it shipped out of here so fast your feet wouldn't touch the ground. The wise decision would be to go with it.'

Gideon grinned as he tucked into the first decent food he'd had for two days. She was a feisty female and if they'd been anywhere else he'd have put his money on her. But it was going to take more than tough talk to shift him. This was his home turf and all the muscle was on his payroll.

She poured herself another glass of water, this time to drink, and needed no encouragement from him to sink onto the lounger beside him.

'Damn, this is good,' he said. Then, glancing at her, 'Aren't you hungry?'

Her only response was to lift her hand an inch or two in a gesture that suggested eating was too much effort. Maybe it was. Now she was lying down, her eyes closed, the I'm-in-charge mask had slipped.

He'd seen it happen a dozen times. Visitors arrived hyped up on excitement, running on adrenalin and kept going for an hour or two, but it didn't take long for the journey, the heat, to catch up with them. It had happened to him once or twice and it was like walking into a brick wall.

'Okay, give,' he said. 'Maybe I can help.'

'You can, but you won't.' She caught a yawn. 'You'll just lie there, eating your illicit chilli and gloating.'

No… Well, maybe, just a little. He was in a win-win situation. He could make things as difficult for her as possible but, no matter what horrors occurred at this wedding, he knew the pain wouldn't show on the pages of *Celebrity*.

Short of the kind of disaster that would make news headlines, the photographs would show smiling celebrities attending a stunningly original wedding, even if they had to fake the pictures digitally.

In the meantime, he had the pleasure of the wedding planner doing everything she could to make him happy.

He smiled as he lifted another forkful of his chef's excellent chilli. Then lowered it again untasted as he glanced at her untouched lunch.

Was she really not hungry? Or was the food…?

He eased himself forward far enough to lift the cover on her plate.

Steamed fish. Beautifully cooked, no doubt, and with a delicate fan of very pretty vegetables, but not exactly exciting. Clearly, she'd taken the ultimate culinary sacrifice to give him what he wanted.

'I won't gloat,' he promised.

'Of course you will,' she replied without moving. Without opening her eyes. 'You're hating this. If you could wave a magic wand and make me, Crystal, Tal and the whole wedding disappear you'd do it in a heartbeat.'

'My mistake,' he said. 'I left the magic wand in my other bag.'

Her lips moved into an appreciative smile. 'Pity. You could have used it to conjure up another couple of rooms and solved all our problems.'

'Two? I thought you were just one room short?'

She rolled her head an inch or two, looking at him from beneath dark-rimmed lids. Assessing him. Deciding whether she could take him at his word.

'Don't fight it,' he said. 'You know you want to tell me.'

'You're the enemy,' she reminded him. Then, apparently deciding that it didn't matter one way or the other, she let her head fall back and, with a tiny sigh, said, 'My problem is the chief brides-maid.'

'Oh, that's always a tricky one. Has she fallen out with the bride over her dress?' he hazarded. 'I understand the plan is to make them as unflattering as possible in order to show off the bride to best advantage.'

Her mouth twitched. 'Wrong. I promise you the bridesmaids' dresses are show-stoppers.'

'Oh, right. The bride has fallen out with the bridesmaid for looking too glamorous?'

'Not that either.'

'The bride caught her flirting with the groom?' Nothing. 'Kissing the groom?' A shake of her head. 'In bed with the groom?'

'That would mean the wedding was off.' Her voice was slowing as she had to think harder to find the words. 'This is worse. Much worse.'

'What on earth could be worse than that?'

'The chief bridesmaid has dumped her partner.'

'Oh.' He frowned, trying to see why that would be a cause for wailing and gnashing of teeth. 'Surely that means you've got an extra bed? You could share her room and the happy couple could have yours. Problem solved.'

'Problem doubled,' she replied. 'The reason she dumped him is because she has a new man in her life and she's not going anywhere without him.'

'Okaaay,' he said, still not getting it. 'One man out, one man in. No gain, but we're just back to square one.'

'If only life were that simple. Unfortunately, her ex is the best man and while I'd love to suggest that you move in with him, solving one of my problems,' she said, still awake enough to wield her tongue with sarcastic precision, 'it seems that he wants to show the world just how much he isn't hurting. To that end, he's bringing his brand new girlfriend with him.'

'You're not convinced that it's true love?'

'Anything is possible,' she admitted, 'but it would have made my life a whole lot easier if he'd declared himself too broken-hearted to come to the wedding…'

All the tension had left her body now. Her hand, beside her, was perfectly still. Her breathing was slowing. For a moment he thought she'd gone, but an insect buzzed noisily across the deck just above her and she jerked her eyes open, flapped at it.

'*Celebrity* would have loved a tragic broken-heart cover story, a nice little tear-jerker to wrap around the wedding,' she said, easing herself up the lounger, battling her body's need for sleep, 'and bump up the emotional headline count. And a new best man would have been easier to find than another room.'

'You're all heart, Josie Fowler.'

'I'm a realist, Gideon McGrath. I've left David juggling the accommodation in an attempt to find some space somewhere— anywhere. Hopefully with sufficient distance between the best man and the bridesmaid to avoid fingernails at dawn.'

'And if he can't?'

'If the worst comes to the worst I'll let them have my room.'

'And where will you sleep?' he persisted as she began to slip away again.

'I can crash in the office,' she mumbled. 'I've slept in worse places…'

And that was it. She was gone. Out like a light.

He took his time about finishing the chilli, wondering where Josie had slept that was worse than David's office floor. Who she was. Where she came from, because she certainly wasn't one of those finishing school girls with cut-glass accents who regularly descended on his office to organise the launch parties for his new ventures.

It wasn't just her street smart, in-your-face image that set her apart. There was an edginess about her, a desperate need to succeed that made her vulnerable in a way those other girls could never be.

It was a need he recognised, understood and, replacing his plate on the tray, he eased himself off the lounger, straightened slowly, held his breath while the pain bit deep. After a moment it settled to a dull ache and he wound out the shade so that when the sun moved around Josie would be protected from its rays.

That done, he tugged on the bell to summon Francis, then he made it, without mishap, to the bathroom.

Maybe he should make Josie's day and keep going while he had sufficient movement to enable him to get onto a plane. Perhaps catch up with Matt in Patagonia.

Just the thought was enough to bring the pain flooding back and he had to grab hold of the door to stop himself from falling.

Josie opened her eyes. Glanced at Gideon.

He was lying back, hands linked behind his head, totally relaxed, and for a moment her breath caught in her throat. She met good-looking men all the time in her job. Rich, powerful, good-looking men, but that was just work and while they, occasionally, suggested continuing a business meeting over a drink or dinner, she was never tempted to mix business with pleasure.

It had to be because she was out of her

comfort zone here, out on a limb and on her own, that made her more vulnerable to a smile. He had, despite the bickering, touched something deep inside her, a need that she had spent a long time denying.

While there was no doubt that he was causing her all kinds of bother, it was as if he was, in some way that she couldn't quite fathom, her collaborator. A partner. Not a shoulder to cry on—she did not weep—but someone to turn to.

She wanted him gone. But she wanted him to stay too and, as if he could hear the jumble of confused thoughts turning over in her brain, he turned and smiled across at her.

The effect was almost physical. Like a jolt of electricity that fizzed through her.

'Okay?' he asked, quirking up a brow.

'Y-yes…' Then, 'No.'

Her mouth was gluey; she felt dried out. Not surprising. It had been a manic forty-eight hours. A long evening at the office making sure that everything was covered while she was away. A quick meeting with the bride, a scramble to pack and get to the airport. And she'd spent most of her time on the plane getting to grips with 'the design', making sure she was on top of everything that had to be done.

'There's water if you need it,' he said, nodding towards a bottle, dewed with moisture, that was standing on the table between them.

'Thanks.'

She took a long drink, then found the stick of her favourite strawberry-flavoured lip balm she always kept in her pocket.

'What was I saying?' she asked.

'That you'd slept in worse places than David's office.'

She paused in the act of uncapping the stick, suddenly chilled despite the hot sun filtering through the trees as she remembered those places. The remand cell. The six long months while she was locked up. The hostel…

She slowly wound up the balm, taking her time about applying it to her lips. Taking another long pull on the water while she tried to recall the conversation that had led up to that.

The shortage of rooms. The wretched bridesmaid and the equally annoying best man. That was it. She'd been telling him about the need for yet another room. And she had told him that she'd sleep in the office if necessary…

After that she didn't remember anything. Weird…

She stopped worrying about it—it would all come back to her—and, in an attempt to make a joke of it, she said, 'You won't tell David I said that, will you? About sleeping on his office floor.

I don't want to give him an excuse to give up trying to find somewhere.'

'I won't,' Gideon assured her. 'Not that it matters. David won't let you sleep in his office. Not if he values his job.'

'His job?' She frowned. 'Are you saying that you'd fire him? When you're one of the reasons we're in this mess?'

'There are health, safety, insurance considerations,' he said. 'You're a guest. If anything were to happen to you while you were bedded down on the office floor, you'd sue the pants off me.'

'Too right.' She'd considered denying it, but clearly it wasn't going to make any difference what she said. 'The pants, the shirt and everything else. Better leave now,' she urged him. Then, just to remind him that he owed her a favour, 'Did you enjoy your lunch?'

'Yes, thanks. Your sacrifice was appreciated.'

Sacrifice? Didn't he know that city girls lived on steamed fish and a mouthful of salad if they wanted to keep their figures? At least when they were being good. She could eat a pizza right now, but the fish would do and she turned to the tray. It wasn't there. There was nothing but the bottle of water.

'What happened to my lunch?' she asked.

'Room service cleared it hours ago.'

'Excuse me?' She glanced at her watch, frowned. It showed a quarter past four. Had she made a mistake when she'd moved it forward?

'You've been asleep for nearly three hours, Josie.'

'Pull the other one...I just closed my eyes,' she protested.

'At about half past one,' he agreed. 'And now you've opened them.'

At quarter past four? No... She looked around, desperately hoping for some way to deny his claim.

The sun had been high overhead when she'd joined Gideon for lunch. The light seemed softer, mellower now and, looking up to check how far it had moved, she realised that someone had placed a shade over her.

'Where did that come from?' she asked, startled. Then, still not quite able to believe it, 'I've really been asleep?' She could have sworn she'd simply closed her eyes and then opened them a moment later. It had felt like no more than a blink. 'Why didn't you wake me?'

'Why would I do that?' he asked. 'You obviously needed a nap.'

'Three hours isn't a nap!' she said, telling leaden limbs to move, limbs that appeared to be glued to the lounger. 'There'll be emails. Messages. I have to talk to the chef. Unpack the linen and check that everything's there. That it's the right colour,' she continued in a rush of panic, forcing her legs over the edge. 'I've got a hundred favour boxes to put together.'

'Relax, Josie. No one rushes around in the afternoon heat. Take your cue from the animals.'

'And do what?' she demanded. 'Slosh about in the river?'

'Not in the afternoon. That's when they find a cool corner in the shade, lie down and go to sleep.'

'Check,' she said. 'Done that.'

'So has everyone else with any sense. Including the chef.' He grinned. 'Now is the time to take a dip.'

She glanced towards the wide oxbow lake that had been formed by the erosion of the bank where the river had once formed a great loop. Animals had begun to gather at the water's edge. Small deer, a couple of zebras and then, as she watched, a giraffe moved majestically towards the water and a lump caught in her throat.

This was real. Not a zoo or a safari park or David Attenborough on the telly and she watched transfixed for a moment before remembering that she had work to do and, turning back to Gideon, said, 'Actually, bearing in mind your advice about crocodiles, I think I might give that one a miss.'

'What do you think the plunge pool is for?'

'Oh, I know that one… "You can simply sit in your own private plunge pool and watch elephants cavorting below you in an oxbow lake while you sip a glass of chilled bubbly,"' she quoted, trying not to think about how good that sounded right now. 'I've read the guidebook.' Or, rather, had it read to her.

'Sounds good to me.' He began to unbutton his shirt to reveal a broad tanned chest with a delicious sprinkling of dark chest hair. 'Get your kit off and I'll ring for room service.'

Jolted from her distracted gaze, she said, 'Excuse me?'

'You're the one who suggested water therapy. I wasn't convinced but the champagne sold it to me.'

Josie was hot, dehydrated and a little water therapy—the delicious combination of cool water, hot skin and the best-looking man she'd met in a very long time—was much too tempting for a woman who hadn't had a date in a very long time.

It was in the nature of the job that events planners were working when other people were partying.

And part of the appeal.

She didn't have to think about why she didn't have a social life when she was too busy arranging other people's to have one of her own.

'You're not interested in water therapy,' she told him. 'You just want a drink.'

'If I wanted a drink,' he said, 'champagne wouldn't be my first choice. But, as a sundowner, a glass or two would help relax the muscles.'

'That sounds like a plan,' she said, well aware that he was simply amusing himself at her expense. Using her desperation to be rid of him to get what he wanted. It was the coffee, the chilli all over again but, even if she had been foolish enough to fall for it, she had far too much to do. And three fewer hours in which to do it. 'I'll smuggle a bottle past the guards for you.'

'I can't tempt you?'

Oh, she was tempted—no question about that—but a splash of water on her face and a reviving pot of tea was as good as it was going to get this evening.

'I'll take a rain check,' she said, forcing herself to her feet. 'The guests will start arriving tomorrow, including a bride and groom who'll be expecting this suite to be waiting for them.'

'Ah…'

'Ah?' She didn't like the sound of that 'ah'.

'I knew there was something I had to tell you.'

'Please let it be that you're leaving.'

'Sorry…' His regretful shrug was so elegantly done that she found herself wondering what he would be like on his feet. How he would move. Imagined the graceful ripple of those thigh muscles…

'No, Gideon,' she snapped, dragging herself back from the edge of drool. She'd tried the placatory approach, been Miss Sugar and Spice. Now she was going to have to get tough. 'You're not in the least bit sorry so don't pretend you are.'

'I am sorry that my presence is causing you difficulties. Why don't you email *Celebrity* and tell them that someone has to stay at home? Couldn't the bride manage with one less attendant? Or maybe just do her own make-up?'

'Was that it?' she enquired. 'What you had to tell me? It's a great idea, but far too late. Most of the guests are already on their way so, if that's it, I've got things to do.'

'No, there's something else. You'd better sit down,' he advised.

'I'm liking this less and less,' she said, but she was still feeling a bit light-headed. Maybe she needed another minute or two to fully wake up and she sank back down. 'You'd better tell me.'

'Tal Newman arrived in Gabarone today. He's got dinner with the Botswana national team tonight and tomorrow he's giving some young-sters a football master class before taking part in a parade giving him the freedom of Gabarone.'

'Yes. I've got the programme. It's just an average day in the life of the world's most famous football player,' she said. 'So?'

'It seems that no one thought to organise something to keep Cryssie occupied so she decided that, rather than hang around in the hotel all day, she'd fly on here and have a quiet day recuperating from the journey and hanging out with you instead.'

'Fly on here? Fly. On. Here.' She repeated the three words slowly, while her brain attempted to translate them into something meaningful. 'You're telling me that Crystal…'and when did he get so familiar with Crystal Blaize that he was calling her Cryssie? '…is on her way here? Right now?' Then, with dawning horror, 'You knew that and you just let me lie there and sleep!'

'No–'

Josie almost collapsed with relief.

'—she arrived just after lunch. She came looking for you, but when she saw how exhausted you were she wouldn't let me wake you.'

'What?' Then, leaping to her feet, 'Ohmigod! Where is she?'

Gideon was too busy making a wild grab for her as the blood rushed from her head to offer a suggestion. Or maybe too short of breath.

It had rushed from her in a little 'Oooph' as his hands circled her ribs.

Rushed from him in a deeper 'Umph' as she made a grab for his shoulders, sank against him.

For a moment she was too winded to move. And even when she managed to suck in some air she couldn't quite manage to lift her cheek from the warm skin of Gideon's neck, her breasts from where they were cosied against his ribs. Disentangle her legs. And the two of them remained that way for a moment, locked together in immovability.

'Are you okay?'

His voice wasn't just sound, it was vibration that rumbled through her, became part of her.

'No.' In the stillness, as they caught at their breath, everything became pure sensation and she was a lot more than all right.

His pulse was pounding in her ear, she could almost taste the scent of his sun-baked skin and, beneath her hands, his strength seemed to pour into her through the hard-packed muscle of his shoulders.

'You?'

'No.'

She lifted her head, afraid that she might have done some irreparable damage to his back, but the visual impact of his stubbled chin, parted lips up so close was like falling a second time.

His 'no' had been the same as hers and the heat that came off him had nothing to do with the temperature but from some fire raging within him, a fire that sparked an answering inferno deep within her. A raw, painful need that burned deep within her belly, sparking at the tips of her breasts, burning her skin.

They had been verbally fencing with one another since he'd teased a cup of coffee out of her. Holding one another off with words while their eyes, their bodies, had been communicating in another language. One that did not need words.

Now there was nothing between them, only the ragged snatch of her breath.

Not a creature moved. Even the cicadas seemed to pause their endless stridulating so that the air was thick with the silence, as if the world was holding its breath. Waiting.

She was so close to him now that all she could see were a scatter of tiny scars high on his forehead, glints of molten silver glowing in the depths of his slate-grey eyes.

His breath was hers, her lips were his but which of them had closed the infinitesimal gap between them was unknowable.

In the still, quiet world that existed only for them, his kiss was slow, thorough, tormenting her with the promise of his power to quench the fire.

His hands softened as he drew her down to him, intensified his kiss and her body moulded naturally to his. But even that was not enough.

She wanted to be closer, wanted to be naked, wanted him in the way that a woman yearned for a man, drawn by the atavistic need to surrender to the illusion of safety within his arms.

Wanted to be held, touched…

As if he could read her mind, his hands abandoned her shoulders and began to move tantalisingly, tormentingly slowly down her body, lingering agonisingly at her waist before descending to her thighs while his tongue plundered her mouth so that in her head she was screaming for more.

He responded to her urgent moan, sliding his hand beneath her short skirt and pulling her into him so that she could feel the sudden hard urgency of his need, counterpoint to the melting softness of her desire.

She wanted to be touched, possessed, loved…

Even as she sank deeper into his embrace and his arms enfolded her, that 'loved' word, that dreadful word, the tool of mendacious men, betrayer of gullible women, splintered through her mind like a shaft of ice and she broke free, slithering from his grasp to the floor before he could stop her.

'Josie—' He followed, crashing onto the deck beside her, his hands reaching for her.

'Don't…'

She flinched, digging her heels into the deck,

scooting away from him. Putting herself out of reach. Dragging the back of her hand over her mouth in an attempt to wipe away all trace of the touch, the taste of his seductive lips, the delicious temptation…

'What have I done?' he asked, but this time making no effort to follow her, hold her. And why would he? She wasn't blaming Gideon. Nothing had happened that she hadn't participated in eagerly, willingly and for a moment, one blissful moment in the warmth of his arms, she had managed to forget, shut out reality. Not this brilliant, sun-filled world, but the darkness within her.

'Nothing… It's not you. It's me. Just…' She shook her head, incapable of explaining. Finding the words to apologise for behaving so badly.

'Don't?' he offered, a great deal more gently than she deserved.

She nodded once. Then, forcing herself to behave normally, like an adult. 'Are you hurt?' He'd come down off the lounger with a hell of a crash.

'Only my pride. I don't normally get that reaction when I kiss a woman.'

That she could believe. It had been the most perfect kiss. So bewitchingly sensuous that for a moment she had been utterly seduced. Nothing less would have stolen away her wits, her determined self-control, even for a moment.

'There was nothing wrong with the kiss, Gideon.' She could still feel the heat of it singing in her blood, telling her that she was strong, could do anything. Tempting her to reach out to him, test her power. 'I just…'

She lifted her hands in a helpless gesture. She'd turned her life around. Was in control. She would never allow anything, anyone to take that from her again.

His eyes narrowed.

'Can't?' he offered helpfully, completing her unfinished sentence for the second time.

She knew that look, recognised the speculation as he wondered what had happened to her. Who had hurt her. Whatever he was thinking, he was wrong. Nothing he was imagining could be as bad as the truth.

CHAPTER SIX

The dress. Individual, unique, it is a statement of everything the bride feels about herself. A matter for secrecy, intrigue and speculation…
—*The Perfect Wedding* by Serafina March

JOSIE steeled herself for the usual prurient inquisition—was it rape or abuse? No man had ever asked her if he'd done something to turn her off. Not that Gideon had. For a moment she had so utterly forgotten herself that she was still shaking with a surge of need unlike anything she'd ever experienced.

But the question never came.

'Don't worry about it, Josie,' he said, so casually that if she hadn't been so relieved she might have felt insulted. 'It was nothing.'

Nothing?

'You don't have to apologise. Or explain.'

'No?'

Easy for him to say. He probably had women throwing themselves at him all the time. Not that she had. Thrown herself. She'd had a giddy spell, had been off balance physically and mentally or she would never have reacted so wantonly to his closeness.

The kiss had not been forced upon her. It had been inevitable from the first moment she'd set eyes on him. She'd recognised the danger, thought she could control it...

'No,' she said, turning the word from a question to a statement as she eased herself carefully to her feet—she didn't want a repeat of that giddy spell... 'Nothing at all.' Then, because he hadn't moved, 'Do you need a hand up?'

He looked up at her for a moment as if considering the physics of the skinny girl/big bloke leverage situation.

'Not a good idea.'

No. It would be too easy to repeat that tumble and it was obvious that he didn't want to risk that.

Nor did she, she told herself hurriedly.

'Shall I call someone?'

'Forget about me,' he said, apparently content to sit on the deck, his back against the hard frame. 'You've got a bride to worry about.'

'Yes…' She backed slowly away—any injudicious move was likely to stir up all those hormones swirling about her body, desperate for action. 'Did she say where she'd be?'

'Her room, I imagine.'

'Her room?' She finally snapped out of the semi-inert state where her brain was focused entirely on Gideon. 'This is her room!' she declared.

'Yes, well, that was the other thing I was about to tell you. Before you threw yourself on me.'

'What a pity I didn't do more damage.'

'Is that any way to speak to a man who, while you were snoring your head off, has single-handedly sorted out your accommodation problems?'

She was fairly sure that the snoring slur was simply his attempt to put up a wall between them and who could blame him?

Ignoring it, she said, 'What did you do? Rub a magic lamp and produce another tree house out of thin air?'

'Is that what you do when, on the morning of the wedding, the bride tells you that a long lost cousin from New Zealand has arrived with all his family and you have to find room for half a dozen extra people at a reception?'

'I don't need magic to produce an extra table,' she snapped back. 'It's my job.' Then, because this was no way to cool things down, she extended a hand, palm out like a traffic cop. 'Stop.' She took a deep breath. 'Back up.' He waited, a questioning tilt to one of those devilish brows while she took another breath. Started again. 'Thank you so much for involving yourself with my accommodation problem, Gideon. Would you care to update me?' she enquired politely.

She got an appreciative grin for her efforts and all those escaped hormones stampeded in his direction and she took a step forward as she almost overbalanced.

Maybe he noticed because he said, 'Sit down and I'll fill you in.'

She did but only, she told herself, because he was having to peer awkwardly up at her in a way that must be hurting his back. Not that he'd been feeling pain a few minutes ago…

Stop. Oh, stop…

Ignoring the low lounger—she wasn't risking a second close encounter with all those free roaming pheromones—she crossed to a canvas director's chair that David had fetched so that they could have a cosy chat over her supine body.

Tempted as she was to pitch in with yet another sarcastic comment, she suspected he was waiting for it and, since she hated being predictable, said, 'When you're ready?'

'The best man and his new girlfriend have been allocated the captain's cabin aboard the river boat. It's not like this, but they'll have the deck for game viewing and the pool if they want to cool off.'

'What about the captain?' she asked.

'He can use the first mate's cabin.'

'And the first mate?' She held up a hand. 'No, I don't want to know.' She swallowed. He was in pain, he didn't want the wedding here, but he'd still gone out of his way to help her. 'Just… well, thank you. That's an enormous help.'

Gideon, the dull ache of unfulfilled lust competing with the hard frame of the sun-lounger digging into his back for attention, was concentrating so hard on Josie that they didn't stand a chance.

A woman had every right to change her mind and she didn't have to apologise. It was obvious, from the moment he'd set eyes on her, that there had been something between them, that rare arc of sexual energy that could leap across a room on a glance. An exchange between two people destined to be naked together in the very near future. For a night, or a lifetime. Or not.

You were with someone else, or she was and there would be a shrug, an acknowledgement of what might have been.

On this occasion it had not just arced, there

had been lightning and it was going to take a lot more than a shrug, a regretful look to make him forget how she'd felt in his arms. That look on her face as she'd scrambled to distance herself from him. Dismay, desperation…

It wasn't what he'd done that had sent her running. It was what she'd come close to doing.

'You've been very kind, Gideon,' she said, her words, like her body, as stiff as a board.

'Well, you know what they say. There's no such thing as a free lunch.' He lifted a brow, hoping to provoke her, get her to loosen up, let go. Get back the Josie who said exactly what she thought instead of what she thought she should say. 'I imagine that surrendering your lunch wasn't an entirely altruistic gesture?'

'Not in the least,' she admitted without a blush.

Better…

'Which brings us to the larger problem of the bridal suite. What'll it take to fix that?' Then she did blush, possibly remembering his earlier comment about incentives.

Much better…

'Nothing. It's sorted.'

'Really?' She brightened.

'We're going to be room mates.'

Gideon saw the blush fade from her cheeks as she rose slowly to her feet.

'Well, you and David have had a busy afternoon,' she said.

He'd known that she wasn't going to be happy about it and, under the circumstances, it didn't take a genius to see what she must be thinking.

'I'm sorry, but David and I went through the guest list to see if there was any way either of us could double up. But, like the Ark, everyone is coming to this wedding two-by-two. We are the only singles.'

'You could leave,' she pointed out.

'I did consider it,' he admitted. 'I even made it as far as the bathroom, but it seems that the very thought of getting on a plane was enough to make my back seize up again.'

'How convenient.'

'You think I'm enjoying this?'

'Oh, God, no,' she said, her face instantly softening, full of compassion, and that made him feel like a heel because right at this moment he was enjoying the situation rather a lot. 'I'm sorry. That was a horrible thing to say…'

He could have told her that she had an instant cure, but under the circumstances he thought it unwise and instead watched as, for the second time in ten minutes Josie struggled to come to terms with a situation she couldn't quite get her head around.

'Is flying a problem for you?' she asked.

He laughed. He knew he shouldn't but he couldn't help himself. 'Are you asking me if I'm afraid of flying?'

'It's nothing to be ashamed of,' she assured him.

'Have you any idea how many miles I fly each year?'

'Well, no, but it's a fact that the more miles you fly the shorter the odds become…'

'Stop. Stop right there. I have a pilot's licence, Josie. I own my own light aircraft. I stunt fly for fun.'

'Stunt fly?'

'It's one of the extreme holidays my company offers.'

'Oh. Right. It's just that if the problem is psychological…' She stopped. 'No. Right.' Then, 'But if you can't move, how are you going to move rooms?' she asked.

'I'm not moving anywhere. You're moving in here.'

Josie frowned. 'Say that again?' she said, hoping that she'd misheard him, misunderstood.

'You're moving in here.'

'Dammit, Gideon, you are not listening to me,' she exclaimed, throwing her arms up in the air, walking around the deck in an attempt to expel all that pent-up emotion she'd been keeping battened down. Refusing to look at him.

'This is Tal and Cryssie's room. It's all been planned.'

'Yes, well, the first casualty of battle is always the plan,' he said. 'You—or rather Cara's aunt—looked at the layout and saw privacy. Cryssie took one look and saw herself isolated about as far from civilisation as it was possible to be and her response was a firm thanks, but no thanks.'

'What?' Josie came to a halt. In front of her, at the water's edge, a line of zebras raised their heads, looking for all the world like a row of startled dowagers at a wedding who'd just heard the vicar swear… 'But she had already approved everything,' she said, turning back to face Gideon.

'Maybe it looked different on paper. Whatever, she flatly refused to be "stuck out here where anything could eat me".'

He put on a high-pitched girly voice and, despite the fact that she was already furious with him on a number of counts, would have happily throttled him at that moment, she snorted with laughter.

'She didn't say that.'

'No? Ask her.' Then he smiled too. 'I really do think you'd have been better off with the petting zoo.'

'It would have been my choice too, but it's too late for that,' she replied. 'So where have you put her?'

'She's in the tree house nearest to the central lodge, which was, fortunately, vacated this morning. David has put the photographer and make-up artist who flew in with her next door.'

'In my room? I close my eyes for ten minutes—'

'Three hours.'

'—and you move someone else into my room.'

'You'd already accepted that you would have to surrender your room, Josie—'

True, but she didn't have to like it.

'—and the rest of the guests won't have gone until the morning. You might believe that we're in need of a major PR hit, but Leopard Tree Lodge is always full at this time of year. Cryssie did turn up a day early with her entourage and she's lucky to have any kind of room.'

'I know and I'm sorry about that, but you should have woken me up.'

'I'm too soft-hearted for my own good.'

'You're too chicken. You knew you'd get an argument and hoped that if I was faced with a fait accompli I'd just roll over.'

'That too,' he admitted, with just enough of a grin to suggest he believed he'd got away with it.

'I'd better go and shift my things,' she said. 'But this isn't over.'

'No need. Alesia did it for you.'

'Alesia…'

Not only her client, but half the staff had apparently walked through here this afternoon. Seen her "snoring her head off". Discussed what was best without reference to her.

He'd been right about one thing. She'd needed the sleep. But that was all he was right about.

This was her job, her responsibility, but she didn't bother to say what she was thinking. Instead, she turned on her heel and went inside.

Her toothbrush was sitting in a glass beside his on the bathroom shelf. Her clothes were hanging beside his cream suit. Her purple wheel-on suitcase was snuggled up cosily alongside his battered soft leather grip.

Even her briefcase had been brought in from the deck and placed tidily on the desk. And she knew exactly what he had done.

He hadn't discussed this with David. Employee or not, as the manager of this hotel he would never have agreed to something like this without consulting her. It was Gideon. Determined not to leave either Leopard Tree Lodge or surrender his own precious tree house to the unwanted bride and groom, he'd told David that this was her idea.

No doubt he'd shrugged, brushed aside the inconvenience, done a good job of presenting himself as the nice guy who was putting himself out to do everyone a favour.

And why wouldn't David have believed him? After all, there she was, fast asleep, totally at home in Gideon's tree house. Jane to his Tarzan.

It was all as neat and nice as the vast bed that Gideon seemed to believe she would share with him.

'Is everything there?' he asked when she emerged, blinking, into the late sunshine. Looking up at her from the deck, where he was looking more comfortable that he had any right to be.

'Oh, yes. They haven't missed a thing,' she said, sliding her dark glasses over her eyes.

'Well, good.' She noted that he sounded a little less certain now. 'I know how busy you are and I thought it would save you some time.'

'You thought that, did you?'

He shook his head. 'Okay. Tell me what's wrong.'

'Wrong?' she repeated, keeping it light, casual as if she had absolutely no idea what he was talking about, all the while holding in the urge to laugh hysterically. 'What could possibly be wrong?'

'I don't know. I've sorted out your accommodation problem. Your bride has got the room she wants. And that bed is big enough for both of us to sleep in without ever finding one another.'

There wasn't a bed big enough in the entire world…

'You were prepared to take the office floor, Josie. This has got to be better than that.'

'Maybe so, but it should have been my decision.'

'I made it easy for you.'

'No, you made it easy for yourself. No argument. Decision made. Everyone happy. Job done.'

He didn't bother to deny it but, with a shrug that could have meant anything, he said, 'I get the feeling you're about to prove to me how wrong I was about that.'

'It's just as well that sleeping on a hard surface is good for the back, or that since you're not going to sue yourself, there can be no objection to you sleeping on the office floor. You are so out of here.'

Josie didn't wait for his response, but went in search of Crystal, muttering a furious 'damn' with every step.

What was really galling was that she knew Gideon was right. She should be grateful to him for taking the time and trouble to summon David and sort everything out, relieving her of at least one worry.

He owned this place and he didn't have to share one inch of his precious space with her. It wasn't even the fact that he was a man that bothered her. She would have moved in with one of the *Celebrity* staff, male or female, without a second thought if they weren't already doubled up.

It was the obvious answer, the grown-up answer, one she might even have got around to suggesting herself, given enough time and a lack of any other option—although she'd still have taken the office floor, given the choice.

But, while he'd no doubt acted from the best of motives, Gideon couldn't possibly know how it made her feel to have control over what she did, where she slept, taken out of her hands.

How helpless, powerless that made her feel.

Or that it was something she'd vowed long ago would never happen to her again.

Stupid, stupid, stupid, she thought, slowing as she approached the last set of steps.

There were two rules.

One—never make a threat you aren't prepared to carry out or, worse, make one that you're powerless to deliver on.

Two—if you can't control the things around you, you can at least control yourself.

She'd just broken them both.

She stopped as she reached the steps to Crystal's tree house. Took a moment to regain control over her breathing, wipe Gideon McGrath from her mind.

Crystal appeared, swathed in a gorgeous silk kimono wrap, before she'd managed either.

'Josie! I was just going for a swim. Want to join me?'

'I haven't got time for a swim, but I'll walk down with you. I'm sorry I was asleep when you arrived. You should have woken me and I'd have sorted out your room for you.'

'No need. Gideon was so sweet; he sorted it all out in a minute. You must have been totally wiped to have slept through all that coming and going.'

'Even so. It's my job, Crystal—'

'Cryssie, please.'

'It's my job, Cryssie. Come to me if you have any problems, okay? Day or night.' Then, 'How's your tree house?'

'Great. Really cute, although I have to admit that when we flew in I thought I'd arrived at the end of the earth. Then, when David took me right out there into the woods…'

'Serafina thought, I imagine, that you and Tal would welcome the privacy.'

'Oh, please. This is a media wedding; there is no such thing as privacy.'

'So why did you do it? It's not as if you're keeping the money.'

She shrugged. The boldly coloured silk wrap shimmered in the sunlight and as they walked through the boma a couple of middle-aged men, showing off their day's 'bag' of photographs over a sundowner, nearly broke their necks as they did a double take.

'People think I'm just another dumb underwear model who's bagged herself an equally dumb footballer,' Cryssie, said, apparently unaware of the stir she was creating. Or maybe she was so used to it that she no longer noticed.

They were much of a height, but that was all they had in common. Cryssie was absolutely stunning and Josie, who'd never worried about her lack of curves or the fact that the only heads that turned in her direction were in disbelief, felt a pang of something very like envy as she realised why Gideon had suddenly become Mr Helpful instead of Mr Obstructive.

Who wouldn't fall under the spell of such beauty?

'We were going to have the press all over us anyway, so we decided to make it mean something.' Cryssie stopped by the edge of the pool, oblivious to the sudden stillness as she slipped off her wrap to reveal a matching strapless swimsuit and a perfectly even tan. 'We're using the money to set up sports holiday camps for special needs kids.'

Not only beautiful, but caring too. Who could compete with that?

'That's a wonderful thing to do.'

'We've been lucky and it's worth the circus to

put something back. But this is the last. We're not going to be living our lives, having our babies on the front pages of the gossip mags. So,' she said, turning a hundred watt smile on Josie, 'we're going to have to give them their money's worth.'

'I'll certainly do my best.'

As she settled on a chair and stretched out, a white-jacketed waiter appeared.

'Sparkling water, please. No ice. Josie?'

Josie glanced longingly at the pool, but shook her head. 'Thanks, but I have to get on.'

'Maybe we could have dinner together later? Talk things through. About seven?'

'Of course. Is there anything you need before then?'

'No. Oh…'

'Yes?'

'There is my dress. I've unpacked it and hung it over the wardrobe door.' She did something with her shoulders that was far too pretty to be called a shrug. 'It's not very big, is it? There's no room inside and we've got a photo shoot tomorrow.'

'You want me to look after it?'

'Please. I don't want Tal to see it before the big day.'

'No problem. I'll pick it up on my way back.'

'Thanks. Oh, and I expect he's told you, but I invited Gideon to the wedding'

'Gideon?' Josie managed to keep the smile pinned to her face but the wretched man had been a problem since the moment she'd first set eyes on him and she'd thought she would be safe at the wedding.

'One extra won't be a problem, will it? You'll have to redo the seating plan anyway because of Darren and Susie's bust-up,' Cryssie said, blissfully unaware of the turmoil in her breast. 'I'll be happy to give you a hand. I've got nothing to do after dinner.'

'That'll be fun,' Josie managed. Rearranging the seating plan was the least of her worries. It happened at every wedding, although, as she'd told Gideon, normally it was simply a matter of a few extra dining chairs. Beds was a new one. 'You can tell me about all the guests at the same time. That way, I'll be prepared for every eventuality. In the meantime, just ask someone to find me if you need me for anything.'

'Great.' Then, 'Oh…'

She waited, wondering what other bombshell Cryssie was about to explode.

'I think Darren's new girlfriend is a vegan.'

She let out a sigh of relief. 'She won't be the only one. I'll make sure that the chef knows about it.'

Her cue to visit the kitchens.

* * *

Gideon stayed where he was for a while, lost in thought. It wasn't that he didn't know what he'd done wrong. Josie had left him in no doubt.

She'd got it all wrong, of course. He hadn't for a moment imagined that she'd throw a virginal strop if he suggested she move in with him. Although maybe kissing her hadn't been such a great idea under the circumstances. If he'd been thinking with his head, it would never have happened. And she'd made it perfectly clear that if she'd been thinking at all, it wouldn't have happened.

But that wasn't what was bugging her.

She wasn't concerned that he'd make an un-welcome move on her. The way that kiss had ended had left him in no doubt that, spontane-ous, passionate, urgent as it had been, she had problems. Despite a very natural urge to hold her, reassure her, kiss her again, taking his time about it, he'd taken his cue from her and backed off, acted as if it had been nothing. Made a joke of it, even though the heat of her strawberry-flavoured lips had been burning a hole through his brain and he'd been feeling no pain.

He knew he'd convinced her; she wouldn't have offered him her hand to help him up if she'd been in any doubt. It would have been too easy to simply pull her down into his lap.

No. It was the fact that he'd taken the

decision without consulting her, choosing to let her sleep on rather than disturbing her, that had made her so mad.

'It should have been my decision.'

And she was right. He should have waited until she'd woken up but he was so used to taking decisions, leaving everyone else in his wake, that he'd forgotten that this was her show, not his.

He hauled himself to his feet. Steadied himself. The back was in a co-operative mood despite the row, or maybe because of it. If it was psychological, stress-related, it wasn't this kind of adrenalin rush that triggered it. But he'd known all along what the problem was.

It had begun on the day he'd decided to offload Leopard Tree Lodge, rid himself of the one resort in his portfolio that he couldn't bear to visit. Couldn't stop thinking about.

He moved carefully across the deck to the tree house; the pain had definitely eased, but he wasn't about to take any chances. Once inside, it took a moment for his eyes to adjust to the different light level, but then he opened the wardrobe door and saw exactly what Josie had seen.

A stunning piece of feminine kit made from purple chiffon hanging next to his suit. A pair of high heeled shoes that appeared to consist solely of straps beside his loafers. His grip, her suitcase.

Alesia had only done what he'd asked her, but the result did not give the impression of two strangers sharing a room out of convenience— her stuff at one end, his at the other. It had the intimacy of the wardrobe of two people sharing a room, sharing a bed because they were together, an item. Because they wanted to.

He could have asked Francis to pack for him, but it was time to go, get out of here. If he called an air taxi now he'd be in time to get away tonight and, without waiting, he bent to pick up his grip.

The chef had been able to spare her an hour to go through the menu for the pre-wedding dinner.

After she'd gone through the menu, including special dietary needs, she'd checked the linen, then she and the head waiter had laid out a table so that they both knew what they'd be doing on the day of the wedding.

She had thought that the colours might be a bit overpowering, but strong light needed rich colours and the orange cloths and pale blue draw sheets looked stunning against the evening sun. The table flowers would be marigolds and forget-me-nots. To her intense relief, there were no balloons; the chance of small pieces of latex being ingested by animals was too great to risk.

It was almost dark by the time she headed back through the trees, but there were solar lamps along the bridge, on the steps and decks, threaded through the trees. It gave everything an ethereal fairyland quality.

'Are you okay on your own?' she asked Cryssie when she stopped to pick up the wedding dress. Now it was dark she could understand why she might not want to be alone out at the far end of the lodge. Might have felt a little nervous herself…

'Absolutely. It's been mad for the last few weeks. It's great to get a bit of peace, to be honest. I'm looking forward to an early night.'

'Well, you know where I am if you need anything. I'll see you later.'

That done, she straightened her shoulders and headed back to face Gideon. Eat a little humble pie.

The deck was bathed in cool, low level light, but there was no sign of Gideon and no candles had been lit inside.

He couldn't have surrendered, surely? Taken her at her word. He could barely move…

'Gideon?' she called, assailed by a sudden rush of alarm.

'I'm on the floor. Please try not to fall on top of me.'

'Where are you? What happened?'

'I'm in front of the wardrobe.'

She felt her way cautiously in the direction of his voice and collided with the edge of the open wardrobe door.

'Ouch!'

'Sorry. I should have warned you about that.'

'I'm okay.' Apart from the crack on her forehead and the odd whirling star.

She felt for the top of the door, carefully hung the dress over it, then got down on her knees and felt around until she'd found his leg. Warm, strong...

'Careful where you're putting your hand,' he warned as she edged forward and she jerked it away.

'What happened?' she repeated. 'Did you fall? Have you hurt your head?'

'No and no. I bent to pick up my bag so that I could pack and my back seized again.'

'You are such an idiot.'

'I've been lying here for hours just waiting for you to tell me that. Where the hell have you been?'

'Doing my job. Talking to the chef, discussing arrangements with David, counting tablecloths.'

Putting off the moment when she'd have to face him, apologise.

'Vital work, obviously,' he replied.

'It's what *Celebrity* is paying me for. Nursemaiding you isn't part of the deal,' she snapped. Then, not sure whether she was more furious with herself or with him, 'Damn it, Gideon, I came back ready to apologise, play nice and you've set me off again.'

'Play nice?' he repeated, with a soft rising inflection that suggested all manner of pleasurable games. 'Well, that's more like it.'

In the darkness, with no visual stimulus, his low, gravelly voice was enough to send a sensuous curl of heat winding through that hidden central core that she kept locked away. Just as his eyes had lit up her body when she'd come face to face with him that morning. As his touch had seduced her into a reckless kiss.

Every part of him seemed to touch her with an intimacy that effortlessly undermined her defences.

Control… Control…

'Are you in pain?' she asked, summoning up her best 'nanny' voice, the one she kept for panicking brides, weeping mothers-of-the-groom and pageboys intent on mayhem. Determinedly ignoring the seductive power of his voice. Blocking out feelings that she couldn't handle.

'It's getting better. Isn't lying on a hard surface supposed to be therapeutic? Maybe bringing me down was my back's way of telling me what it needs.'

'Smart back. Maybe you should sleep down here,' she suggested.

'Is that your best offer?'

'Oh, shut up. I'll light the candles,' she said, shuffling back the way she'd come so that she could move around him. She misjudged his length, caught his foot with her knee.

'Ouch!'

'Sorry…'

She backed off carefully, crawled towards the bed, banged her head against the wooden frame. 'Ouch!'

Gideon began to laugh.

'It's not funny!'

'No. Sorry…'

That was enough to set her off and, as he peppered his laughter with short scatological expletives each time he jarred his back, she broke down and, helpless with laughter, collapsed beside him, provoking another, 'Ouch!'

For a moment the two of them lay, side by side in the dark, trying to recover. It took an age for her to smother the outbreaks of giggles, but every time she said 'Sorry' it set them both off again. Then his hand found hers in the dark and all desire to laugh left her.

CHAPTER SEVEN

Some brides want to include a much-loved
dog, pony or other animal as part of their
big day. This can be a challenge…

—*The Perfect Wedding* by Serafina
March

'THAT'S better. Are you okay?' Gideon asked as
she hiccupped and gasped as she tried to get her
breath back.

'I th-think s-so.' No question. Infinitely better.
She'd had no idea that a man holding your hand
could make you feel so safe. 'You?'

'A lot better than I was ten minutes ago.' She
felt, rather than saw, him move his head and she
knew that he was looking at her. 'They do say
laughter is the best medicine.'

'That would be why you were swearing so
much.'

'Sorry…'

'Don't!' she warned and Gideon's hand tightened as, for a moment, neither of them dared to breathe. When, finally, Josie was certain that she was safe from another fit of the giggles, she said, 'I'd better light the candles.'

'No hurry. This is good.'

Before she could react, the bell rang at the foot of the steps, and then a dark figure appeared in the open doorway.

'*Rra*?'

'We're here, Francis. Give us some light, will you?'

'Are you hurt, *Rra*?' he asked as he lit the candles and the room filled with soft light. 'Oh, madam, you are here too. Can I help you?'

'Just see to the nets, Francis,' Gideon said. 'We're fine where we are.'

Nets?

Josie watched Francis unfasten them from the bedposts and spread them out so that they turned the bed into a gauzy cloister. Her turn to let slip an expletive. She'd thought they looked romantic, but they were mosquito nets.

'Is there anything I can bring you? *Rra*, madam?'

'A large single malt whisky for Miss Fowler and a bottle of mineral water for me, Francis. And I'm sure Miss Fowler would welcome something to nibble on. It's a long time since she had lunch.'

'Yes, *Rra*.'

'A long time since lunch?' she challenged, the minute he'd gone. 'I didn't have any lunch. And the monkey ate my breakfast. It's no wonder I nearly passed out on you.'

'Don't worry, I'll share.'

'I won't. I hope you enjoy your mineral water.' Then, 'Why didn't you let Francis help you up?'

'No rush. It's therapeutic, remember? Just lie there quietly until he comes back.'

'I haven't got a bad back,' she reminded him. Not because she didn't want to stay where she was, her hand feeling small and feminine tucked in his. But it wasn't wise, not when just being close to him was jump-starting emotions that she'd successfully held in stasis for so long that she'd become complacent, assuming herself to be immune.

'Maybe not, but you don't want to risk another dizzy spell. It being so long since you've eaten.'

'You are soooo thoughtful.'

'That's me. A man you can count on in a crisis.'

'A man you can count on to cause a crisis,' she retaliated. Then, before they started in on one another again, she said, 'Oh, for goodness' sake. I have something to say so will you just lie there and be quiet for a moment so that I can get it off my chest?'

'An apology? They're worse than a trip to the dentist,' he said sympathetically.

She was forced to bite her lip, take a breath. He really, really didn't deserve one, but she would apologise if it killed her. 'The thing is, Gideon… What I have to say is…'

'I'm not sure that there's time for this before Francis comes back.'

'You're not making this easy.'

'Sorry…'

It was a deliberate attempt to set her off again, she knew, but she held her breath, stared straight up at the ceiling, refusing to be distracted.

'What I want to say is that I might… just…be a little bit of a control freak—'

'What a coincidence. I'd have said that too,' he broke in, so that she lost the momentum of the apology she'd been rehearsing as she'd counted tablecloths.

Just from his voice, she knew that he was smiling, undoubtedly with smug self-satisfaction. That was his problem, not hers, however, and, before he could say something that would make her forget every one of her good intentions, she pressed on.

'As I was saying, I have a very real problem with people taking over my life, leaving me without a choice…'

This was where he was supposed to interrupt,

say that he understood, that he had been heavy-handed and was sorry. Instead, there was a long pause, then Gideon said, 'Is that it?'

'…and, as I was saying before I was rudely interrupted, I apologise for my overreaction to your high-handed actions,' she spat out through gritted teeth. Then, when he still didn't leap in to agree that he had been high-handed in the extreme, she added, 'Although, to be honest, I believe I would have been perfectly justified in dumping you over the railing and leaving you to the mercy of the crocodiles.' She allowed herself a smile. 'Okay, that's it. I'm done.'

'Well, that's a relief. I was beginning to think I was the one who should be feeling guilty.'

She didn't say a word.

'I see. Right, well, here's my version of the take it or leave it non-apology. In my company I make the decisions and I expect everyone to do what I tell them—'

'You must be such fun to work for.'

'I'm a generous and caring employer—'

'And maybe just a little bit of a control freak?'

'On the contrary. I welcome the involvement of my staff, I leave them to run their own departments—which is why I didn't know about the wedding—and people stay with me because I'm successful.'

'Yes?' she prompted, since he seemed to have forgotten the apology bit.

'But in the future I'll do my best to remember that you don't work for me.'

'In other words, you'll have a full and frank discussion with me before you start rearranging my life? Even if it means waking me up.'

'I wouldn't go so far as to say that.'

'No? I can see why you're so at home here, Gideon.'

'Go on,' he said, 'give me all you've got.'

She shrugged. 'It's obvious. A leopard can never change his spots.'

She'd expected him to come back with a smart answer, but he didn't say anything.

'Gideon?' she prompted after what seemed like an age.

'Yes,' he said, obviously coming back from somewhere deep inside his head. 'I have no doubt that you've hit the nail firmly on the head.'

What? She turned to look at him. He too was staring up at the ceiling but, sensing her move, he turned to look at her. Smiled. Not the slow killer smile that melted her inside. It was superficial, lying on the surface, a mask...

'Now we've got all that out of the way, are we going to be room mates?' he asked. 'Or, since it's too late to fly out of here tonight, am I to be banished to the office floor?'

She sighed dramatically. 'I thought my apology covered that, but here's how it is. One,' she said—she would have ticked it off on her finger, but he still had her hand firmly in his— 'since I've been informed by Cryssie that you accepted her invitation to the wedding, it's clear that you have no intention of going anywhere until after the weekend.'

'We were both just being polite,' he assured her.

'Cryssie is a sincere and charming woman. She certainly meant it, even if you didn't so you'd better start thinking about a wedding present.'

'Done. And two?' he said.

'What?'

'You said one. I'm assuming there was a two, possibly a three.'

'Oh, yes. I just couldn't get past how quickly you could sort out a wedding present.'

'I'm making a donation to their new charity.'

'She told you about that? You two did have a nice chat.'

'Such a sincere and charming woman,' he agreed. 'And there's no such thing as free PR. Two?'

'Two,' she said, playing for time while she recalled her train of thought. Oh, yes… 'Since Health and Safety rules cover everyone—even the boss—it seems that, like it or not, we're stuck with one another. Control freaks united.'

'And three?' he enquired hopefully.

'There's no three.'

'Pity. I liked the way that was going.'

'Okay, here's three,' she said, finally breaking the connection, letting go of his hand and sitting up. 'You've got a reprieve from the office floor, but I haven't yet decided whether or not you're going to sleep on this one.' Then, as he pushed himself up so that he was leaning against the timber wall, 'Well,' she said, 'didn't you make a fast recovery once you got your own way.'

'I didn't say I couldn't move. I just didn't want to take a chance on it going again and knocking myself out on the wardrobe door.'

'Just left it for me to walk into,' she said, getting up and crossing to the wardrobe, picking out a change of clothes. 'So you really will be leaving in the morning? I'll be happy to pack for you,' she offered quickly, afraid her voice might have betrayed the little flicker of disappointment that had shimmered through her at the thought of him leaving. 'Just in case your back decides it would rather stay here.'

'What about the wedding?'

She glanced back at him. He had that delicious rumpled look that only men could pull off without having to spend hours in front of a mirror getting it just right. Too tempting.

'If the donation was big enough, I'm sure

Cryssie would forgive you. Didn't you say something about having to be in Patagonia?'

'Did I?' He shook his head. 'My deputy has gone in my place.'

'But you're a control freak. Won't leaving something that important to a deputy cause you serious stress?'

Gideon hadn't given Patagonia a thought since Josie Fowler had waltzed onto his deck wearing nothing but a bathrobe that morning. He'd been having far too much fun teasing her, enjoying the fact that she gave as good as she got, but as she closed the wardrobe door he saw the white full length dress cover hanging over the wardrobe door.

'What the hell is that?' he demanded, all desire to tease draining away at the shock of seeing it here, in his room.

'It's Cryssie's dress.'

'Obviously. What's it doing here?'

'We've got a photo shoot in the bridal suite tomorrow,' she reminded him. 'Exquisite gossamer-draped bed, candles, rose petals, fabulous PR for Leopard Tree Lodge and—'

'I don't want it in here,' he said, on his feet before he had even thought about it.

'Gideon!' She put out a hand as if to support him.

'I'm fine!' he said, brushing her away.

She didn't back off, but stayed where she was for a long moment. Only when she was sure that he wasn't going to collapse did she finally let her hand drop, take a step back.

'It's not only the photo shoot,' she said, shaken by his reaction, anxious to make him understand. 'Tal will be arriving tomorrow afternoon.'

'So?'

'Well, it's obvious. He can't see it before the big day. It would be unlucky.'

Unlucky...

The word shivered through him and he put his hand flat on the wall, not because of his back but because his legs, having taken him up like a rocket, were now regretting it.

'It's not staying in here,' he said stubbornly.

'This is my room, Gideon,' she returned with equal determination. 'Your decision, remember? And that dress is my responsibility. It's not leaving here until I take it to Cryssie on her wedding day, along with a needle and thread to put the last stitch in the hem, just as I do for all my brides.'

'Tradition, superstition, it's a load of damned nonsense,' he said furiously. 'What about the tradition that he doesn't see her before the wedding? They're sleeping together, for heaven's sake.'

'That's on the day of the wedding, Gideon. And he won't. Her chief bridesmaid will spend the night before the wedding with Cryssie and Tal is going to bunk down with his best man…' Her voice trailed off and she groaned as she realised that plan had flown out of the window when the number one bridesmaid had switched partners.

'Problem?' he asked.

'Just another challenge for Mr Fix-it,' she replied sharply. Then, her face softening in concern, 'Maybe you should sit down before you try, though. You look a bit shaky.'

'I'm okay,' he said and, pushing himself off, he made it unaided as far as the sofa before the bell rang again. He remained on his feet, helping himself to the whisky from the tray Francis was carrying, downing it in one.

'*Rra*!'

'Sorry,' he said, replacing it on the tray. 'Wrong glass. You'd better bring another one.'

'That won't be necessary,' Josie said quickly.

'Bring one,' he repeated angrily. He wasn't used to having his orders countermanded. 'What's special on the menu tonight? Something tasty for Miss Fowler, I hope?' he continued, not because he was hungry, but because he wanted to annoy her. Wanted her gone…

'Chef is recommending a tagine of lamb, *Rra*.'

'What do you say, Josie?' he said, turning to look at her. 'Do you fancy that?'

'Don't worry about me, Francis,' she said, ignoring him. 'I'll get a drink in the bar if I want one. And I'll be eating in the dining room, too. Just bring Mr McGrath whatever Chef's prepared for him.'

'You can tell Chef that—'

'Gideon!'

He lowered himself carefully onto the sofa and said, 'You can tell Chef that I am sorry he's been put to such inconvenience, Francis.'

'He is happy to do it for you, Mr Gideon. We all want you to be better. My wife is hoping that she can welcome you to our home very soon. She wishes to thank you for the books.'

'I won't go without visiting her,' he promised.

'You bring his wife books?' Josie asked when Francis had gone.

'For their children.' Then, before she could make something of that, 'So, you're abandoning me for the delights of the dining room?'

'You don't want my company, you just want my lamb,' she replied. 'I'm sure whatever the chef makes for you will be delicious.'

'Low-fat girl food,' he retaliated. 'The chilli didn't do me any harm. Quite the reverse. I was on the mend until you decided to kick me out.'

Until she'd turned up with a wedding dress.

'I'm not keeping you here,' she reminded him. 'And, since you seem to be mobile, there's no reason for you to stay.'

'Who's your date?' he asked, ignoring her blatant invitation to remove himself.

'Now you're on your feet you can come to the dining room and find out,' she said sharply, taking her tone from him. 'Now, if you'll excuse me, since I've been working, I'm going to take a shower.'

'Don't forget the matches. You'll need to light the candles,' he said as she opened the door. 'Although, personally, I prefer to shower under starlight.'

'Have you ever tried to put on make-up by starlight?' She shook her head. 'Don't answer that.'

'What's the matter?' he asked as she hesitated in the doorway.

'Something…scuttled.'

'What sort of something?'

'How the heck would I know? It's dark.'

'You're not scared of spiders, are you?'

'I can handle the average bathroom spider,' she said, 'but this is Africa, where the spiders come larger, hairier. And they have teeth.'

'Fangs.'

'Fangs. Great. That makes me feel so much better.'

'The thing to remember, Josie, is that they're more frightened of you than you are of them.'

'You know that for a fact, do you?' she asked as she returned for the matches.

'Any creature with two brain cells to rub together is more frightened of us than we are of them. From hippos to ants. They only lash out in panic.'

'Well, that's reassuring,' she said. 'I'll do my best not to panic it, whatever it is.'

'Do you want me to come and guard your back while you're in the shower?'

She glanced at him and for a moment he thought she was going to say yes. Then, with a determined little shake of the head, 'I don't need a guard, I need a light.'

As she looked quickly away, the nets, glowing in the candlelight, moved in the light breeze coming in off the river and she was held, apparently entranced.

'You don't get that kind of magic with electricity,' he said as her face softened.

'No…' Then, abruptly, 'I'll make sure to mention it to the photographer. *Celebrity* will like that nineteenth century effect.'

'I'd be happier if you liked it.'

The words slipped out before he'd considered what they might mean. But then unconsidered words, actions had marked the day. He hadn't

been entirely himself since he'd smelled the tantalising aroma of coffee, caught a glimpse of
Josie through the branches.

Or maybe he was being himself for the first
time in a decade.

'It's a mosquito net,' she pointed out. 'What's
to be happy about?'

'Of course. You're absolutely right.'

She looked at him as if she wasn't sure whether
he was being serious. That made two of them…

'So what am I likely to find in the bathroom?'
she demanded. 'I'm assuming not hippos.'

'Not great climbers, hippos,' he agreed. 'It's
probably just a gecko. A small lizard that eats
mosquitoes and, as such, to be welcomed.'

'Well, great. But will it take a bite out of
me?' she asked.

'Not if you're polite,' he said, wondering if
perhaps he might, after all, have hit his head. He
didn't appear to be making much sense. 'Step on
it and all bets are off.'

'Oh, yuck…'

'I'm kidding, Josie. They live high on the
walls and the ceiling and, anyway, you'll be safe
enough in those boots. Just make sure you shake
them out before you put them on in the morning.'

She glared at him.

'Basic bush-craft.'

Her response to that was alliterative and to the

point as she struck a match and, braving the dark, advanced to where a row of tea lights were set in glass holders on a shelf. The flames grew, steadied and were reflected endlessly in mirrors that had been carefully placed to reflect and amplify the light.

'Okay?' he called.

'I can't see anything that looks as if it's about to leap out and devour me,' she replied. 'But, while this is all very pretty, I want lamps available for every bathroom. Big, bright gas lamps that will shine a light into every corner.'

'Where's the excitement, the adventure in that?' he asked.

'Believe me, Gideon, I've had all the excitement I can handle for one day.'

'It's not over yet,' he reminded her. 'Better leave the door open, just in case. All you have to do is scream…'

There was a sharp click as Josie responded by shutting the bathroom door with a firmness that suggested he was more trouble than an entire bath full of spiders.

Maybe she was right.

Gideon set down the glass, his grin fading as he leaned his head against the back of the sofa and closed his eyes to avoid looking at the wedding dress.

He'd get up, move it in a minute. For now he

was content just to sit there, listening to the shower running in the bathroom, the comforting sound of another person sharing his space. Even if she was getting ready for a 'date'.

Obviously, she was having dinner with Cryssie but the fact that she'd chosen to tease him a little about it brought the smile back to his face. That she'd made the effort to provoke him, maybe make him jealous was a result and he could use that.

Even as the thought slid into his mind he recoiled from it.

He'd been using her all day, having her make phone calls, fetch and carry for him—admittedly with mixed results; she was no pushover. And she hadn't handed her lunch over without an ulterior motive.

He refused to accept that he was a control freak as she'd suggested, but he was single-minded, totally focused on growing his business.

He'd sorted out her bed shortage simply to prove that he could do it when no one else could.

That was what he did. New challenges, more exciting resorts, ever more extreme adventure breaks—the kind that his father had dismissed as ludicrous.

Who on earth would want to travel across the world to bungee jump? Go dog-sledding in the far north of Canada? Trekking through the Kalahari?

Nothing had mattered more than proving himself better than the adults who, stuck in the past, had been too stupid to listen to a teenage boy who'd seen the future.

Not his family.

Not even Lissa, the woman whose genius for design had turned this place from a basic boy's own safari lodge, much like any other, into a place of beauty. Who'd taken the utilitarian and made it magic with candles, mirrors, nets.

The wedding dress taunted him and, unable to bear it a moment longer, he hauled himself off the sofa, lifted it down and stuffed it inside the wardrobe so that it was out of sight.

He used his arm to wipe the cold sweat from his face, then leaned against the door, forcing himself to let go of the tension that had snapped through him like a wire the minute he'd seen it hanging there, like a ghostly accusation.

He'd come here to draw a line under the past but, instead of closure, it seemed to be pursuing him, hunting him down.

What was it his doctor, Connie, had said? '…sooner or later you're going to have to stop running…'

The water was still running in the shower, tantalising him with its promise of soothing, reviving heat. With the image of being crammed in there with Josie, her hands on his shoulders, sliding down his back, easing away the pain with those capable hands. Just the thought of it warmed the muscles, eased the ache, sent a hot flood of desire coursing through his veins as he imagined her small breasts against his wet skin as she kneaded away the aches, dug into the hollow at the base of his spine. In his heart…

He recoiled from the thought. Dammit, he was still using her, even inside his head.

Not good. Forget hot— what he needed was a cold shower and he opened the bathroom door just wide enough to grab a towel from the rack. As the candles flickered in the draught something moved, catching his eye, and he opened the door a little wider. It wasn't a gecko that had lost its grip sitting in the middle of the floor, but a hunting spider on the prowl for supper.

Suddenly everything went quiet as the water was turned off. He had one, maybe two seconds before Josie stepped out of the shower, saw the spider and screamed.

His chance to be a hero.

His reward, a naked woman in his arms.

As the shower door clicked, he dropped the towel on the spider, scooped it up, shut the door quietly behind him.

He steadied himself, then carried it outside, shook it carefully over the rail.

CHAPTER EIGHT

Wedding favours were traditionally five almonds to represent health, wealth, long life, fertility and happiness; the modern wedding planner will add something that memorably reflects the couple's interests.

—*The Perfect Wedding* by Serafina March

JOSIE pulled down a towel, wrapped it around her, opened the shower door, paused to take a careful look around.

The bathroom was a myriad of reflected lights, stunningly beautiful, and there wasn't a creepy-crawly, or even a friendly lizard, in sight.

'You are such a wuss, Josie Fowler,' she said as she dried off. Then she brushed her teeth, applied fresh make-up, used some wax on hair that had wilted in the steam and finally emerged, wearing the fishnet T-shirt she kept for evenings beneath a simple slipover, ready for the next round with her nemesis.

'It's all yours,' she said to an empty room.

Gideon was nowhere to be seen. Neither was Cryssie's wedding dress.

'Gideon!' she yelled, surging out onto the deck.

He emerged from the outdoor shower, dark hair clinging wetly to his neck, his forehead, wearing only a pitifully small towel—stark white against his slick sun-drenched skin—wrapped around his waist.

Standing straight, he was so utterly beautiful that for a moment she struggled for words.

'You shrieked?' he prompted.

She made an attempt to gather herself. 'The dress…' She swallowed. 'What have you done with Cryssie's dress?'

'I put it out of harm's way,' he said. 'In the wardrobe.'

'Oh…'

'What did you think I'd done with it? Tossed it into the trees for the monkeys to play with?'

'No. Sorry. It's just—'

'Your responsibility. I heard you, Josie. This is your room and you've every right to keep whatever you want in it.'

'It was just that you were so obviously disturbed by its appearance, angry even—'

'Forget it,' he said, so fiercely that she drew back a little. 'Let it go, Josie,' he said, rather more gently. 'It's not important.'

Clearly it was. His dislike of weddings was obviously rooted in something rather deeper than an aversion to long white dresses. But it was equally obvious that he didn't want to talk about it.

'I realise that all this is nothing but a huge pain in the backside for you, Gideon—'

'A little higher than that,' he suggested, doing his best to make light of it by making fun of her.

'Dammit, Gideon!' she snapped. 'This is really important to me. Sylvie has taken a huge gamble making me a partner and so far I haven't been exactly trampled in the stampede of women desperate for me to plan their weddings. I have to get this right…'

'Why?'

'Why?' she repeated, confused. 'Surely that's obvious?'

'Why was it a gamble?'

She sucked in her breath. He wasn't supposed to ask that. She shouldn't have said it, wouldn't have let it slip if she hadn't been so wound up. So desperate that everything should go without a hitch.

'You're motivated, enthusiastic and you care deeply that Cryssie's big day is special,' he pressed. 'In her shoes, I'd rather have you than

Cara's scary Aunt Serafina holding my hand on my big day.'

If Sylvie had been here, it was exactly what she would have said and she was forced to blink hard to stop a tear from spilling over.

Not good. Determined not to lose it completely and blub, she took her eyes on a slow ride down that luscious body until she reached his feet. Then she shook her head.

'Sorry, Tarzan, they wouldn't fit.' And, just to prove to herself that she was firmly back in control, she made herself look up, meet his gaze. Nothing had changed. He knew what she was doing and he wasn't diverted. The question was still there…

Why was it a gamble?

'And, to be honest, embroidered, beaded satin slingbacks really wouldn't be a good look for you,' she added a little desperately.

For a moment he continued to look at her, challenge her and she thought he wasn't going to let it go, but finally he shrugged. 'You think the beads would be pushing it?'

'The bigger the feet, the less you want to draw attention to them,' she replied.

He looked down at her boots, lifted an eyebrow, said nothing.

'Cryssie will be waiting,' she said, desperate to escape. 'I'll…um…just get my briefcase.'

Gideon followed her inside. 'It's a working dinner?'

'We've got to rearrange the table layouts. Then we're going to start on the favour boxes.'

'Favour boxes?'

'Little table gifts for the guests. The boxes have been specially created to look like Tal's football strip. We have to slot them together, then fill them with all the bits and pieces,' she explained. As if he'd be interested.

'Could you do with an extra pair of hands?'

'Excuse me?' A tiny laugh, pure disbelief, exploded from her. 'Are you offering to help?'

'Now I ask you, is that likely?' he replied. 'I was going to suggest that you ask Alesia and some of the other girls to give you a hand. I've no doubt they'd love to be involved.' He shrugged. 'Just a thought.'

Just a thought. A crazy, foolish thought. The very idea of him sitting around with a bunch of women making wedding favour boxes was so ridiculous that anyone would laugh.

Everyone knew that he didn't do weddings. The engraved invitations arrived once in a while, *Gideon McGrath and Partner* inscribed in copperplate—he was never with anyone long enough for his family, friends or colleagues to be sure who it would be. Not that it mattered that much. The invitations were a formality. They knew he wouldn't attend.

The excuse would be solid. The gift generous.

Yet here he was, stuck in the middle of the biggest wedding of the year, a wedding he wanted nothing to do with, and, like an idiot, he'd volunteered to help and even Josie Fowler, who'd known him for less than a day, had understood how ridiculous it was. Assumed that he had to be kidding.

And why wouldn't she?

He could scarcely believe it himself.

'Josie!'

'Sorry,' she said as Cryssie claimed her wandering attention. All through dinner, while Cryssie had been chattering away, telling her how she'd met Tal, about the country estate they'd bought, her mind had kept drifting back to Gideon on his own back there in the trees.

His casual, 'Could you do with an extra pair of hands…?'

Not him. He couldn't have meant him.

He was so anti-weddings that he'd ordered Cryssie's dress out of his room. Her room. Their room!

And yet, even as he'd dismissed the idea out of hand, suggested asking Alesia, waved her away, urging her not to keep the blushing bride waiting, she'd felt a little sink of uncertainty. The feeling that she'd thoughtlessly spurned something rare.

That she'd hurt him…

'Where are you sitting?' Cryssie asked. 'I can't find you.'

'I'll be running things behind the scenes,' she said absently.

'That's just rubbish. I'm going to put you on this table,' she said, carefully pencilling her in. 'Right here, next to Gideon.'

'No, really,' she protested. The fact that she cared whether she'd hurt him was the biggest warning yet. Far bigger than drooling over his gorgeous body. Much more dangerous than losing her senses and kissing him. Fantasising about dribbling oil over his back and soothing the pain away. That was physical.

Caring about his feelings was on a whole different level.

But Cryssie wasn't listening.

'I want you both at the pre-wedding dinner too.'

Falling back on the need for professionalism, she summoned up the book of rules to support her. 'Serafina March would not approve.'

'Really?' Then, with a burst of giggles that attracted indulgent smiles from other late diners, 'Well, to be honest, I wouldn't have asked her.'

Josie glanced at the bottle of champagne Cryssie had insisted on ordering and sighed.

'Why don't you leave the rest of this to me, Cryssie?' she said, gathering everything up. 'It's going to be a long day tomorrow and you'll want to look your best for your photo shoot.'

'But I was going to help you with the favours,' she protested.

'Better not risk it,' she said. 'You might damage your nails.'

Cryssie extended a hand to display her exquisite extensions and giggled again. 'They are great, aren't they?'

'Gorgeous,' she said. Definitely time to get her up the wooden hill… 'Come on. I'll put this stuff in the office and then walk you back to your room.'

The champagne had made Cryssie talkative and more than a little weepie as she cleaned off her make-up. Josie just held her for a while as she babbled on about her mother, her dad.

'You will be there, Josie?' she sniffed, a long way from the poised young woman who, a few hours earlier, had dismissed this whole wedding as a media event.

'Every step of the way,' she promised, fighting back tears of her own. She did a good 'hard' act in the office, tried to remain detached, professional, throughout even the most touching event.

Weddings, though, were an emotional quagmire, with a trap for the unwary at every turn. 'Come on. Into bed. Tal will be here tomorrow.'

Cryssie was asleep by the time Josie had hung up her discarded clothes. She blew out the candles, leaving her like Sleeping Beauty, enclosed within the gauzy nets, the little torch within hand's reach in case she woke in the night, while she returned to the dining room.

It was empty now. Everyone had moved on to the open fire pit in the boma, the candles had been extinguished and there was only the low level glow of the safety lighting.

As she fetched her boxes from the storeroom she could hear bursts of laughter as they drank their nightcaps and told tall stories in a wide range of accents. People had come from all over the world to stay here, experience this. By the morning they'd all have moved on to other camps, other sights. Crossing the desert, taking in the Victoria Falls, going into the mist to find the gorillas.

She, meanwhile, had more than a hundred favour boxes to deal with. She'd normally have the girls in the office doing this in spare moments, but she couldn't even call on Alesia to give her a hand. The reception desk was closed with only an emergency bell.

She found a box of matches on the service

trolley, moved three candles to one of the larger tables, lit them, then spread herself out and set to work, tucking in the flaps of the flat-packed little boxes. Losing all sense of time as people gradually drifted away to their rooms, the fire died down and, within the small world of the candlelight, everything became quiet.

This wasn't a resort where people stayed up late.

They would all be up before light to grab a cup of coffee and a muffin before heading off at first light to get in another game drive, guided walk, or to glide through the reeds in a canoe in the hope of catching one of the rarer beasts on an early morning hunt or drinking at the water's edge.

'Josie?'

She started, looked up. 'Gideon…' He looked ashen in the candlelight. 'How did you get here?'

'Slowly,' he said.

'Oh, God… Sit down,' she said, leaping up, pulling out a chair. 'Do you need someone? Can I get you anything?'

'No. I'm fine. Don't fuss…' Then, as he sank carefully on the chair, 'What the hell do you think you're doing? Have you any idea what time it is? I thought you must have fallen off the bridge…'

'You were waiting up for me?' she asked, astonished.

'I've been lying down all day. I'm not tired.' Then, 'Yes, I was waiting up for you.' He didn't wait for her to laugh at him again, but looked around. 'So much for everyone pitching in to help. Where's Cryssie?'

'I put her to bed. She had a glass or two of champagne and got a bit emotional.'

'Nerves?'

'No. She was missing her mum,' she said, sitting back down, reaching for another box, concentrating hard on putting it together.

'Oh, right. When's she arriving?'

'She's not. She died when she was a teenager. Hence the tears.'

'I didn't know. That's tough.'

'Especially at moments like this. You go through the day-to-day stuff, managing, but…'

And, without warning, it got her, just as it had caught Cryssie. One minute she had been giggling with excitement, full of the joys, the next there had been tears pouring down her face at the prospect of facing the biggest, most important day of her life without her mother to support her.

It would have been so easy to break down and weep with Cryssie, but she'd held back the tears, knowing that to join in would have dragged them both down into a black pit. But it had got to her and now Gideon had provided the emotional catalyst. A stranger, a man she barely knew, staying up to make sure she got home safe. It was years since anyone had done that and, without warning, the box in her hand crumpled and, just as she'd known the moment to reach for Cryssie, he was there, solid as a brick wall, to prop her up as the memories flooded back.

The times when she'd been frightened, angry, in despair. The times when something amazing had happened. That day when, just before Sylvie had gone into church to be married herself, Sylvie had hugged her and told her that she wanted her to be her partner.

She'd been so happy, thought she might burst with pride and the only person she'd wanted to tell was her mother. Just to let her know she was all right. That everything had worked out, that she was okay…

'Sorry,' she said as her tears seeped into his shirt. 'It's been years since anyone waited up to see me home safe.'

'How many years?'

'Nearly eight.'

She let her head lie against his chest, letting the scent of freshly washed linen fill her head. That was a good memory too. Being tucked into clean pyjamas, feeling safe, protected…

'I was seventeen, almost eighteen. There'd been a party at college. It was late when I got home but Mum was sitting up for me as she always did. Pretending to be engrossed in some old movie. She made us hot chocolate and we sat in the kitchen while I told her about the party. About some boy I'd met who'd walked me home. Just talked, you know, the way you do in the middle of the night when it's quiet and there's no one to butt in.' Her throat closed with the ache of that last night of pure happiness. 'Being still like that, with no distractions, no radio…' without her mother's second husband yelling for a beer or a sandwich or his cigarettes '…I suddenly saw how tired she looked. That her clothes were hanging on her. And I knew then. Knew she was sick.' A little shiver ran through her as she recalled the fear. 'I said that maybe she should make an appointment for one of those well-woman clinics. Just for a check-up…'

But she'd already seen the doctor.

She sniffed and, as she pulled away, hunted in her pockets for a tissue, looked helplessly at the crushed mess of blue and orange card in her hand.

He made no attempt to hold her, just took the useless box from her and replaced it with a hand-kerchief. A proper one. White. Folded. Perfectly ironed. And that nearly set her off again but Gideon, playing the calm, unemotional role, said, 'I hope there are spares.'

'Loads,' she said, mopping up the dampness

on her cheeks, grateful for the fact that she never used anything but waterproof mascara—panda eyes was such a bad look at a wedding. 'They had to be printed specially and you never know the exact number until the last minute.'

He picked one up, turning it over to examine it, before fitting it together as if he'd been doing it all his life.

'Maybe you should save some. I bet they'll go for a fortune on eBay after the wedding.'

'They'd go for a lot more if they were complete.'

'That's the next job? Filling them?'

She nodded.

'Better not waste time then.'

She watched for a moment as he placed the box he'd finished with the others, then picked up another and handed it to her before carrying on. Folding, tucking, lining them up in serried ranks of little football shirts on the table.

'Are they all the same?' he said when it was obvious they had a lot more than fifty. 'Don't the women get a Cryssie lookalike in a blue dress with orange ribbons?'

'That is such a sexist remark,' she replied, doing her best not to grin, but failing. 'This is an equal opportunities wedding.'

'I know, but it made you smile.'

'Yes, it did. Thanks.'

'Any time.'

Probably… Then, because that wasn't a wildly sensible thought, 'I'm sorry about weeping all over you.'

'I'll dry out. I'm sorry about your mother.' She fumbled with another box, dropped it, but as she bent to pick it up he stopped her.

She gave a little shake of her head and, not wanting to think about that terrible year, she began to quickly count the boxes off in tens.

'Okay, we've got enough,' she said, stacking them carefully in a couple of collapsible plastic crates that David had provided. 'Would you like a cup of tea? Coffee?'

'There won't be anyone in the kitchen at this time of night.'

She rolled her eyes at him. 'You might need a fully qualified chef to boil a kettle but I'm not that useless.'

'Throw in a sandwich and you've got me,' he said.

'I've already got you. It's getting rid of you that's defeating me.'

'You're right. I've been pushing myself into your business all day,' Gideon said, much too gently. 'I'll get out of your way.' He eased himself carefully to his feet, touched her arm in a small, tender I'm-here-if-you-need-me gesture. 'I'll leave a light on.'

'Don't…'

Josie didn't want him to go. He'd been driving her crazy all day, but only because she wanted to show the world that she didn't need anyone. That she could do this on her own. That she was worthy...

'You start a job, you finish it,' she said, concentrating very hard on ripping open a box containing the little nets of sugared almonds. 'You can make a start on those while I get us both a sandwich.'

He didn't say anything, but he didn't move either. She risked a glance. His expression was giving nothing away, but there was a damp patch on his shirt, right above his heart, where she'd cried on him and that told her pretty much everything she needed to know about Gideon McGrath.

He might be a little high-handed, inclined to take over, want to run things, but he wasn't afraid of emotion, wouldn't quit when something mattered to him. He wasn't her enemy, he was her ally.

'A good employer understands that feeding the workforce is vital,' she told him, growing in confidence as he stayed put. 'Especially if they're working unsociable hours.'

Gideon watched Josie battle with herself, wanting him to stay, asking in the only way she knew how. Unable to bring herself to say the

simple words. Please stay… Please help…
Wondered what had happened to her that had
made her so afraid of opening up.

He was seized by an overwhelming urge to
grab her, shake her, tell her that life was a one-
off deal and she should live it to the full, not
waste a minute of it.

He fought it.

'I don't work for cottage cheese,' he said, responding in kind, making it easy for her. Making
it easy on himself.

'Oh?' One of her brows kicked up. 'So what
will it take?'

'That's for me to know and you to find out.
Let's go and take a look in the fridge.' He caught
his breath as he turned awkwardly and his hand
landed on her shoulder as he steadied himself.

'Sit down. I can manage,' she said anxiously.

'It's not a domestic kitchen. You'll need help.'

'I spent a year working as a hotel scullery assistant,' she replied. 'Believe me, there's nothing
you can tell me about hotel kitchens.'

'Great, I'll direct, you do the work,' he said,
putting the obvious question on hold.

Accepting that he wasn't going to take no for
an answer, she took his hand, eased beneath it so
that his arm was lying across her shoulders, then
tucked her arm around his waist. 'Okay, let's go.'

There was nowhere to sit in the kitchen, so she

propped him against a handy wall while she filled
the kettle from the drinking water container, lit
the gas, then opened one of the large fridges.

'Right. Let's see. There's cheese, cold meat,
cold fish…' She peered at him around the door, all
violet eyes and hair. 'What can I tempt you with?'

Not food…

'How about something hot?' he replied.

'Hot?'

Josie could still feel the heat where she'd been
pressed up against Gideon as they'd walked to
the kitchen and now her cheeks followed suit,
warming in response to something in his voice
that suggested he wasn't talking about food.

'Chilli hot or temperature hot?' she said, glad
of the cool air tumbling out of the fridge.

'You're doing the tempting. You decide.'

'Okaaay…'

He wanted tempting, she could do tempting…

'I'm thinking white bread,' she said. 'Butter,
crispy bacon, eggs fried so that the yolks are still
running and…'

'And?'

Was he a ketchup man or a brown sauce man?

'A great big dollop of brown sauce,' she said,
going for the spice.

'With a sandwich like that you could tempt a
saint, Josie Fowler.'

'I think we both know that you're no saint,

Gideon McGrath,' she replied, taking out a catering pack of bacon, piling on the eggs and butter before closing the fridge door.

She expected him to be grinning, but he was looking at her with an unsettling intensity and for a minute she forgot everything. What she was doing, what she'd been thinking…

Before she could collect herself, he'd pushed away from the wall and relieved her of her burden.

She still hadn't moved when he took down a pan from the overhead rail, set it on a burner and began to load it with slices of bacon.

'You've done that before,' she said, sounding like an idiot, but she had to say something, anything to break the silence, restore her balance. It had been out of kilter all day. An endless journey, her body clock bent out of shape, Cryssie's tears… She scrambled for all the reasons why she should be reacting so oddly. Any reason that didn't include Gideon McGrath.

'Once or twice,' he admitted as he lit the gas. 'And, this way, I'll be the one in the firing line if the chef decides to throw a tantrum in the morning.'

'He won't. He's a sweetheart,' she said, seizing on the chance to focus on something else. 'I was worried about his reaction to Serafina choosing an outside caterer for the wedding breakfast, but he was really sweet about it.'

Gideon shook the pan to stop the bacon from sticking, then glanced at her. 'The wedding is on Sunday, isn't it?'

'Yes. Is that important?'

'Paul belongs to a church that doesn't permit its members to work on Sunday.'

'Oh?' She reached up for a spatula. 'Shall I take over?'

'I'm good,' he said, taking it from her, adjusting the heat. 'You could butter the bread,' he suggested.

'Gee, thanks,' she said. 'My natural place in the kitchen. Taking orders from a man who thinks he knows best.'

'This is my kitchen,' he reminded her. 'When we're in your kitchen you can give the orders.'

'Don't hold your breath.'

'I never do.' He pointed with the spatula. 'You'll find the bread through there.'

She fetched the bread from a temperature-controlled storeroom, cut four slices, then tested the butter. It was too hard to spread and she ran some cold water, stood the butter in it. Waited.

Apart from the sizzle of the bacon, the faint hum of the refrigerator, the kitchen was unnaturally silent. Her fault. She'd chopped the conversation off at the knees. It was a protective device.

Her automatic response to anyone who said or did anything that suggested more than a superficial acquaintance. Not just men. She did it to women, too. You couldn't lie to friends.

'How're you doing there?' he asked.

She half turned. 'Give me a minute.' Then, desperate to resume communication but on a less risky level, she said, 'How do you know all that? About Paul. I thought you don't involve yourself with the day-to-day running of your hotels and resorts.'

'I don't. I can't. But Leopard Tree Lodge was my first permanent site and Paul has been with me since it opened. I interviewed him myself. He'd been working in a big hotel in South Africa but they couldn't accommodate his religious observances within their schedule.'

'But you could.'

'I told you,' he said, 'I'm a generous and caring employer.'

'Oh, right. You brought books for his children, too?'

He glanced across at her, a small smile creasing the corners of his mouth, sparking something warm and enticing in his eyes. 'They're all grown up now. His youngest is studying medicine in London.'

And he was still buying the books, she'd bet any amount of money, she thought, doing her best to resist an answering heat that skittered dangerously around her abdomen. Just bigger and more expensive ones.

'The butter should be soft enough by now,' he said, flipping the bacon. Then, as she tested it with the knife, then carried it across the work surface, 'Tell me about being a scullery assistant.'

'What's to tell?' she replied, concentrating very hard on buttering the bread. 'I scrubbed, I washed, I peeled. End of story.'

'What about college? Even if you were going into catering, starting at the bottom, a year seems like a very long apprenticeship.'

She carried on spreading. She sensed that he was looking at her, but dared not risk looking across at him.

'I didn't finish my course,' she said, bending down for plates. 'My mother was dying. Someone had to nurse her.'

'She had a husband.'

'Yes. Did we decide on coffee or tea?'

'This late? I think we should stick to tea, don't you?'

'We should probably be having cocoa,' she said, but she was happy to go along with whatever he said, as long as he was thinking about something other than her career path. Her stepfather.

She took one of the teapots lined up for the

morning trays, spooned tea into the cage, poured on boiling water.

'His back prevented him from doing very much, I imagine,' Gideon said, picking up the bacon and laying it across the bread.

Mugs, milk…

'Without my mother's salary, one of us had to work but I'd have rather starved than left her to his neglect,' she finally replied as he cracked the eggs on the side of the pan, dropped them in the hot bacon fat so that the whites bubbled up. 'The prospect of spending time with his dying wife effected a miraculous cure and he found himself a job pulling pints of beer in The Queen's Head.' She shrugged. 'Well, it was, in many ways, his second home.'

CHAPTER NINE

The wedding breakfast, great food, is at the heart of the celebration.

—*The Perfect Wedding* by Serafina March

GIDEON could feel the deeply buried anger that was coming off Josie in waves. She was covering it with the sharp sarcasm she used whenever she felt threatened, but there was a brittle tension about her, a jerkiness about her movements that was at odds with her natural grace.

That she despised the man her mother had married was obvious, but there was more to it than that. There was also a *don't go there* rigidity to her posture that warned him not to push it.

'Couldn't you have returned to your course after your mother died?' he asked, taking a different tack. Coming at her sideways. Wanting to know what was driving her. What emotional trauma was keeping her prisoner.

'No.' She poured the tea into two mugs, everything about her stance screaming, *Don't ask...* 'Milk? Sugar?' she asked calmly, her voice a complete contradiction to the tension in her body.

'Just a splash of milk,' he said, compassion compelling him to let it go.

She added the milk, returned it and everything else to the fridge while he turned the eggs, then lifted them onto the bacon. Began to clean down the surfaces while he fetched the brown sauce, moved onto the stove. Then dealt with the pan in the swift, no-nonsense manner of an experienced kitchen hand.

'I'll bet they missed you when you left the kitchen,' he said, picking up the plates, heading back to the dining room.

Josie picked up the mugs of tea and followed him.

'Maybe they did. I certainly didn't miss them,' she said, not looking back.

Not one of them.

They'd treated the youth who'd been locked up for snatching some old lady's handbag better than they'd treated her.

It was as if there had been a fence around her hung with warning signs.

She'd been given all the worst jobs. Had to

work twice as hard as anyone else, do it before she was asked. Do it better than anyone else. Never answer back, no matter what the provocation. Never give Chef—who'd treated her like a leper—the slightest excuse to fire her.

Gideon bypassed the table where they'd been working on the favours, crossing to one at the far side of the dining room where it overlooked the river far below them.

There were animals near the water, creatures taking advantage of the darkness, tiny deer no bigger than a dog, animals she didn't recognise.

'Your back seems easier,' she said as Gideon pulled out a chair for her.

'It's amazing what interesting company, the prospect of good food will do.'

'Interesting? Mmm…' she said. 'Let me think.' Glad to escape the dark thoughts that had crowded in while she was in the kitchen, she put a finger to her lips as if she was considering what he'd said. '"I had supper with an *interesting* woman." Is that something a girl wants to hear?'

He smiled, but dutifully rather than with amusement, she thought, and said, 'If I was offered a choice between spending time with a beautiful woman or an interesting one, I'd choose interesting every time.'

'Oh, please,' she said. 'Give me a break.'

And then he did laugh, which was a result and, content that she'd finally distracted him, she gathered the sandwich, now oozing egg yolk, and groaned with pleasure as she bit into it.

'What I said about holding your breath, Gideon,' she mumbled, catching a drip of egg yolk and licking her finger, 'forget it. You can do this for me any time, anywhere.' Then, 'If I was given a choice between spending time with a good-looking man or one who could cook, I'd go for the cook every time.'

Gideon hadn't bothered to light a candle; the moon had risen, almost full, silvering the river, the trees on the far bank, the creatures gathered by the water's edge, offering enough light to see him smile.

Encouraged, she said, 'Where did you learn to do this?'

'I spent a lot of time camping out by myself in the early days,' he said, sucking egg from his thumb. 'Trekking, walking, canoeing. Trying out ideas to see if they worked before I sent paying customers out into the wild.'

'Is that how you started in the business? Adventure holidays?'

'Not exactly. My family have been in travel since Thomas Cook started it all in the mid nineteenth century. It's in my blood.'

'And here I was thinking that you were some kind of go-getting entrepreneur blazing the trail for adventurous souls who like to risk their necks for fun.'

'Yes, well, that's the problem with family businesses. They get top-heavy with generations of nephews and cousins, most of whom are little more than names on the payroll. Everyone is too polite, no one is prepared to take charge, innovate, shake things up. And while the same people come back year after year, followed by their children and their children's children, it survives. A family business for family holidays. That was the selling slogan.'

'A bit nineteen-fifties. I did a design course,' she explained when he threw her a questioning look. 'I guess the Internet changed all that with cheap online flights.'

'They sleepwalked into it. I saw the danger, tried to convince my father that he had to do something to counter the threat. But fifteen years ago he was too busy playing Captain Hook in the local panto to listen to a kid babbling on about how computers were going to change everything, let alone some newfangled thing called the Internet.'

'It's so much a part of our lives now that we forget how fast it happened. Cheap flights, online booking. Who needs a travel agent these days?'

'People who are looking for something different. When I was at university there were all these students keen to go off somewhere after taking their finals and do something crazy before they settled for the pinstriped suit. One of them was moaning about it in the bar. How endlessly time-consuming it was if you wanted to do anything except book two weeks on the Costa del Sol. I asked him what he wanted to do and sorted it for him. He told all his mates and, when the lecturers started to come to me for advice, I realised I had a business.'

'And the family firm?'

'It staggers on. They've closed a dozen or so branches and when staff retire they're not replaced. The cousins have discovered that if they want to draw a salary they have to put in a day's work.'

'You're not interested in turning it around?'

'I tried. I went to my father, showed him what I was doing. His business, he told me, was family holidays, not daft jaunts for youngsters. His customers didn't go bungee jumping in New Zealand, dog sledding, white water rafting. Except, of course, they do. People of all ages want to feel their hearts beat faster. Feel the fear and do it anyway. Leap out of an aeroplane, walk across the desert, take a balloon ride over Victoria Falls…'

'Go on a walking safari in Botswana,' she prompted when he stopped. Because that was where all this was leading. Here. To this river-bank.

'A walking safari in Africa,' he agreed. 'I'd met someone at university whose father worked here for the diamond people. She'd raved about the Okavango delta, the birds, the wildlife and when I called her, asked for her advice, she invited me to visit, offered to be my guide.'

She?

'She brought me to the places she knew. We walked, camped, made notes. Made love.'

Yes. Of course they had. She'd known it from the minute he'd said 'she'.

'On our last night, we pitched camp here. Cooked over an open fire, sat out beneath the stars and, as the moon rose, just like this, I caught the glint of a pair of eyes in a tree on the far side of the river. A leopard lying up, waiting for dawn to bring its prey to the water's edge. We thought we were the watchers, but it must have been there all evening, watching us.'

Josie felt the hairs on the back of her neck rise. She shivered, glanced nervously across the river as she remembered Marji saying that the area was famous for leopards.

'Will it be there now?'

'Not that one but a descendant will certainly

be out there, somewhere close. It seemed like an omen. The walkers love the birds, the insects, everything, but everyone wants to see the cats.'

'Do they?' She gave a little shiver. 'I love my little tabby, Cleo but I'm not sure about the big, man-eating kind.'

'I'll show you, tomorrow,' he said.

She didn't bother to argue. Tell him that a London sparrow was about as exciting as she wanted the wildlife to get. She knew that this had nothing to do with her; she was just a conduit for his thoughts.

'That's why you built this lodge?' she prompted. 'Because of the leopard?'

'Lissa...Lissa immediately spotted the potential for a permanent camp. A destination. Somewhere to mark the end of the journey, to relax after the walking, the hard camping in the wild.'

Lissa.

Beautiful? It was a name that fitted a beautiful woman. Elegant, sophisticated, unlike her own solid, workmanlike name.

Interesting?

And clever too, she thought with a pang of envy that tore at her heart. Not jealousy. She had no right to be jealous. But something in his voice invoked a longing to claim that special tenderness in his voice as he'd said Lissa's name for herself.

'I was thinking about something fairly basic.

Tents with plumbing similar to those I'd seen at smaller campsites in Kenya,' he said. 'Lissa was dreaming up this.'

He lifted a hand, no more than that, but it encompassed her vision.

Beautiful, interesting, clever and he loved her...

'She sounds like a very special woman,' Josie said, doing her best to hold herself together. Trying not to think of the way his mouth had tasted, the way his body had fitted hers or how he'd told her there was no one waiting for him. That he was no different—

'She was an extraordinary woman,' he said. 'She knew so much. When she was out here she seemed to feel things, notice things that I would have missed.'

Was?

No...

He wasn't looking at her now, but at the riverbank below them.

'We opened a bottle of champagne on the day we drove in the first deck supports. Drank a glass, poured one on the hot earth in gratitude for letting us be here. Then I asked her to marry me.'

Everything was beginning to fall into place and she didn't want to hear it, hear his heart breaking. But it was equally obvious that this was why he was here. And why he was in such pain.

He needed to talk and she had always known how to listen.

'What happened, Gideon?'

He turned from the river, looked directly at her.

'I was here, overseeing the final work on the lodge. Bedding in the systems, testing everything, getting to know the staff. Lissa was at home, organising the wedding.'

He turned away, looking across the water, but she doubted if he was seeing anything.

'We were going to come here afterwards for our honeymoon. Just us, with the whole place to ourselves for a few days before the first guests arrived.'

They'd have spent their honeymoon in the last tree house, she thought. As far as they could get from civilisation. Making love. Making a life. Watching the leopards watching them.

'The communications systems had finally been installed and my first call was to let her know what flight I'd be on. She wanted to come and meet me but I told her to stay home in the warm, that I'd make my own way from the airport.'

No…

'I let myself in, called her name. When I

didn't get an answer I went upstairs. Checked all the rooms. She'd picked up her wedding dress and it was hanging up in the spare room in a white cover—'

Her hand flew to her mouth as she tried to stifle the groan, but he didn't hear her. It was clear that he was somewhere else, in another world, another life…

'— and I was just thinking that she wouldn't want me even that close before the big day when the doorbell rang. It was a policeman. Apparently, Lissa had decided to surprise me, meet my plane.'

No, no, no… She didn't want to hear this.

'She must have been lying there on the freezing road, dying while I was travelling warm and dry on the train. If I hadn't called… If I'd just got on the damn plane…' Something snagged in his throat.

'You've never been back here, have you?' she asked.

He shook his head.

'Why now?' she asked, not for her—she understood the need for closure—but for him. Because anyone with half a brain cell could see that this was the stress, the cause of all his pain. He'd locked up all that grief, blaming himself and it was breaking him apart. He needed to say the words, open up.

'I had an offer for the Lodge from a hotel group a while ago and I thought well, obviously, that's the answer. Cut it away, set myself free.'

'It's not that easy.'

'No,' he said, 'it wasn't easy at all. There were just so many things that kept cropping up. The security of tenure for the staff. Paul's Sundays. And Francis had been here, taking care of us from the start. He was the first person to congratulate us on our engagement. Lissa was godmother to one of his children…'

'You take care of them.' Not a question.

'I send them things. Pay school fees,' he said. 'I don't give them what matters. What they deserve. But when it came to selling this place cold…' He shook his head. 'I couldn't do it. Not until I'd been here, told them face to face. Told Lissa…'

'I'm so sorry, Gideon.'

'Me too,' he said, doing his best to make light of it. 'It was a damn good offer.'

'Good enough?' she prompted.

And the attempt at a smile faded. 'No. Now I've been here I know that I can never let it go,' he said. It's part of her. Part of me. I was wrong to stay away.'

'Yes,' she said. 'You were.'

Because he wasn't looking for sympathy, only truth.

'It's a very hard thing to acknowledge, but I'm

a lot more like my father than I ever wanted to believe,' he said, reaching out, taking the hand that had been aching to reach out to offer some human comfort. Afraid that if she touched him it would shatter the moment. Now he took it, held it, as if he was the one comforting her. 'Avoiding painful reality is, apparently, a family failing.'

'That's a little harsh.'

'Is it? His displacement activity is dressing up and raising money for charity. Mine is to discover ever more exotic holiday destinations. We are both very good at ignoring what we don't want to face.'

'Most people do that,' she said. Her mother had blanked out the blindingly obvious until she couldn't ignore it any longer.

Her own tragedy was that she couldn't. But this wasn't about her.

'What would Lissa have done?' she asked.

'If she'd been the one left behind?' He didn't have to think about it. 'She wouldn't have run away from Leopard Tree Lodge. She'd lived close to nature all her life and understood that death is part of life. Something to be accepted.'

Thinking about that did something to his face. He wasn't smiling exactly, but it was as if all the underlying tension had drained away.

'She'd have come here,' he said. 'She'd have lit a fire, cooked something special, opened a bottle of good wine. She'd have scattered my ashes on the river, poured a glass of the wine into the water to see me on my way. One into the earth to thank it for what it gave us. One for herself. Then she'd have eaten well and got on with her life.'

Josie thought that the wine would have been watered with tears, but he surely knew that. It was being here, making a fitting end that was important.

'We all deal with loss in our own way, Gideon. You've built an empire on her vision,' she reminded him. 'She lives in that.'

'I wish that were so, Josie, but the truth is that I was so busy making new places that I forgot this one. Running,' he said. 'That's what my doctor told me before I left London. That I was running on empty…'

'You're not running now,' she said. 'You could have left at any time. A private air ambulance would have taken you anywhere you wanted to go. You fought me to stay here.'

'That isn't why I fought you.' His hand tightened imperceptibly over hers and she caught her breath. 'You know it's not. It's been ten years, Josie. I haven't been celibate in all those years, but you are the first woman in all that time that I've…' he paused, searching for the right word '…that I've seen.'

'Yes...'

That was the word. She had seen him, too. From that first glimpse of him through the leaves, it was as if a light had come on in her brain.

A red light. Danger...

'It's the purple hair,' she said quickly. 'And now I understand why you were so angry about the wedding.' She'd never forget the look on his face when he'd looked up and seen Cryssie's dress hanging over the wardrobe door. She'd have to find another home for it... 'It must have been like coming face to face with your worst nightmare.'

He shook his head. 'I've already been there, Josie. This is just a wedding. Speaking of which, we still have work to do,' he said, releasing her hand, easing back his chair so that he could stand up. Then, as she joined him, he caught her arm. 'There!' he said. 'Do you see him?'

She didn't want to take her eyes off Gideon, but his urgency was telegraphing itself from his hand to her brain and she turned to look across the river. It took her a moment, but then she saw the cat's eyes reflected back from the safety lights.

'What is it?' she whispered. But she already knew and he didn't answer, only his hand tightened in warning as the big cat streaked to the ground, struck some hapless creature near the water's edge. It happened so fast that before she could react, think, it was over; cat and prey were back in the tree.

'What was it?' she asked, turning instinctively to bury her face in his sleeve.

'A small deer. A dik-dik probably. It's nature's way,' he said, putting his arm around her as, sickened by the savagery of it, she shuddered. 'It's the food chain in action. When a leopard kills, everything feeds. Jackals, birds, insects lay their eggs, the earth is enriched.'

She looked up into his face. 'Life goes on?'

He hesitated but, after a moment, he nodded. 'Life goes on. It's a circle. Birth, marriage, death… This weekend it's marriage. Something to celebrate. Come on. Let's finish those favours.'

'It's very late.'

'That's okay.' He picked up the mugs and, taking her arm, he said, 'You can keep me awake by telling me a fairy story.'

'Sorry?'

'Who waved the magic wand and transformed you from scullery assistant Cinderella to partner princess?'

The teasing note was back in his voice, a little gentler than before, maybe, but the black moment had, apparently, passed.

'Oh, I see,' she said, grabbing for that and responding in kind. 'You've shown me yours, now I'm supposed to show you mine?'

'We could do that instead, if you prefer,' he replied with a questioning tilt of the head, that break-your-heart grin that assured her he was kidding.

'Let's stick with Plan A,' she said, glad that there was only the flickering candlelight as the heat rushed to her cheeks anyway. Betraying a need that he had touched within her to be a whole person. Not in the physical sense, although that was undoubtedly part of it; she was attracted to him in ways that she'd never dreamed possible.

It was the emotional vacuum within her that ached tonight. A longing to reach out to someone you could trust, love with your whole heart and know that he would be there, no matter what.

Not the role for a man eaten with guilt because he wasn't there. For a man still in love with his dead fiancée.

'But if you've got that much energy, you can make a start on the sugared almonds while I wash up,' she said, taking the mugs from him. 'One net in each box. Don't miss any.'

She didn't wait for the comeback. She needed a back-to-earth moment on her own, her hands in hot dishwater while she composed herself.

She didn't get it.

'Well, you were quick,' she said as he followed her into the kitchen, turned on the tap at the handwash sink.

'I didn't think you'd want bacon fat all over your pretty boxes,' he said, soaping his hands, drying them on a paper towel.

She swilled the plates, rinsed them, put them to drain, accepted the paper towel he pulled from the dispenser and offered her.

'Thanks.'

He was looking at her quizzically, as if wondering what on earth was so bad about a Cinderella rags-to-riches success story that she wouldn't talk about it. And obviously, if that was all it had been, there wouldn't have been a thing.

But that wasn't the story. Beloved daughter to rags was the story and the only person she'd shared that with was Sylvie.

'Do you want to help me get the rest of the stuff from the office?' she asked, hoping that the more he had to think about, the less he'd bother about her. 'Since I've got an extra pair of hands, we might as well do it all at the same time.'

'The guests don't just get the sugared almonds?'

'Oh, right—' she laughed '—that would go down well. No. Five sugared almonds to represent health, wealth, long life, fertility and happiness. And, to reinforce the wishes, we have five favours. The almonds, a packet of seeds— love-in-the-mist is popular—a mint silver coin with this year's date, something individual to mark the day and the box itself to keep them all in.'

She picked up a paperknife and ripped open a box that was packed with dozens of small turquoise chamois leather pouches.

'Tiffany?' Gideon said, taking one and tipping the contents into the palm of his hand. It was a stunning sterling silver key ring with a fob in the shape of a football, enamelled with Tal's colours and engraved with both their names and the date. 'Very pretty.'

'Everything done in the best possible taste,' she agreed as he replaced it. Then, as he made a move to pick up the box, 'No!'

'What?'

'Your back. Here, take these,' she said, thrusting the feather-light box of seed packets at him before he could argue. 'I'll bring these last two.'

Arguing over that did the trick. By the time she'd conceded, allowed him to carry the heavier boxes, they were off the dangerous subject of her past and for the next hour conversation was minimal as they concentrated on filling the boxes as quickly as possible before stowing them safely away under lock and key in the office.

By the time she'd staggered back to the tree house, Gideon at her elbow, she was too tired to worry about sharing a bed with him.

It was all she could do to remove her make-up, brush her teeth, pull a nightie over her head. She didn't even bother to ask him which side of the bed he preferred. Just staggered out of the bathroom and fell into it.

Gideon waited on the deck until he heard Josie's bare feet patter from the bathroom to the bed. He'd asked Francis to have it—and Cryssie's bathroom—checked thoroughly for anything that might have fallen onto the deck and crawled in there, although she was so exhausted she probably wouldn't have noticed an elephant hiding in the corner.

He stayed for another moment, looking out across the river, remembering the past. Remembering that it was the past, that nothing he could do would change it. That he could only change the future.

Then he went inside, closed the doors, rolled up the sidings, fastening them in place so that the air could circulate, leaving only the screens between them and nature to keep out flying insects.

For the first time in years, he wanted nothing to come between him and the sounds of the earth coming to life at the beginning of a new day.

The rooms would all have been sprayed while the guests were at dinner, but he lit a coil to discourage any mosquito that had escaped. Straightened the nets where Josie had collapsed through them and crawled beneath the sheet.

She was lying on her stomach, her arm thrown up defensively, her shoulders, her cheeks, her eyelids luminous in the candlelight.

Why hadn't he thought her beautiful when he'd first seen her? he wondered. Was the perception of beauty changed by knowing someone? Cryssie was stunning, sweet too, but twenty minutes had been enough for him to know that an hour of her company would be too long.

Josie, on the other hand, kept him on his toes. Challenged him every step of the way. Never gave an inch. Had the toughness of tensile steel. A natural tenderness. A fragility that called to every protective instinct.

She also cried messily and somewhere in her past had got so screwed up that she couldn't talk about it, not even when he'd opened up to her about Lissa. He understood that. It had taken him ten years to find the right moment, the right person, someone who knew how to listen.

He bent over her, touched his lips to her shoulder, murmured, 'Sleep safe…' before he tucked the nets around her, doused the candles.

He normally slept naked and, since she'd clearly gone out like a light the minute she'd hit the pillow, Josie wasn't about to have a fit of the vapours. But he'd been ribbing her all day about getting some action, had come closer to it than he had done in a long while. Now it was too important to risk her waking up and getting the wrong idea so he kept his shorts on as he climbed into the vast emptiness of the far side of the bed.

And did not feel alone.

CHAPTER TEN

A well planned wedding should run like clockwork, but always be prepared for things to go wrong.

—*The Perfect Wedding* by Serafina March

'JOSIE…'

She brushed away the sound, the tickle of breath against her ear, burrowed deeper into the pillow.

'Wake up.'

Who was that? Where was she? Who cared? It was dark, definitely not time to get up.

'Go 'way…'

'It's important,' the voice insisted and, finally, the urgency of the summons began to seep through to her brain.

'What is it? What's wrong?' she said, blinking to unglue her eyelids. Yawning. Stretching… Oh, shoot! 'Gideon!'

He was fully dressed, shaved, while she was... She was wearing a nightdress that had twisted around and would undoubtedly be missing some of the important bits.

She didn't look, just grabbed the sheet, glared at him.

'What?'

'I thought you'd like to see an African dawn.'

'You are so wrong about that.'

'Trust me, you'll love it. Francis has brought coffee, muffins warm from the oven...' He waved one under her nose so that she leaned forward, following it like an eager puppy.

Certain that he'd finally got her attention, he whisked it out of reach. 'On the deck. Fully dressed. You've got ten minutes.'

'Or what?' she demanded.

'Or you'll regret it for the rest of your life.'

Not a chance, she thought, staggering to the bathroom, peering at herself from beneath lids that needed matchsticks to keep them open.

Coffee, yes. Muffin, yes. Then she was going back to bed until morning.

She pulled a shirt, the first pair of trousers that came to hand, to cover her modesty. Emerged to the scent of warm earth, coffee and muffins, the air filled with the sounds of insects tuning up for the day.

Gideon handed her a cup of coffee. 'Sit down.'

She needed no second bidding, but he wasn't concerned that she was going to fall down. The minute she had collapsed into a chair, he produced a pair of socks from his pocket and said, 'Give me your foot.'

Then, as she responded without thinking, 'What are you doing? Are they my socks?'

'They were in your boots,' he said, sliding them onto her feet. 'You can change them when you come back.'

'Come back from where?' she asked as he picked up one of her boots and continued dressing her as if she were a three-year-old.

'I've made sure nothing's crawled into them in the night,' he said, sliding it over her foot, lacing it up.

'The only place I'm going is back to bed,' she declared.

'If that's an invitation, you're on,' he said, the second boot in his hand. 'If not, let's go.'

'Where?' she demanded as he laced up boot number two.

'To feel the fear and do it anyway. You can bring the muffin.'

'I remember you,' she grumbled, grabbing the muffin and following him down the steps. 'You're the guy who issues an invitation as if it's an order.'

The dining room was already buzzing with

visitors gathering for dawn walks and drives, but Gideon turned aside before they reached it, heading for the jetty she'd been shown on her tour. It was where the river boat, due in later that morning, would tie up.

By the time they'd reached a boatman, waiting beside a boat that looked a little like a cross between a punt and a canoe, the sky had begun to pale.

'*Dumela, Rra. Dumela, Mma,*' he said.

'*Dumela, Moretse. O tsogile?*'

'*Ke tsogile, Rra,*' he replied with a full-beam smile. Then he turned to Josie, repeated the greeting. She looked at Gideon.

'He asked if you rose well,' he said. 'You say "*ke tsogile*".'

She obediently repeated the phrase, then said, 'And what's the response if I was hauled out of a deep sleep by a man who refused to take no for an answer?'

'It's like "How d'you do?", Josie. There is only one answer.' Then, 'He's waiting for you to get into his boat.'

'I was afraid of that,' she said, looking at the very small craft. 'Here goes the last of the Fowlers,' she said as she stepped in, choosing the rear of two front-facing seats.

'Don't you want to sit in front?' Gideon asked.

'No. I'm good,' she assured him. 'I'll hide behind you and, if we meet anything on the prowl for breakfast, it'll see you first.'

He grinned.

'I'm serious,' she said as he took the seat in front of her, said something to the boatman. 'Don't, whatever you do, smile at any passing crocodiles.'

And then they were off, moving silently, smoothly through water turning pink to reflect the sky where tiny bubbles of cloud were threaded like gold sequins against the red dawn.

Gideon said something to the boatman and he nodded.

'What?' Josie asked.

'He thinks the rain will come early this year.'

'Not before Sunday,' she begged. 'Tell me that it won't be before Sunday.'

'Probably not for another week or so.' Then, 'There's a heron.'

A tall white bird looked up as they passed, but didn't move. Deer of all shapes and sizes, zebra, giraffe had come to the water to drink.

Gideon named them all for her. Shaggy waterbuck, tiny dik dik, skittish gazelles. Pointed out birds that she would never have seen. Identified a vivid flash of green as a Malachite Kingfisher.

Before she knew it, Josie was leaning

forward, her hand on his shoulder, eager to catch everything. The zebra lined up as if waiting to be photographed, as if you could capture this in a picture. It wasn't just the sight of animals in the wild; it was the scent of the river, the strident song of the cicadas, the grunts and snorts, the screams of monkeys overhead in the trees. The splash of an elephant family having an early morning bathe. The sun bursting above the horizon like the first dawn.

And Gideon.

He'd given her this and, as they drifted back towards the jetty, she laid her cheek against his back. Said, 'Thank you.'

He turned, smiled, responding almost absently to her thanks with a touch to the cheek, before crossing to the majestic river boat which was in the process of docking alongside the jetty.

By the time she had showered, turned herself back into the 'wedding lady', the florist had arrived with a planeload of flowers. The photographer, with the hair and make-up girl in attendance, grabbed Cryssie and bore her away, taking the chance to get some pictures of her around the lodge, while she and the florist worked to create the fantasy bridal suite.

By lunchtime, all the main players had arrived, apart from the groom and, as anticipated, she was soon fielding complaints about the lack of a phone signal from both men and women.

'Problems?' Gideon asked, joining her as she was being berated by one particularly irate young man.

'This is ridiculous. I've got to talk to my agent today—'

'And you think that shouting at Miss Fowler is going to make that happen?'

'What?' Gideon had spoken quietly but, even with the buzz in the room, the man's attention was instantly engaged. 'Who are you?' he demanded.

'Gideon McGrath,' he said, not offering his hand. 'I own Leopard Tree Lodge so if you have a complaint, bring it to me.'

Accepting that as an invitation, he forgot all about her, turning to someone with the power to help him. 'I can't get a signal on my mobile and I have to talk to my agent—'

'After you've apologised to Miss Fowler.'

The man blinked, clearly not used to being interrupted.

'Or you could call your agent from Gabarone. There's a plane leaving in the next five minutes.'

'Gideon,' Josie said, stepping in quickly to avert disaster, 'may I introduce Darren Buck? He's one of Tal's teammates. And his best man.'

'Really?' Gideon said, without a flicker to

suggest that he was in the least bit impressed, either by his iconic status as a football star or the fact that he was an important player in the forthcoming event. 'That explains a lot.' Then, 'Which is it to be, Mr Buck?'

Darren Buck, the hottest thing on two legs, apart from the groom, was no taller than Gideon and had an angelic smile that made him a *Celebrity* favourite, but he was built like a brick outhouse and had a famously short fuse. Josie held her breath as the reality of the choices he was being offered sank in. Gideon clearly had no idea of the danger but, as the two men faced off, it was Darren Buck who backed down, favoured her with that famous smile.

'I'm sorry, Miss Fowler. My agent is negotiating a TV deal for me but that's no excuse for shouting at you. If I can help in any way, please don't hesitate to ask. My apologies, Mr McGrath.'

Gideon nodded once and, as if released, the man turned and walked away.

Josie's breath escaped like steam from a pressure cooker. 'Have you any idea what you just did?' she demanded, not sure whether to slap him or hug him.

'Darren Buck is a bully, but this isn't a football field,' he replied, as calm as he'd been throughout the confrontation. 'I have no doubt that you could have handled him with one hand tied behind your back, but I won't have my staff subjected to that kind of behaviour.'

'I'm sure he'll be on his best behaviour from now on,' she said. It wasn't her that Gideon had stepped in to protect, but his staff. People he cared about. 'But thank you, anyway.'

'How is everything going?'

'Fine. Cryssie has her bridesmaids to gossip with. The bridal suite looks stunning.' She looked up as another plane circled overhead. 'And guests are pouring in. All we need now is the groom.'

'Does that mean you're free for lunch?'

'Theoretically,' she said. 'I'll even share forbidden treats, but you'll have to put up with non-stop pleading for email and phone access. Hiding out in the tree house isn't likely to save us.'

'I'll get David to send round a notice,' he said, 'but in the meantime I thought you might like to escape this madness for two or three hours. Have lunch out.'

'Lunch out?'

No! The way her heart had picked up a beat warned her that she was already too deeply involved with this man. Cared too much. Was looking for him whenever she turned a corner, entered a room. Missed him when he wasn't there. How had that happened?

No, no, no…

Then, as the incongruity of what he was asking struck her, 'Where do you go out for lunch around here?'

'There's a place just along the river I'd like to show you.'

'Oh…' Of course. There had to be other places like this. Well, maybe not quite like this, but success bred competition.

'I thought it would give you a break while everyone settles in. It's our job to handle any queries.' His eyes creased in that slow smile that reached her toes. 'We're quite good at it.'

'Yes. I noticed,' she said, fighting off an ear to ear grin.

'Ten minutes? I'll be waiting outside in the compound. Bring a camera if you have one. And your passport.'

'My passport?'

'We're right on the border here. It's always best to be prepared.'

'Oh. Right,' she said. It was only when he'd disappeared into the office that she realised that she seemed to have accepted his invitation, despite her determination not to.

'I feel as if I'm playing hooky,' she said as Gideon drove through the compound gates, raising a plume of dust in their wake. A touch light-headed, as if mind and body weren't quite connected.

'Is there anything you have to do in the next three hours?' he asked.

'No, but…'

'You worked half the night.'

'That's par for the course.'

'No doubt. But the next two days are going to be non-stop. You need down time. Am I right?'

'Absolutely right,' she said, laughing.

'Hold that thought.'

'Yes, sir!' Then, as she saw a twin-engine plane parked in the shade, 'Oh, this is the airstrip.'

'Full marks for observation. Let's see what else you notice,' he said as he pulled up alongside, came round to offer her a steadying hand as she jumped down.

'Er… When you said "just along the river" what exactly did you have in mind as a scale of reference?' she asked.

Gideon shrugged. 'At home you drive out into the country for lunch at some village inn. Africa's bigger. Here you hop in a plane.'

'I've done all the checks, Gideon. Filed your flight plan,' the pilot said. 'She's all ready to go.'

'Thanks, Pete. Enjoy your lunch.'

Josie watched as the pilot climbed into the four-by-four and, before she could gather her wits, drive off with the only transport back to the Lodge.

She turned to Gideon, who was walking slowly around the plane, visually checking that everything was there, despite the pilot having assured him that he'd already done it.

It should have filled her with confidence, but she was too angry to think about that.

'Do you recall me saying to you that I have a very real problem with people taking over my life, leaving me without a choice?' she said.

Gideon looked up, frowned. 'I invited you to lunch, Josie.'

'And my passport? Where are we going? I want to know.'

'You won't trust me?'

The way he'd trusted her last night, when he'd laid his broken heart out in little pieces for her. Talked about things he'd kept bottled up for years. That was what he was asking.

'It's not a question of trust,' she protested.

'Isn't it? You didn't ask where we were going when you thought it was just a ride along the river in a Land Rover. What's the difference between getting in a canoe with me on a river swarming with crocs and hippos, taking off into the bush on four wheels, or climbing aboard an aircraft so that we can do in an hour what would take all day to do by road?'

'I gave you an argument this morning, if you remember, despite the fact that I was half asleep. Even though you didn't bother to mention the crocs and hippos.'

She'd started to give him an argument about lunch, but he'd deflected her, just as he'd deflected Darren Buck.

'I didn't want you to be worrying about anything this morning. I just wanted you to feel the wonder so that when you thought of Leopard Tree Lodge you wouldn't remember it filled with people like Darren Buck. Only the quiet, the peace, the beauty of it.'

Josie knew she was making a fool of herself. That Gideon McGrath was offering her something rare. His time. A part of himself.

'Do you believe I'd do anything to hurt you?' he asked when she didn't respond.

'No.' It was a sincere question and she answered it honestly. 'Not intentionally.'

He couldn't help it if she lost her head, her heart... Because she was very much afraid that the only thing she'd remember when she thought about Leopard Tree Lodge would be Gideon McGrath. That first heart-stopping smile. Standing over the kitchen range as he'd cooked supper for them both. Spilling his heart out in the moonlight.

'That's the best anyone can promise, Josie,' he said. 'You can walk around all your life trussed up in emotional armour plating in case someone gets its wrong. Or you can take the risk.'

Feel the fear and do it anyway…

'So?' he prompted. 'Do you want to climb aboard? Or shall we walk back to the Lodge?'

As she drew in a long breath of the warm, earthy air she looked back along the track to the Lodge. She could scurry back there, hide away in her emotional burrow. But it no longer felt like a safe retreat. It felt dark, stifling, suffocating…

When she'd been locked up, shut away, she'd had no choice but to endure. Learn to control her feelings so that she could be free. This prison, she realised, was of her own making and the only thing keeping her there was her own fear.

She turned back to Gideon, waiting patiently for her decision. 'Let's go,' she said stiffly, afraid that if she didn't hold herself tightly together, she might betray just how big a deal this was.

He was too busy buckling himself into the seat beside her, calling up air traffic control as he taxied out onto the airstrip, concentrating on take-off to notice one way or the other.

He banked over the Lodge and headed east, keeping conversation to pointing out the sights as they flew over them. A family of elephants at the water's edge, giraffe and zebra grazing together. A herd of antelope.

She'd been too tired to take much notice when

she'd flown up from Gabarone. Now she took in everything. The dark green snake of vegetation that marked the river. The endless dry bush spread beyond it. The occasional village. The astonishing sight of a town set in what appeared to be the middle of nowhere.

And then, off in the distance, she saw a mist rising from the earth. 'What's that?'

'It's what I've brought you to see. *Mosi O Tunya.*'

'Oh?'

'The smoke that thunders,' he prompted, clearly expecting some response. 'You haven't heard of it?'

She shook her head.

'The first European to see it was Dr David Livingstone. He did what all good explorers do and named it after the reigning monarch.'

She frowned. 'Livingstone? Nineteenth century? Queen Victoria…' Then, as she caught up, 'The Victoria Falls?' She looked from him to the mist, closer now. 'I had no idea it was so near. Is that the spray?'

'That's the spray,' he confirmed, picking up the radio and calling air traffic control. Then, 'Make the most of it if you want pictures; I can only go round once.'

Josie had her cellphone with her, but she left that in her bag. She didn't want to look at one of the natural wonders of the world through a view-finder; she wanted to see it, feel it at first hand.

As he circled she could see that it wasn't an open waterfall like Niagara, but dropped, over a mile wide, into a deep gorge. The size, the scale of it was awesome, breathtaking and she didn't say a word until, a few minutes later, they had landed on the Zambian side of the Falls.

'That was incredible, Gideon. Thank you so much.' Then, 'I'm sorry for being such a—'

'Don't,' he said, pressing his fingers to her lips to stop the word. 'Don't apologise for saying what you thought, felt. You were honest.' Then, letting his hand drop, 'Do you want to take a closer look?'

At that moment the only thing she wanted to get closer to was him, but he had already turned to a waiting car.

'Gideon, man! Good to see you,' the driver said. They did that man-hug thing and then Gideon turned to her. 'Josie, this is Rupe. Rupe, Josie.'

'Let me guess,' she said, a little overwhelmed that he'd not only thought to bring her here, but had arranged a car to pick them up. But then that was his business… 'You've been here before.'

'One of my earliest ventures was organising trips for the bungee jumping nuts. From that,' he said as they passed a great wrought iron bridge laced with a rainbow where the mist was lit up by the sun. 'It's still a favourite.'

'Have you ever tried it?'

He just grinned. Of course he had.

'Before you suggest it,' she said, hurriedly, 'no. Definitely, absolutely, a thousand times no.'

'Smart woman,' he replied. Then, 'Here we are.'

He got out first, offered her his hand as if she were visiting royalty, walked her across to a point where there was a clear view of the mighty Zambezi pouring into the gorge in a dizzying rush.

'Words are inadequate,' she said after a while.

'Did you bring a camera?' he asked. 'I'll take your photograph.'

'Just this,' she said, handing him her phone.

'You should be looking at the Falls, not me,' he said. She turned obediently.

'Do you want me to take one of the two of you?' Rupe said.

Before she could rescue him from the embarrassment, Gideon had handed the cellphone to Rupe, put his arm around her and, looking down at her, said, 'Say, cheese, Josie.'

'Cheese, Josie.'

'Okay. Let's eat,' he said, retrieving her phone, checking the picture before handing it back to her, glancing at his watch. 'Pick us up in half an hour, Rupe,' he said, taking a cold bag the man was holding. 'Come on, this way. Take care; the steps are wet. Better hold my hand.'

He went first, leading her down steps cut from the rock that led down into the depths of the gorge. He didn't go far before he placed the cold box on a large flat rock.

'Help yourself to a step,' he said. 'It's not the Ritz but the service is quick,' he said. 'Soda or water?'

'Water, please,' she said, and held the bottle to the pulse throbbing in her neck, before opening it and taking a mouthful.

'This is amazing,' she said. Everywhere was overgrown with ferns and tropical plants dripping with moisture in the steamy atmosphere. It reminded her of the tropical hothouse at Kew, except this was the real thing. 'A bit Garden of Edenish.'

And they were the only people in it.

He looked in the box. 'Sorry, no apples. There's a naartje, will that do?'

'Tell me what it is and I'll let you know.'

'A small orange—a bit like a tangerine,' he said, showing her.

'It's green.'

'It's ripe, I promise.'

'Okay, hand it over. What else have you got in there?'

'Nothing exciting. Sandwiches. A Scotch egg. I'll do better next time.'

Next time? He was saying that there would be

a next time? No... But she couldn't believe how much she wanted there to be a next time.

'Cheese, egg, salad?' he said, looking up, catching her staring.

'Salad. Thanks,' she said quickly.

'Are you okay, Josie?'

'Yes,' she said quickly. Then, because he was still looking at her, 'No...'

Next time meant a future and that meant telling him everything, just as she'd told Sylvie when she'd offered her a job. Because she had a right to know and if she hadn't been honest someone else would have told her. Warned her...

And she had to do it now, before there was the possibility of any next time. Before they went back to Leopard Tree Lodge. Now...

CHAPTER ELEVEN

Create a fragrant memory for your guests
by choosing wedding flowers with beautiful and distinctive scents.
—*The Perfect Wedding* by Serafina
March

JOSIE put down the sandwich, rubbed the back
of her hand over her forehead.

'You asked me if I trusted you,' she said.

He handed her a sandwich, leaned back
against the rock. 'You answered that by getting
into a plane with me, even though you didn't
know where I was taking you.'

'That was a physical thing. The trust that you
wouldn't hurt me.'

'Not intentionally,' he said. 'I understood the
qualification. The vulnerability we all feel when
we open ourselves up to someone. Expose our
weaknesses, our fears.'

'You said it was the most we could hope for,' she said, looking up at him, trying to see behind those dark eyes. Find something in them to reassure her that he would understand what she was about to tell him. 'Will you kiss me, Gideon?'

Gideon felt the plastic pack collapse beneath his fingers, crushing the sandwich inside.

Would he kiss her?

Did she have any idea what she was asking?

Last night, as they'd worked together, knowing that she was doing everything she could to distract him from asking her about her past, all he'd wanted to do was hold her, tell her it would be all right. Instead, he'd concentrated on the job in hand, showing her how he felt by doing what he could to help.

He'd lain propped on his elbow half the night just watching her sleep, memorising her face. The shape of her ear, the little crease that appeared by her mouth from time to time as if she were smiling in her dreams, the long inviting curve of her neck.

She had no way of knowing that when she'd leaned her head against his back this morning in the canoe, a wordless gesture that was more speaking than a thousand thanks, he'd had to force himself to walk away before he did something stupid. He'd seen how she'd reacted to a kiss that she hadn't seen coming. The fear…

When he'd seen that idiot Darren Buck shouting at her, it had taken every atom of self-control to stop himself from grabbing the man and pitching him bodily out of the Lodge.

Now, because of something he'd just said, she'd decided this was the moment to share whatever horror lurked in her past. What? What had he said? He reran the last few moments in his head.

Next time...

The words dropped into the waiting slot with an almost audible clunk. He'd said them without thinking, because he hadn't needed to think about it. This was different from his earlier attempts to move on, date. That had taken effort. This was—had been from the moment he'd first set eyes on Josie—effortless.

Next time. The possibility of a future...

But first she had to lay the ghosts of her past. And she was asking him to kiss her now, before she told him, because she was afraid that afterwards, when he knew, he might not want to.

Would he kiss her? In a heartbeat.

Should he?

Suppose, afterwards, he was so repelled by what she told him that he couldn't bring himself to kiss her again? How much worse would she feel then? How could he live with himself if he confirmed everything that she most feared?

Not intentionally...

She was looking up at him with those huge, impossibly violet eyes. The same eyes that had wept for her mother last night, had looked at him with such compassion as he'd spilled out his heartache, guilt. Could he do any less for her?

He dropped the sandwich back into the cold box, squeezed himself onto the step beside her.

'Sure?' he asked, hoping that she wouldn't pick up on the uncertainty in his voice.

'No.' She shook her head. 'Sorry. I shouldn't have asked…'

'Be still,' he said. Then again as, startled, she looked up at him and he captured her face between his hands, lowered his lips to hers, 'Be still…'

Her lips were soft, strawberry-flavoured, sweet and he was trembling as he fought to keep his kiss light, tender, when everything was telling him to go for broke, take her over the edge so that she would forget whatever nightmare she was about to reveal. To make her his, there in a steamy grotto as old as time.

Or was it Josie who was trembling?

He leaned back, looked down at her. 'Okay?'

She nodded and he put an arm around her shoulder so that she could lean into him, so that she wouldn't have to look at him. So that she couldn't see his face.

She didn't speak for a while, and when she did

it was about those last months with her mother. 'She was terrified of hospitals, Gideon, wanted to die at home.'

'You nursed her? How long?' he prompted when the pause had gone on too long.

'Months. Six, seven, maybe. Alec didn't help much.'

'Alec? He was your stepfather? What happened to your father?'

'He was killed in the first Gulf war. It was really hard for her and Alec was funny, charming, had all the moves and Mum must have been desperately lonely. She also had the house that her parents had left her, a war widow's pension and a nice little part-time job. He couldn't wait to move in. But Mum didn't do that. He had to marry her before he could get his feet under the table.'

'And you? Did he ever touch you?'

'No. He knew I could see right through him, would have leapt at the chance to get him out of the house. He was always very careful around me.' Then she drew back, looked at him. 'That's what you thought when I freaked out?'

'It crossed my mind.'

'No one hurt me like that, Gideon. It's just losing control. That's what sex is about, isn't it? Surrendering yourself totally?'

It was a question, not a statement, as if she

was seeking confirmation. As if it was something she'd never done.

'It's an equal surrender, Josie. A mutual gift.'

'Equal?' It was as if some light had gone on
inside her head. 'I never thought of it like that.'

It was true. He could scarcely believe it, but
this feisty, modern, in-your-face woman didn't
know. Had never experienced it for herself.
Turned off, maybe, by the smooth operator who'd
taken advantage of her mother. Seen it as a
weapon…

'What happened, Josie?' he said, rather
more urgently.

'The nurse who came in twice a day told me to
go out, take a walk around the park, get some
fresh air. That she'd sit with my mother. Alec was
at work so I felt safe leaving her. It was a lovely
day. I sat on a bench in the sun near the roses,
sucking up the scent. I fell asleep, Gideon. I was
gone for over an hour and when I got back the only
person home was Alec. He said that my mother
had started to fit just after the nurse left and he
hadn't known what to do so he'd called an ambulance. He'd been waiting to tell me. By the time I
got to the hospital they had her hooked up to all
kinds of machines, exactly what she'd feared.'

'It wasn't your fault, Josie.'

'Of course it was.' She shook her head. 'I stayed
with her for three days. He never once came near

and when I went home to tell him that his wife, my mother, was dead, I found him sitting in her kitchen with the barmaid from the Red Lion. She was wearing one of my mother's dressing gowns, drinking tea from one of her cups…'

'Oh, love,' he said, but she shrugged off his attempt to comfort her.

'I went crazy, Gideon. Lost control. I smashed the cup from the woman's hands. Smashed everything from the table. The teapot went flying and she began to scream that she was scalded and, as Alec came for me, to grab me, I suppose, stop me from doing any more damage, I picked up a chair and hit him.'

The air was so still. Nothing stirred. And the only sound was the muffled roar of the Falls.

'The police came and took me away. But I was uncontrollable and a doctor had to be called to sedate me and, when he heard what had happened, he had me sectioned under the Mental Health Act. Locked up for twenty-eight days for my own safety.'

Josie swallowed hard, her throat tight with anger, even now. But it had been her fault her mother had died in hospital. Her fault she wasn't there to see her decently laid to rest.

'I was never charged with anything.'

'Well, that's something, I suppose. Hospital has to be better than prison.'

She turned on him. 'Do you think so? Do you really think so?' she demanded. 'Being banged up for assault would at least have given me some kind of street cred but there's a stigma to mental illness that you can never shake off. I was in there for six months, Gideon.'

'Six months? But you weren't sick; you were angry, grieving…'

'I hurt two people, Gideon. When I realised, understood what I'd done, I was appalled. But sorry is just a word. Anyone can say it. I was watched, monitored, drugged until I learned to control every emotion. Eventually, when I was good and obedient and stopped fighting them, they let me go.'

'What did you do?'

'I went home.' She could still remember exactly how she'd felt walking up to the door of her home. Having to knock. The door being opened by someone she didn't know. But even then she hadn't understood… 'He'd sold my mother's house. There were strangers living there. Other people's children playing on the swing my dad built for me.'

'But your life was there. How could he do that?'

'There was an old will leaving everything to me that she'd made after my dad died, but apparently they become invalid the minute you marry. My mother couldn't have known that and, as her husband, Alec automatically inherited everything. I went next door to a neighbour to find out where he'd gone. I didn't want to cause trouble,' she said quickly. 'The last thing I wanted was to go back into that hospital. But I didn't have any clothes. Nothing. Not even a photograph of my mum, my dad. His medals…'

She heard the crunch as the plastic sandwich carton she was still holding crushed between her hands and Gideon unhooked his arm from around her shoulder, took it from her, stood up to dump it in the box. He took out a bottle of water, opened it, took a long drink.

'The neighbour?' he asked when he finally turned back to face her. 'What did she do?'

She shook her head. It didn't matter. She'd seen his reaction. He couldn't wait to put some distance between them. Couldn't bear to look at her.

'Josie?'

'She told me to wait. Shut the door on me while she called Social Services to come and get me. She was afraid of me.' She'd never forget that look. 'She'd known me all my life but she was terrified.'

She sighed.

'I was found a place in a hostel, a job in a hotel kitchen where the most important thing I was trusted to do was scrub pots. Obviously I couldn't be trusted to peel vegetables. That would have meant giving me a knife.'

'Wasn't there anyone you could turn to?'

'You think I'd have lived in that horrible place if there was?' she snapped. This was so not like telling Sylvie. She'd just listened. No questions. Just let it all come out. Then she'd made her a cup of tea and asked her if she wanted the job. End of story. Not this…anger.

'I'd gone berserk, Gideon. Scalded a woman for daring to drink out of one my mother's cups,' she said, cutting it short, wanting it over. 'Brought a chair down on my stepfather's head. Would you want me in your house?' She didn't wait for an answer. The Garden of Eden had lost its charm and she stood up. 'It's hot down here. I'm going back up—'

'Someone wanted you,' he reminded her before she'd taken a second step. 'Sylvie.'

Sylvie. Just the name was enough to bring her back from that dark place. 'You called her my fairy godmother and she was. Still is. She'd been let down by the agency supplying waiters for a reception at the hotel and the duty manager rounded up anyone he could find to fill in. You can tell how desperate he was…'

She'd done the work of five that night, bossing the chambermaids who hadn't got a clue—after all, no one in their right mind was going to argue with her—made sure the food and drink kept coming. Whisked away a very drunk actress who was about to make a fool of herself and found her a room where she could sleep it off. She'd seen an opportunity to impress and seized it with both hands.

'You must have been amazingly good for her to take you on without experience,' Gideon said.

'I just wanted it more. I was the only one who stayed to help her clear up when it was all over. Help her pack up her stuff. Sylvie comes from some really swanky aristocratic family but she'd had a rough time, lost her mother, her home, too. We bonded, I suppose.'

She took another step.

'How long has it been? Since the scullery.'

'Nearly five years.'

'And now you're here, taking charge of the most important wedding of the season.'

'Marji wanted Sylvie,' she said impatiently, taking another step. Wishing she'd never started this. Next time. There was never going to be a next time... 'But she's on maternity leave.'

'And there was no other wedding planner prepared to drop everything and grab the biggest job in town?'

She stopped, turned. 'What are you saying?'

'That maybe you're the one who needs to let go of the past, Josie. Stop worrying about what you think other people think about you. They really don't care as long as you do your job.

What happened to you is shocking. This man stole everything from you. Your home, your memories, but unless you can let go you're handing him your future, too.'

'Well, thanks, Gideon. Like I haven't heard the pull yourself together, get laid and stop feeling sorry for yourself speech before.'

He shrugged. 'I couldn't have put it better myself. If you need any help with the second part of the plan, let me know.'

'If you have any ideas in that direction, the office floor is still vacant,' she said, and this time when she started up the steps he did nothing to stop her.

The car was waiting and she climbed into the back. She hoped Gideon might get into the front seat alongside his old friend Rupe, but he wasn't done.

'You were honest with me yesterday, Josie. I don't know what else I could have said.'

'Nothing,' she said. It wasn't what he'd said. It was the fact that he couldn't wait to get away from her.

'Did you ever look for him?'

She frowned. 'Alec? You're kidding? If I'd turned up on his doorstep he'd have called the police, told them I was harassing him.'

'I wondered if you'd made any attempt to get back your personal things. The photographs.'

'Oh, please. They would have gone into a skip with the rest of the rubbish when he moved.'

'Do you think so? Photographs are—'

Josie heard a bleep. 'Did you leave my phone on?' She took it from her bag. 'Well, what do you know?' she said, feigning enthusiasm. 'I've got a signal. Do you mind? I need to deal with this.'

She opened her messages and spent the next few minutes answering them, calling her office, using the time to block out the presence of the man beside her. Rediscover the Josie Fowler who'd left London. Tighten up the armour plating. Re-establish a safe boundary between her and her emotions.

He must have got the picture because he dropped the subject of her past while she kept her eyes on the scenery, straining to see the mist from the Falls for as long as it was visible. Then on the horizon. But she needed her sunglasses to keep her eyes from watering in the brilliant light.

The four-by-four was waiting for them when they landed and she didn't wait for him to help her down when they reached the compound.

'Thanks, Gideon. Great lunch,' she said, swinging herself down before he could help. He didn't follow her and at the door she glanced back, realised he was still sitting in the Land Rover. 'Are you all right?' she asked with a sudden pang of concern. 'Is it your back?'

'No,' he said. 'It's not my back. It's my foot. I appear to have got it firmly lodged in my mouth.'

'No.' He couldn't help his feelings. At least he hadn't tried to pretend. 'You were honest,' she said. 'And that is all any of us can hope for.'

Anything else was pie in the sky and she didn't hang around to embarrass him any longer.

She kept herself busy. Not looking for Gideon whenever she turned a corner, walked into a room. Not looking so hard, in fact, that she didn't see him even when she walked into the dining room. Not until he half rose, as if to invite her to the table he was sharing with some of the guests.

For a heartbeat there was nothing else. No sound, no movement, nothing but the two of them locked into some space where the world was in slow motion.

Then Cryssie grabbed her arm, wanting to tell her something and the noise rushed back and she turned away.

It was going to be a long day tomorrow and she ordered supper on a tray, then checked to see if there were any messages before heading for the tree house to obsessively check her lists.

She'd done it half a dozen times before she gave up waiting for him to return and went to bed. Lying in the dark, listening to the party going on until late. Pretending to be asleep when he did finally make it back.

There was no dawn call with coffee and muffins. Instead, she left him sleeping, grabbed a quick breakfast in the dining room with the photographer waiting for Cryssie and Tal, who were going out on a game drive to be photographed in the wilds.

Later, while the women took over the swimming pool and talked clothes non-stop as they had their nails done, Gideon took the men, needing an outlet for their pent-up energy, off to the nearest school to give the children a football master class.

Josie, meanwhile, kept an eye on the florists, back with even more flowers. Decorated the top deck of the river boat, laid up the tables for the dinner that night.

'You haven't laid a place for yourself,' Cryssie said when she came to see how it looked.

'Honestly, Cryssie…'

But Cryssie, it seemed, had an unexpectedly determined streak that belied her blonde bombshell image.

'There's an uneven number on that table,' she said. 'It looks untidy.'

And untidiness was, apparently, not to be tolerated.

Gideon had beaten her to the bathroom, changed and gone by the time she was finally satisfied that there wasn't another thing she could do and rushed back for her one minute shower, a quick pass with a pair of straighteners she'd borrowed to perk up her hair and the fastest make-up job in history.

She only had one posh frock with her and the vintage designer dress, midnight-purple chiffon, backless almost to her bottom, a handkerchief hem around her knees, was going to have to do double duty for tonight and the wedding.

Hair and make-up done, purple stockings so fine that they were practically non-existent clinging to her legs, she slipped it over her head. Fastened two velvet chokers studded with crystals around her neck. Pushed her feet into a pair of vertiginous Mary Janes. Checked her little black and purple velvet evening bag for the basic kit. Took a last deep breath.

'Game on,' she said, then she turned and came face to face with Gideon.

He was wearing the cream suit she'd seen hanging in the wardrobe, a dark open-necked shirt. Forget dinner. He looked good enough to eat.

'Cryssie sent me to look for you.'

'Why?' she asked. 'I wasn't lost.'

'No?' He extended a hand. 'Let's go.' And, when she hesitated, 'I'm not prepared to risk you stumbling on those heels.'

She hadn't seen him looking at her feet, but then she had no idea how long he'd been standing there before she'd turned around. She didn't argue but surrendered her elbow to his hand, allowed him to escort her along the bridge and down to the jetty.

What had been a plain wide wooden deck was now lined on either side with flowers, lit with lanterns that were reflected in the dark water. Small tables had been placed along its length where guests were being served pre-dinner drinks, canapés.

'It looks stunning, Josie. You've done a great job.'

'Let's get tomorrow over before you start congratulating me. Stay and have a drink,' she urged. 'I need to go up on deck, to be there, make sure everyone finds their seat.' She didn't wait for his answer, but broke away, walked quickly to the boat and climbed up onto the deck, took one final look around before nodding to the maitre d' to ring the ship's bell to summon everyone on deck.

'Penny for them?' Gideon asked.

The table with the odd number had been where Gideon was sitting and Cryssie had written her name on a place card and set it next to him. Josie had switched it so that he was at a table at the far end of the room, adjusted the table plan and reprinted it.

While she was directing people to their seats,

someone had switched them back and, from the little grin that Cryssie had given her, she knew that she'd been rumbled.

'I was thinking about the food,' she replied. 'It's superb. I really wish that Paul and his team were catering the wedding tomorrow.'

'I'll tell him.'

'All your staff have been great, Gideon. You should be proud of them, proud of what you've made of Lissa's dream.'

Before he could answer, Tal rose, said a few words to welcome everyone to his and Cryssie's wedding. 'Make the most of it,' he urged them before he sat down. 'Neither of us will be doing this again.'

It got a laugh, a signal for the small band that had set up on the jetty to start playing.

'Are you free now?' Gideon asked. 'You don't have to rush off and do anything?'

'I'll have to restore order here…'

'Not until after the party.'

'Well, no…'

'It's just that I had the feeling you might have been avoiding me.'

'Me? Avoiding you?'

'You say that as if it was the other way around. I came looking for you last night but you'd disappeared. Then this morning you were up before dawn.'

'The one was linked to the other. Early to bed, early to rise. And you didn't appear to be lacking for company. An entire bouquet of bridesmaids hanging on your every word the last time I saw you.' That, at least appeared to amuse him and she was afraid she knew why. 'But thanks for taking the guys off our hands this afternoon,' she said quickly to cover her slip. 'Did you have fun?'

'The footballers were great with the kids. They had a whip-round for the school funds, too. Darren Buck was especially generous.'

'That'll go down well with the readers of *Celebrity*.'

'Do you dance, Miss Cynic?' Gideon asked as they joined the crowd drifting down the stairs, his hand to her back to steady her. Cool against her naked skin, raising gooseflesh even though the night was warm.

'No.'

'Never?'

Not when she wanted to keep her head.

'I don't think you'll be short of a partner,' she assured him. Then, as an altercation broke out between two of the women, 'Go and find Darren Buck, tell him to a get a grip on his women,' she said, hurrying to step between them just as the chief bridesmaid's replacement swung a left.

If she'd been wearing her boots she would have

taken the full force of it, but the high heels gave her no purchase and she went down as if poleaxed.

'Josie!'

She blinked, slightly dazed by the speed of it as Gideon ran his fingers lightly over her cheek. 'That's going to be one hell of a bruise.'

'Just as long as the bridesmaid wasn't marked,' she said, wincing as she sat up, testing her jaw.

He grinned. 'You took the hit for the bridesmaid?'

'If she had to drop out it would make the numbers uneven,' she said. 'Is she okay?'

'Her mascara's run. Is that fatal?'

She snorted. 'Stop it. Help me up.'

'Put your arm on my shoulder.' She did as she was bid but, instead of helping her to her feet, he scooped her up and carried her inside.

'Gideon, put me down. Your back…'

'There's nothing wrong with my back.' He pushed open the swing door to the kitchen. 'It was a stress thing.' He stopped, looked down at her. 'Thanks to you, I'm not stressed any more.' Then, before she could say anything, 'Crushed ice here!'

It was Paul who made up the ice pack, but it was Gideon who applied it with the utmost gentleness to her jaw. Waved away Cryssie, who'd come running to make sure she was all right.

'I'm so sorry, Josie.'

'No problem,' she said. 'I just lost my balance. Gideon warned me about these heels. Could you make sure Darren's girlfriend is okay? She could probably do with some of this ice for her hand.'

'If you're sure there's nothing I can do?'

'I'll take care of her,' Gideon said. 'Go and enjoy your party.' Then, when she'd gone, 'Let's get you to your room.'

'You're not going to carry me!' she warned. 'I can walk.'

'Really? Well, that's a relief.'

'You have hurt your back!'

'No, but I very well might if I had to carry you all that way,' he said.

She jabbed him with her elbow but didn't object when he put his arm around her waist to support her as they walked slowly back along the bridge. He sat her on the bed, gave her a pain-killer. By then her head was throbbing so badly that she didn't care that he was undressing her. She was just grateful to lie down and have someone tuck her in. Give her a kiss goodnight.

Gideon watched her all through the night but Josie slept easily, only stirring as the sky turned pink.

'Hey…' he said. 'How do you feel?'

'Ouch?' she said with a rueful grin.

'Sorry…'

She laughed, then pulled a face as it hurt.

'Noooo…' She put her hand to the bruise along the edge of her jaw that threw the faint white scar into prominence. 'Does it look bad?'

'Nicely colour coordinated. I'll bet her knuckles are worse.'

'She was probably provoked.'

'No excuse.'

'No,' she said. 'There is never any excuse.'

Wanting to distract her, he ran a finger gently along the line of the scar. 'You seem to have a habit of leading with your jaw.'

'Oh, that. I was climbing on the back of the sofa, fell off and caught my chin on a table.' She looked up at him. 'Did you think it was the wicked stepfather, Gideon?'

'I couldn't have been more wrong about him, could I?'

'He used his good looks to take advantage of a lonely woman, but he was too lazy to be violent.' Then, 'Can you move? I need the bathroom.'

'Hold on,' he said. He climbed off the bed, fetched a robe, fed her arms into it as if she were a kid.

'I'm not an invalid.'

'No? How many fingers am I holding up?'

'One.'

'Do you feel dizzy? Sick?'

'No, I just need to –'

'Just checking.'

'I know,' she said. Touched his cheek, very gently. 'Thanks for taking care of me.'

Then she swung herself out of bed as if nothing had happened. An act? Or was she really that tough?

She emerged after the fastest shower in history, towelling her hair dry as she walked out onto the deck.

'Isn't there supposed to be coffee?' she asked hopefully.

'Any minute…' He stopped as the bell jangled on the steps but it wasn't Francis, it was David. 'Josie…' he said, coming to a halt when he saw her. 'How are you?'

'Fine. No real damage.'

'Right. Good.'

'What's up, David?' he asked.

'I'm afraid we've got a bit of a problem.'

'What kind of problem?' Josie asked, letting the towel fall.

'I've just had a call from Gabarone. The owner of the catering company is missing. The staff turned up early to prepare the wedding food this morning to find the premises locked and deserted.'

'But I spoke to him two days ago,' she said.

'Apparently there have been rumours that he was in financial difficulty. When someone eventually managed to get into the premises, there was nothing there.'

'Nothing?'

'Completely stripped. No equipment. No food.'

Gideon saw the colour drain from Josie's face and he turned to David. 'What have we got in the chill room?'

'Lamb, beef, poultry, but we haven't time to make an elaborate five-course wedding breakfast from scratch. Even with Paul…'

'No. It'll have to be something simple. A *braai*? The saffron rice salad you do with pine nuts. Tabbouleh. Salads. Get Pete on the phone. Tell him what you need. And fish, whatever he can grab off the early flight from the coast.'

'Excuse me?'

He turned to Josie.

'What's a *braai*?' she asked.

'A barbecue. I know it's not elegant, but I promise you'll have a feast that no one will ever forget.'

She swallowed. 'I'm sure it will be great. There's just one thing.'

'What?'

'The cake.'

He was brought to a juddering halt.

'The cake?'

'They were commissioned to make the cake. Three tiers of the finest fruit cake, almond paste, royal icing…'

He glanced at David, but he shook his head.

'We can't do that. With the best will in the world, Josie—'

'No,' she said. 'We're going to have to make those big cupcakes. Serafina doesn't approve of them—'

'Already I love them,' he said.

'We can use muffin cases. David?' she prompted.

'The cases aren't a problem, but we're running on skeleton staff today. Breakfast, cold lunch… I allowed everyone we didn't need to go home last night to leave the kitchen clear for the caterer.'

'I'll make them,' she said. 'The ingredients are basic enough. We can use white frosting but we need decorations.' She turned to him, totally focused on the wedding now. 'Can Pete find those on a Sunday morning?'

'He'll get them,' Gideon said. 'What do you want?'

'Whatever he can find in pale blue and orange. And we'll need cake stands. The three-tier kind.'

'Cake stands. Got it,' David said. 'I'll…um… go and get the ball rolling.'

'We'll be right behind you,' Gideon said.

Josie broke the news to Cryssie. Explained what they were going to do.

'Is there anything we can do to help?' she asked.

'No. You stay here, have your hair and make-up done. But, if I have your permission, I might round up one or two of your guests? Beating batter might keep them from beating each other. It'll make great copy for *Celebrity*.'

'Good plan. And tell Gideon that if he needs help with the barbecue, the lads will pitch in.'

'Thanks. I'll do that.'

Josie commandeered a corner of the kitchen and set up a cupcake production line. The brides-maids all pitched in but none of them appeared to have ever made a cake before and the minute the photographer had got pictures of them, giggling and splattered with batter, she shooed them away as more trouble than they were worth.

Gideon scrubbed up and came to help the minute he'd got the barbecue pit set up. At least he only needed to be told once, although he wasn't above wiping a finger round the bowl like a kid. She caught him red-handed, slapped him with a spoon and, instead of licking it himself, he offered it to her.

'Come on,' he said, tempting her. 'Tell me you can resist.'

She looked up into hot liquid silver eyes and

for a moment completely lost her head. She could not resist him. Not for a moment and, closing her lips around his finger, she surrendered to the dizzying tug of desire and, as the sweetness melted on her tongue, she thought she'd pass out.

'Good?' he asked. And when she struggled to speak, 'Maybe I should try.' He didn't wipe his finger around the bowl, but lowered his head, touched his tongue to her lips.

'Josie Fowler?'

She jumped, spun around. There was a man standing in the doorway.

'I've got two leopard cubs. Where do you want them?'

The wedding was perfect. The florists had done their thing again, this time surrounding the open air boma and poolside with huge swathes of bird of paradise flowers. Twining the posts of the thatched open-sided rondavel that had been constructed for the ceremony with roses and tiny fairy lights.

Josie was waiting at the steps to put the last stitch in the hem, then slipped into her seat beside Gideon at the back.

The bridesmaids came first, show-stopping in clinging dresses made from animal print silk with tiny ostrich feather fascinators. The lion, the zebra, the giraffe, and finally the leopard leading two tiny cubs on orange and blue ribbons.

Then it was Cryssie's turn. She was breathtaking in a strapless white gown cinched in with a basque that had been embroidered and beaded with the team's colours and, as she was led by the team's manager through the guests to take her place beneath the thatched canopy beside her groom, there was only a sigh.

This was always the moment that caught her out. The look of pure love on a groom's face as he saw his bride coming towards him.

Usually, she'd be sitting alone at this moment but today Gideon had been at her side from first light and, as the tears welled up, he reached for her hand. Startled, she turned to him and saw in his eyes that same look for her.

Afterwards, Cryssie hugged her. 'You are the best, Josie. And the cakes…' The tiny sparkly sprinkles that Pete had found had perfectly matched the beading on her dress. 'If they'd been designed for the wedding, they couldn't have been more perfect. You have been a star and I'll make sure everyone knows. Thank you both so much,' she said, looking past her to Gideon. 'And you two. Will you get married here?' she asked.

'No!'

'No,' Gideon said, beating her to it by a

fraction of a second. 'We'll find a place of our own, Cryssie, and when we do, you'll be at the top of the guest list.'

She spun around to stare at him.

'Gideon, I…' She didn't say any more because he was kissing her.

It was the kind of kiss that Prince Charming would have given Cinderella. A sweet, true, for ever-and-ever kind of kiss.

And afterwards she couldn't think of a thing to say because whatever it was wouldn't be adequate. Would shatter the moment.

'Come on,' he said. 'You've been on your feet since dawn. Let's leave these people to enjoy themselves.'

'Gideon…'

'Three days.' He looked down at her. 'That's what you were going to say, isn't it? That we've only known one another for three days.'

'Yes.'

'That's a good sign, you know. Being able to read one another's minds. Do you want to have a guess at what I'm thinking?'

'I haven't a clue.'

He looked at her, grinned. 'That's not strictly true, is it?'

'No.'

He kissed her again. 'We're adults, not kids. I've wanted you from the moment I first saw you, fell in love with you, somewhere between the coffee and the chilli.'

'No… It's not possible.'

'That's the nature of love. I wasn't supposed to be here. Neither were you. "There is a destiny that shapes our ends…", Josie. Trust me; I recognise the real thing when I feel it.'

She wanted to believe it so much…

'But when I told you about what I'd done, I saw the look on your face. You couldn't wait to get away from me.'

'That's what you thought?' He pulled her to him, holding her. 'Angel, when you asked me to kiss you, I knew it was going to be bad. I wanted to wrap you up in my arms, hold you, make it go away in the only way a dumb man knows how. But you needed me to hear it and I had to listen. If I looked horrified it was not because of what you'd done, but because so many people had let you down. Hurt you. I was so angry that I made a complete mess of it.'

'You could make all the hurt go away,' she said, leaning into him, feeling the steady, powerful beat of his heart against her cheek. 'Right now.'

'Maybe, but that's not you.' He pulled back to look at her. 'We're not a couple of kids, Josie. We're adults. I love you. I'm here for you and I always will be. Everything else can wait until we're married.'

The thought that such a man loved her enough to wait until she trusted him enough to marry him overwhelmed her.

'I don't know what to say.'

'We'll have a very short engagement?' he offered.

'The quickest in history,' she said. Then, 'So what do we do until then?'

'We'll date. I'll take you to the cinema, to dinner, for walks in the park, to meet my parents. You'll cook me supper. We'll have a really nice time and, when you are really, really sure, we'll set a date and get married.'

I'm sure, she thought. Never more sure of anything in my life…

'And tonight?' she whispered.

'Tonight…' He looked up to a velvet African sky. 'Tonight we'll count the stars.'

The marriage of Josie Fowler and Gideon McGrath took place three months later on a tropical island that the tourist world had not yet discovered. It was a simple affair. No bridesmaids, just Sylvie at her side. No hothouse flowers, only the orchids growing wild and, the only creatures, the birds, crickets, tree frogs. The guest list didn't trouble *Celebrity*. This was not a public occasion, but something precious for the two of them and those who were closest to them. Gideon's family, close colleagues. Sylvie, her husband and her baby girl. And friends, including Cryssie and Tal. And Josie's staff, who were, for once, simply there to enjoy the day.

Josie's dress was a simple white column of silk, over which she wore a little bolero, scattered with tiny amethyst beads.

Her hair had been restrained into a short bob with only one vivid splash of purple that echoed the colour of her eyes. As they stood beneath the trees, the air scented with vanilla orchids, hand in hand as they said the vows that made them one, Gideon felt such an overwhelming sense of peace, love, joy.

They ate simple food served in the open and then, as the sun set, they left the party to walk along the beach to the cottage that Gideon had found for their honeymoon.

They started sedately enough, but the minute they were out of sight they began to run, arriving laughing and breathless at the open French windows where Gideon picked her up and carried her inside, not stopping until they reached the bedroom.

Sitting in the centre of a bed scattered with flower petals, there was a large white beribboned box.

'More presents?'

'This one is special.'

'Gideon, I don't need presents, I've got you…'

'For ever,' he said, 'but I think you'll want this.'

'It's heavy. Not diamonds, then…' she said, pulling on the ribbons.

'More precious than that.'

'Really?' She looked up at him but there were no clues to be found in his beloved face. 'What?' she asked, laughing.

Then, as if she could see into his mind, she knew.

'Gideon?'

He said nothing and she turned back to it. She hadn't thought her heart could beat any faster than it had today, but this was different and she could hardly breathe as she lifted off the lid.

The first thing she saw was the box containing her father's medals. She picked it up, opened it, touched them. Laid them aside. Opened an album of photographs.

Her mother as a girl.

'Oh,' she said as she saw her father, unbelievably young, in his uniform. Their wedding. She sat down, turning the pages. Groaning over school photographs. Remembering trips. 'That's me on my first bike.'

'And guess what,' he said. 'You're wearing a purple jumper.'

'My mother knitted it for me…'

She leaned against him and gasped, exclaimed, laughed, cried as she turned each page. 'It's my life. My history.' Then, turning to him, 'Did I ever tell you how much I love you?'

'Not more than twenty times a day.'

'It's not enough. I don't know how you got this…' She put her hand over his mouth before he could tell her. 'I don't want to know. I only know that you could not have given me anything more precious, more perfect. But this is my past,' she said. 'You are my future.' And she cradled his face in her hands, kissed him. 'From this day forward, Gideon…'

THREE TIMES
A BRIDESMAID...

BY
NICOLA MARSH

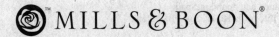
MILLS & BOON

First published in Great Britain 2010
Harlequin Mills & Boon Limited,
Eton House, 18-24 Paradise Road, Richmond, Surrey TW9 1SR

© Nicola Marsh 2010

ISBN: 978 0 263 87667 3

Printed and bound in Spain
by Litografia Rosés, S.A., Barcelona

Nicola Marsh has always had a passion for writing and reading. As a youngster she devoured books when she should have been sleeping, and later kept a diary whose content could be an epic in itself! These days, when she's not enjoying life with her husband and son in her home city of Melbourne, she's at her computer, creating the romances she loves in her dream job. Visit Nicola's website at www.nicolamarsh.com for the latest news of her books.

What people are saying about Nicola's books:

'Sterling characters…
and crackling sexual tension make for a great read.'
—*RT Book Reviews* on A TRIP WITH THE TYCOON

'Nicola Marsh's PRINCESS AUSTRALIA
has a delicious hero and sparkling dialogue!'
—*RT Book Reviews*

For my gorgeous, talented, intelligent friends
eagerly awaiting a trip down the aisle.

I'm looking forward to a boogie after your bridal waltz!

CHAPTER ONE

DREAM dates were difficult to find. Eve Pemberton should know. She'd tried. Boy, had she tried.

With an exasperated sigh, she prodded at the gilt-edged, gold-embossed, ludicrously expensive wedding invitation propped in the middle of her desk.

It didn't budge, folded on its crisp columbine cardboard edges, immovable, rigid, taunting her with its stand-up stiffness.

She knew what she had to do.

She just didn't want to do it.

Taking a deep breath, she swept the invitation aside and flipped open her laptop. Now was as good a time as any to continue her quest to find her dream date.

'This is business,' she muttered, her fingers flying over the familiar keys as she skimmed a few new search engines before finding what she was looking for.

Here goes nothing.

Squinting at the screen, covered in tacky ruby hearts, she stabbed at the enter key, hoping this wouldn't take too long. She had a million things on her to-do list today, starting with chasing recalcitrant subcontractors for one of the corporate marquees at the Australian Tennis Open to ensuring it was all systems go for an event kicking off the AFL season at the Melbourne Cricket Ground.

She loved her job as events coordinator and would much rather be scoping out Aussie Rules footballers than finding her dream date via a dating agency on the Internet but she had to do this.

She had no choice.

The first profile flickered to life on the screen and her tense shoulders relaxed a tad. Not bad. Nice face, nice smile, just...nice. Pity she didn't want nice. She wanted drop dead gorgeous.

While her fingers clattered and she viewed close on twenty-five guys, her hopes sank. There wasn't a stand out among them, not the kind of guy she needed to impress *the bridal babes*— her friends Linda, Carol and Mattie—with. She'd been single at every wedding within their social circle for too long and she'd had enough. Throw in the hoo-ha associated with being a bridesmaid, the only unattached bridesmaid at each wedding, and she really needed to pull this off.

Though they never said anything, she'd caught their pitying glances, their frantic scanning of the guests for a suitable 'fix-up' at each wedding, or worse, the occasional 'accidental' introduction to a long-lost second cousin.

She may as well arrive at every matrimonial shindig with the words 'dateless desperado' tattooed on her forehead.

Not this time. Mattie, the last of her single friends to tie the knot, was always extra-sensitive to her moods and she'd be damned if she spoiled her friend's day, inadvertently, by turning up alone.

Just one last wedding to attend, one last bridesmaid dress fitting… The thought perked her up for a moment and she renewed her search with vigour, reluctant to admit defeat when the fiftieth bland profile blurred before her.

All these guys sounded the same: searching for friendship with a view to a relationship, likes walking on the beach, enjoys cosy dinners.

Well, she didn't need friendship or a relationship or any of that other stuff, thank you very much. She was an industrious businesswoman who needed a date, nothing more, nothing less. She used the Net all the time for work, so finding a date via this medium should've been a cinch, right?

She'd already been on five dates—five excruciatingly boring, painful, blah dates—and nothing. Not a dream date among the shoddy lot.

This was her last shot, the last online dating agency she hadn't tried and, right now, her chances weren't looking crash hot.

With a disgusted snort, she pushed back from her desk, rubbed the bridge of her nose, when a grainy photo in the corner of the news home page caught her eye.

She clicked on the icon to bring up the story, her breath instantly catching as the photo sprang to life, filling half her screen with twinkling blue eyes, a charismatic smile and a cheeky dimple which lent the striking face a boyish charm.

She'd wanted drop dead gorgeous.

She'd got her wish.

Only problem was, Bryce Gibson knew exactly how hot he was and, worse, knew exactly how he affected her.

Determinedly ignoring the adorable dimple she remembered all too well, she speed-read the article.

'"New headhunted hotshot advertising exec arrives in Melbourne from Sydney...needs to prove himself...expecting big things..." yada, yada, yada...' she mumbled under her breath, finding her gaze unwittingly drawn to the picture again.

Oh, yeah, Bryce Gibson hadn't changed

a bit. Still too confident, too charismatic, too…everything.

He'd had charm to burn, and she'd faked immunity. Until Tony's twenty-first, the night that had changed everything.

She stared at his picture, remembering her brother's coming of age party, her coming of age night.

That night had been the catalyst for where she was today: new look, new confidence, new personality.

She should thank Bryce: for flirting, for teasing, for making her feel like a woman for the first time in her life. Or she should kick him for what came after. After that almost-kiss…

Either way, she'd love Mr Overconfident to see her now…

Eve sat bolt upright and snatched her hand off the mouse as if she'd been burned.

Oh, no.

Bad idea. A very bad idea.

You need a date. A 'sexiest guy on the planet' date. The type of date to show your friends you're fine, you *can* hook a hot guy; you just choose not to.

Yeah, but this is Bryce cool-McCool Gibson we're talking about. Remember him? The guy who teased me? Who turned on that legendary charm until I blushed? The guy who went out of his way to pay me attention when I didn't want it, then, when I did, froze me out?

Yeah, but that was then. This is now. Wouldn't you like to show him how far you've come? Where's your pride?

But he'll think I'm some kind of desperado, asking him out on a date. Or, worse, that I still like him. And, besides, using a dating agency was all about business. A no-frills, no-expectation date.

And your point is? Why can't Bryce be about business?

Telling her voice of reason to be quiet, Eve shook her head and glared at Bryce's picture.

He fitted her date criteria in every way: attractive, successful, charming, the type of guy to turn heads, the type of guy who would prove once and for all to her friends she could pull a date like him, she just chose not to because of her career.

Drumming her fingers on the desk, Eve knew she had no choice. The guys she'd dated so far were below par and this last dating agency's potentials were a no-go, while she had the perfect date staring her in the face.

Her belly trembled as her fingers inched towards the phone, barely touching the receiver before she snatched them back.

She couldn't do it.

No matter how far she'd come, she couldn't

just pick up the phone and ask him to be her date.

It was ludicrous.

It was crazy.

And the longer she stared at those deep indigo eyes, those tempting lips, remembering how close they'd once been to hers, it was a foregone conclusion.

They'd shared a spark, a hint of something she'd never dreamed possible that special night and, while it may have ended badly, there was nothing like a trip down memory lane to give a girl a confidence injection.

She'd used what had happened as a catalyst and had reinvented herself after that night.

Wouldn't it be great to show him how far she'd come, a kind of *in your face, Gibson, this is what you missed out on?*

But it was more than that and therein lay the problem. She may be wary but she'd be a fool to believe she'd be totally immune to him, even after eight years. Girls like her never fully got over guys like him.

No matter how many designer dresses or trendy haircuts or killer shoes she had, no matter how many events she presided over like a queen, no matter how many bookings she had for the next year, there was that small, insecure part of her that hoped he wouldn't take one look at her and walk, like he had at the end of that night.

Rules, she needed rules. Clear-cut, don't-mess-with-her-head rules. Rules that would give her heart a resounding whack if she contemplated, even for a second, anything other than using him as a stopgap date for the wedding functions.

Eve's French-manicured fingernails absent-mindedly tapped a stack of documents in front of her as she debated the wisdom of cold-calling a guy she'd once liked and asking him to be her date for a specified period of time.

Wisdom? More like insanity, but, as her gaze drifted over the documents, all perfectly logical and precise, and back to Bryce's picture, she knew she could do this.

She was a successful businesswoman, used to following processes and procedures to the nth degree. And that was exactly what dating Bryce for the next month would be—a process to get what she wanted: her friends convinced she was okay and a stress-free wedding for Mattie.

She could do this.

Ignoring a zoo's worth of butterflies in her stomach, she focused on that taunting wedding invitation and reached for the phone with a shaky hand.

No time like the present to see if hotshot

Bryce with his hypnotising eyes and magnetic smile would come to the party—literally.

'Nice view, huh?'

Bryce turned away from his office window towards his colleague Davin; the Melbourne cityscape was great, but decidedly less glamorous than the million dollar Sydney harbour views he'd given up when he'd taken on his new role here at Ballyhoo Advertising Agency.

No big deal; he'd cope without the view, considering the scope of this opportunity. Ballyhoo was big in the advertising world, real big, and he couldn't wait to get stuck into this new challenge.

'Not bad. Though I won't be spending much time staring out the window with all this to keep me busy.'

He gestured to the tower of manuals Human Resources had dumped on his desk, making a mental note to start sifting through them and prioritising ASAP. He needed a jump-start here, needed to stay one step ahead.

'Have you met with Sol yet?'

Bryce shook his head, dropped into his executive leather chair. 'He's in Auckland for the day, said we'd touch base when he got back.'

'Right.'

Davin propped himself on the desk, opened

his mouth as if to say something before shutting it again.

'And?'

His uneasiness increased as Davin fiddled with the pen holder, didn't quite meet his eye.

'You know we're the number one ad agency in Melbourne, right?'

Oh, yeah, he knew. Solomon Perlman, CEO of Ballyhoo, had extolled the agency's virtues at length when he'd headhunted him for the position. He'd been blown away by the company's mission statement, reeled in by the lure of new challenges, and Sol had rammed home his offer with a salary package that would make the Prime Minister blink.

Working for a company as big as Ballyhoo would send his career into the stratosphere, something he'd worked towards for the last few years, something he deserved after the hard yards he'd put in.

'Yeah, Sol might've mentioned the "premier agency" thing a time or two. What's your point?'

Davin squirmed slightly, his expression shifting between furtive and ingratiating, setting his smarm radar on high alert.

'We're number one because Sol only goes for the big contracts. He won't tolerate anything less.'

'I already know all this.'

'Rumour has it you've been brought in as

some kind of proposed shake-up. Sol knows the clients you courted in Sydney; he wants the same results here, pronto.'

'Takes months to build up contacts in this industry. Sol knows that.'

'Just telling you how it is. Sol expects results and he's not a patient man.'

'And you're telling me this because?'

The avaricious gleam in Davin's beady eyes told him exactly why his new colleague was acting so buddy-buddy before he said a word.

'We're on the same team now.'

So when he brought in the big bucks, Davin would bask in the glory too. He'd seen his type in Sydney, had worked alongside hangers-on, the slack employees only too eager to ride the coat-tails of a go-getter.

'Speaking of teams, a bunch of us are heading out for drinks tonight. You in?'

The last thing he felt like was socialising with guys like Davin but he needed to scope out his co-workers, get a feel for how things worked around here and the quickest way was over a beer.

'Sure.'

'We usually head around the corner to the Elephant and Wheelbarrow around six.'

'No worries.'

'Later.' Davin raised a hand as he sauntered out of the office, a smug grin on his podgy face.

Relaxing into his chair, Bryce linked fingers and stretched forwards, wishing he could dispel Davin's words as useless drivel. But he couldn't. Ballyhoo was top of the advertising heap and he'd just signed on as the newest executive. Sol would expect results, fast.

What if he couldn't deliver?

Doubt unfurled like a poisonous python, uncoiling, stretching and threatening to strangle his hard-fought confidence.

Failure didn't sit well with him. Never had.

Dropping his hands, he swivelled on his chair to stare out the window, hating the flicker of unease creeping through the deepest, darkest part of him—the doubting part, the part he'd conquered a long time ago with every successful deal he'd clinched.

The phone rang and he grabbed it, annoyed he'd let one iota of his old doubts creep in today, on what should be the start of another giant leap up the career ladder for him.

'Bryce Gibson speaking.'

'Bryce, it's Eve Pemberton. Tony's sister.'

He didn't need clarification. He knew who Eve Pemberton was. What he wanted to know was what she'd done to her voice. She'd never sounded this mellow as a teenager. Then again, she'd barely spoken back then. Until that night he'd rather forget.

'Hey, Eve, how are you? Long time, no hear.'

'I'm fine, thanks.'

She paused and his curiosity ratcheted up. What would mild-mannered Eve want with him, especially after how things had ended between them?

As if reading his thoughts, she hurried on. 'I have a business proposition for you. Are you free to meet me for a drink after work?'

'Actually, I'm busy…'

The words died on his lips as he caught the softest sigh on the other end of the line. If he didn't know better, he would say she sounded disappointed. Why? Apart from Tony, who he hadn't seen since he'd moved to New York eight years ago, they had nothing in common.

'The geek', some of the kids had called her behind her back, exactly why he'd gone out of his way to talk to her. He knew what it was like being the odd one out, even if he'd done his damnedest at the time to make sure nobody knew it.

'What about tomorrow?'

If he'd barely caught her disappointed sigh, there was no mistaking the hint of desperation audible in her dulcet tone.

Cool, quiet, aloof Eve Pemberton desperate? As if.

'Business proposition, huh?'

He deliberately lowered his voice, insinuating

a different type of proposition, and almost laughed out loud at her sharp intake of breath.

Eve wasn't a woman he should flirt with. He'd tried it once; look how that had turned out.

'With you being new to Melbourne, it's in your best interests to meet with me.'

He opened his mouth to cite a prior engagement when she murmured, 'You won't be disappointed.'

He ricocheted upward so fast his knee clunked the overhang under his desk and he silently cursed while staring at the phone as if she'd reached through it and tweaked his ear.

The Eve he'd known had never sounded like that: soft, breathy, with an underlying hint of promise. Except the night of Tony's twenty-first, a night he'd deliberately erased from his memory, a night filled with promise, a night ended in shame.

Shaking his head, he pressed the phone to his ear, knowing he was crazy for hearing anything other than brisk politeness in her tone.

'Bryce?'

Making the type of snap decision he was famous for in the ad world, he double-checked his diary.

'I have to put in an appearance at a work function around six this evening. Maybe we can catch up later?'

'How about the Aria bar at the Langham Hotel? Around seven-thirty?'

'No worries.'

'Great. See you then.'

'How will I know you?'

He made a joke of it, wanting to end their weird conversation on a light note, wondering if he'd imagined the desperation.

'I'm sure you'll have no trouble recognising me.' Her tone, tremulous and uncertain as she hung up, left him staring at the phone in confusion.

Shaking his head, he punched the details into his BlackBerry. Eve Pemberton wanted to discuss business. But what business could they possibly have in common after all these years?

Come seven-thirty, he had every intention of finding out exactly what that was.

CHAPTER TWO

SHE'D lied.

Not only did Bryce have trouble recognising the lithe, leggy goddess walking into the swank Aria bar, he would've pegged her as someone other than Eve Pemberton by the confident toss of her highlighted hair swinging in a shiny dark chocolate curtain over her shoulders.

The Eve he knew had never been confident. She'd slunk around with shoulders slouched, huddled over a mountain of books, pushing her bottle-thick glasses up her nose while nibbling on the end of a pencil.

Gone were the glasses, as were the wide-leg jeans, baggy T-shirts and shapeless cardigans she'd worn like a compulsory uniform back then.

His gaze travelled the length of her, from the deep purple trouser suit the colour of ripe plums to the matching two-tone shoes. Designer, all of it. The kind of outfit that screamed success—and showed off a body he'd never imagined in his wildest teenage fantasies.

She scanned the room, her gaze locking on his as he smiled, waved her over, surprised by her answering grin. Genuine. Warm. Dazzling—the type of smile that made every man in the room turn his head to watch her wind her way between the tables.

'Bryce, good to see you.'

She held out her hand and he shook it reflexively, stung by the uncharacteristic urge to kiss her in greeting.

They weren't exactly strangers…not after the confidences they'd shared that night, the same confidences that had prompted him to act like a heel when his mates had laughed at their almost-kiss and he'd laughed along with them.

The memory shamed him and, with a mental slap to the head, he gestured for her to take a seat.

'You too. You look great, by the way.'

A tiny flicker of uncertainty flashed across her face before she sat down with a toss of her hair. 'Amazing what contacts and a new wardrobe can do for a girl, huh?'

It was more than that, much more. There was a self-belief about her, an inner poise that couldn't be faked or manufactured and her self-assurance had him intrigued.

What had happened over the last eight years to turn the shy girl he remembered into a sophisticated, elegant woman who apparently didn't have a qualm about calling him up and asking him to meet her after all this time, after that night?

'I would've recognised you anywhere.'

He smiled—the same smile he'd used to great effect over the years to woo clients and influence women—as he gestured a waiter over. 'Eight years isn't that long.'

Her eyebrows shot up in an *are you kidding me?* inverted comma.

'Still the charmer, I see.'

Leaning forward, he braced his elbows on his knees, staring straight into her deep brown eyes.

'Is it working?'

She laughed, a soft, sweet sound he'd heard many times the night of the party, when she'd responded to his witty banter rather than ignored him, as she usually had.

'I didn't come here to be charmed. Though some of that might come in handy for the deal I want to propose.'

'Deal?'

If her new persona hadn't intrigued him, the mention of a deal did. There was nothing he liked better than sealing deals.

The arrival of a waiter stalled their discussion and he sat back, resting his arm across the back of the chair, content to watch her turn the young guy into a red-faced fool with a nonchalant smile and a twirl of her hair around her finger as she placed an order for sparkling mineral water with a twist of lime.

Eve Pemberton, shy bookworm, had morphed into a chic woman. He'd been expecting standoffish Eve with average dress sense and aloof demeanour, not this…this… *babe!*

'Right, where were we?'

She turned back to him, her eyes glowing like warm molasses, and for a second he forgot the surprise of her call, forgot her fascinating deal, forgot the cringe-worthy finale at Tony's party, and wondered what it would be like to be sitting here on a date with her.

'The deal you mentioned?'

'That's right, the deal.'

Taking a gulp of his usual after-work caffeine hit, he tried to ignore the secretive smile playing about her mouth, the intriguing sparkle in her eyes.

He was an expert at reading non-verbal body cues, had mastered it from a young age to make up for his other shortfalls, and, if he was reading her correctly, this deal was more than business…

As if. Seeing her again, seeing her like this, had thrown him more than anticipated and his mind, used to creative flights of fantasy in devising innovative advertising pitches, was having fantasies of an entirely different nature.

'It's quite simple, really.'

She leaned forward, the smile fading as her eyes fixed his in a no-nonsense stare.

'I have a business proposition for you. One I think you'd be hard-pressed to pass up.'

'I'm listening.'

For the first time since he'd seen her, she appeared less than confident as she toyed with the serviette beside the drinks coaster. She picked it up, opened it, refolded it, pleated it before balling it into a crumpled mess and throwing it on the table and leaning back, hands clasped in her lap.

'I read that you're new in town, working at some top ad agency?'

He nodded, eager for her to cut to the chase. The faster they wrapped up this business stuff, the faster they could get onto more interesting topics, like what she'd been doing for the last eight years, who she'd been doing it with, was she still doing it with any significant others?

'Ballyhoo. The CEO made me an offer I couldn't refuse.'

'Congratulations. The article mentioned something about you chasing big contracts to prove yourself. Is that right?'

'It's the way the ad world works, yeah.'

Why he'd entered the field, why he kept working at being the best. He loved striving, loved proving himself over and over.

'Good. In that case, how would you like a personal introduction to some of Melbourne's biggest business names?'

'Great.'

What's the catch?

One of his first lessons in the business world had been—*if something sounds too good to be true, it usually is*—and this out of the blue phone call from Eve, combined with her suddenly false, brittle brightness, screamed that there was more to this.

'I just need one thing from you in return.'

'What's that?'

She paused, nibbled on her bottom lip, a strangely erotic movement that had him focusing on its fullness, its sheen, its teasing curve, remembering how close he'd come to kissing her, really kissing her, that night too long ago...

'I need you to be my date for a month.'

CHAPTER THREE

BRYCE'S eyes widened, his jaw sagged slightly. Not that Eve could blame him. It wouldn't be every day some desperate female in need of a quick date dressed up her ridiculous proposal in business terms.

He recovered quickly. Typical. Nothing had fazed young Bryce, the guy who'd swaggered around school halls as if he didn't have a care in the world and didn't give a damn what anyone thought of him.

He'd stood up to kids and teachers alike, famous for his wisecracks, cutting people down to size in the flick of an eraser. She'd avoided him for that very reason. Plagued by enough insecurity to keep Cinders scrubbing floors for a decade rather than attend a ball, she hadn't needed some cocky know-all turning his razor tongue onto her.

Not that he'd deigned to notice. If anything,

he'd gone out of his way to chat to her. Nothing major, just small talk—small talk that came with a gorgeous smile and a twinkle in his startling blue eyes. Though only when he'd dropped around their house; at school, he was a year ahead and way too cool to acknowledge a dweeb like her.

She couldn't remember when she'd first developed a crush on him. Early teens? Later? But somewhere between Tony bringing him home for skateboarding and finishing high school, she'd looked forward to their brief encounters, even though she retreated inwards with every chat.

The more he noticed her, the further she withdrew, hiding behind aloofness because she didn't want him knowing what an insecure mess she was inside and how much she liked him. Besides, how could a guy like him consider noticing a girl like her—baggy clothes, glasses, a bookworm—as anything other than the sister of his best mate?

Tony's twenty-first had changed everything because she'd wanted to take the first fragile step towards acknowledging her femininity and what better way than testing out her meagre courage on the guy she'd secretly liked for years?

When he'd approached her out of politeness, she'd responded to him for the first time ever,

blown away when he hadn't dumped a punch
cup in her hand and headed back to the dance
floor with a beautiful blonde on each arm.

Instead, he'd talked to her, flirted with her,
feeding her teenage crush until it'd been inevitable they'd kiss.

Almost kiss. Big difference; yet another thing
she'd regretted about that night.

These days, she didn't have time for regrets,
which made her entrance ten minutes ago all
the sweeter—when she'd seen him almost fall
out of his chair when he'd first laid eyes on her.

'You want to *date* me?'

His lips kicked up at the corners and her
wavering resolve dived for cover as she gripped
her bag, ready to make a run for it. Her fingers
dug through the leather to the stiff wedding invitation beneath, a none-too-subtle reminder of
why she was here, humiliating herself like this.

Only one month. One month of wedding fes-
tivities before she could return her attention back
to what she did best: business.

'No, I don't want to date you; I want you to
be my date. There's a difference.'

She relaxed her death-grip on her bag, forced
herself to relax. 'My last single friend is getting
married and I need a date to accompany me.'

His smile broadened. 'Sounds easy enough.
I'm flattered you asked—'

'Don't go getting any ideas. This will purely be a business arrangement. You accompany me to a few functions in exchange for introductions to the upper echelons of Melbourne's business world. That's it.'

It had to be. She wouldn't be foolish enough to think for one second that sexy, dimpled smile was anything other than a practised move known to charm, that the appreciative glow in his cobalt eyes was solely for her.

Bryce Gibson was mesmerising, always had been, and he'd had girls swooning from the time he'd put on his first pair of those ripped, frayed denim jeans he used to wear. If she'd thought he was cute as a kid, it was nothing on the magnificent male before her now.

He was one hundred per cent drool-worthy, from those playful eyes to those kissable lips, from his broad shoulders encased in crisp cream cotton to his long fingers caressing a very lucky coffee cup.

She'd wanted drop dead gorgeous to impress the bridal babes and Bryce would deliver. As long as she didn't go getting any crazy ideas—like how much fun it would be to date him for real.

She didn't date as a rule, found the whole process tedious at best, mortifying at worst. Guys were intimidated by her success or used her to get to the starlets she arranged functions for. She'd had three short-term relationships, if two months of dating apiece constituted a relationship. When casual verged on commitment, she quit. Not from some deep-seated phobia against long-term; she'd just never found the right guy.

So, rather than put herself out there, she preferred a quiet night in over making inane small talk with overconfident guys hell-bent on making a false impression.

Yet, with Mattie marrying, and her being the last bridesmaid standing, so to speak, she couldn't help but feel she was missing out on something, that being single and successful wasn't all it was cracked up to be.

Bryce sipped at his coffee—long, leisurely sips designed to make her wait, driving her anxiety levels sky-high—and she squirmed, wondering if she should've stuck to the Internet after all.

Staring at his picture on a screen was one thing, having those too-blue eyes focused unwaveringly on her another.

Laying his coffee cup on the table, he sat back and casually draped an arm across the back of his chair as if he were propositioned by crazy event managers every day of the week.

'Tell me more about these business contacts.'

This she could deal with: cold, hard facts. Facts to impress him, facts to woo him, for she had no doubt his business brain would jump at the chance to meet who she had in mind.

'You would've heard of Hot Pursuit?'

'Biggest sporting company in Australia?'

'That's the one.'

She paused for dramatic effect—completely unnecessary, for any ad exec worth their pitch would jump at the chance to meet AJ.

'I know Angus Kilbride quite well. He's the groom. So I'm guessing an intro to him at the pre-wedding dinner, a well-wish at the wedding, a casual beer or two at the post-wedding barbecue and a friendly hand of poker at the cocktail night video viewing mightn't be a bad thing?'

She snapped her fingers, throwing out the line a little further, ready to reel him in.

'My friend Linda is married to Anton Schultz, of the German Anton jewelers, and another friend Carol's husband is Duane Boag, of Australia's biggest real estate chain.'

She wouldn't have been surprised to see dollar signs light up his eyes but Bryce had class as well as looks for he fixed her with a steady stare, as if trying to ascertain her real motives, and she was the one forced to look away.

'Impressive contacts.'

He shrugged, a dismissive gesture that had her hopes for a dream date to dazzle the bridal babes with fading fast.

'I'll be honest with you; I could do with an introduction to businessmen of that calibre.'

'But?'

His gaze stabbed her, probing, questioning, demanding answers she had no intention of giving.

'I'm wondering why you've asked me. A woman like you would have her choice of dates. Why me?'

Especially after how things ended at Tony's party. The unsaid hung between them, as if he was prompting her to bring it up, get it out in the open. And she would, if he agreed to her deal. If not, she'd relegate the memory to the dim, dark recesses of her mind where she'd stored it as fuel for her new life.

Secretly thrilled he was deluded enough to think she could pull any guy she wanted, she shrugged.

'Would you believe it's fate?'

His eyebrow shot up in a perfectly inverted V as his mouth twitched. 'No.'

'It was. I was working online when I came across an article on you and when I heard you were new in town…'

She trailed off, hoping he'd buy her little white lie, aware he hadn't by the knowing glint in his eyes.

'You took pity on me. Yeah, I get it.'

His hint of bitterness surprised her but,

before she could get a read on his mood, he chuckled. 'I'm also intrigued. And I could do with some new contacts, so it looks like you've got yourself a deal.'

'Great!'

Could she be any more pathetic? Being thankful he'd agreed to her dating deal was one thing, practically jumping out of her seat and pumping the air with a raised fist another.

'I still don't get why you had to approach me, though.'

She'd hoped he'd leave it alone. Now she'd have to give him some snippet of the truth.

'I'm a businesswoman, a busy one. I run my own events management company so I socialise for a living, day and night.'

She picked up the drink the waiter had deposited a moment earlier and took a sip. 'What little down-time I get, I spend at home. Basically, I don't have much spare time to date.'

Or trade mindless small talk, pretend to be interested in over-inflated egotistical ramblings or fend off the inevitable grope after one drink, which most of the guys she'd dated seemed to expect.

Give her a big kitchen, fresh ingredients and the latest recipe book to hit the stands and she was much happier. Though gourmet cooking wouldn't show the bridal babes she wasn't a sad case and, right now, the guy staring at her with increasing intrigue in his eyes would.

Suddenly, an awful thought insinuated its way into her head and she almost groaned aloud.

'I'm sorry. I didn't ask if you were seeing someone.'

How stupid could she be? She'd been so caught up in her plan to secure him as perfect date material she'd overlooked a very salient point: his availability.

He wiggled his ring-free left hand in front of her.

'No attachments here. No wife, no girlfriend.'

Leaning forward, he crooked his finger at her, leaving her little option but to shuffle forward on her seat, ending up way too close to him.

This close, she could see the sea-green flecks in his eyes, the faintest end-of-day stubble prickling his cheeks and the sexy groove bracketing his mouth on the right.

She'd always had a thing for dimples, could almost reach out and touch it. Trace it. Dip a fingertip in it...

'I'll let you in on a little secret. I wouldn't have agreed to date you if I was seeing someone. What kind of guy do you think I am?'

His conspiratorial wink merely added to his roguish charm and she inhaled sharply, needing some air to clear her fogged head. The tantalising scent of freshly brewed coffee and crisp citrus filled her senses, making her want to reach out, haul him closer and bury her nose in his chest.

'On second thoughts, don't answer that.'

He laughed and sat back, breaking the intimate spell and she clamped her lips together to stop herself from reneging on the daft deal right this very minute.

'So how's Tony? I haven't heard from him in years.'

'He's fine. Taking Wall Street by storm.'

'Still in merchant banking?'

She nodded, wishing her only family didn't live half a world away.

'Yeah, he hasn't been back to Australia in years. I'm surprised you two didn't keep in contact.'

'Guys tend to drift apart. We started moving in different circles after high school.'

But he'd been at Tony's twenty-first, so they hadn't lost contact totally.

That night was imprinted on her brain. She'd felt gauche and awkward and out of place in her new formal dress, the only dress she owned, a bright blue stiff taffeta that had made odd crinkly noises when she'd moved, while Bryce had swaggered into the party wearing a cocky grin as if he owned the place.

And he had. He'd been the life of the party, had talked and laughed his way through the first hour while she'd stayed in the shadows like a wallflower, wishing a guy like him would notice a girl like her.

As if by some inexplicable, intangible force, her wish had come true. He'd spied her on the outskirts of the room, edging towards the balcony of the trendy Albert Park club Tony had hired for the party, and followed her.

For the next hour they'd talked, laughed, ribbed, and she'd come alive under his attention. She'd never felt that way before, had been stunned that a few minor changes in her appearance—contact lenses, new dress, lipstick, high-heeled shoes—could give her the power to flirt with a guy like Bryce.

Even after what had happened later, she'd never forgotten that feeling, how good she'd felt, had been desperate to reproduce it. She had—reinventing herself after that night, hadn't looked back.

And wouldn't start now, not with Bryce staring at her, that dimple only a lip quirk away.

'Last time I saw him was at his twenty-first.' His gaze flicked over her suit, leaving a trail of tiny goose bumps as if he'd touched her. 'You too, remember?'

Oh, yeah, she remembered every tiny detail, from the faded denim jeans he'd worn to the tan bomber jacket he'd slung around her shoulders when she'd shivered, more from his attention and proximity than the cold.

She remembered him handing her a champagne, the touch of his fingers brushing hers giving her more of a buzz than the bubbles sliding down her throat.

She remembered leaning on the balcony railing, gazing out at the stunning view, lights reflecting in the shimmering surface of Albert Park Lake with Melbourne's city skyline in the background, with him standing behind her, close behind her, his body spooning hers, until he'd held her arms, turned her around and…

She blinked in a desperate attempt to obliterate the memory of what came next, knowing they had to acknowledge the unspoken but not wanting to discuss it now.

His lips curved into a sexy smile as he reached out, placed a finger under her chin and gently tipped it up.

'We need to talk about what happened that night.'

She couldn't move, couldn't look away, trapped in the heat of his stare, her skin prickling beneath his fingertip.

This wasn't good, this…this…*awareness*. How could she keep things strictly platonic between them if she reacted like a schoolgirl with a giant crush on the high school jock the second he turned his charm on her?

And he would, of that she had no doubt. Charm

was as natural to Bryce as breathing and it meant nothing. She'd watched him exercise it at will as a teenager, had seen girls literally lean against walls with weak knees as he'd strutted past.

Not her. Uh-uh, no way.

She'd been smarter than that, had hidden her reaction behind coolness; that did little to stop him. She'd been a brainiac, could never explain her aberrant reaction to a guy with a glib line and a flirtatious dimple he used as a weapon. Until she realised something. Not everything had a logical explanation and, with a guy like Bryce, her reaction had been instinctive, hormonal, visceral.

Not any more. Please, Lord, not any more.

Forcing a laugh, she ducked her head and glanced at her watch. 'As much as I'd like to stay and reminisce about old times, I've got work to do.'

'Right,' he drawled, leaving her in little doubt he didn't buy her lousy excuse to escape. 'How about we schedule another time to catch up?'

'Catch up?'

His smile widened, as if he knew exactly how flustered he made her.

'If you want your friends to think I'm dating you, surely we need to get together before the first function and get our stories straight? Practise acting lovey-dovey, that sort of thing?'

Practise acting lovey-dovey...

Heck, what had she got herself into?

Her horrified expression must've clearly shown her trepidation for he laughed and squeezed her hand. 'Relax, I'm kidding. But we do need to chat because we're going to get asked the basics like how we met, was it love at first sight, all that kind of stuff.'

'You're right.'

She'd intended to set up a meeting to do just that, until he'd befuddled her senses with his potent presence.

'Can I give you a call? I'm kind of swamped with a few events at the moment.'

'No worries.'

He laid a steadying hand under her elbow as she stood and, with his innocuous touch sending sparks shooting through her body, she knew it was easy for him to say.

No worries, indeed.

CHAPTER FOUR

BRYCE tried to focus on Sol droning on about profit margins but his mind kept drifting back to his meeting with Eve.

He'd been over it in his mind countless times, replaying everything she'd said, every nuance, every expression and he still didn't get it. Sure, he'd bought her story about not having time to date and wanting this to be just business but that was where his confusion kicked in. She'd said she socialised for a living, would know loads of guys on a platonic basis, so why hadn't she asked any of them to be her date?

And why him, especially with how things had ended at the party? She couldn't even talk about it, yet had proposed a convenient arrangement, one he'd been more than happy to accept, considering her terms. While Eve may be singing the dating deal tune, he knew there was more to it. And he had every intention of finding out what that was.

'Bryce? Where are you at with new clients?'

Wrenching his attention back to the meeting, he withdrew several meticulous lists from his portfolio. His colleagues in Sydney had labelled him the 'list king' and it had stuck. Not that he cared. He'd always worked that way, found lists helped him organise and prioritise and focus, keeping him at the top of his game, right where he wanted to be.

'I've made a list of contacts I'm in the process of following up.'

Sol narrowed his beady eyes, probing, assessing. 'Who?'

'Angus Kilbride. Anton Schultz. Duane Boag. For starters.'

'Impressive list.'

Sol rubbed his chin, one of several, before pinning Davin with an intimidating glare. 'Isn't there a rumour the Hot Pursuit contract is up for grabs soon?'

Davin's head bobbed so furiously it was a wonder it didn't fall off. 'No rumour; it's fact. One of the major players on their last campaign just quit and hasn't been too circumspect with information.'

A shot of adrenalin pumped through Bryce's veins. Man, was he glad he'd agreed to Eve's deal. Not only would he get an informal intro to Angus, he might have inside running to nail the lucrative contract.

'Right.' Sol's gaze swivelled back to him, calculating and predatory. 'If Kilbride is on your hit list, make sure you secure the Hot Pursuit contract.'

'Got it.'

And he would. Failure wasn't an option, not here, not now, not ever.

Sol's steely gaze lingered on him a tad longer, as if trying to size him up before sweeping over the rest of the conference table. 'As for the rest of you, I want to see results by next week.'

He thumped the table while Bryce smothered a smile. He was used to the theatrics of the ad world. He'd worked with the best, had seen some shows in his time with keen up-and-comers trying to secure big campaigns.

Personally, he'd rather let his work do the talking, the creative ideas that flowed like a steady stream when he took on a new project, something he never doubted and thanked the big guy upstairs for every day.

'I want each of you to bring a new client to the table this time next week. Bryce, you get a month because you're new in town and aiming high. That's it. Get to work, people.'

A month? He'd landed bigger fish in Sydney

in a fortnight. But who knew, maybe things worked differently in Melbourne? Maybe the networking circles were harder to break in to? Which was exactly where Eve came in and the thought of pretending to be her date made him do an inner high-five. All that hand-holding, cuddling, maybe a kiss or two for authenticity's sake…

'You really think you can land Hot Pursuit?'

Shoving documents into his folder, Bryce stood and gave Davin a perfunctory nod.

'I wouldn't have said it otherwise.'

The calculating gleam never left Davin's eyes for a second. 'If you need a hand, don't hesitate to ask.'

The day he asked the toady for help was the day he'd admit defeat: never.

'I'll keep that in mind.'

Sending a pointed glance at his watch, he picked up his paraphernalia, gave Davin a casual wave and headed for the door. Now the meeting had wrapped up, he had another to attend. One that would prove a lot more fun.

Eve slid her hand into a potholder and lifted the lid, inhaling deeply as the delicious aroma of slow-cooked Moroccan lamb filled the air in a burst of cinnamon fragrant steam.

Humming to herself, she sprinkled a generous

handful of torn coriander over the top and turned the stove to low, letting the dish simmer before replacing the lid.

She shouldn't have gone to all this trouble but she'd been nervous and, when she was nervous, she cooked. Other people worked out, went for long walks or meditated. She cooked.

She'd cooked her way through high school.

She'd cooked her way through her dad's death when she was eighteen.

And she'd cooked up a veritable feast the minute Bryce had said he'd be dropping around tonight so they could go over their dating story.

Cooking was therapeutic. Cooking was relaxing. But, as she stared around the kitchen, noting the fluffy couscous with preserved lemon, the roasted vegetable pilaf and the Mediterranean stack of chargrilled eggplant, zucchini and Roma tomatoes, she knew there'd been little unwinding and loads of stress involved in the culinary masterpieces she'd concocted.

She reached for her wine glass, took a healthy sip, too wound up to savour the divine Clare Valley Shiraz.

He'd be here any moment. The guy she was supposed to be dating, the guy who had to convince her friends she wasn't a desperate singleton.

One more bridesmaid stint, one more wedding—one more teensy-weensy wedding—before the last of the bridal babes were married off and she wouldn't have to fake the whole *I'm cool and successful and happy being single* at another ceremony.

She was happy being single most of the time, but there was something about this wedding, something about Mattie joining her other friends in matrimonial smugness that grated.

The slight condescension that came with being part of a happy couple wasn't intentional—the girls would never do that to her—but being surrounded by it had worn thin. The constant touching and eye-contact and in-jokes were fabulous—if you were the one involved in the relationship.

And while she loved hanging out with her best friends and their men, the constant pressure of being the only unattached female in blissful coupledom left her feeling like a third wheel most of the time—and somewhat miserable, if she was completely honest.

Hopefully, turning up with Bryce in tow would give her a legit excuse to beg off a few gatherings after the wedding rice settled.

Once she'd survived the next month and all the wedding events, she could return to doing what she did best: work. And unwinding on her terms, in her place, without the expectations of socialising with the aim to find a partner.

She couldn't rely on people. She'd learned that the hard way. Her business, her home was steady, dependable and she liked it fine.

A sharp knock sounded at the front door and she gulped the rest of the Shiraz in record time, shooting a last frantic glance at her reflection in the oven door before smoothing her hands over her favourite beaded top and heading down the hallway at a deliberately slow pace when in fact she felt like bolting—in the opposite direction.

With a deep breath, she opened the door, sending Bryce the confident smile she'd spent weeks practising when she'd first opened Soirée. With Bryce staring at her as if she were a gorgeous goddess, it was all worth it.

'These are for you.'

He handed her a bunch of beautiful gerberas in tangerine, buttercup and garnet. No standard issue carnations or clichéd roses for Mr Tall, Dark and Charming. Uh-uh—when he wanted to impress a girl, he went all out.

'Thanks, but you didn't need to.'

With a slow conspiratorial wink, he stepped over the threshold.

'Ah, but I did. I'm getting into practice for my role as your date.'

Disappointment filtered through her before

she gave her conscience a swift, sharp kick. She wanted him to do this right. So why the momentary lapse in reason, the split second where she'd wished he'd brought her flowers just because he wanted to, because she was deserving of them?

'Good idea; come through.'

She marched up the hallway, instantly regretting her rather brisk response. Where were some of those deportment skills when she needed them?

'Something smells great.'

'Hope you're hungry,' she said, smiling at the irony of the statement.

She could've catered one of Soirée's premier events at the Town Hall with the amount of food she'd cooked, let alone feed one hungry charmer. Entering the kitchen, she made for the stove, knowing the exact moment he followed her into the room.

'What the…'

Turning around, she laughed at his stunned expression and beckoned him to take a seat at the island bench dominating the room.

'Are we expecting company?'

She shook her head, picked up a wooden spoon and gave the tagine a last minute stir before switching off the stove.

'I like to cook. It's my relaxation.'

'Gourmet, by the looks of it.'

He picked up one of the crudités and dunked

it into her special smoked salmon and Camembert dip before popping it into his mouth, his satisfied expression soothing her chef's heart.

She liked cooking but she also liked seeing people enjoy food and, by the look of sheer bliss on Bryce's handsome face, he was really enjoying it. Imagine how he'd look during other activities he really enjoyed...with a shaky hand, she filled a wine glass for him, refilled hers.

'This is great.'

'Try these too.'

She shoved a platter of tiny samosas and curry puffs under his nose, pleased when he popped three into his mouth in rapid succession, happy to feed him the entire contents of the counter if it kept them from talking.

Crazy, considering they needed to get their story straight if Linda, Carol and Mattie were going to believe this was real but, having him here, in her home, had rattled her more than she'd anticipated.

Her home was her sanctuary, the one place she could shut out the world and be herself. Her confidence mask slipped off the minute she removed the contacts from her eyes and wiped off the day's immaculate make-up, her posture relaxing the instant she shrugged out of her designer suit and donned her oldest frayed jeans and tatty T-shirt.

She'd spent years building a professional persona to hide the insecure girl she'd once been but, the moment she stepped through her front door, she slipped into her old skin, more comfortable than ever.

Picking up her wine glass, she gestured to the backyard. 'Do you want to sit outside for a while or are you starving?'

Patting his stomach, he wrinkled his nose. 'After the number of those tasty treats I just demolished, let's sit for a while.'

Eve knew she should respond, should put one foot in front of the other and head for the door, but she couldn't think, couldn't move, for the second he patted his stomach her gaze had riveted to his jet-black polo shirt and the way it highlighted flat, to-die-for abs.

She could see the faintest ripple of muscle, the delineation of the fabled six-pack and her mouth watered, having little to do with the heady aromatic spices of the tagine and everything to do with his great body.

'You've changed.'

His soft words lingered in the air and she wrenched her gaze up to meet his, recognising a flicker of desire which mirrored her own.

'Guess I'm not a geek any more, huh?'

He visibly started before quickly masking his shock with a rueful smile. 'Kids can be cruel.'

Oh, yeah, she knew that first-hand. Her less than cool clothes, her thick glasses and her IQ hadn't exactly endeared her to her classmates back in high school. Then again, she hadn't really cared. She'd never had the confidence to match it with the cool girls, or the sporty ones for that matter. The only time she'd cared was on the odd occasion when Tony had brought Bryce home…and he'd been a balm, treating her as if she wasn't a dork, making her fall a little bit in love with him every time for noticing her, let alone talking to her.

She picked up her wine and headed for the back door.

'I was a geek. The kids just called it as they saw it.'

He followed her, his stare boring into her back and sending heat flushing through her.

'I never called you that.'

'What I could never figure out was why.'

She pushed the door, held it open for him. With a puzzled glance he stepped through, grabbing her arm when she made to move past him.

'I know you don't want to talk about this, but we have to,' he murmured, his long, strong fingers hot on her skin, his equally hot gaze lighting an instant fire between them.

'What happened that night is irrelevant.'

'I don't think so.'

Giving her arm a gentle squeeze, he dropped his hand.

'I was an idiot that night.'

Something dark, almost painful, shifted in his eyes, at odds with the cocky, brash kid who'd commanded attention without trying, at odds with the confident, powerful man he was today and, for a guy who wore his self-assurance like an aura, the hint of vulnerability was beyond appealing.

'Not for all of it.'

'When it counted most.'

His compelling stare locked on her, imploring her to remember. She needed little reminding as her gaze dropped to his lips, remembering the exact moment their entire evening had gone pear-shaped—the second before his lips had touched hers.

'Don't beat yourself up. So we almost kissed? And your mates saw us. They teased you; you said it meant nothing.'

She gave him a little shove towards her patio table. 'You were right; it didn't. Now, take a seat and I'll bring out the hors d'oeuvres.'

By the determined glint in his eyes, he wanted to labour the point, to discuss how she'd down-played what had happened, but she was through playing the reminiscing game. If she was going to get through the next month, she needed to focus on now, not the past and the embarrassing crush she'd had on a guy out of her league.

'Eve, it wasn't like that—'

'Back in a sec.'

Desperate for time to reassemble her wits after he'd shot them down in a conflagration of flames with that innocuous touch on her arm, she fled.

Bryce let Eve go, despite the urge to…what?

Get her to acknowledge what a jerk he'd been that night? Get her fired up so he copped some well-deserved anger? Get her to admit most of that night had been amazing until he'd screwed up?

What was he going to do—badger the woman in her own house?

From the stack of cookbooks piled in higgledy-piggledy disarray in the cosy kitchen to the sprawling English cottage garden filled with wild flowers spread before him, he could see she invested time in her home.

She'd always been a homebody, had filled her childhood home with vases of violets, had done most of the cooking for her dad and Tony. Their mum had died when they were toddlers and, while Tony had never spoken about it, he wondered if that was the reason behind Eve's nurturing side, her urge to create a home beyond a simple house.

Not having a mum must've been tough on her, especially as a teenager, when she hadn't fitted in. He'd seen the hurt in her eyes when she admitted knowing about the geek nickname, had felt it like a kick in the guts and, while he'd never called her that, he'd thought it.

He'd almost blurted out the truth right then and there—anything to wipe that pain away—but what good would it do? He was here to act as her impressive date, not give her reasons to doubt him.

The screen door creaked open as she backed through it, arms laden. He leaped up to help, but not before he let his appreciative gaze linger on her fine butt, clad in denim, her funky top riding up as she elbowed the door, giving him a tantalising glimpse of tanned skin above her waistband.

She'd always been lean, athletic, but this new and mature Eve had filled out in all the right places, lending her a softer feminine edge—an edge that had him itching to run his hands all over her.

'Let me help you.'

'Thanks.'

She handed him a platter filled with vol-au-vents, smiled her thanks—a small, shy smile at odds with the confident, go get 'em woman she'd been when they'd met at the bar.

He admired the successful businesswoman she'd become—doing a Google search had clued him in to exactly how successful she was—yet found this homely version as appealing.

He, who only dated models and soap actresses and 'It' girls, who hadn't had a home-cooked meal in for ever, who didn't like houses for the very fact they screamed to be filled with noisy kids and the entire family kit and caboodle, was attracted to a woman so obviously connected to her home? The cleaner Melbourne air must be getting to him.

Pulling out her chair and scoring a dubious look for his trouble—he had to remember that; she wasn't used to chivalrous guys—he sat opposite.

'Apparently our past's off-limits; let's talk about our deal. How do you want to play this dating thing? Do you want your friends to know we used to hang out or am I the new love of your life?'

Her stare could've withered the violets on the table between them, though the corners of her mouth twitched.

'We never used to hang out, though I think we ought to pretty much stick to the truth.'

'Which is? That I'm your new main man and you can't keep your hands off me?'

Grinning, he popped several crudités into his mouth, enjoying the faint blush staining her cheeks. Oh, yeah, he loved this susceptible side to her, the soft core of the confident city girl.

'Speaking of which…' Her blush deepened and she bolted down half of her wine before continuing. 'We might have to hold hands, drape an arm around waists, that sort of thing to make it look authentic. Hope you don't mind.'

Mind? Was she kidding? The first opportunity he got, he'd be sliding an arm around her waist and cuddling her close. If she was this delightfully flustered just talking about it, he couldn't wait to see how she'd react when they did it for real. He might've mucked up royally the night of Tony's party, he'd be damned if he made the same mistake twice.

Biting on the inside of his cheek to keep himself from chuckling, he mustered his best guileless expression.

'What about kissing?'

'No kissing.'

She stuffed a samosa into her mouth, chewed frantically, masticating the thing to mush in less than a second.

'Couples kiss all the time. It might add to the authenticity of your plan. You want them to believe we're dating for real, don't you?'

She muttered something that sounded decidedly unladylike before sending him a slightly tremulous smile which had him wanting to leap over the table and haul her into his arms. She was adorable, every contrasting inch of her, and going through with this crazy dating scheme was going to be more fun than he'd thought.

'Let's just take it as it comes, okay?'

Keeping the victorious grin off his face, he nodded before reaching across the table and taking hold of her hand, his pulse picking up tempo as her tongue darted out to moisten her bottom lip.

'You don't have to worry. I'm going to be the model date.'

By the flicker of doubt in her expressive chocolate-brown eyes, that was exactly what she was afraid of.

CHAPTER FIVE

EVE had known that inviting Bryce into her home would be a bad idea but she'd gone ahead and done it anyway.

Madness, when every move she made in the business world was calculated to the nth degree. She hadn't turned Soirée into Melbourne's number one events management company without some sound decisions, including changing her image. She'd hired a wardrobe consultant, make-over artist, hairstylist to the stars, even done a stint at a deportment school to improve her posture, to project the image she wanted—that of a poised, confident businesswoman at the top of her game.

She'd handled huge events with aplomb, mingled with the upper echelons of Melbourne society, prided herself on cool, methodical decisions. So what was with the fuzzy brain syndrome ever since she'd approached him to be her dream date?

Watching him fork the last of her pistachio panna cotta with honey syrup into his mouth, a satisfied sigh escaping his lips as an expression of sheer bliss spread across his handsome face, she had her answer.

Staring into those indigo eyes, seeing that groove flash in and out of his right cheek at will, those lips curved in a permanent smile, what chance did a girl have to think straight?

Patting his stomach—she wouldn't look, she wouldn't look, oops, there she went, catching a quick peek—he groaned, an all too sexy sound as he pushed back from the table.

'That was categorically the best meal I have ever had.'

Thrilled by his praise, she pushed her own plate away, surprisingly relaxed considering they hadn't nutted out the dating logistics yet.

'I find that hard to believe, considering hotshot ad execs like you would be wining and dining clients in five star establishments all the time.'

His eyes crinkled adorably when he smiled. 'And, like I said, this is still the best meal I've ever had.'

'So let me get this straight. A simple lamb tagine with baby carrots, a bit of couscous and a super-sweet dessert does it for you?'

The instant the words left her mouth she knew

she'd said the wrong thing, for his eyes darkened to midnight, the resident cheeky glint replaced by something more seductive.

'You have no idea what does it for me,' he murmured, searching her face for—what? Agreement? As if he'd get any argument from her! 'But I guess, as my date for the next month, you're about to find out.'

Oh, boy.

She began gathering up crockery at record speed, unprepared for his hand to snake across the table and still her forearm.

'Leave them. After a meal like that, the least I can do is clear away and wash the dishes.'

Her skin burned beneath his palm, hot, fierce, as a sizzle of sensation zinged up her arm, jolting her into realising she'd better lay down some firm ground rules for their dating quick-smart before her haywire hormones had other ideas of what dating Mr Charming entailed.

'Okay. But don't wash them. Just give them a quick rinse and stack the dishwasher. I'll turn it on later.'

Oh-oh. Poor choice of words again and she quickly slid her arm out from under his hand, needing to establish some physical distance between them.

With her mind in a tizz, her body joined the party in a big way, popping champagne corks and flinging streamers and stringing up a banner bearing the message, *Surprise! Eve Pemberton still has a monster crush on Bryce Gibson.*

'Sit tight; I'll be back in a minute.'

Watching him gather plates, stacking them with the cutlery on top, she couldn't help but notice his strong forearms dusted in a smattering of dark hair, his long, almost elegant fingers and the sure way he handled her precious crockery.

Her gaze drifted upwards; his polo shirt pulled taut across his broad shoulders as he leaned across the table, his biceps flexing deliciously while he piled his arms high.

Mmm…definite benefits to having him clear up and as she tried, and failed, to not look over her shoulder as he strode through her back door, a little sigh of longing escaped her lips.

Bryce Gibson was seriously gorgeous.

Not just in a physical sense; the time they'd spent together tonight had proved she'd misjudged him all those years earlier.

Maybe he'd been trying to fit into the cool crowd, maybe he'd had issues she didn't know about, maybe he'd just been growing into his own skin, as most young guys did, but the man she'd pinned as a jerk at the conclusion of Tony's party was nothing but charming and lovely and utterly irresistible.

'Must be some mighty nice thoughts to put that smile on your face.'

Lost in her musings, she started as he slid into the chair opposite. 'You don't want to know.'

Unable to do anything but return his disarming smile, she wondered why he made her feel so inept. It wasn't as if she'd never handled flirtatious guys before. She met all types in her work, socialised with people from all walks of life, from mega-wealthy CEOs to office gofers. Yet Bryce could undermine her with a flash of his even white teeth beneath the curve of those sensual lips.

He interlocked his fingers, stretched them behind his head. 'Oh, I get it. You were thinking about how I'm going to be a great date.'

She tried to quash the bubble of laughter at his mock smugness and failed, chuckling when he pretended to check himself out.

'Not that I blame you. I'm pretty irresistible.'

Considering he'd just echoed her very thoughts, he'd get no arguments from her. But she couldn't let him know how he still affected her, how much she really liked him, how much she wished they were dating for real, and the sooner they discussed specifics about their dating the sooner she could bundle him out of the door and try to vanquish images of enigmatic blue eyes and deep dimples.

'Modest too. Let's talk about the upcoming functions before I lose my head completely in your overwhelming masculine presence.'

'Are you making fun of me?'

She held up her thumb and forefinger about an inch apart. 'Just a little?'

His eyes twinkled with delight as he reached across and closed his fingers over hers, sending her into instant meltdown. Heat raced up her arm, swift, scorching, warming her better than the spicy lamb she'd served.

So much for vanquishing. She needed to get this briefing done ASAP before the cravings of her body overrode her sensibilities.

'Teasing is good,' he murmured, his tone low and husky, undoing her as much as his sexy smile. 'Teasing is what dating couples do, so nothing like getting in a little practice.'

Yeah, right, practice. That was what she'd been doing. Not.

'Exactly.'

Sliding her hand out from his on the pretext of taking a drink of water, she ended up guzzling the entire glass in several unladylike gulps, desperate to douse the flames burning her up from the inside out.

This was sooo not going to work, this *let's keep our relationship platonic while you pretend to be my date; it's all business* plan she'd concocted.

But she couldn't back out now. She'd already had Mattie on the phone this afternoon, subtly suggesting she buddy up with a third or fourth cousin removed at the wedding rehearsal dinner, so she'd done the only thing possible and blurted out the truth about Bryce.

Well, an adulterated version of the truth: that she'd met someone, they were dating and he'd be accompanying her to all the wedding functions.

Mattie had oohed and aahed, and Eve knew she would've barely made it off the phone before her enthusiastic friend had conference-called Linda and Carol to give them the goss. Both girls had rung her mobile a scant half hour later and she'd let the calls go through to messages, too busy working out her stress in the kitchen at the time.

She'd been wound up enough about Bryce's imminent arrival without having the bridal babes tag-teaming her with their special brand of, *Is he the one? Is he gorgeous? Is he rich? How long before you're walking up the aisle and having his babies?*

She loved her friends but, boy, did they have one-track minds when it came to weddings and the fabled happily-ever-after—hence the nickname she'd given them years ago.

'Top up?'

He held the ceramic water pitcher out to her

and she shook her head, eager to get this evening back on track.

'No, thanks. I'd really like to chat about our arrangement.'

'Okay, then, down to business.'

He whipped a notepad and pen from his pocket, scribbled a few headings and drew up columns.

'You're taking notes?'

'I want to make sure I get the details correct.'

The tightening around his mouth eased as he pointed at his notepad with the pen. 'You want to convince your friends, right? Well, I need to make sure I remember the little things and it pays to put in the hard work.'

She couldn't fault him for that ethos, so why the niggle of doubt that there was more to it?

'You've mentioned the functions I have to attend; how about you give me a little background on your friends?'

'Mattie is the bride. She's a flight attendant, which is how she met AJ.'

'Angus Kilbride is AJ?'

'Angus James Kilbride. Everyone calls him AJ.'

Bryce raised an eyebrow, as if questioning the informality of calling Australia's biggest sporting empire mogul by his initials as he scribbled notes.

'Right. What about your other friends?'

'Carol's married to Duane Boag, who you've heard of. Biggest chain of real estate agencies in the country. And Linda's hubby is Anton Schultz, the jewel king. She's a publicist, Carol's a copywriter. The babes are the best.'

'Babes?'

His other eyebrow shot up to join the first and she laughed. 'I call them the bridal babes. Ever since Linda first walked up the aisle, they've been obsessed with weddings. I've been a bridesmaid at each of their weddings and, thankfully, this one is the last.'

She waited for him to trot out the trite 'always a bridesmaid, never a bride', grateful when he didn't.

'You didn't mention you were a bridesmaid.'

'Foregone conclusion with the bridal babes. No one in our circle is released from duties such as trying on hideous satin dresses, enduring hair trials with Edward Scissorhands and getting buffed and spray-tanned to within an inch of our lives.'

He grimaced. 'Sounds painful.'

'You don't know the half of it!'

They laughed. 'So, if they're obsessed with weddings, does that extend to getting you partnered off?'

She nodded, instantly remembering embarrassing 'coincidental' meetings with *suitable friends* at Linda's infamous dinner parties, Carol begging her to accompany her to work functions, only to discover a desperate and dateless colleague she *had* to meet, and Mattie setting her up on a blind date with a pilot who'd yawned through the entire evening—short-lived as it had been.

And she wasn't even thinking about the parties where some poor unsuspecting single guy would be foisted on her or both weddings, where she'd been shoved towards a lone best man or groomsman.

'They just don't seem to get it, the fact I'm happy with my job and don't need some guy to complete my life.'

With a playful wink, his lips curved into that oh-so-sexy smile that turned her insides to mush. 'So that's why you haven't just picked *some guy* to impress them; you picked me.'

Chuckling at his teasing, she waggled a finger in front of him. 'Don't go getting an inflated ego. You just happened to pop up on my computer screen at the right moment.'

'You were looking for a date on the Net?'

Battling a surge of embarrassment guaranteed to heat her cheeks, she nodded.

'I thought it'd be quick and easy. Log onto a dating site with all those guys at my fingertips and choose one. I use the Net for business every day so it should've been a cinch.'

'So what happened?'

You, was what she wanted to say.

You, with your incredible blue eyes and your cute dimple and your smile that could melt a nun at a hundred paces.

You, with your broad shoulders and sensational abs and charisma that practically oozed through the PC screen and was so much more potent in reality.

Instead, she chose her answer with care.

'Honestly? I'd been on a few dates and nada. The guys on those dating sites all sound the same, like they'd rehearsed answers to get chosen.'

His lips twitched. 'Let me guess. Walks on the beach. Cosy dinners. Weekends at B&Bs in the countryside.'

'How did you—'

'I did a campaign for one of the biggest sites in Sydney. My research was thorough.'

'Sure was.'

They laughed, their easy-going camaraderie reminiscent of the past and that one fabulous night where she'd captured his attention for an all-too-brief moment in time.

Eight years was a long time and she hadn't expected to like him this much. She'd thought they'd get the ground rules of this dating arrangement established, make a bit of polite small talk and that was it. No way had she expected to be blindsided by his charm, struck

by his natural warmth and friendliness all over
again.

Bryce was something else. The bridal babes
would be blown away—her intention all along.

But what if she was blown away too?

What then?

CHAPTER SIX

POISE.

Plan.

Precision.

The words she'd once read in some self-help tome reverberated through Eve's head as she stood in front of her wardrobe, her hand uselessly trailing along the season- and colour-coordinated clothes.

To be poised for the rehearsal dinner and her grand entrance with Bryce, she needed a plan— a solid plan to follow with precision.

So far, her plan to wow Bryce and boost her confidence with a fabulous dress had hit a snag—a big one.

She didn't own the type of dress she needed.

A va-va-va-voom dress, a knockout dress, a dress that would make a guy like Bryce unable to tear his eyes off a girl like her.

That dress wasn't in her closet. She should

know; she'd been through every single one of her expensive designer dresses: all very sleek and elegant and lovely, but not a hint of va-va-va-voom in sight.

With a disappointed sigh, she unhooked a hanger and held her newest little black dress at arm's length. Knee-length, fitted, V-neck, its cut clung and flattered in all the right places.

But it wasn't a knockout and she thrust it back into the wardrobe and slammed the door, glancing at her watch and groaning as she realised it was too late to make a dash down Chapel Street before the boutiques closed.

It was at times like this she missed having a mum. She'd never had someone to help her choose clothes or do her hair or show her how to apply make-up, had been envious of the other girls in her class when they'd rolled up to the school gates with their yummy mummies dressed in fashionable clothes and dazzling smiles and bestowing hugs on reluctant daughters.

She would've given anything to have that kind of relationship but her mum had died when she was too young to remember and, while her dad had done his best, she often wondered if she would've been more outgoing, more confident if she'd had a woman's advice.

In her teens, while girls her age were dressing

in hip denim and experimenting with make-up, she'd been at home experimenting with fresh herbs and recipes. Not that she'd ever begrudged cooking meals or housekeeping for her dad and Tony, but every time she'd seen a classmate stroll through the school gates in the latest wedges with mascara-enhanced eyelashes, a small part of her had really wished she had a mum.

Staring daggers at her uncooperative wardrobe, she turned away, her gaze lighting on her open laptop where she'd been doing a bit of work earlier.

'You dolt,' she muttered, plopping onto the bed on her tummy and yanking the laptop close, her fingers flying over the keyboard as she Googled several chic Australian designers and came up with a plethora of online boutiques.

If she'd found the perfect man online, she should've known finding the perfect dress there would be the obvious place to look.

A tingle of excitement grew exponentially as she scanned the various sites, seeing some killer dresses but not *the one*. Until her eyes landed on a new up-and-coming designer with an unpronounceable name and she jolted upright, slapping her hand over her eyes, too scared to look in case the picture she'd seen was a figment of her wishful imagination.

Spreading her fingers a centimetre apart, she peeked through, letting out an excited squeal as she saw it.

The dress.

With enough va-va-va-voom to make an entire male revue cast take notice.

Clapping her hands in glee, she leapt off the bed, did a little shimmy before darting a glance at the price, not particularly caring how much it cost. She worked hard; she deserved to own the most heavenly dress on the planet.

Even on the computer screen the dress shimmered and danced, its bold silver sparkling, catching her eye and making her yearn to run her hands over the gleaming fabric.

She had to have it.

Plonking down on the bed, her fingers shook as she placed the order, express delivery.

Come tomorrow, she'd have the dress.

Come tomorrow night, she'd have the man.

Since when did her life get so exciting?

'No last minute pep talk before I wow your friends?'

Sending Bryce a tremulous smile that hid a wealth of nerves, she said, 'Glad to see you're not short on confidence.'

He patted her hand tucked under his elbow and winked.

'With a gorgeous woman on my arm, you bet I'm confident.'

Slipping into routine, assuming a role, that was all he was doing, yet with his smouldering gaze skimming her body and his touch doing crazy things to her insides, she almost believed him.

'So we're straight on our stories? How we met, that sort of thing, how—'

'Relax.'

He brushed her cheek with the back of his knuckles, a soft, barely-there caress that sent her belly into freefall and her limited bravado with it.

Relax? Was the guy insane? How could any woman relax with someone as sexy and suave and sophisticated staring at her as if she was his girlfriend for real?

Relax, indeed.

'Come on, the faster we get in there, the faster you'll relax.'

Not on your life, she thought as he held her hand, intertwining their fingers in such a way that felt way too comfortable, way too right. They shouldn't fit like this and tonight should-n't feel like a real date.

But it did. And had, ever since she'd slipped into the Silver Streak, her knockout dress. The dress was beyond va-va-va-voom—way beyond—and the second Bryce had first laid eyes on her and his jaw had sagged she'd known it was worth every cent.

He'd recovered quickly, the shock in his eyes replaced by something much more potent, much scarier as he'd started at the top and worked his way down, his hungry gaze devouring her.

Her skin tingled at the memory and her grip inadvertently tightened, wishing she could back out of this ludicrous plan now, knowing it was too late.

'You're having second thoughts.'

It wasn't a question, and the fact he could read her mind so easily, could sense her unease, had her more worried than his hand holding hers.

'Am I crazy doing this?'

He smiled, and the power behind that one simple action slugged her all the way down to her toes.

'You're a professional businesswoman who doesn't have time to date. There's no shame in being single.'

He tipped up her chin and she gulped, hoping he couldn't read the rush of anticipation his touch elicited. They were so close—close enough for him to duck his head and…

'But if you want to show up with a date for all the wedding tribulation, I'm all yours.'

If his caress on her cheek a few moments ago

had unnerved her, his thumb brushing her bottom lip almost undid her completely.

Bryce Gibson was all hers, even if it was only for a month. Why the heck was she hesitating?

Hoping a toss of her hair would distract him from her wobbly knees as she swayed towards him, she nodded.

'Let's do this.'

'That's my girl.'

With a squeeze of her hand, they climbed the few steps and pushed through a giant glass door, pausing at the entrance of The Anchorage.

Butterflies alternated between tap-dancing and slam-dancing against the walls of her belly as she took a deep breath—several—only a matter of time until one of her friends caught sight of her.

A sudden hush fell over the intimate restaurant and she could've sworn she heard a collective indrawn breath as Mattie caught sight of her, followed by Linda and Carol in quick succession, courtesy of several sharp elbow jabs in the ribs from the bride-to-be.

'We've been spotted.'

Bryce's broad grin screamed he loved every minute of the unfolding drama as he ducked his head to whisper in her ear, 'Do you want me to kiss you now for an extra convincing touch?'

'No!'

His low chuckle broke the tension, his twinkling eyes with the endearing creases going a long way to soothe her nerves. Not a moment too soon as the bridal babes wound their way through the tables, making a beeline straight for them.

'Show-time.'

Sliding an arm around her waist, Bryce sent her friends a charismatic smile as they descended into bedlam.

'Hey, hon, you look fabulous.' To Mattie's credit, she managed to mouth 'wow' at her dress before her curious gaze zeroed in on Bryce. 'And you must be Eve's new man. Pleased to meet you.'

Refraining from rolling her eyes as Linda and Carol elbowed each other out of the way for next in line introduction honours, Bryce handled her crazy friends with aplomb.

With an encouraging squeeze of her waist, he dropped his hand to shake Mattie's. 'Bryce Gibson. Pleased to meet you.'

Making room so Linda and Carol could squeeze in, he said, 'So which of you lovely ladies is the blushing bride?'

They all twittered like excited birds presented with a juicy worm as Eve silently applauded. She had to hand it to him; rather than being put off by her friends' whirlwind introductions and non-stop chatter, he was in his element, bestowing smiles and winks and charming compliments.

Thrilled he was living up to his end of the

bargain, she slipped a hand into his, hating how good it felt, loving the dimpled smile he bestowed on her.

'Meet Mattie, Linda and Carol.' She waved to each of them in turn before doing a theatrical hand flourish back at him. 'Girls, Bryce.'

'Charmed, I'm sure.' Carol's casual once-over started at Bryce's hand-made Italian leather shoes, ended at his twinkling blue eyes and encompassed everything in between as she gave her a thumbs up sign of approval behind her back.

'Great to meet you, Bryce.' Linda's effusive greeting and wicked grin matched Carol in the subtlety stakes and Eve stifled a groan as Mattie slid a possessive hand through his other elbow.

'Come and meet the guys while we interrogate our friend.'

Squeezing her hand for reassurance, his lips curved into a sexy grin that kick-started her stalling heart as he allowed Mattie to lead him away. 'Be gentle with me.'

Mattie chuckled. 'No promises.'

'Girlfriend, we have got to talk,' Carol muttered under her breath as she and Linda propelled her to follow.

'You have some serious explaining to do, young lady!'

* * *

Eve's best innocent look was lost on Mattie as her friend all but dragged her into the swanky Ladies' room while the rehearsal dinner was in full swing. Linda and Carol were already waiting on the plush persimmon velvet chaise longues in the cosy foyer, none too patiently by the way they jumped to their feet as soon as they entered.

'Eve! Oh, my God, where did you find that man? He is absolutely gorgeous!' Linda gushed, grabbing her arm and tugging her towards a chaise longue while Carol all but shoved her down with a 'He is a total hottie! Tell all!'

Laughing, she held up her hands. 'Can you girls give me a minute here?'

She shrugged off their clinging hands and smoothed down her silver sheath with deliberate slowness, knowing it would drive the inquisitive trio barmy.

'Eve Pemberton, if you don't tell us right this very minute what's going on, I'm afraid we'll be forced to take drastic action.'

Mattie stood over her, hands on hips, her Titian ponytail bristling like a sunburnt hedgehog.

She knew better than to cross the babes in full inquisition mode and she held up her hands in surrender.

'Okay, okay, just let me catch my breath.'

She paused for effect and exhaled slowly. 'Trying to keep up with Bryce has me exhausted.'

'You mean—'

'Have you two already—'

'You go, girl!'

Laughing, she crossed her legs at the ankles, admiring her sky-high silver stilettos. She'd caught Bryce checking them out, though he hadn't stopped there.

In fact, when she'd opened the door to him a few hours earlier, he'd taken a good long look at her clingy dress and sparkly shoes before holding out his hand to her, twirling her around and murmuring a soft, sweet, 'You look absolutely stunning.'

Coming from him, she felt stunning and in that magical instant he'd obliterated the awful memory of him leaving her alone on that balcony, her skin pebbling with cold, her face flushed in mortification, as he'd rejoined his friends, who were laughing at her.

She'd never worn anything like the Silver Streak, had never had the confidence to wear something so fitted, so glittery. But tonight demanded it and, if Bryce's gobsmacked expression and hungry gaze had been any indication, her confidence boost had worked.

The Eve he'd once known—ugly duckling—had transformed into the proverbial elegant swan.

While she still felt the same on the inside—uncertain, confused and bamboozled by his attention—it was great to gain the admiration as an attractive woman she'd once hungered for from him.

Not that she was trying to prove a point. They'd moved past that the moment she'd walked into the Aria and seen the genuine male appreciation in his heated blue-eyed stare.

Uh-uh, this was about her—all about her. She'd spent an inordinate amount of time over the years building her image, shedding her old look, building a confident outer shell to the world that no one could breach. She never went out in public without full make-up, contact lenses and stylish clothes.

The babes, her three closest friends in the world, teased her about it. Then again, she'd never seen any of them look anything other than immaculate, stylish and chic. Crazy, but they were friends from her 'new' life and a small part of the old her, insecure, craving approval, wondered if they'd still like her if they saw the real her. The Eve that Bryce knew.

He was the only one who'd seen her back then, apart from Tony, who loved her as a sibling regardless. And the old Bryce had walked away from her without a backward glance.

Which brought her full circle to the

dress…and ensuring he saw how far she'd come, how little his rejection meant.

Rolling her eyes, she pushed off the chaise longue and headed for the mirror, lipstick at the ready. 'Relax, ladies. We've only been dating a short time. We're still getting to know each other.'

'Oh.'

The babes sighed in disappointed unison and she shook her head, chuckling at their morose expressions.

'Cheer up, girls. I'll be sure to let you know when anything juicy happens.'

Yeah, right. Not that she hoped anything remotely report-worthy would happen…right?

Mattie fanned her face and plopped onto the chaise longue. 'With a guy like Bryce, juicy is only a matter of time. Phew, is he hot or what!'

Surprised by the niggle of jealousy at her gorgeous red-headed friend finding Bryce attractive, and more surprised by the tiny flicker of hope at what juicy with him might entail, she played it down.

'I thought you girls might be impressed.'

'Impressed?' Carol smoothed her sleek bob as if the man in question had just entered the room. 'Eve, honey, that man is beyond impressive.'

'Hear, hear,' Linda chirped up, her resident cheeky smile alerting the rest of them she was about to drop one of her classics. 'I recently read an article comparing guys' sex appeal to chocolate and, in Bryce's case, he's the finest Swiss ever invented.'

Bryce…chocolate…yum…

As three sets of curious eyes swung her way, Eve briefly wondered if she'd said that last bit out loud.

As she rejoined them on the chaise, Mattie laughed and patted her arm. 'That expression on your face says it all.'

She had an *expression?* She couldn't, not when this dating thing with Bryce was strictly platonic.

Uh-uh, no way would she be silly enough to read more into it, just because he'd stroked her arm, held her hand and casually touched her every chance he'd got tonight. They'd discussed it, remember? Small physical displays of intimacy would be expected from a dating couple if she wanted to convince the girls.

Carol and Linda smirked and headed for the mirror for a quick make-up repair job. 'Come on, leave the girl alone. Can't you see she's so gaga over the guy she can't wait to get back out there?'

'I'm not gaga,' Eve said, desperately ignoring the sinking feeling that maybe she was.

Bryce was in his element.

Great party, great food, interesting people,

sparkling conversation—and a stunning woman by his side.

Eve chose that moment to enter the room and his gaze zeroed in on her, his gut instantly tightening with longing as he watched her sashay between the tables towards him.

She was something else.

He'd dated models and soap opera starlets, women as uninterested in commitment as he was, but none of them held a candle to this beautiful woman. It was so much more than appearance. Her quiet confidence, her subtle class combined with a killer brain had him wanting to get to know his faux date a lot better.

Reaching his side, her glossed lips curved in a tentative smile—a smile that tugged on his heartstrings, a smile that insisted he sweep her into his arms and show her exactly how gorgeous she was with a kiss to end all kisses.

But it wasn't the time or place. Or was it?

She wanted to convince her friends they were dating; what better way than to…?

'Whatever you're thinking, get it out of your mind right now,' she said, the flare of heat in her eyes making a mockery of her words.

'Where's the fun in that?'

He whipped out her chair, placing a hand in the small of her back to guide her down, not surprised by the slight stiffening.

Eve may have made it clear she didn't want anything from this dating deal beyond what they'd agreed but her body didn't lie and right now it was begging him to put their platonic agreement to the test.

'The girls are very impressed.'

'With me?'

'No, with my new BlackBerry.' She rolled her eyes as he laughed. 'What do you think?'

'I think I'm going to have a lot of fun convincing your friends we're a couple.'

'You've already done a good job so far.'

'Bet I can do better.'

He ran a finger down her bare arm, lingering in the hollow at her elbow, savouring her sharp intake of breath as he continued downward to caress her pulse point, the frantic beating a clear indication he was having the same effect on her as she was on him.

'I think you've done enough.'

Her voice sounded shaky but she didn't move away and, emboldened by her nearness, her intoxicating vanilla fragrance so reminiscent of the delicious dessert she'd concocted the other night and the heat simmering between them, he slid an arm around her waist and pulled her flush against him.

'Not nearly enough,' he murmured as his gaze locked on hers, daring her to stop him, hoping like hell she wouldn't.

'This isn't part of the deal—'

He kissed her, driven by an all-consuming need to discover how she responded to him as a man, how she felt in his arms, how she tasted.

He'd aimed for a gentle testing kiss, an affectionate kiss between a couple just getting to know each other. However, when she angled her head ever so slightly and parted her lips on a small satisfied sigh, he lost it.

Completely.

Everyone, everything faded into oblivion as she came alive in his arms, kissing him back with a surprising hunger that fired him, inspired him and showed him what he'd missed out on all those years ago by foolishly walking away from her.

'I've wanted to do this since I first laid eyes on you tonight,' he whispered as he momentarily broke the kiss, hating his misplaced chivalry that demanded he give her time to pull back, wanting her more now than ever.

To his amazement, she touched her lips to his again, tentatively at first, before demanding a response he was only too willing to give.

Sliding his hand into her hair, he cradled her head while deepening the kiss to the point of losing control, losing his mind, losing sight of the real reason he was here.

Business. Where failure wasn't an option.

And being the platonic date Eve wanted for the duration of the month was paramount to success at his new job.

So what the hell was he doing taking a chance like this?

Breaking the kiss, he pulled away to look into her eyes, expecting censure, indignation, even anger.

The unguarded yearning glittering in the expressive dark depths had him reassessing the situation in an instant. If Eve wasn't mad about the kiss, if she looked like she wanted more, maybe he had a chance of making the next month more pleasurable than anticipated?

Why couldn't they date for real? Have a little fun, considering they both knew the score—that it wouldn't lead to anything, apart from what they both wanted out of it?

'Eve?'

'Hmm?'

'Did I just score a ten out of ten in the convincing stakes?'

'Don't know about them but I'm convinced.'

Her soft tone bordered on wistful as she raised a hand to her mouth, skimming her fingertips over her lips while a dazed half smile played there, a smile that had him hankering to do it all over again.

'So am I.'

Unable to stop himself, he leaned forward and brushed a lingering kiss across her lips again, a kiss that promised more.

'You're good at this acting thing.'

Her blunt words doused him more effectively than if she'd flung her chilled wine in his face.

She thought he'd kissed her as part of the charade they were perpetuating. While it might've been his original plan when they'd first discussed this crazy deal, his intentions had changed along the way. Kissing her had nothing to do with proving a point to anyone and everything to do with the vibrant woman gnawing on her bottom lip and staring at him with confusion in her eyes.

He should leave it alone, let her go on thinking this was all part of the deal they'd figured out. That was the easy way, the uncomplicated way. Then again, since when had he ever done easy?

Sliding his hand into hers, intertwining their fingers, he said softly, 'What if I wasn't acting?'

Her eyes widened in shock, huge and dark and mesmerising, her teeth leaving off worrying her bottom lip only to be replaced by the tip of her tongue darting out to moisten it.

'B-but our plan—'

'Plans change.'

He tightened his grip on her hand, his thumb tracing slow, lazy circles on the back of it.

'They evolve. They grow. They develop into new and exciting possibilities.'

She didn't look convinced and, just as he expected her to yank her hand out of his, she smiled, a sunny radiant smile that warmed his heart better than the flush of success after his first promotion.

'You're good, Bryce Gibson, very good. I'm still not convinced at your motivation behind that kiss but I'll let you off this time.'

'With a warning?' He grinned right back at her, hoping she'd flirt with him and not retreat back into her cool, elegant shell.

Shaking her head, she said, '*You* should come with a warning.'

'And what would that be?'

'Dangerous goods, handle with care!'

He laughed, wondering how far he could push her. 'Come on, admit it.'

'Admit what?'

Her smile slipped as he focused on her mouth, on her deliciously plump, thoroughly-kissed lips, staggered by how badly he wanted to do it again.

'How much you enjoyed it.'

Folding her arms, she tilted her nose in the air like every disapproving teacher he'd ever back-chatted. 'I'll do no such thing.'

She even sounded like them, all prim and

proper and stern, which only served to egg him on.

'I won't let up until you do.'

Sliding an arm across the back of her chair, he deliberately let his fingers ripple across her skin in the barest of caresses, vindicated by the slight shudder beneath his fingertips as she stiffened.

Ducking his head, he nuzzled the tender skin behind her ear. 'I've got all night to keep this up and, believe me, I'm just getting started.'

'All right, fine, I enjoyed it. Satisfied?'

Her rigid back and hands-off posture would've been enough of a signal to have him backing down, if it weren't for the momentary fear he glimpsed in her eyes.

She wouldn't be scared if that kiss hadn't affected her as much as it had affected him and it gave him hope.

'A few more of those incredible kisses and I might be well on the way.'

'Oh, for Pete's sake.'

Her mock exasperation was blown when the corners of her mouth twitched and he chuckled, his arm sliding off the chair to rest on her shoulders, hugging her gently, bringing the side of her sensational body into luscious contact with his own.

'You enjoyed it as much as I did.'

She laughed, placed both palms flat against his chest and pushed lightly.

'Anyone ever tell you you've got confidence and then some?'

'In my job, it pays to be confident. Guess it's become a part of who I am.'

Damn, where had that come from? Curiosity shifted in her eyes but, thankfully, she didn't push him for answers he wasn't ready to give.

'Speaking of your job, how did you go with AJ? Any male bonding yet?'

He reached for his beer, grateful the heavy moment had evaporated quicker than his job if he didn't deliver what the boss man Sol wanted.

'He seems like a nice bloke. Duane and Anton too.'

Strangely, work had been the furthest thing on his mind since they'd arrived at the rehearsal dinner. He'd been focused one hundred per cent on Eve, all too aware of her long tanned legs stretched out beneath the table next to his, by the way the tight shimmery dress ended an inch above her knees, how it clung to her body and outlined every delicious inch.

He'd hung on her every word, had flirted and laughed with her, had concentrated on her and her alone, his plans for networking coming a distant second to ensuring she had a good time on their first date.

'They're all great, even though I had to face an inquisition of mammoth proportions from the bridal babes when I went to refresh my lippie.'

'They wanted to know about me, huh?'

She nodded, her lips curving in a playful smile. 'Every single detail.'

'What is it with women and the baring soul thing?'

Her smile faded, a wary expression darkening her eyes to the richest bittersweet chocolate.

'We look out for each other.'

He knew in an instant she was feeling guilty at deceiving her friends. He could see it in her down-turned mouth, in her tense shoulders, in her expressive eyes.

Squeezing her hand, he said, 'If you're worrying about us being here together, about you and me dating, don't. We're old buddies hanging out together for a while and I don't know about you but I'm having a great time. We'll stay in touch after all this is done, so don't feel bad. It doesn't have to be any more compli-cated than that.'

Okay, so he'd stretched the truth a tad. They'd never been buddies, far from it, but he wanted to make her feel better, to bring back the lively sparkle she'd had all evening.

Thankfully, she relaxed enough to lean into him and murmur in his ear, 'Thanks for that. You're a good guy.'

'Just good?'

Sending her an exaggerated wink, he raised his glass in her direction.

'To being the best dating buddies.'

'I'll drink to that.'

If only he could focus on the buddy part and forget how much he'd like to move on to being so much more.

CHAPTER SEVEN

LYING to her friends didn't sit well with Eve.

They'd been genuinely excited for her at the wedding rehearsal dinner and it wasn't until later, when she'd been casually chatting with Bryce, did the depth of her deception hit her.

These girls cared about her; they wanted her to be happy. Yet in their eyes she needed a man for that. A theory she usually scoffed at but, with Bryce sending her into a tizz every time he glanced her way, she couldn't help but wish for that fabled happily-ever-after her friends were so good at touting.

Great, she was starting to believe her own hype. This plan was crazy but she'd have to perpetuate the deception a tad longer, go through with it until after the wedding, and when she'd shucked her bridesmaid dress for the last time she'd tell them the truth.

Which was what, exactly?

Groaning, she flipped open her laptop and brought up her diary for the day. Better to focus on work and forget how complicated the situation with Bryce was.

The guy was too irresistible for his own good. She'd wanted drop dead gorgeous to impress her friends; little did she expect she'd be the one equally impressed!

If dinner at her place had opened up a world of possibilities between them, pretending to be his girlfriend at the rehearsal dinner had been sheer and utter torture.

He'd been attentive, charming and utterly captivating all night. She'd barely noticed the divine oven-roasted duckling on a confit of new potatoes with five-spiced peach chutney and the mouth-watering apple and macadamia crumbled tart drizzled with hot caramel sauce—her, the queen of gourmet cooking!

She'd paid scant attention to her friends, who'd thoughtfully given her space to...what? Stare into Bryce's blazing blue eyes all evening? Chat with him like old friends? Flirt outrageously like she'd never flirted in her entire life?

As for those kisses...she squeezed her eyes shut but nothing could erase the memory of how he'd made her feel—like a desirable woman, a woman who could attract a guy like him.

It had been the dress, of course. He'd never

seen her like that, had responded by slipping into a role he was an expert at playing: charming, flirtatious, gallant, a master at making a woman feel special.

It had been great while it lasted but she was under no illusions. If Bryce had seen her later—contacts out, make-up off, faded grey cotton pyjamas—he would've run, just like he had years ago.

Okay, maybe a tad unfair, as she hadn't been wearing anything remotely interesting the night of Tony's party, the peacock blue taffeta formal dress a reject from the eighties and, while she'd loved it, being the first dress she'd ever bought, she'd seen the aghast glances from fashion-conscious bimbos wearing slinky LBDs.

He'd seemed just as interested in talking to her that night, had made her believe for an all-too-brief time that he actually liked her for her brains, that appearances weren't important.

Until his friends had intervened and he'd acted like a loser. Now, like then, Bryce could turn. Once their deal was over, what if he reverted to ignoring her, pretending that none of this had happened? Wouldn't be the first time.

One kiss, and already things were getting way more complicated than anticipated. And if she felt this torn after one kiss, how the heck would she hold up until the end of the month?

Better to assume the kiss meant nothing, that Bryce had been playing the role assigned to him. She'd assumed he was performing but there'd been something in his tone, something in his eyes when he'd asked her, *'What if I wasn't acting?'*

Her heart had stopped when he'd said that, her over-sensitised body ready to jump him on the spot. Being the scaredy-cat she was, she'd laughed it off but he'd gone on to complicate matters by talking about things developing and growing and goodness knew what.

While *developing* something out of dating Bryce sounded appealing, she couldn't do it. She knew better than anyone how becoming too attached to someone could end.

Uh-uh, she wasn't cut out for the dating game, let alone a relationship, no matter how much she secretly craved it.

A knock sounded at the door and she opened it, ushering one of the AFL's marketing managers into her office.

The Australian Football League, a major customer, had helped propel Soirée to the top of events management in Melbourne, but as the slick guy droned on about his requirements for the upcoming Grand Final Ball she found her mind constantly wandering: to the way Bryce had filled out his suit at that first meeting at the Aria, the way he'd cleaned up the dishes at her house, the way he'd kissed her senseless at the dinner.

She managed to nod and smile and sound articulate with the client, saying all the right things like how she'd theme the ball, include special effects, organise the entertainment, devise a suitable food and beverage package and organise everything from invitation design to VIP concierge service, but all the while she couldn't forget the way Bryce's lips had felt moving against hers, how he'd been tender yet passionate, skilful yet reverent, as if expecting her to rebuff him.

As if. The moment he'd kissed her she'd forgotten every sane reason why they shouldn't be doing it and had instantly been transported out of this world—to a planet where ugly ducklings really did end up with the prince.

Okay, so she was seriously mixing her metaphors but the memory of that one kiss brought a goofy smile to her face every time she thought about it.

'Any venues in mind, Miss Pemberton?'

Annoyed she'd been daydreaming when she never let anything interfere with her professionalism, she handed the client a filled brochure.

'I love using unique locations so whatever you want I can do. For other functions I've taken over disused warehouses, showgrounds, forts, passenger terminals, trains, swimming baths, building rooftops, quarries, islands, you name it, anywhere that's special I can arrange an event there to be remembered.'

The client, a dead ringer for a young Mel Gibson—did she have Gibsons on the mind or what!—appeared suitably impressed and she went with a decisive conclusion to her pitch.

'Just so you know, I don't rely on traditional props or well-worn themes. I like to come up with exciting, innovative ideas, the kind of tailored package you won't find with any other event company.'

Mel's double sent her a long penetrating stare before holding out his hand as he stood.

'I need to take this back to my marketing team but I can't see a problem. Looks like you've got yourself an AFL gala to coordinate, Miss Pemberton.'

'Thanks. You won't be disappointed.'

Shaking hands, she escorted him to the door, leaning against it and exhaling in relief after he'd left.

She'd done it. Added another celebrated event to Soirée's impressive portfolio, the type of event that would bring mega-exposure.

When she'd landed big events previously she'd usually rush home, cook up a storm involving loads of quality couverture chocolate and lashings of cream, and listen to her favourite soul CDs as she curled up on the couch and savoured her victory.

So why the insane urge to pick up the phone, ring Bryce and share her good news with him? Or, worse, go out for a celebratory drink? Her, the antisocial queen out of work hours?

Madness. Pure and utter madness. Dating Bryce was about convincing the girls she wasn't desperate and dateless, that was it. No getting involved, no developing fanciful ideas about what it would be like to date the gorgeous Bryce for real.

Her wavering gaze drifted to the phone perched on her desk at a jaunty angle, taunting her, and her palm itched to cross the room, pick it up and dial.

No, she couldn't. She wouldn't.

The mobile in her pocket sang out its jingle at that precise moment and she sighed in relief, answering it without checking caller ID.

'How's my fabulous date today?'

Clenching the phone to her ear, she couldn't control the surge of sheer joy sweeping through her at the sound of Bryce's deep voice.

'Fine. Just thinking about you, actually.'

Cringing, she slapped the side of her head with her free hand. What was she thinking, telling him that?

The rumble of low laughter washed over her,

rich and warm and oh-so-sexy, telling her exactly why she'd said that. She couldn't think when she heard his dulcet tones, let alone formulate a coherent, witty response.

'All good things, I hope.'

'I was thinking about work stuff.'

'Sure you were.'

His teasing tone brought a blush to her cheeks as she alternated between silently cursing him for reading her mind and cringing with embarrassment because he knew how much she liked him.

'Speaking of work, AJ contacted me and invited me to a product launch for Hot Pursuit.'

'Great.'

She was pleased for him. If she got what she wanted out of this dating deal, it would be good for him to get something out of it too.

'He suggested I bring my girlfriend. It's a partner thing too so Charlie's Angels are going to be there, along with buyers.'

'Charlie's Angels?'

He chuckled, a low, seductive sound that raised the hairs on her nape and sent heat flooding to places that hadn't been flooded in a long, long time.

'My nickname for your friends. What with Linda being blonde, Carol brunette and Mattie a redhead, it kind of fit.'

Joining in his laughter, she crossed the room

on shaky legs—drat the man and his effect on her, even via the phone—and plopped onto her comfy ergonomic chair. 'Bridal babes, Charlie's Angels, wonder what the girls would think if we let them in on our little secret.'

'Which one?'

Not willing to acknowledge her guilt at not telling her friends the truth yet, not now, when she was on a high after her latest coup, she brought up her diary with a few clicks of the keyboard, thrilled when she realised her last client of the day had cancelled.

'Talking about secrets, how would my secret date like to come out and have a celebratory drink with me? I've just scored a major event.'

'Congratulations. A drink sounds great. Where and when?'

Wrinkling her nose at the stack of contractor invoices piled neatly on her desk, she said, 'How about I wrap up things here, which should take an hour, then I'll text you the details?'

'Sounds good.'

He paused as she heard the murmur of voices in the background, impatient voices by the sound of it, before he came back on the line.

'Sorry about that. New boss expects results like yesterday. So you'll come with me to the Hot Pursuit gig, yeah?'

'Sure.'

She had no choice. The girls would think there was a problem between her and Bryce if he showed up and she didn't.

'Good. Better get going. Chaos here. Looking forward to that drink.'

'Me too. Bye.'

She rang off quickly, eyeing the stack of invoices. The sooner she dealt with them, the sooner she got to let her hair down with Bryce.

As long as that was all she let down around him, for she had a distinct feeling if she let her guard down there'd be no recovering from it.

Eve smiled her thanks at the doorman as he opened the door to Bryce's apartment and waited until she entered before leaving.

This felt wrong, entering his apartment when he wasn't there, but he'd insisted and, rather than spending another forty-five minutes at the bar where they'd initially arranged to meet, she'd agreed to wait for him here.

Stepping into the lofty open-plan room serving as lounge, dining and entertaining area, her mouth fell open as she took in the black sheer drapes framing the floor-to-ceiling windows and the giant chandelier hanging from an ornate ceiling, the leopard-print furniture, the black marble floors and the eclectic mix of candelabras, African animal figurines and coloured glass bottles.

A few dimmed down lights reflected off the ebony marble floors, shimmering like an oil slick beneath her feet while Melbourne's city skyline glittered through the sheer black chiffon like jewels scattered against an ermine cape.

The overall effect was surreal, sophisticated and decadent. A bit like the man himself, the man she'd first glimpsed in that photo accompanying the article online: suave, confident, a guy on top of his game, a guy ready to take on the world and win.

Bryce's apartment was very James Bond while her home in a quiet South Yarra street channelled *Little House on the Prairie,* from its green and cream chequered sofas to its soft-honey oak polished boards, its antique fireplace to the lemon walls.

The two places were worlds apart.

Standing in his apartment reinforced what she'd always thought, always known: they were two very different people.

She'd been kidding herself.

All his tender gazes, gentle hand-holding and intimate smiles had fooled her temporarily, his desirability blinding her to the facts.

Fact: Bryce was a charming, irresistible extrovert who could wend his way into the heart of any unsuspecting female, while she was an introspective introvert who faked confidence on a daily basis for her job.

Fact: Bryce was fun-loving and spontaneous and enjoyed partying, while she shed her cool image the second she walked in her front door and curled up on the couch with a book rather than go to a bar.

Fact: Bryce was her opposite in every way and, while he might be dating her to further his own ends, there wasn't the remotest chance he'd develop feelings for her.

The type of feelings she knew deep down were already starting to blossom in her guarded heart, feelings she'd harboured as a teenager but dismissed as a crush, feelings that had flared to life the night of Tony's party, only to be doused by Bryce's cavalier attitude at the end.

Could she be any more pathetic? She'd been the one raving on about keeping their dating strictly platonic, about sticking to business and furthering their agendas.

Ha, ha, looked like the laughs were on her.

She'd come here to celebrate with the one person who had lit her world in a short space of time and she'd been daft to do it, to harbour a secret fantasy that dating him could become real.

That kiss had changed everything, had shifted the boundaries she'd been so desperate to establish and, no matter how hard she tried to act like it was nothing, it had been something. A cataclysmic something, a something every bit as incredible as what she'd imagined when their first kiss had been aborted all those years ago.

Taking one last look around the sensual, evocative room, she shook her head. She had to leave, get out of here while she still could, before he came home and she fell under his spell a little more.

Trying to convince her friends she was dating Bryce was one thing, falling into a trap of her own making another.

Snatching a notebook out of her handbag, she scrawled a quick note and stuck it on the glass-topped hall table. She needed time to marshal her defences, to cool things down between them.

As she slipped from the apartment, she had a feeling she'd need the entire Melbourne fire brigade to do that.

Bryce never bounded out of the lift. Unless he had some swank party to attend, that was. He hated coming home, preferring to stay out and about.

Old habits died hard.

His school days had been the same. Going home meant endless questions and probing and recriminations—or worse, if his dad was there on one of his rare shift changes from the hospital.

If the illustrious Victor Gibson happened to

grace them with his presence there'd be the inevitable put-downs and condescension and disappointment.

How could the only child of a brilliant, world-renowned obstetrician and a talented midwife be so stupid? Easier to stay away and, while he had no one nagging him these days, he still preferred to spend as little time at home as possible.

Not that the ultra-cool apartment Ballyhoo had organised as part of his salary package felt like a home. Every time he stepped through the thick, shiny black door he felt as if he'd entered a film set.

Tonight was different. Tonight he had a spring in his step and he whistled under his breath as he opened the front door, for standing on the other side of it was the most intriguing woman he'd ever met.

'Eve, you here?'

Silence greeted him as he dumped his leather satchel at the door and bumped it shut with his hip, frowning as he glanced at his watch.

He'd come up the private lift from the underground car park so he hadn't checked with the doorman if she'd arrived yet. Considering the late hour, she should've been here ages ago after he'd rung and said he'd be running late.

'Eve?'

Slipping out of his suit jacket, he swung it

over his shoulder and, in doing so, knocked a piece of paper off the hall table. Picking it up, he scanned the cursive, flowing script, taking his time, as he always did.

Hi Bryce,
Sorry I couldn't wait around. Took a call, had to leave on business. You know how it is. Speak soon.
Eve

He should've been relieved. Things were getting a little too cosy between them if he was the only person she wanted to celebrate with after landing a big event.

Combine that with the odd glances she'd been sneaking him when she thought he wasn't looking, and the way she'd responded to his impromptu kiss at the rehearsal dinner, and he should definitely be relieved.

Why the utterly deflating disappointment?

He couldn't get in too deep with Eve. When she discovered his secret—inevitable if they got together for real—he couldn't stand her pity. An intelligent, successful woman like her would definitely pity him, and if there was one thing he hated more than people judging him, it was their pity.

It was better this way.

While she'd cited business as an excuse to leave, he knew better. She'd sounded genuinely eager to see him on the phone earlier, her excitement audible. He understood. He got the same buzz when he nailed a pitch, wanted to shout it to the world.

Her invitation for a drink had surprised him, when he'd expected her to retreat after that kiss last night. The kiss he should've followed through on eight years ago, when he'd been a naïve jerk hell-bent on hiding his secret from those who knew him by doing what he did best: playing the fool.

He'd bet every dollar he had that, once the initial high had worn off, she'd arrived here and started second-guessing: him, the kiss, everything.

Not that he could blame her; he'd been doing a fair amount of that himself since last night. While he'd quashed his second thoughts at the wisdom of this dating game in deference to his all-important career, and achieving the goal that might change things between them, Eve obviously hadn't.

She'd bolted. He should be grateful; it gave him an uninterrupted evening to put in some solid work hours.

Crumpling the note in his hand, he lobbed it into the nearby bin and headed for the phone.

Takeout for one tonight; just the way he liked it.

Then why the bitter taste in his mouth?

CHAPTER EIGHT

'HAVING fun?'

With Bryce's breath fanning her ear, Eve stiffened before forcing herself to relax as she turned towards him.

'Sure. The ceremony went off without a hitch, I didn't trip up the aisle and take out the rest of the bridesmaids and this reception is amazing, so you bet I'm having fun.'

'This tells me otherwise.'

He reached out and smoothed a finger across her brow, gently, slowly, the simplest of touches, setting her skin alight. 'You were frowning.'

Damn, she'd thought she'd mastered her cool, unflappable face. Looked as if it was about as successful as her efforts to shield her heart against this incredibly sexy man dressed in a designer tux staring at her with concern.

Relieved when he stopped touching her, she shrugged. 'It's the events coordinator in me.

Guess I keep wondering how the staff here managed to pull this off.'

By his dubious expression he didn't buy her excuse for a second but let it slide. 'The Melbourne Aquarium is an interesting location for a wedding reception.'

'I've done other functions here, corporate cocktails and team-building sessions, but never a wedding. It has a certain something, don't you think?'

'If you like being in an underground room surrounded by floor-to-ceiling water, separated from man-eating sharks and stingrays and a host of unappealing deep-sea nasties by what appears to be the thinnest of glass, sure, it has an ambience.'

She laughed at his tortured expression. 'I forgot you don't like the ocean.'

'Who told you that?'

Puzzled by his wary tone, she shrugged. 'Tony must've mentioned it. Or maybe the way you piked on our regular jaunts down to the coast gave it away.'

A clear image flashed across her mind of Bryce strutting in the back door of their family home, catching sight of their duffel bags loaded with crisps and sodas and sunscreen, boogie boards propped nearby, and taking a step backward.

He'd begged off that trip to the beach and

every one after, and she'd put it down to her un-
welcome presence as the one and only time he'd
gone down to the Peninsula had been with Tony.

Aiming to lighten the mood, she punched him
lightly in the arm. 'Not that I blame you. Let me
guess, Tony made you navigator like he did me.
I hated reading all those maps and signs with
him demanding constant updates on our
location.'

Rather than smiling as she expected, his lips
thinned. 'Yeah, me too.'

The band started up their first set at that
moment and, before she could make a quick
escape—dancing up close and personal with
Bryce would be pure torture, considering her
decision to cool it after that kiss—he slipped
his hand into hers.

'Come on, let's dance.'

She couldn't say no. Not with him tugging on
her hand as he strode to the makeshift dance
floor set in one of the tunnels with water all
around, not with the blood pounding through
her veins and drowning out every common sense
reason why she shouldn't, and certainly not with
her feet flying to keep up with the inner happy
dance she was already doing.

Slipping one arm around her waist and holding
her other hand with the lightest of pressure, he
tugged her closer until their bodies brushed, her

breasts skimming his chest, their thighs touching, the current buzzing between them having little to do with the static electricity of their clothes and everything to do with the underlying physical attraction between them that wouldn't quit, no matter how much she tried to ignore it.

'Now, this is more like it,' he murmured, moving his feet in time to the music, guiding her with an expertise she'd expect from a guy used to socialising.

The guys she knew, including AJ, Duane and Anton, who stood off to one side nursing beers, would rather bungee jump naked from the top of the Rialto building than dance so Bryce's sudden urge to trip the light fantastic had been a decisive escape from their conversation.

She'd clearly made him uncomfortable, discussing the past. Not that she could blame him. It wasn't a time she particularly enjoyed revisiting. But there'd been something more behind his reticence, something that might explain why he'd done such an abrupt turnaround from treating her with respect years earlier to going cold in front of his friends to showering her with warm affection now.

It wasn't an act, no matter how hard she'd tried convincing herself otherwise. You couldn't fake that kind of thing and his gregarious, spontaneous personality oozed genuine warmth, most of it directed at her. What chance did a girl have of shielding her heart?

'Relax, you're tensing up.'

His hand slid from her waist up her back, stroking her, burning a trail through the flimsy chiffon of her bridesmaid dress.

He expected her to relax when he was doing *that?*

His fingertips skimmed her spine, sending delicious tingles spreading through her body like the far-reaching tentacles of the octopus swimming lazily by without a backward glance.

She bit down on her lip as he dipped his head, his warm breath tickling her ear, his masculine scent combined with the faintest citrus filling her senses until she swayed, punch-drunk on sensation, in tune with him far more than the music.

'There are some definite perks to being your date.' His hand released hers to trail down her bare arm before linking with the other behind her back, circling her, holding her, cherishing her while she secretly wished he'd never let go.

'Dancing being one of them?'

Brushing the barest of butterfly kisses against her temple, he said, 'Holding you like this being one of them.'

She managed a mute nod, unable to speak as a sudden lump of emotion lodged in her throat.

When he held her like this, touched her like this, spoke to her like this, she felt special, desirable and for that one infinitesimal moment she forgot all the reasons why she shouldn't be in his arms and gave herself over to the sheer unbridled pleasure of it.

'You dance like a dream.' His head dipped, his cheek grazed her temple, his body swayed in perfect sync with hers and she sighed, swept away in a fantasy they were dating for real.

Closing her eyes, she rested her head against his shoulder, savouring his proximity, the subtle citrus scent embedded in the fine wool of his tux, his soft hum in tune with the old dance hit reverberating through his chest.

The perfect moment, with the perfect man...

She, of all people, knew there was no such thing as perfect.

Her eyes fluttered open as she reluctantly lifted her head, wishing she could capture this fragment in time for ever, a treasured memory to resurrect on one of those long winter evenings when she liked to curl up on the couch in front of the open fire sipping her favourite cocoa.

She loved those evenings: the peace, the cosiness, the freedom to relax in her oldest yoga pants and T-shirt, make-up-less, with her glasses sliding down her nose like they always had.

But she'd be lying if she didn't wish for someone to share it all with and being held in the protective circle of Bryce's strong arms, with his male scent infusing her senses and the welcome warmth radiating off his body bamboozling her, resurrected that wish in an instant.

'Don't you hate it when the song has to end?'

He smoothed her hair back, his fingertips entwining through the strands, gently massaging her scalp and she shivered involuntarily, his touch eliciting a fiery need in the deepest recesses of her neglected body.

With what was probably a practised touch, with those incredible blue eyes wide with desire and a small sexy smile playing about his lips, she knew, whatever she may wish for in the heat of the moment, Bryce wasn't it.

He couldn't be, no matter how much she wanted him for real.

She slipped out of his arms. 'Everything has to end some time.'

He scanned her face, a tiny crease appearing between his brows, and she quickly mustered a smile.

'Come on. I think dessert's being served.' She turned on her heel and headed towards their table, silently cursing her foolishness in falling for a guy who would run a mile if he saw deep down she hadn't changed a bit, still harboured a giant crush that, if anything, had increased with age.

Bryce pulled up outside Eve's house and switched off the engine. He wanted her to invite him in. He willed her to do it, hoping she wanted to explore this connection they shared as much as he did.

As she turned towards him, her expression closed, her eyes guarded, he knew the only place he was headed tonight was his cold, empty apartment.

'Thanks for tonight. I had a great time.'

Trite words, general words she could've said many times to countless other guys. Empty words with a distinct hollow ring, when what he wanted to hear spill from her lush mouth were genuine words of warmth and excitement and honesty in recognition of this undeniable attraction simmering between them, despite their initial platonic deal.

He could've answered in the same *I did too* vein but he hadn't got this far in life without taking risks and he'd be damned if he sat here and pretended there was nothing between them.

'I'm not going to play this game, Eve.'

Her pupils dilated, large and dark, wide with alarm, as her glossed lips parted in a small surprised O.

'What game?'

'The one where we dance around each other, hiding behind this dating deal we made, when we both know damn well there's more going on.'

There, he'd said it, put it out there, demanding a reaction, a recognition she felt half as bemused by all this as he did.

She quickly averted her gaze, staring out the windscreen at the deserted street, her fingers fidgeting with the hem on the slinky dress that had driven him wild all day. Or, more precisely, the way her lithe body had filled it out so perfectly.

The few weddings he'd been to, the bridesmaids had worn boring satin numbers in God-awful bright colours, but the soft pale-pink dress draping Eve's body had shifted and shimmered as she moved, making him itch to touch it, see if it felt as soft as it looked, to touch her.

'There's nothing going on.'

'Liar,' he murmured, leaning across to capture her chin, his touch insisting she look at him.

Words were cheap but her eyes couldn't lie. Not those wide, dark brown pools of honesty. She used to hide them behind glasses but not any more and he'd seen how much she wanted him: after their first dinner, their first kiss, and tonight, their first dance.

He waited, unaware he was holding his breath

as her gaze fixed on his bow tie, moved upwards with slow regret until their gazes collided, his blunt and assessing, hers shadowed and reluctant. But the shutters didn't last and the second the dark chocolate melted into warm desire he breached the short distance between them and kissed her.

Their first kiss might've initially been a prove-a-point kiss that quickly got out of control but this one was wild from the start, a no-holds-barred, candid kiss from the heart, filled with passion and wonder and soul-deep need.

She made a soft mewling sound as he slanted his mouth across hers repeatedly, her hands clutching his lapels as she pulled him closer, opening her lips beneath his, meeting him halfway, pressing against him with urgency.

He'd wanted an honest answer—looked like he had it—as his tongue traced the soft fullness of her lips, sweeping into her mouth, exploring, teasing and she gave herself wholeheartedly in return, her mouth ravenous, demanding a response he was more than happy to give.

Blood pounded through him, coursing through his veins hard and fast, impossible to slow or steady. Not that he wanted to.

This was what he'd been fantasising about since the first time he'd tasted her sweet lips, this pulsing, passionate, very real expression of how she was feeling, a frank response that she wanted him as much as he wanted her.

She trembled, her breath coming in short, soft pants as he slid his mouth across her cheek, feathering tiny kisses all the way to her ear before ducking down her neck in slow, exquisite detail.

His body ached for her, his pulse quickening as she released his lapels to slide upwards, her fingertips skimming his face, exploring it with delicate finesse before trailing downwards again, toying with his collar, tugging on his tie.

'Eve?'

'Hmm?'

Her lips found the pulse point in his neck and he groaned, letting his head fall back as her tongue traced tiny circles, her mouth nipping him until he thought he'd combust on the spot.

'You know this isn't faking it, right?'

She stilled on a reluctant sigh, her mouth ceasing its playful exploration, and he instantly wished he hadn't spoken.

But he had to know, had to make sure she wasn't doing this out of some warped sense of cementing their deal, had to ensure it was all about him and how he made her feel rather than guaranteeing he stuck around to convince her friends they were a couple.

'Define faking it.'

Her forced chuckle sounded exactly that,

forced, and he cradled her face in his hands, leaving her no option but to meet his gaze head-on.

'I don't know about you, but somewhere along the line this dating scheme of yours has gone beyond platonic. Guess I was wondering how you feel about that.'

Her eyes searched his—for what? Reassurance? Sincerity?

Hell, he'd had no intention of getting involved with her at the start. He never got involved with anyone, preferring to keep his love life tangle-free. A huge misnomer—*his love life.*

He didn't do love. Too complicated, too messy and too revealing, for there was nothing surer than his secret getting out if he let a woman get too close.

She'd almost slipped under his guard the night of Tony's party but he'd prevented it by acting so awfully.

So what was he doing cosying up to her now? She was smart, wouldn't take long before she guessed why he'd fled all those years ago, why he had every intention of keeping her at arm's length now.

But he couldn't stop this…this…*thing* between them. Ignoring their attraction would be like admitting failure on a campaign and the chances of that happening were a big fat nil.

He'd started down this road of honesty. He'd have to take it all the way.

Her eyes shimmered with wariness but she had nowhere else to look and, as she met his gaze, he saw exactly what he'd been hoping for: blatant desire.

She wanted him as much as he wanted her, but would she admit it?

'I don't want this to get too intense,' she said softly, her lower lip trembling, undoing his resolve to push her.

'It doesn't have to be.'

He dropped his hands, shook his head at potentially making a mess of this.

'I just wanted you to know I'm not jerking you around.'

He ran a hand through his hair, wishing he was more articulate. How was it he could nail a pitch with his eyes closed, yet couldn't string two coherent words together in front of this savvy woman?

'What I mean is I'm not taking advantage of our deal and playing up to you just for the hell of it. I like being with you. For real.'

She didn't say a word. Instead, she reached out and slid her fingers through his, squeezing his hand gently.

'Thanks for being honest. I'm enjoying this too. But I don't want it to get complicated.'

His jubilation at her admission evaporated in an instant. 'What's complicated?'

She didn't like confrontation. He could see it in her look-away glance, her fiddling fingers as they plucked at the hem of her dress, the rigidity of her slim shoulders.

'I don't have time for a relationship. It's not what I want right now so, yes, I acknowledge we've got a spark but I think we leave it at that.'

A spark? Very understated considering they'd almost ripped each other's clothes off a few moments earlier.

He should leave it alone but he couldn't, spurred on by an uncharacteristic urge to push her for answers he could barely contemplate himself.

'So we keep going as we have been? Dating for the next month and that's it?'

She hesitated and, in that split second before she dropped her gaze to stare at her white-knuckled clenched hands, he glimpsed pure unadulterated fear.

What had her running scared? So scared she wasn't willing to take a chance on having a little fun?

'That's it.'

Her soft, tremulous words echoed in the car, a cloak of vulnerability shrouding her shoulders like the finest mink.

He wanted to bundle her into his arms and

comfort her but, considering how much he wanted her, touching her right now wouldn't be the brightest thing he'd ever done so he settled for hiding his true feelings as he always did: with quick wit.

'In that case, let me escort my date to the front door before this car turns into a pumpkin and I trade the tux for a frog suit.'

She smiled as something indefinable and infinitely scary shifted in the vicinity of his heart.

She was right.

They had to stick to the original plan.

Contemplating anything else would be crazy.

CHAPTER NINE

Eve braced herself for the oncoming onslaught as she spied the bridal babes weaving their way through the picnic tables, gazes determined, smiles resolute.

Not that she blamed them. She'd done a fine job of avoiding them so far, staying glued to Bryce's side, hanging on his every word, feigning interest in the corny decorations featuring intertwining As and Ms festooning the place.

Ironic, considering Bryce was the last person she wanted to be close to after last night.

That kiss in his car after the wedding had been an unmitigated disaster. Not the kiss itself. That had been spectacular. It was the aftermath that had her cringing and wishing she'd never devised this zany scheme in the first place.

If their first kiss at the rehearsal dinner had shocked her, their second had sent her good intentions to hold him at arm's length up in a sizzle of lust.

She'd gone from independent career woman secure in her home and business to yearning romantic mess who craved a guy totally wrong for her with a passion. A strong, unquenchable passion that throbbed and blossomed and grew as she stood here, watching him chat with the guys like they'd been mates for ever.

She'd tried so hard to keep her burgeoning crush under control, fooling herself into believing that first kiss at the rehearsal dinner had been all show, an attempt on both their parts to authenticate their dating.

It had worked until that mind-blowing kiss in the car last night. They hadn't been on show then, so every astonishing, scintillating second had been all about them—pure pleasurable delight. She tingled all over from the memory alone and, struggle as she might, she couldn't wipe the grin off her face as the girls approached.

'Well, well, will you look at that? Someone's looking mighty pleased with herself.'

Mattie sidled up to her and handed her a glass of champagne. 'Not that I blame you, hon. The more I see of Bryce, the more I understand why you haven't dated much.'

Carol popped an olive in her mouth, swirling

the rest of her Martini. 'Yeah, you've been waiting for top notch rather than wasting time dating dregs.'

Eve laughed. 'You girls haven't done too badly yourselves.'

She gestured towards the barbecue where AJ, Duane, Anton and Bryce were raising beer bottles in a toast of some sort.

Carol sighed, a dreamy look on her face. 'Looks like we've all hit the jackpot.'

Guilt pierced Eve, niggling like a deep spur, but now wasn't the time or place to tell the girls the truth. Mattie was still floating, the guys were bonding and she couldn't take the risk of them thinking badly of Bryce.

She'd got them into this; he'd been good enough to help her out. What would her friends think when they learned the truth? Worse, what if the guys felt that they'd been duped and ostracised him from the business community completely?

An awful thought insinuated its way into her brain—something she hadn't considered when she'd first hatched this scheme. Bryce needed to make contacts in Melbourne and she'd dangled AJ, Anton and Duane in front of him for that purpose. But what if it all went horribly wrong when she told the girls the truth and the guys tarnished his business reputation? All three had the power to make Bryce's name mud in Melbourne; where would he be then?

Heck, she couldn't tell the girls, not now, no matter how much it grated to hide the truth from them.

Then again, what was the truth?

Watching Bryce throw back his head and let out a belly laugh, she couldn't ignore the insistent feeling she was dating him for real, despite all protests to the contrary.

'Hey, what's up?'

Mattie placed a hand on her arm as Eve wrenched her gaze away from Bryce, needing some sound relationship advice for the first time in her life.

'Can I ask you girls something?'

'Anything,' they said in unison, chuckling as they linked pinkies in a jinx sign girls the world over did at primary school.

Eve knew she was taking a risk. In asking the girls her question, she was risking revealing a part of her deepest insecurities. And that was scary. Beyond scary.

The bridal babes had never seen her anything other than confident, cool, successful, a city girl on top of her game. They did brunches, met up for snatched lattes over BlackBerrys, had cocktails to catch up on gossip. She'd cooked gourmet dinners for them, went to the ballet, shared a laugh at salsa lessons.

But she'd never revealed her old insecurities to her friends, never told them how she'd deliberately chosen a career that thrust her into a social whirlwind because being surrounded by beautiful things, beautiful people, made her feel beautiful.

She'd never told them that a few hours of intense male attention at a party eight years ago had transformed her life, had made her yearn to feel that good all the time, had propelled her into making life choices that she revelled in every day, yet she was still the same shy girl deep down, petrified Bryce would walk again if he discovered the real her.

'Wow, this looks serious.'

Linda slung an arm over her shoulder while beckoning Mattie and Carol closer. 'This could be something really important, like a birds and bees question.'

They all cracked up and Eve sent her intuitive friend a grateful look for breaking the tension.

'Actually, you'll probably laugh at this, but I was wondering when you girls let your partners see the real you.'

'The real me?' Mattie wrinkled her nose as if the thought of AJ seeing her in anything other than her favoured Gucci was totally foreign.

'You know,' Eve persisted, 'without make-up, in around the house clothes, with your hair unstyled and not looking the glamorous god-desses you usually are.'

Carol frowned and patted her sleek bob. 'Oh, you mean *that* real!'

Silence descended on the group as they pondered the question, while Eve shifted her weight from heel to heel. Was it so difficult to answer?

'Well?'

'I'm thinking.'

Linda tapped her red lipsticked mouth with a matching fingernail. 'I think I dropped the whole make-up thing at home with Anton within the first month.'

Fear lanced Eve, swift and sharp. She could never contemplate showing any guy, let alone Bryce, the real her in that amount of time. Ironic, considering that was the amount of time she had with him if they stuck firmly to their deal.

Mattie's perfectly plucked eyebrows shot hea-venwards. 'That soon? Heck, I don't think AJ saw me without make-up till we were engaged.'

'Really?'

Carol held her French-manicured nails at length, studying them intently. 'Well, I don't think Duane's ever seen me totally au naturale.'

'What?'

Once again, they spoke in unison, though this time there were no jinx signs. They were too focused on their perfectly polished friend without a hair out of place.

Carol shrugged. 'I believe in always being well-groomed for your husband. Keeps them interested, you know.'

Mattie shook her head. 'Girlfriend, you sound like you've just stepped off the Ark! And, in case you haven't noticed, Duane thinks you walk on water, so he'd love you whether you wore make-up or turned green like the Incredible Hulk.'

'Nothing wrong with being well presented.' Carol must've noticed her expression. 'Right, Eve?'

She couldn't agree more. People looked at you differently when you were well presented, they treated you differently, they thought you were a somebody rather than a nobody, no matter how smart you were.

She knew that better than anybody and, while Carol's response didn't reassure her, what Linda and Mattie had said struck a chord.

'If you're worried about Bryce, don't be. Anyone can see he adores you.'

The tiny bud of hope deep within her heart unfurled its petals a smidgeon. Was he that good an actor? Was he merely playing the dating role she'd assigned him or did he feel something for her? His actions and words last night implied he did, especially as they hadn't been on display for her friends.

'Yeah, he gets the look whenever you're with him,' Linda said, nodding.

'What look?'

Mattie patted her cheek. 'The "I'm smitten and don't know what the hell to do about it" look. We've all seen it before.'

Yeah, on your guys, not mine, she thought, managing a breezy smile as the man in question chose that moment to catch her gaze across the garden and sent her a cheeky wink.

'See? Smitten,' Mattie said smugly. 'Relax, hon, it may be early days for you two but he's a keeper. I have a feeling the babelicious Bryce won't blink an eye if you strut around with mud on your face and a garbage bag for a dress.'

And, just like that, some of Eve's old insecurities receded. What if she was making too much of this, letting old insecurities stand in the way of her happiness? Right now, Bryce made her happy. And she had a feeling that if she let go of her reservations, she could be the happiest she'd ever been.

'Thanks,' she said, downing the rest of her champagne, buoyed by her new determination.

She was going to do it.

Tell Bryce she wanted to date him—for real.

Chuckling, the babes linked arms along with her. 'Come on, let's grab a champagne top-up before we wander over to that barbecue where there are some seriously hot guys with our names stamped all over them.'

I wish, Eve thought as she happily wandered towards the bar with her friends, *I wish.*

Bryce watched Charlie's Angels flutter around Eve like busy butterflies, each exotic and beautiful in their own way.

As attractive as they might be, they couldn't compete with the gorgeous woman in their midst, looking cool and elegant and oh-so-delectable. He wanted her with a staggering fierceness and, while she didn't want anything beyond their dating deal, he had other ideas.

It wasn't as if he was proposing marriage. They could date for the month she'd stipulated and walk away at the end. He never dated longer than that usually anyway, so this thing with Eve wouldn't be any different.

A win-win for them both.

Then why did he feel like a loser at the thought of walking away from her again?

'So, Bryce, I hear you're working for Ballyhoo these days?'

Nodding, he focused his attention on AJ. 'Yeah, it's a great opportunity.'

AJ nursed a beer and ran a hand across his chin. 'I may have another one for you. Hot Pursuit's advertising contract is up for grabs. I've never used Ballyhoo before but you seem like a stand up guy. How'd you like a shot at it?'

A shot at one of the biggest ad contracts in Australia? He refrained from punching the air and letting out a whoop—just.

'That'd be great. Thanks, mate.'

Much more sedate, much more professional but AJ must've sensed his jubilation for he grinned and raised his beer bottle in his direction.

'No worries. Ring my PA and tee up an appointment. Just so you know, we've got three other companies vying for it and the pitches are scheduled for next month. Timeline not too short?'

Not at all, not if he worked night and day between now and then. And he would, for this was the break he was looking for.

When he'd agreed to Eve's outlandish scheme, he'd hoped to make contacts but never in his wildest dreams had he expected to be given an opportunity like this.

If he could land the Hot Pursuit contract his career would shoot into the stratosphere. Landing the ad campaign for Australia's biggest sporting company could only lead to international work. He'd be set for life, would reach his goal, with his past well and truly behind him.

Clinking his beer bottle against AJ's, he said, 'I like working to tight deadlines. It won't be a problem.'

'Good. I'm looking forward to seeing what you come up with.'

Chugging back his beer, AJ's gaze wandered to the women.

'And don't think this has anything to do with Eve. She didn't ask me for any favours and, even if she did, I don't let my personal life mix with business. I've checked into you, like what I've heard and as we've hung out a few times…' he shrugged '…I'm interested in seeing your work. Now, if you don't mind, I see my new bride making eyes at me. Later.'

As Bryce watched AJ make a beeline for Mattie, his jubilation evaporated. He'd been so busy doing mental high-fives he'd completely forgotten about Eve and what this could mean for them.

Once he reached his goal, he would have no excuses not to pursue her.

His goal had been the reason he'd steered clear of commitment, hadn't been interested in anything other than dating all this time, but now, achieving the ultimate success in business had the potential to lead to his ultimate downfall.

Hell, he hadn't thought this through.

Wanting to pursue her, to see if the attraction between them could explode into a raging inferno of passion for the month they were together was one thing. Achieving his dream and discovering a woman who could make the rest of his secret dreams come true was another.

His brain whirred with the ramifications of nailing this pitch and while a small part of him said leave it, the driven, proud part of him that had struggled for recognition his entire life screamed that he had a brilliant opportunity, one he couldn't afford to pass up.

As he watched Eve flick her shiny brown hair over her shoulder and laugh at something AJ said, he knew what he had to do.

Concentrate on business. Cool things off with Eve, despite the insane urge to do otherwise. And if he nailed the pitch, reached his goal, he'd worry about the rest of his dreams then.

Eve willed the miles between AJ's bayside mansion and her place away.

She had a plan. Get home, whip up her favourite prosciutto-wrapped chicken breast with fennel butter, followed by sticky date pudding and then subtly—or not—tell Bryce she'd changed her mind.

She wanted to date him, every scrumptious inch. His many facets intrigued her—suave and confident one minute, fun-loving and boyish the next. He'd slotted into the gang as if he'd known them for years, and while she'd wanted a date to impress them, he'd far surpassed expectations.

'You're awfully quiet.' He indicated, checked over his shoulder in his blind spot and pulled off the freeway. 'In fact, you've been silent the whole trip.'

'Just thinking.' If he only knew. 'I could say the same about you.'

'Business on the brain. You know how it is.'

'Yeah, I do.'

Though, lately, Soirée hadn't been occupying all her thoughts as it usually did. Uh-uh, he had pride of place there, easily superseding the upcoming AFL gala and the Spring Racing Carnival bonanza she had planned.

Her house came into view as he drove up the street, the cream-rendered bricks, Brunswick-green trim and terracotta window frames giving her a warm thrill, the same secure, satisfied feeling she had every day when she arrived home after a hard day's work.

'Would you like to—'

'I have to—'

They laughed and he waved his hand towards her. 'Ladies first.'

'I was wondering if you'd like to come in. I

can whip up some dinner. Open a bottle of wine.
Unwind a bit.'

His smile faded, his expression guarded, the
first time he'd looked at her with anything other
than warmth. 'Thanks, but I can't. I've got loads
of work to do.'

'Right.'

She forced a smile while silently chastising
herself for making such a hash of things last
night. She'd told him she wasn't interested and
he'd obviously taken her at her word.

'Another time, maybe?'

He paused, as if searching for the right words,
and her heart sank further.

'AJ has given me a shot at pitching for Hot
Pursuit's new ad campaign.'

She let out a long, low whistle through pursed
lips. 'Wow, that's great. Congratulations.'

'I haven't done anything yet. Which is why I
need to get my butt into gear. I have less than a
month to come up with the winning pitch.'

'Bet you'll do a brilliant job.'

She had no doubts. She'd Googled him when
she'd first seen that Net article, had read up on
his stellar career and lightning-fast rise to the top
of the ad world. He'd taken Sydney by storm,
bursting onto the scene from nowhere and now
he had his sights set on Melbourne.

She should be thankful. He'd never have

agreed to pose as her date if she hadn't dangled the contacts in front of him. She should be downright ecstatic her introductions had gone so well. Instead, she had the faintest sour feeling that now he had what he wanted he couldn't wait to see the back of her.

'We're still on for the launch party next week?'

His slow nod added to her growing foreboding. 'I'll have to see how things go work-wise. If I've got the basics down for the pitch, we'll go. Otherwise, I'll have to give it a miss.'

'That's fine.'

It wasn't and her impending sense of doom increased when he glanced at his watch, as if she was taking up too much of his precious time.

Slinging her bag over her shoulder, she opened the door. 'Thanks for accompanying me today.'

'My pleasure.'

Hating how needy she sounded, she said, 'I'll call you and let you know when the cocktail party for the video night is scheduled. Mattie isn't sure if they'll take a few extra days on their honeymoon or come back early for AJ's launch so she said she'd confirm by e-mail. Is that okay?'

'Sure.'

Sadness seeped into her heart, warring with embarrassment, making it ache the same way it had that night he'd turned his back and walked away from her.

Actually, no, this was worse—much worse. Back then, she hadn't known how wonderful he was, how warm and spontaneous and funny. Now she knew, having him shut down on her, using monosyllables for responses rather than the ribbing she'd grown accustomed to, hurt. More than it should.

'Bye.'

She held up a hand and almost tumbled out of the car in her haste to leave.

'Eve?'

Biting down on her bottom lip to stop it quivering, she forced herself to turn around.

'Yeah?'

'Thanks.'

Dusk cast long shadows over his car, over his face and she couldn't see his expression in the growing darkness so she had no idea if the wistful regret in his voice was real or a figment of her wishful imagination. 'For what?'

'For understanding.'

Nodding, she spun on her heel and headed for the door.

Understanding?

She didn't understand any of this, least of all the devastation wreaking havoc on her emotions as he gunned the engine and slid away from the kerb.

CHAPTER TEN

BRYCE shut down his PowerPoint presentation, scanning the conference table for some sign that his initial pitch wasn't complete rubbish.

Sol's ruddy face remained impassive, while Davin's complexion turned a pale shade of green, clear indication his presentation couldn't have been all bad.

'That's my initial idea. Angus Kilbride has never used Ballyhoo before so I thought I'd go in bold, with a fresh, new, in-your-face campaign. What do you think?'

Pin-drop silence, punctuated by the quiet shuffling of papers. No one wanted to say a thing, waiting for Sol to pronounce judgement before they backed him up like lapdogs.

He'd seen it all before. Creative copywriters waiting for the go-ahead before letting their imaginations run free, execs holding their breath for approval.

He'd been there, done that but this meant a whole lot more. Sol's endorsement of his Hot Pursuit pitch would make or break his career in Melbourne. The big guy had spelled it out for him and he'd make damn sure he delivered. Despite the potential minefield success would mean for his personal life.

Steepling his podgy fingers together, Sol leaned forward and fixed him with a probing stare.

'How soon can you get the rest done?'

'I'm working on it day and night.'

It consumed him, this quest to nail the Hot Pursuit contract. He'd always been driven, ever since he'd slaved nights to gain his high school diploma and, later, his economics degree.

No one had thought he could do it. He'd shown them all. And, when he secured this campaign, his professional reputation would be set. As for the rest…he'd decide what to do about the Eve situation when he reached his goal, not before.

Sol drummed his fingers together, his bulbous nose almost getting trapped between them, before he sat back and thumped his palms on the conference table with a decisive bang.

'Good work. And if you land this account it'll be nothing short of brilliant. Now, I want all of you to give Gibson whatever assistance he needs over the next fortnight to make this happen. Got that?'

Casting a look that meant business around the table, Sol left the room and everyone gave an audible sigh of relief.

Glowing inwardly from the high praise from a man of few words, he gathered up his laptop and presentation notes, eager to get cracking on the next stage of his pitch.

'Impressive.'

He glanced up at Davin, perched on the edge of the table, a sour-cum-smarmy expression on his face.

'Thanks.'

'How did you get an opportunity with Angus Kilbride? Rumour has it he's a hard nut to crack.'

'The usual meet and greet stuff. You know how it is.'

Davin's forehead crinkled in fake concentration. 'Actually, I don't. I've been scouting a meeting with the big guy for ages and no-go. Yet here you are, new to the Melbourne scene, and not only do you get to meet him, you get to pitch. Wish I knew your secret.'

'Hard work,' he bit out—*something you'd know nothing about.* 'Speaking of which, I have to get back to it. Later.'

Turning his back on Davin's speculative stare, he stalked from the conference room.

Thanks to Eve, he had a shot at this—a real

shot. And how had he thanked her? By burying his nose in work—work he still needed to complete to nail this campaign. He'd missed her—really missed her—and it had only been a few days.

While he may have wowed the boss with his preliminary outline, he needed to take this all the way and that meant keeping his distance from a guaranteed distraction in the form of one luscious woman.

Then again, since when had he ever not taken a risk?

'Thought you were too busy to attend this launch party?'

Bryce handed Eve a champagne flute filled to the brim. 'It's work. Gives me a feel for the current mob Hot Pursuit are using, hopefully gives me an edge for my pitch.'

'Right. Work.'

She sipped at her champagne, her melted chocolate eyes fixed on him as if she could see right through him.

Work was the excuse he'd cited for being here while the beautiful woman with a knowing glint in her eyes and coy smile curving her lips saw it for the feeble lie it was.

He was here because of her, because he couldn't stay away, no matter how focused he was supposed to be on business, how terrified he was of achieving his goal and losing his excuse not to pursue her for real.

Biting back a grin the longer she stared at him with awareness making her eyes sparkle, he pointed to a giant billboard-size poster of the latest and greatest athletic shoe.

'See that? I'm feeling inspired just looking at it.'

Her smile widened as she lowered her champagne flute. 'Oh, really? And what type of slogan would you come up with for that? Have shoe—will travel?'

She tapped her bottom lip—her deliciously full, glossy bottom lip—as she pretended to think. 'These shoes were made for jogging and one of these days these shoes will run all over you?'

He chuckled as she snapped her fingers. 'I've got it. How about blue suede running shoes?'

'You've missed your calling. You should be in the ad business.'

She crooked her finger and he happily leaned forward, all too glad to inhale her soft vanilla fragrance, to have her arm brush against his jacket.

'And give you some stiff competition?' Laughing, she patted his cheek. 'I wouldn't be that mean.'

Touching his cheek had been a joke, part of

the word play, but the instant her soft palm
scraped against him he wanted to haul her into
his arms and have her touch him all over.

The thought inflamed him further and he
needed a distraction, needed to deflect some of
the heat back on to her. If not seeing her for a
week did this to him, how the hell would he
survive when their month came to an end?

When her hand dropped, he quickly grabbed
it, sliding his fingers between hers and holding
on tight.

'What's got into you?'

She blushed, glanced away. 'I don't know
what you mean.'

Tipping up her chin so she had no option but
to look at him, he said, 'I think you do.'

Her eyes widened with understanding before
snapping shut, shutting out the heat flaring
between them, the heat slowly simmering to
burning point.

'You've been different tonight. More chatty,
more lively, more at ease.' He squeezed her hand
before drawing it up, unfurling her fingers from
between his and placing a soft kiss on the palm.
'As for touching my cheek, you don't usually
initiate physical contact, so I'll repeat the
question. What's got into you?'

Curling her fingers over the kiss, he took pity
on her, dazed expression and all, and released

her hand. 'Not that I mind, but I'm curious. Does absence make the heart grow fonder?'

'You're teasing me.'

She rolled her eyes, but not before he'd glimpsed a shimmer of fear—genuine fear—as if he'd asked a question she had no hope of answering.

He'd known that feeling back in school way too many times to be comfortable. If she used a smart-assed comeback, he'd know she was floundering out of her depth as much as he used to.

'As for what's got into me, this stuff will do wonders for giving a girl false ideas of flirting grandeur.'

She raised her half-empty champagne glass in a silent toast. 'With the absence thing, it's only been seven days, five hours and thirty-three minutes. Give a girl some time to miss you.'

Oh, yeah, she was definitely out of her depth. And if she kept looking at him with stars in her eyes, he'd know the feeling.

'There you go again. Cracking a funny.' Bending down, he whispered in her ear, 'Almost flirting!'

Batting her eyelashes, she pulled back enough to give him an outrageously false innocent look. 'Is it working?'

'Hell, yeah.'

Before he could think or rationalise or second-guess himself, he backed her into a nearby corner and kissed her, pouring all his pent-up frustration and desire and driving need into it.

God, he'd missed her. Missed being near her, missed hearing her laugh, missed basking in her warmth cloaked in the elegant cool only she did so well.

A small moan escaped her lips as he manoeuvred them deeper into the shadows and he eased off the pressure, giving her a chance to stop this madness.

In response, her hands snaked around his neck, pulling his head closer, and he didn't need a second invitation as he took her mouth again, teased her lips apart, tasted her, feasted. His mouth was ravenous, his entire body on fire as they kissed as if there were no tomorrow.

But there was a tomorrow, and a day after that, and another after that, each and every day filled with work he couldn't lose sight of, no matter how tempting the distraction.

Gently disengaging, he leaned his forehead against hers, murmured, 'Wow.'

Her soft, ragged breathing did little to calm his libido and he reluctantly straightened, needing distance, needing perspective, needing a cold shower. A month's worth to cool his desire for the woman staring at him with the same dazed passion reflecting in his stare.

'You keep making a habit of that.'

'Some habits are harder to break than others.'

Dragging a hand through his hair, beyond rattled when it shook slightly, he settled for thrusting it into his pocket to stop himself from reaching for her. 'And you, Eve Pemberton, are fast becoming one habit I'd very much like to keep.'

Her gobsmacked expression had him mentally slapping a hand over his mouth. Damn his hormones for making him run off at the mouth.

He should've kept this light-hearted, in the spirit of the casual flirting they'd been doing all evening. Instead, he'd blurted what he'd been thinking and now had to do some serious back-pedalling.

'Then again, I've learned to manage my habits, bad ones and all.'

Her hand crept up to her mouth, her fingertips absentmindedly touching her bottom lip, and he gritted his teeth to dampen the urge to do the same.

'Are you saying I'm bad for you?'

'I'm saying you're bad for my concentration.'

'And you need to concentrate right now because?'

'Work, remember? The reason I'm here.'

'The only reason?'

She wouldn't let him off the hook, damn it.

'Because, while this is coming up with perfectly logical rationale—' she pointed to his head '—this is having a hard time keeping up.'

She rubbed her thumb along his bottom lip and he bit back a groan, wondering where this temptress had emerged from, desperately needing the old Eve to put in an appearance right about now.

'No more kisses. Promise.'

'Too bad.'

With a last longing glance at his mouth, she sauntered away, leaving him cursing his impulse to come tonight, cursing her power over him and cursing the day he'd agreed to this stupid dating deal.

Eve knew he'd come after her.

Bryce was that sort of guy. Always up for a challenge. And she'd been stupid enough to issue one. All fine and dandy in the heat of the moment with his lips robbing her of all rational thought, but now her meagre supply of courage had run out, she was in trouble. Big trouble. The kind of trouble that couldn't be erased with more fake flirting or steamy eye contact.

She'd wanted to prove a point tonight, to show him she'd changed her mind about her *I don't want a relationship* stance.

What had she said to him in the car last week? Something along the lines of, 'I don't have time for a relationship. It's not what I want right now.'

Yeah, right. Not only had she changed her mind, she'd lost it completely. If the Silver Streak had worked a treat, the Red Peril she'd worn tonight was in a class of its own. Tight. Sprayed-on tight. Sleeveless, knee-skimming, cleavage-peeping. If the cut didn't grab a guy's attention, the colour would, the gorgeous pomegranate crimson making her stand out in a crowd of Melbourne black.

She'd never worn anything like it—probably wouldn't again—but, for tonight, for the last few hours, she'd felt like a different woman, had acted like a different woman.

If Bryce didn't get the idea now he never would and, when he came after her, she'd tell him. Once she'd downed another champagne or ten.

'Hey, wait up!'

He grabbed her arm, the instant sizzle of heat licking along her skin like an electric shock.

'I'm after a refill.' She held up her empty flute, knowing a bottomless glass wouldn't give her enough courage to carry through with the rest of her plan tonight. 'Back in a sec.'

'Eve, this isn't going to work.'

Her heart stalled, her confidence rapidly dwindling in the face of his sombreness.

'It's only another champagne—'

'You look amazing.' His gaze raked her body, set it alight, as she clutched her glass to stop herself from folding her arms over her chest where the evidence of just how much she burned for him was on clear show. '*You're* amazing but I can't do this right now.'

She could've pretended to misunderstand him again, could've made another joke but the time for kidding was over.

This was too important to her. *He* was too important to her.

'Why?'

His lips compressed, his determined stare bored into her, willing her to understand.

'Because nailing this pitch is critical.'

She clamped down on the little exasperated snort that escaped before she could stop it. 'Lots of people date and work. Most of the known universe, in fact.'

'Sorry, I have goals.' Shaking his head, he thrust his hands into his pockets. 'I can't afford the distraction.'

'Guess I should be flattered I can distract you.'

Her sarcasm elicited an instant response, mischief sparking his eyes.

'You could distract a monastery of meditating monks.'

Her mouth twitched at his analogy but she wouldn't let this go. She'd come this far; she would use up the last of her courage before she rehung the Red Peril in the closet and reverted to unruffled, non-confrontational Eve.

Jabbing a finger at him, she said, 'You're the one who's kissed me repeatedly and who's pulled back. What gives?'

'Kissing you was a mistake.'

'Oh, thanks very much,' she snapped, hating the blossoming hurt making her heart ache.

If she'd harboured any doubts she wasn't in over her head with this so-called platonic dating deal, the spreading pain in the vicinity of her masochistic heart put paid to that little delusion. Over her head? She was seriously drowning.

'I didn't mean it like that.'

He cupped her cheek, stroked it with his thumb and her heart lay down and waved a white flag in surrender.

'Kissing you was a mistake because I want to do it again and again and again. It's a mistake because I don't want to stop there.'

His hand dropped but his beseeching gaze never left hers. 'But, most of all, it's a mistake because when I kiss you I can't think of anything else and I can't afford that. Not now.'

Motivational music blared at that moment, loud and uncompromising, as AJ wandered onto a stage with several lithe models clad in minimal Lycra and Hot Pursuit's latest and greatest sneakers.

The fanfare didn't impress her but Bryce's eyes lit up as he scanned the scenario, taking it all in.

She had her answer right then.

'This is everything to you, isn't it? Winning this ad campaign?'

He tore his gaze from the stage, refocused on her and she knew his response before he spoke.

'I need to do this.'

'And us?'

Regret clouded his eyes. 'We carry on as we agreed at the start.'

Clamping down on the urge to rant and rave at the injustice of sticking to a stupid deal of her own invention, she nodded. 'Business as usual. Got it, loud and clear.'

This time when she walked away, she knew he wouldn't follow.

CHAPTER ELEVEN

Eve had cooked up a storm.

For the last four days straight.

When she wasn't at the office she was in the kitchen, taking out her frustrations by pummelling dough, tenderising meat and kneading pasta. All perfectly good venting activities involving loads of fist-thumping and hammering and wringing—the type of activities she'd like to practise on the man who'd caused this cooking frenzy in the first place.

The therapeutic cook-off hadn't worked. She was still mad—mad as hell. She was over it, over him.

Maybe not quite over him… Okay, okay, she had as much chance of getting over him as strolling down Chapel Street in her Ugg boots and tracksuit *sans* make-up.

Bryce blew hotter and colder than a Melbourne spring change. Kissing her one minute, citing business the next.

If he'd done it once she might've accepted his brush-off and believed he was a workaholic. But he'd done it several times, had hinted he wanted more from their dating deal at the rehearsal dinner with all that guff about plans evolving and changing, before backing off quicker than the boys she'd asked to take her to the prom.

It didn't add up.

She hadn't made it to the top of Melbourne's events consultancies without being able to read people and, right now, Bryce was hiding something.

For a moment she'd wondered if he was as fickle as she'd pegged him at Tony's party, ditching the nice act the moment he'd been given a shot at AJ's advertising contract, but common sense said otherwise.

By the heat of his kisses, his reluctance to stay away despite citing business, his reaction every time he kissed her, then backed off, she'd say he was torn.

Why? Darn it, none of this made sense.

She could always ask him.

Wrinkling her nose at the thought, she stirred the chilli con carne faster, moving the wooden spoon in concentric circles, the rhythmic action soothing, as always.

She did need to call him, to hand over some documents AJ had given her via Mattie. Her first reaction had been to fob them off but how would it look, a girlfriend not passing on documents to her boyfriend, who they assumed she'd see before them?

Prevaricating for the last few hours, she'd picked up the phone several times, only to drop the receiver and resume cooking, ignoring the pile of papers that taunted her from their place in the corner.

She had to hand over the documents, no choice; great, she'd known things would get complicated the longer she perpetuated this fraud.

With a defeatist groan, she propped the spoon in its holder, turned down the stove and picked up the phone. Punching in the numbers, she waited, rearranging the spice rack with fiddling fingers as she gritted her teeth through the first ring…the second…the third…

'Hello?'

'Bryce, it's me.'

'Hey, Eve. How's it going?'

No hesitation, which had to be a good sign, right? And he sounded genuinely pleased to hear from her, another plus, so she ploughed on before she lost her cool.

'Great. Thought I'd give you a quick buzz and let you know AJ gave me some documents you might be interested in for your pitch.'

A pause followed—a long, loaded pause

where her heart almost burst out of her chest. Even if he didn't want to see her, surely he'd want the documents for his all-important work?

'Thanks, I'll swing by and pick those up some time but right now I've got a ton of work to do.'

'Me too.'

'Look, I have to duck out and have dinner anyway so why don't I drop by afterwards? Promise I won't stay long.'

Her gaze drifted to the simmering chilli on the stove, the tantalising aroma making her nose twitch. She'd cooked enough for a hungry posse; wouldn't it make sense to invite him to share as he'd be coming over anyway? How bad would it look when he dropped by, saw all the food and realised she hadn't asked him to dinner?

But sitting together at the table, sharing dinner, reeked of intimacy and he'd made it clear he wanted to keep his distance.

'Eve, if it's a problem, I can—'

'No problem. It's just that I've cooked a huge batch of chilli, so if you're busy with work, rather than wasting time ordering takeaway, why don't you eat here?'

He hesitated and she screwed up her face in embarrassment.

'Honestly? I've had my nose to the grindstone all day, I haven't had time to eat and the thought of your chilli is making me even hungrier.'

At least her cooking could achieve what she only dreamed about her body doing.

'In fact, I'm starving. I'll be there in half an hour. Do you want me to bring anything?'

You—only you.

Shaking herself out of her wishful reverie, she propped the phone between ear and shoulder as she opened the oven, donned mitts and slid freshly baked tortillas out.

'Yeah, a healthy appetite. I have enough food here for a small army.'

'A healthy appetite, huh?'

Her flushed cheeks had nothing to do with the wave of heat emanating from the oven and everything to do with the sudden shift in tone from light-hearted to sexy in a second.

Gulping, she desperately wished for a free hand to fan her scorching cheeks. 'Uh-huh. See you soon.'

She rang off and slid the baking tray onto the stove top before she burned her hands.

Considering the way she reacted to a simple shift in Bryce's mood, she hoped that was the only thing at risk of being burned.

He was a sucker for a pretty face.

That was Bryce's excuse and he was sticking to it as he trudged up the manicured path to Eve's front door, hoping he didn't lose his cool completely and give in to this incessant, over-whelming need to make Eve his.

He'd been neck-deep in work when she'd called, cursing the phone when it broke his concentration, but the instant he'd heard her voice, warm and soft and tentative, he'd wanted to hang up and race to her house ASAP.

Sucker.

She stimulated on every level: intellectually, physically and, for the first time ever, emotionally.

He'd never had such a connection with anybody and it scared him. He'd always faced his fears—faced and conquered them—and he'd be damned if he let an inconsequential, irrational fear of falling for Eve stop him from being her friend.

It was the least he could do after she'd given him this amazing opportunity through AJ and, while he may not be able to date her, why couldn't they hang out together as buddies?

Yeah, buddies. He could do that.

However, as she opened the front door to his knock, being buddies with this incredibly beautiful woman was the last thing on his mind.

'Hi, come on in.'

She held the door open and he struggled not to gape as the muted hall light streaked russet through her warm molasses hair, falling in disarray around her face. Her brown eyes shone with welcoming warmth and her designer jeans and T-shirt clung to her sleek frame as if they'd been poured on.

Breathtakingly, heart-stoppingly beautiful. Not in the classic sense of the word but, put together in a dazzling combination, Eve was all that and then some.

With a rueful smile, she rubbed her nose. 'Have I got a chilli smudge here?'

Mentally kicking himself for staring when he was supposed to be playing it cool, he shook his head. 'No, I think my eyes are glassy from staring at the computer screen too long. Sorry if I was rude.'

Her smile widened, genuine and perceptive; she didn't buy his woeful excuse and he didn't blame her. For someone good at thinking on his feet, that had been lame.

'Not at all. My eyes get that way too.'

Stepping into the hallway, the rich aroma of chilli and toasted bread filled the air and his tummy rumbled, reminding him of exactly how long it had been since he'd eaten.

'Sounds like someone's ready for dinner.'

She chuckled at his emphatic nod and ushered him through to the kitchen. 'We'll eat first, then I'll get you that paperwork.'

'Good idea,' he said, instantly entranced by the warmth, the smells and the vision of Eve totally at home behind the kitchen bench as he placed his load on a dresser in the corner.

He'd never had this. His mum's work hours at the hospital delivering babies had almost been as maniacal as his dad's and he'd rarely had a home-cooked meal. Not that he'd minded. The less he saw of his folks the better. The rare times they were home they'd only paid him cursory attention anyway, once they discovered he wasn't the child prodigy they'd hoped for.

Occasionally, after winning a pitch, in the quiet of his apartment, nursing a cold beer, he'd wonder if that was why he'd set himself the goal of achieving financial success before he would ever consider pursuing his secret dream—the warm, loving family he'd never had.

Did he equate success in his chosen field with being worthy enough to win the love of a good woman?

It had worked for his dad; his mum had eyes only for him, had barely acknowledged her only child and, while he'd shrugged off their unforgivable coldness growing up, he wondered if his yearning for a family the opposite of his was what drove him every day, what drove him towards his goal despite the deep-seated fear of what he'd have to risk once he achieved it.

'Need a hand?'

He headed for the island bench, propped

himself on a stool and the warmth in her answering smile had him wanting to vault the bench and kiss her silly.

'Thanks, but I've got it covered. Fancy a wine?'

I fancy you.

His body clamoured to re-create the sparks they'd ignited with their kisses, to explore the heat simmering like their dinner on the stove. But he'd made his choice. Business over pleasure and he had to stick to it. Achieving his goal depended on it.

'I'd better not. Need to keep a clear head while I put the finishing touches on my presentation.'

She quirked an eyebrow as she ladled out chilli con carne into a serving dish. 'Wow, you have been working night and day if you're nearly finished.'

He gathered up the plates and cutlery, followed her to the cosy dining table, where he set two places before pulling out her chair.

'I'm manic when I have a deadline.'

'So I gathered. Tortilla?'

'Thanks.'

Somehow, his mention of work stifled their conversation and they ate in silence, the quiet punctuated with the odd 'pass the salt' or 'more water'.

As far as meals went, the food was fantastic

but he missed the easy-going rapport they'd had when she'd cooked for him before, missed the sassy sparkle in her eyes, the playful smiles.

Then again, he wanted it this way, remember?

Buddies was good, anything more potentially disastrous.

This wasn't a good idea.

The fraught silence over dinner had bothered him so, rather than grabbing AJ's documents and making a run for it, he'd suggested he look over them here, over coffee.

One problem: how was a guy expected to concentrate on work when he had one big distraction wrapped up in a too-snug cardigan sitting opposite him?

It wasn't as if Eve was interrupting him, far from it. While he pretended to peruse the documents, Eve had sat down to work, ducking behind her laptop screen, tapping away on the keyboard, jotting down notes on a giant yellow notepad.

In fact, everything on her desk was yellow, from an oversized stapler to her Filofax, with a huge bunch of yellow roses in a clear cut-glass vase in the middle. It was a bright, sunny environment to work in, even on a darkening spring evening. He briefly wondered what she'd make of his work station at home: clear, functional, uncluttered.

He needed it that way to help him think, to help him use the methods he'd learned to optimise his performance. A performance in dire straits if he didn't concentrate on his presentation and not on the intriguing woman opposite.

He dropped his gaze back to the documents as she shifted in her seat but found his gaze unwittingly drifting upwards again when she resettled.

Picking up a pencil, she tapped it against her notepad, lost in thought, absentmindedly gnawing on her bottom lip, the action almost making him groan out loud with the frustration of how much he'd like to do the same.

Unfortunately, he must've made some sound because she looked up, her eyes wide and enquiring.

'Just thinking,' he said, linking his hands and stretching overhead, hoping she'd buy his nonchalant act.

Her gaze drifted to his chest and the spark of interest there had him wanting to drag her across the desk and into his arms, nonchalance be damned.

'How's it coming along?'

'Not bad.' He held up his Eee PC where he'd been making notes. 'This new software I'm using is great.'

'Anything I could use?'

Silently cursing his slip of the tongue, he shook his head. That was all he needed—for her to take a look at it and see why he used something like it.

'Doubt it, it's ad specific.'

'Okay.'

Her dubious glance had him gripping the end of the table to prevent himself from ducking around the other side and hugging her for sounding like a grouch.

'I don't know about you, but I've been at it all day and my brain's entering meltdown mode.'

She waved towards the screen, a slight frown puckering her brow. 'Me, too. The AFL are major league with their demands. Think I'm having a mini confidence crisis.'

'Don't. Your business success speaks for itself. You must be brilliant at what you do.'

Gratitude shimmered in her eyes before her gaze flickered back to the screen again. 'Thanks for the pep talk. I need it to pull this off.'

He studied her—so serious, so dedicated—and he was instantly transported back to their high school days when he'd wander into their kitchen with Tony, only to find Eve permanently seated at the table with her nose in a book. He'd always thought she was cute, even with those god-awful glasses and clothes she used to wear. Something about her eyes and her shy smile had tugged deep.

'What happened to your glasses?'

Her gaze snapped up to his, wary and shuttered. 'Contact lenses. More user-friendly.'

'I remember how you used to push those glasses up your nose constantly when they slid down.'

He also remembered how she'd bake choc-chip cookies for her dad, just because he liked them, how she'd buy sourdough bread because Tony wouldn't eat any other kind, how she'd managed to keep house and cook and excel at her studies, while having a ready smile and a kind word when Tony and her dad walked through the door.

She'd been amazing—was amazing—and he'd been a fool for hurting her the night of Tony's party, for letting her believe he didn't care, when he did.

'You remember?' Her eyebrows shot up at a rate of knots. 'That's right; you used to tease me about them.'

Remorse prickled him, along with a nasty urge to tell her the truth. But he couldn't. If he told her, she'd either pity him or go all soft and comforting. He was having a hard enough time holding her at bay now; what chance would he have if she turned soppy and wanted to hug him?

'I didn't call you four-eyes, though.'

'Bet you thought it.' She scrutinised him, her stare cool and assessing. 'Can I ask you something?'

'Sure.'

'Why did you acknowledge me at our place and not at school?'

Damn, he should never have gone down the reminiscing track. Now he'd have to make up something halfway plausible so that she wouldn't probe him for the truth.

'Because I was an obnoxious little jerk?'

She didn't buy his lame attempt at humour. 'Tell me why.'

Hell, she wouldn't let this go.

Pushing back from the desk, he placed the Eee PC on the desk and folded his arms. He'd have to opt for partial honesty. By the astute expression on her face, she wouldn't settle for anything less.

'Honestly? You intimidated me.'

'What?'

Her mouth dropped open, a surprised O.

'Crazy, huh? At home, you seemed more approachable. At school, you were this super-smart brain, always with your nose in a book and I was a goof-off, the kid who used his mouth to get a few laughs rather than get ahead. Guess I didn't want to run the risk of you cutting me down to size with some of those big words you knew.'

By the softening around her mouth and the appreciative gleam in her eyes, she believed him.

Sad thing was, he almost wished he could tell her the rest—the real reason why she'd intimidated him.

That was what happened when you had a belly full of food and a woman staring at you with a scary mix of need and warmth and understanding in her entrancing chocolate-brown eyes.

'I would never have done that.'

She reached over and placed a comforting hand on his forearm and he gritted his teeth to stop himself from placing his hand over it.

'Yeah, but I was an egotistical brat. My behaviour had nothing to do with you. You asked why I did it; I told you. Now, do you mind if I get back to this?'

Their growing intimacy shattered with his sharp comeback and she snatched her hand away before ducking behind her screen again.

'Fine.'

He'd hurt her. She'd only been concerned and he'd clammed up because she was getting too close.

He should be glad, for there'd been several tension-filled moments during dinner where he'd seen the need in her eyes, the passion bubbling below her cool exterior.

He'd almost given in, almost gone for it, despite the precious campaign. But his goal was ingrained, programmed into his psyche and he couldn't bomb, no matter how much he wanted her.

His jaw clenched, stifling the urge to explain, before he forced himself to relax. 'Eve, I'm sorry—'

'Don't be. I'm the one who's been a fool, hoping there was more to our friendship than my dating deal, trying to get a handle on what makes you tick, but hey, don't worry. I was obviously wrong.'

'This isn't what you think.'

Her gaze pierced him, fierce, angry.

'Then what is it?'

Shaking his head, he ran a hand through his hair, searching for the right words, his brain a scary jumble of letters and combinations he remembered all too well.

'Don't answer that. I know what's going on here. This dating thing is a business transaction, nothing more. I won't make the mistake of reading more into it again.'

He could've refuted it, could've blurted a truth he'd kept hidden from everyone for a lifetime but, instead, he nodded, shut down his small PC and picked up the paperwork.

She avoided looking at him as he stood and, while his feet urged him to make a run for it, he couldn't leave like this.

'Thanks for a great meal.'

He moved past her before stopping and laying a hand on her shoulder, his heart lurching when she stiffened. 'I wish things were different.'

He didn't stick around long enough to hear her whisper, 'Me, too'.

CHAPTER TWELVE

'YOU'VE got yourself a deal.'

Bryce stared at AJ, hoping his growing grin came across as professional and not goofy.

He'd done it.

His pitch had won Hot Pursuit's advertising campaign for the next year. All his hard work had paid off, all his sacrifices, namely losing any chance he had with Eve to benefit his career.

Was he happy? Hell, yeah, but the thought of what he'd potentially lost with Eve took the gloss off what should be a watershed moment.

'Great, thanks very much.'

He shook AJ's hand, sent a polite nod around the table at the sporting company's execs.

'We'll schedule another meeting for early next week to get the ball rolling, okay?'

Laughter followed AJ's statement as he tossed a football into the air and, once again, Bryce was struck by the mateship he'd seen in evidence at this company.

Sure, he hadn't been at Ballyhoo long but their meetings never had this kind of feel, a sincere camaraderie between colleagues who genuinely loved their job. Come to think of it, none of the agencies he'd worked at in Sydney had been like this either, but then the ad world was probably more cut-throat than sporting goods.

'I'll tee up the appointment.'

Gathering his presentation, he waved to the group. 'Nice meeting you all. Look forward to working with you.'

He left on a general chorus of goodbyes, waiting until he got outside the conference room to punch the air with a satisfying, 'Yes!'

He couldn't wait to get back to the office and tell Sol the good news.

His job was secure.

Until the next pitch.

The thought pulled him up short, garnering strange looks from the young receptionist behind the front desk.

Where had that come from? He was used to the competitive nature of his field, usually thrived on it. What was different this time? He should be shouting his success from the top of his apartment building, yet something had taken the edge off his victory and he knew exactly what that was.

Eve.

He couldn't get her out of his head, particularly the hurt look in her eyes when they'd had dinner.

He'd avoided her since, citing work issues to soothe his niggling conscience. Not that she'd called and, considering the way they'd left things, she probably wouldn't. The cocktail party and wedding video night was tomorrow and after that she wouldn't want to see him again.

How easy it had sounded at the beginning: act as her date, walk away at the end with a few business contacts under his belt. He'd never expected to feel like this. Surprised, uncertain, scared, a stupid, irrational fear that in playing this dating game, he'd come out the loser.

He hadn't expected to like her this much, hadn't expected the kindling spark the night of Tony's party to still be there; worse, for it to flare to life in a scorching whoosh of flames that threatened to consume them both.

Sealing this deal had been a major goal. Not just establishing his reputation at Ballyhoo, but financially. Ever since he'd started work he'd had a plan. Reach five million in earnings and maybe he'd have something to offer a woman, enough for her to take a chance on him, encumbrances and all.

He'd plucked the figure out of the air at the time, not interested in a relationship with anyone, focused solely on success.

Now he'd achieved his goal. And there was a woman in the picture. A beautiful, intelligent woman he could now offer something to without guaranteed rejection. Not that money would matter to her—Eve was successful in her own right, had a lucrative business and a house in a posh suburb with all the trimmings—but it mattered to him in a non-mercenary, vindicating achievement way. He'd battled long and hard to get where he was today, had consistently avoided getting close to anyone.

What if he didn't want to walk away this time?

Pity he'd made a mess of things. Maybe if he devoted half as much time to figuring out what he really wanted with Eve as he had to his pitch he might actually stand a chance at resurrecting the burgeoning relationship he'd botched before it had really begun.

He'd give it a go.

What did he have to lose?

If Eve had to force another brittle smile, her face would crack.

She hated this. Pretending everything was okay with Bryce, having him back to his usual flirty self, putting on a show for her friends while they tossed popcorn at each other and made rude jokes about Mattie and AJ as they did a bit of dirty dancing, bridal waltz style, on the video.

She should be good at acting. It was what she did every day, put on a brave face to hide the insecure mess she was inside.

But tonight was different. She'd reached the end of her tolerance and knew when Bryce dropped her home she'd be struggling not to bawl, or hang onto him, whichever was worse.

'Who's up for another piña colada?'

Mattie held up the jug to a chorus of affirmative cheers while Eve surreptitiously nudged her half-empty glass under the coffee table. That was all she needed, for the alcohol to make her more maudlin.

'You okay?'

Hell, no. She hadn't been okay since she'd first caught sight of his picture on the Internet and was stupid enough to coerce him into dating her to prove a point to her friends.

But she couldn't say that—any of it—with Bryce staring at her with concern.

'I'm fine. Alcohol always makes me sleepy.'

'Well, no more for you, then. We still have another hour or so of making fun of the bride and groom to go yet.'

She forced a smile again, surprised her cheeks didn't seize with the effort.

Leaning closer, he murmured in her ear, 'I know you're not okay. Do you want to leave?'

She shook her head, horrified he'd seen

through her act, and bit down on her bottom lip to keep from crying.

'Hey…' He slipped an arm around her waist and cuddled her close, not giving an inch when she initially refused to lean into him. 'You haven't been yourself all evening and I'm betting the last time we met has something to do with that. I promise we'll talk after we leave.'

She didn't want to talk. She'd already tried that and look where it had got her—with him telling her he didn't want to get involved.

No, it was past time for talking. Way past time considering the hollowness deep in her soul, the empty ache because she was missing out on something great.

'Excuse me.' She surged off the floor and made a beeline for the bathroom, needing space to collect her wits before she fell apart.

As she slammed the bathroom door, leaned against it and took great shuddering breaths, she knew it would take a lifetime to get past this feeling, this feeling she daren't name for recognising how monumentally stupid she might've been in falling for a guy like Bryce.

She waited a full five minutes before reopening the door, only to be confronted by the bridal babes lined up against the opposite wall, arms folded, expressions concerned.

'You ok, hon?'

Mattie rushed forward first, slipping an arm around her waist, while Carol and Linda crowded her from the other side.

'You don't look so good,' Carol said, while Linda merely tut-tutted.

A hand flew over Mattie's mouth. 'You're not…?' She sent a pointed look at her belly.

Eve shrieked, 'No way!'

'Right, guess that settles that.' Linda, the ever pragmatic one, bustled them towards the backdoor. 'Pow-wow. Now.'

Eve loved her friends but talking was the last thing she felt like right now. She wanted to get this evening over and done with, and never have to see Bryce again.

Then why did the thought of watching him walk out of her life send her into an emotional free fall she had no hope of recovering from?

'Something's wrong, hon, and if you don't tell us you know we're going to drag it out of you eventually.'

Mattie's belligerent expression was matched by Carol and Linda and she knew from past experience they wouldn't leave her alone until she gave them something, so she blurted the first and foremost thing in her head.

'I'm in love with Bryce.'

'But that's great!'

Mattie clapped excitedly while Carol and Linda did a little jig.

'It's about time. We'd just about given up on you, what with you burying yourself in work or holing up at home.'

She shook her head, trying not to blame the girls for getting her into this predicament. She might've wanted to avoid being the only single bridesmaid among all their gushing wedded bliss but she'd been the one stupid enough to fall in love with a guy so wrong for her.

Shaking her head, she plopped down onto a garden bench and sagged against it.

'It's not great.'

'Why?'

She waited until the girls sat next to her, jostling for the position closest to her, before she continued her sorry tale.

'I've lied to all of you. Bryce and I aren't dating for real.'

Three mouths dropped open in unison.

'You're always so gung-ho at weddings. Roping me into bridesmaid duties, making sure I don't feel left out. Either that or you're feeling sorry for me and, honestly, I'm tired of being single and I didn't want you worrying about me at Mattie's wedding so I got Bryce to agree to be my date.'

Mattie was the first to close her mouth, only to open it again a second later. 'But this doesn't make any sense. You two are the real deal. Anyone can see that. The way he looks at you, the way you glow around him—how can that be fake?'

Carol laid a hand on Mattie's arm. 'Let her finish.' Sending her a curious look, she said, 'There's more, isn't there?'

Eve nodded, relaunched into her story.

'Bryce was my brother's best mate in high school. We used to chat a bit back then but I didn't really know him.' Discounting that one amazing night when she thought she had, only to have him walk away regardless. 'We're opposites in every way imaginable and I was the one who stipulated our dating be platonic but...' She trailed off, struck once again by how pathetic she was in falling for him.

'But you went and fell in love for real,' Linda finished, reaching out to rub her back. 'It's okay, sweetie. Why don't you tell him how you feel? I think you'll be verbalising what he's feeling too.'

Shuddering at the thought of having that particular conversation with Bryce after he'd said a resounding no to dating for real, she shook her head.

'Aren't you guys the teensiest bit mad I deceived you?'

To her amazement, they laughed before Mattie leaned forward and chucked her under the chin.

'Hon, we get it. It's hard being single, even harder having your friends fussing over your personal life and making you trudge up the aisle in front of them repeatedly. We just want you to be happy and now you are.'

'But I'm not, I'm miserable.'

'With the potential to be happier than you've ever been if you *talk* to the guy.'

'But he doesn't feel the same way.'

Linda rolled her eyes. 'Trust us on this one, sweet-cakes. He does feel the same way. We've seen his look before—on Anton, Duane and AJ. The guy's not only smitten with you, he's head over heels.'

Fear, potent and consuming, churned in her gut. She'd already tried talking to Bryce and look where that had got her: with a swift *thanks, but no thanks*.

He simply wasn't interested in her that way and everything that had happened between them had either been an act for the benefit of her friends or a spur of the moment thing. What guy wouldn't say no to a girl who was practically draped all over him and, sadly, that was how she must've come across: desperate and dateless. She shuddered and swiped a hand across her eyes.

'Hon, you have to do this. Otherwise, you may lose out on the best thing that ever happened to you.'

Tired of talking, exhausted down to her bones, Eve knew she'd have to agree to get the girls to leave her alone. Right now, she wanted to head home, relax and wallow in her misery. If that happened to involve drowning her sorrows in a litre tub of cherry ice cream, all the better.

Standing, she brushed off her skirt. 'Thanks for the advice, and for being so understanding. I think it's time I headed home and did something about this.'

Like delete Bryce's number from her phone's auto dial.

Mattie jumped to her feet and clapped her hands. 'That's the way. Tackle these guys head-on. Trust me, they don't know what hits them.'

Linda and Carol chuckled and, as the girls headed back inside, Eve knew there'd be no tackling Bryce.

About anything.

'Man, have you got it bad.'

Bryce wrenched his attention away from the window and back to AJ, passing another round of beers to the guys.

'Sorry, what did you say?'

Duane sniggered and Anton placed a thumb in the middle of his forehead.

'Mate, she's got you under her thumb already

and you aren't even hitched yet. Let me tell you, it only gets worse from here.'

Bryce darted another quick glance out of the window. 'I'm worried about her.'

AJ nodded and raised his beer in his direction. 'See? Smitten.'

Duane toasted him too. 'Yeah, Eve's not in the room for a few minutes and you can't stop looking out for her.'

'But she bolted out of here like there's something seriously wrong.' And he had an awful sinking feeling he knew why.

Duane slung an arm around his shoulders. 'Listen, mate. I'm going to give you some free advice. Women are impossible to understand so there's no use even trying. And once you fall for them it gets a hundred times worse. So chill out. Go with the flow. Whatever's bugging her, she'll tell you soon enough. Trust me, she'll spend hours telling you, going on and on and on…'

The guys laughed while Bryce knew he'd blown it. Something he hoped to change later tonight. He'd give it his best shot; a small part of him hoped she wouldn't be acting this way unless she cared.

Anton's speculative look held a hint of steel beneath. 'Just make sure you treat her right. Eve's had it tough.'

He didn't want to talk about her like this, not

with a bunch of guys he'd only recently met. He didn't know what galled him more: the fact these guys knew her better than he did or the fact he wanted to glean as much info from them about her as he could.

'How tough?'

'Carol said Eve's dad died when she was eighteen and she lost the family home. Then her brother ups and leaves for overseas a few years later and she's been on her own ever since. She works damn hard, rarely dates, likes her solitude.'

AJ scratched his head, crinkling his forehead. 'Come to think of it, you're the first guy we've ever seen her date.'

Duane chuckled. 'Yeah, so there's no pressure on you or anything.'

Anton and AJ joined in. 'And don't forget you have to answer to us if you muck her around.'

These guys genuinely cared about Eve and it warmed his heart. He'd already judged them to be good guys and seeing how much they cared about her raised them in his esteem more.

Plonking his beer down on the table, he stood up. 'Thanks, guys, but I have no intention of mucking Eve around. She's too special for that.'

He strode towards the door amid catcalls and wolf whistles, determined to tell her. However, he didn't get five steps before his mobile rang and, fishing it out of his pocket, he groaned when he saw Sol's number on call display.

'Work,' he mouthed to the guys before heading into the kitchen to take the call.

'Hey, Sol, what's up?'

'I need you to come into the office now. There's a potential glitch in the Hot Pursuit contract I want ironed out ASAP.'

As he watched Eve stroll across the backyard towards the house, soft and pretty and ethereal in the moonlight, the words, *Can't it wait till morning?* died on his lips.

The sooner he took care of business, the sooner he could be back at her place discussing their future.

'No worries, Sol. I'll be there in half an hour.'

'Good. See you then.'

Sol rang off and Bryce thrust the phone back into his pocket and headed for the door.

He had some serious business to take care of…once he'd ironed out the contract.

CHAPTER THIRTEEN

EVE found a shady patch of lawn and curled her feet under her, flipping open the pages of the latest spy novel.

She needed to take her mind off things, namely the fact that Bryce had said he'd drop by last night after he'd taken care of some urgent business at the office.

He'd wanted to talk. She was still waiting.

He'd sent her a text message around midnight saying he was caught up at the office and wouldn't make it and, rather than being disappointed, she'd been relieved. She didn't want him turning up at her home any more, not now.

Their deal was done.

He'd acted as her date, she'd acted like a love-starved fool and fallen for him and, rather than talk about it as the girls suggested, all she wanted to do was put the whole sorry month behind her.

She'd been crazy to concoct the scheme in the first place, though it *had* meant she hadn't been the only single bridesmaid at the wedding for once, and it *had* been fun hanging out with him, *had* been beyond flattering being charmed by him…

Shaking her head, she forced herself to concentrate on the book. Thinking like that would be self-defeating and if there was one thing she'd learned the hard way it was to think positive.

A confirmed optimist, that was her: which explained why a small part of her couldn't help but hope when Bryce had mentioned he wanted to talk, he'd meant about them.

Forget about him.

Easy for her voice of reason to say; the rest of her was having a hard time catching up.

Lifting the book in front of her face, she leaned back against the maple tree, its rigid trunk a solid comfort behind her back. She loved sitting out here on a fine day, lulled by the buzz of bees going about their business as they flitted through her flowers, tuning out the hazy traffic noise of nearby Chapel Street and Toorak Road.

This was what she could depend on, not some hotshot exec who thought nothing of dating a woman he barely knew to advance his own career.

Determinedly ignoring how unfair that was, she buried her nose deeper in her book, reading the same paragraph for the third time.

Bryce found Eve this way, her long bare legs stretched out in front of her, a pair of rimless glasses sliding down her nose and her hair in a sexy, mussed, just-out-of-bed mess.

With her frayed cut-off denim shorts and baggy red T-shirt, she looked cute and rumpled and at one with her surroundings, making him feel like an intruder. Hopefully, he wouldn't feel that way once she heard what he had to say.

Clearing his throat, he took a few steps towards her but she didn't look up, engrossed in the latest spy novel he'd heard about but hadn't had time to read yet.

It wasn't until his shadow fell across her pages did she glance up, her mouth falling open as she leaped to her feet.

'What are you doing here?' she yelled, and his welcoming smile died on his lips as he registered her horrified expression.

'Your line was busy when I called so I left you a message on your mobile. Didn't you get it?'

'Do you think I'd be looking like this if I did?'

Her hands flapped between trying to smooth her hair and tug down the hem of her shorts, adding to her air of delightful dishevelment.

'You look fine.'

He breached the short distance between them to reach out and pluck a piece of bark off her

T-shirt but, to his amazement, she shrank back and held up her hands to ward him off.

'I'm a mess. You can't see me like this!'

Dropping his hand, he thrust it into his pocket, at a total loss. Why was she freaking out like this?

'What's wrong?'

'You. Being here. Dropping in unannounced.'

Her choppy words were punctuated by short breaths as her hands resumed their fidgeting and it took all his willpower not to reach out and stop them.

'It's no big deal. It's not like we're strangers, right?'

Hurt flickered in her eyes and for the life of him he couldn't figure out what he'd said wrong this time.

'This isn't a good time for me.'

Yeah, she looked like she was super-busy, but he kept that to himself. Sarcasm would only fuel her fire at the moment, whatever had lit it.

'I'm sorry I didn't make it back last night but I need to talk to you, which is why I'm here.'

She looked straight past him, her gaze darting around as if searching for the quickest escape route.

'I'm not leaving till we talk.'

Her wary stare swung back to him, her frantic hands finally stilling as she pushed her glasses up her nose before folding her arms.

'There's really nothing left to say, is there? You don't need to act as my date any more and I'm sure you've got plenty of work to do, so—'

'I know I've been sending you mixed messages but that's why I'm here, to sort it out. Why are you acting like this?'

He couldn't bear her cold indifference a second longer and stepped into the shade, taking hold of her upper arms, hating it when she stiffened.

Her bottom lip wobbled and he almost bundled her into his arms but he needed to find out what had caused her funk, move past it and concentrate on their future. Together.

'Eve, please, talk to me.'

For a split second her gaze warmed to melted treacle before her lips thinned and she tossed her hair back as if it was immaculately coiffed rather than resembling a bird's nest.

'You can drop the charm act.'

Shrugging out of his grasp, she backed away, stopping short when she bumped into the rose arbour at her back.

'See this?'

Her hands resumed their butterfly impersonation, flapping and flitting all over the place. 'No make-up. Frizzy hair. Glasses. Comfy clothes. This is the real me.'

Her shoulders drooped ever so slightly but the fire in her eyes didn't dim one iota.

'Still the same girl underneath all the trappings. Go ahead, look, really take a good, long, hard look.' She did a bizarre little twirl as he finally twigged what this was all about. 'See? No designer clothes. No sleek hair. No contact lenses. Just plain old Eve, the girl you used to know. Not too impressive, huh?'

'Eve, you're beautiful.'

He knew he'd said the wrong thing the moment the words left his mouth for she straightened, sending him a withering glance that spoke volumes.

'You've got what you wanted out of this so there's no need to pretend any more.'

'I'm not!'

Deriving little satisfaction from her shocked expression, he lowered his voice with effort and took a deep breath. 'I'm here because I care about you. You, not the clothes you wear or how neat your hair is. Surely you know that?'

Her eyes narrowed, cool, assessing, finding him lacking when she shook her head. 'How would I?'

His heart sinking, he opened his mouth to convince her but she held up a silencing hand.

'For a while there I would've given anything to hear you say that, but not any more.'

'Why?'

'Because I can't compete with your first love.'

His confusion must've shown because she continued, 'Your work. It'll always come first.'

He opened his mouth to protest and she leapt in again.

'You can't deny it. Every time we've grown closer over the last month you've chosen your precious career over exploring what we may've started.'

Waving towards the gate, effectively dismissing him, she continued, 'We're too different, you and I. Your job is the most important thing in your life; for me, it's this place. Being able to unwind at the end of a long day, home-cooked meals, quiet time. For you, I don't think it would ever be enough.'

She tilted her chin up, challenging him to correct her. 'Go on, tell me I'm wrong.'

What could he say? He did thrive on the buzz of business: the networking, the social dinners and drinks, the party schmoozing.

So they were opposites? Big deal. Her cool, unflappable personality intrigued him, was a balm to his outgoing gregariousness. They could make this work, he had no doubts.

'Guilty as charged on the work thing but ever heard of opposites attracting?'

With a resigned shake of her head, she leaned

back against the arbour. 'Tell me what you do in your spare time.'

'What?'

'Go ahead, tell me.'

'I play golf, the occasional game of tennis, ski in the winter.'

'Alone?'

'No, usually with work colleagues or clients…' He trailed off, seeing where she was going with this.

'Want to know what I do? I volunteer at the RSPCA. Riveting stuff for a guy like you.'

Figured. She had always used to rescue wounded birds and animals as a kid, another reason he'd steered well clear of her at school back then, not wanting to be treated as another one of her strays if she'd discovered the truth.

Holding his hands out to her palm up, he kept his tone cool, controlled.

'None of this stuff matters. We're individuals; none of that has to change. We'd only be dating, for goodness' sake.'

The instant the fire in her eyes blanked and her expression shut down, he knew he'd said the wrong thing again.

'Eve, honey, we can work this out.'

His mobile rang and he muttered a curse, wishing he'd remembered to turn it off.

Sending a pointed look at his pocket, she said

in a saccharine sweet voice, 'Hadn't you better answer that?'

'No, look—'

'But it could be important. More valuable business?'

With their relationship hanging in the balance, he was inclined to say business be damned but Sol had been riding his case last night, hassling him over every little thing with the Hot Pursuit contract.

He couldn't afford to mess up with that, no matter how much he wanted her. Perhaps he could sneak a peek at the caller ID… No, this was too important. *Eve* was too important.

His hesitation cost him dearly. He could see it in the derisive curl of her upper lip, the disappointment in her eyes.

'You know something? I pity you. Even now, when we're trying to have a heart-to-heart here, you can't tune out from work.'

Only three little words resonated out of her speech.

I pity you.

No one pitied him.

Ever.

He'd had a gutful of it growing up and he sure as hell didn't need the woman he loved pitying him now.

Loved? *Loved?*

Damn, he'd always had lousy timing and it looked as if this was no exception. What a dumb time for him to realise he'd fallen in love with her, when he had no option but to walk away.

Ignoring the unusual ache in the region of his heart, he thrust his hands in his pockets. Ironically, his phone stopped ringing the moment he touched it.

'You're right. I can't. Goodbye, Eve.'

With that, he swivelled on his heel and stalked across the garden, oblivious to the beauty of dahlias and hyacinths and chrysanthemums clambering for space in her beautifully wild garden, dappled sunlight and the warmth of a perfect spring day.

He'd just laid his heart on the line.

And lost.

Eve watched Bryce stomp off, her heart splintering into itty-bitty pieces.

She'd wanted to drive him away, had done a mighty fine job of it, but she'd never expected to see genuine hurt as she'd flung her final comment at him.

He'd looked devastated, as if her opinion really mattered to him and, rather than being glad he'd gone, it took every ounce of willpower not to run after him and apologise.

She'd overreacted. Big time. Glancing down

at her oldest denim shorts and awful shapeless red-faded-to-pink T-shirt, she wrinkled her nose and sank onto the grass, resting her folded arms on her knees, her chin atop them.

No one ever saw her like this—ever—and the last man she wanted to see her so dishevelled was Bryce. She'd seen him checking her out and, while he hadn't run screaming from her yard in horror, there was no way he could be attracted to someone like her.

'You're beautiful.'

She squeezed her eyes shut, blotting out the memory of him saying those words with a tender expression in his eyes.

Was the guy blind? Delusional? Both? She looked like a fright and he'd paid her a compliment like that?

What if he'd meant it? What if she was letting the same old insecurities ruin any chance of happiness she could have with the love of her life?

Her eyes flew open as the impact of her thoughts struck her anew.

The love of her life.

Bryce was the love of her life.

Oh, heck.

Leaping off the grass, she dusted off her butt and raced towards the house. However, as she neared the back door and heard him gun the engine of his Aston Martin, her steps slowed.

What was she going to do—accost him after booting him out of the door? No, better to give him some time to cool down, get herself tidied up and then work out what she was going to say.

For she had absolutely no doubt when she spoke to him next, it would be the most important speech of her life.

CHAPTER FOURTEEN

HE'D failed.

Him, the guy who never, ever let the F word enter his head, let alone his vocabulary, had failed spectacularly with Eve.

And he hated it.

She may have acted like a crazy person when he'd showed up at her place but he'd overreacted too, stomping out like a sulky brat.

Now he'd had time to think, he knew what he had to do. He'd never failed at business, he'd be damned if he sat back and let his relationship with Eve fail before it had really begun.

She was right. He always put business first, always had. He'd never questioned why, never had any reason to. Until now. Falling in love, potentially losing that love, had him doing some serious soul-searching and, as much as it pained him, he had to face up to a few home truths.

He'd finally figured out why business was everything, why his drive to succeed went above and beyond rational human emotion.

He had to tell Eve all of it if they were to have any chance.

Now this.

When he'd landed the Hot Pursuit campaign, he had no idea he'd be based in Sydney for a good part of the next year.

It was an opportunity too good to pass up, an opportunity he'd worked his ass off for. But if they couldn't maintain a fake relationship in the same city, what hope did he have of convincing her to give a real relationship a shot, long distance?

Sitting on a plane bound for the Harbour city to start the ball rolling had given him plenty of time to think, time to plan...

When he returned, they'd have that chat he'd wanted yesterday.

This time, he wouldn't settle for anything less than gut-wrenching honesty from both of them.

He'd upped and gone to Sydney.

Just like that.

Leaving her aching and depressed and heart-broken.

She couldn't concentrate at work, couldn't face her friends and couldn't be bothered entering her kitchen, a sure sign she was in a bad, bad way.

Only one way to deal with this—head-on—

and, thankfully, some creepy colleague named Davin had let her into Bryce's office, saying it was okay to leave a note.

She sank into Bryce's chair behind his desk and reached for a pen. Her plan was to leave him a note so he wouldn't have the option of not answering her call, a likely proposition after she'd behaved like a shrieking shrew yesterday.

The memory alone made her cringe and, grabbing a pen, she found a notepad tucked under a stack of paperwork. Tapping the end of the pen against her bottom lip, she searched for the right words, mentally rehearsing a few different versions of what she wanted to say before deleting them all.

'Well, isn't this just peachy,' she muttered, the pen rapping faster and faster as she racked her brain to come up with something that didn't sound pathetic or desperate or an embarrassing combination of the two.

Her gaze drifted to the notepad, idly scanned the scribble, seeing it without actually reading it.

The squiggles soon coalesced, yet she still couldn't make sense of it and she peered closer, intrigued by the precise documentation of digital times in the left-hand column with a printed jumble of words in the right, like some kind of weird shorthand.

Probably some weird ad-world-speak and, annoyed she'd become distracted, she flipped the top page and started writing 'Dear Bryce'.

She still had no idea what she was going to say but, as the words dribbled out, she knew one thing. She owed him an apology *and* an explanation and, if he didn't respond to her note, she'd camp out on his doorstep to get him to hear her out.

He'd walked away from her once without an explanation. She'd be damned if she stood by and let him do it again.

Eve had just baked her last batch of double choc fudge brownies when the phone rang.

Wiping her hands on a dishcloth, and trying not to notice the staggering array of comfort baking on the benchtop, she answered.

'Eve, it's Bryce.'

Her heart soared as she sagged against the doorway in relief that he'd called. 'How are you?'

'Just back from Sydney, got your note.'

'Good.'

'I'd like to see you.'

He paused, as if weighing up his next words. 'Which is why I'm ringing first, of course.'

She heard the wary amusement in his tone and she couldn't help but laugh. 'Smart guy, considering my little performance the last time you dropped by. I'd like to see you too. Are you too tired to pop over now? I've baked brownies.'

'Sounds good.'

'And apple pie. And lemon tart. And a mountain of shortbread.'

His deep chuckles washed over her, low and sexy. 'Lucky I didn't eat much on the plane. I'll be there in fifteen minutes.'

'Great.'

There was so much she wanted to say, starting with *I'm sorry* and ending with *I love you*.

She settled for, 'I'm really looking forward to seeing you.'

'Same here, sweetheart.'

She rang off on a sigh, clutching the phone to her chest, his endearment reaching down to the lonely place in her soul and filling it with blossoming warmth.

Fifteen minutes.

Her gaze instantly flew to the glass cabinet opposite, seeing her reflection in all its mussed glory. She had loads of time to make herself presentable, yet, as she swivelled towards the hallway leading to her bedroom, her steps faltered.

What happened to being completely honest with him? Was a trowel-load of make-up, blow-dried hair and a designer outfit the real her?

Uh-uh. He was coming to see her and, for once, she was going to let him see the real her, without qualms, without reservations. It would make her admission all the more sincere, would put her old insecurities to rest, once and for all.

She'd been terrified he'd bolt if he saw the real her without all the trappings, the same way he'd bolted eight years ago, yet he was coming over despite seeing her at her worst that day in the garden.

Probably to tell her she was loony, but hey, he was making the effort and the least she could do was keep an open mind. She'd desperately wanted this opportunity, now all she had to do was not mess it up.

Casting one last longing look in the direction of her bedroom, where a plethora of beauty paraphernalia and designer outfits awaited her, she deliberately turned her back and returned to the benchtop.

Icing cupcakes would keep her hands busy and her mind off the terrifying thought that, despite everything she planned on saying to Bryce, he could still walk out her door and never look back.

Bryce had never been scared of anything.

He'd learned early on to face his fears, grapple and conquer them. It was how he'd survived school, how he'd gone back and got his high school diploma, how he'd got to where he was in the advertising world today.

Yet, right now, standing on Eve's doorstep clutching a bunch of her favourite violets with a very important document tucked into his jacket pocket, he had to admit to a certain amount of trepidation.

He'd come here to tell her the truth.

Would she think less of him? Would she pity him? Or, worse, would she open her heart to the possibility of them having a relationship because she considered him one of her strays who needed mollycoddling and nurturing?

He couldn't stand any of those options but he had to give it to her straight if they were to have any chance at the future he so desperately wanted.

As he raised his hand to knock again, the door swung open and he smiled, a purely instinctive response to the fresh, vibrant woman standing before him with a flour smudge on her nose and chocolate streaking her right cheek.

'Thanks for coming,' she said, holding the door open, her eyes lighting up when she spied the violets he brought out from behind his back.

'These are for you.'

'Thanks.'

She buried her nose in them, her gently mussed hair draping over the soft purple petals in a beautiful contrast of dark chocolate against deep amethyst.

He loved her hair like this, loose and curling, with that 'just out of bed' look rather than sleek and styled to within an inch of its life like she usually wore it.

Straightening, she caressed one of the petals, her genuine smile shooting straight to his heart.

'Come on in. There's a bakery's worth of cakes and pastries awaiting you.'

'Sounds great.'

He fell into step beside her, following the delicious trail of apples and cinnamon and vanilla permeating the air.

'And smells even better.'

'I think I went overboard.'

She waved towards the benchtop, and the table, and the stove. Every conceivable surface was covered in a staggering array of mouth-watering delicacies and, while his stomach grumbled accordingly, all he could think about was how much he'd like to taste the chocolate smearing her cheek.

'You like baking. Nothing wrong with that.'

'I cook when I'm nervous.'

Her gaze flickered to his and what he saw there shocked the hell out of him.

Fear.

She was as scared as he was.

Hoping his smile reassured her, he brushed his thumb against her cheek.

'Chocolate smudge,' he said when she raised an eyebrow. 'And flour here.' He tweaked her nose and she laughed, the sound warm and familiar. 'So why are you nervous?'

'The million dollar question.'

Cradling her violets like a precious bundle, she headed for the sink, rummaging for a vase underneath and giving him ample opportunity to study her.

Apart from the afternoon he'd surprised her in the backyard when she'd gone crazy, he'd never seen her so casual: worn denim jeans frayed at the cuffs, plain white singlet top and flip-flops.

He liked it, liked the fact she felt comfortable enough around him now not to get all tizzed up. In fact, the more he thought about, he realised he'd never seen her looking anything other than immaculate.

Personally, he liked looking good. His job demanded it, but there was nothing like kicking back in jeans and a T-shirt on the weekends with a healthy three-day growth.

'Are you going to answer the question?'

Sending him a wry grin, she stood and filled a cut glass vase with water. 'How much time have you got?'

'All the time in the world.'

Crossing to the breakfast bar, he pulled out a

stool and sat. 'Besides, the sooner we chat, the sooner I get to devour all this.'

Her chuckle sounded forced, nervous as she busied herself unwrapping the violets and arranging them in the vase as if she were auditioning for florist of the year.

'The flowers can wait.'

He reached across the bench separating them and laid a hand on her forearm, not surprised it gave a little tremor.

Yeah, she was as nervous as he was, but he'd be damned if he backed down now. She had to hear what he had to say.

All of it.

With a long heartfelt sigh, she placed the vase on the windowsill and nodded. 'You're right. Guess I'm just not sure where to start.'

'Don't tell me you've got some deep dark secret to unburden too?'

He'd meant it as a joke, a bit of light-hearted banter to get the ball rolling. Instead, her eyes clouded with pain and a faint blush stained her cheeks.

'Hey, I was kidding.'

She gnawed on her bottom lip, twisting a strand of hair around her index finger. 'Why don't you go first?'

'Okay, but maybe you should sit down.'

'That bad, huh?'

'Depends on your definition of bad.'

Once again, his attempt at humour fell flat as a tiny crease appeared between her brows and it was then it struck him.

She was wearing glasses again. Funny how it hadn't registered at first, but then, it was all she used to wear in high school and, while this new rimless variety was more trendy than the thick plastic frames she used to wear, they seemed a part of her, a part of the girl he knew and liked and respected, despite acting like a jerk whenever they crossed paths.

'Let's go through to the lounge room and make ourselves comfortable. Fancy a drink?'

He shook his head. 'Thanks, but I'd rather just talk.'

'Suit yourself.'

She preceded him into the lounge room and it took all his willpower not to reach out and touch her softly curling hair swinging over her shoulders to see if it felt as silky as it looked.

He deliberately waited until she chose a seat, doing an inner high-five when she sat on the three-seat sofa and he sat next to her. To her credit, she didn't scoot away or flinch but he saw the wariness in her eyes, the tension around her mouth.

And that was before he started his spiel.

Leaning back, the document in his pocket

gave a noisy crackle, as if reminding him there was no better place to start than the beginning.

Slipping his hand into his pocket, he drew it out, tapping it against his thigh, searching for the right words before deciding to jump straight in.

'I'd planned on telling you the truth that night I was going to come by but never made it because of work. And then things got botched when I dropped around that afternoon you weren't expecting me. But there's something you need to know before I explain why I went to Sydney and what it has to do with us.'

Flipping the document between his fingers, he clenched his fingers around it before holding it out. 'Here. I think you should take a look at this. It might make things clearer.'

Her puzzled frown intensified as she unfolded the paper and read it, the tip of her tongue protruding as she moved down the page at a speed he'd never hope to match. Reading wasn't his forte. Along with spelling, writing and telling the time.

Confusion creased her brow as she rattled the paper in her hand. 'What's this?'

'Remember that book report on *Pride and Prejudice* we had to submit to pass English Lit in Year Ten?'

'Uh-huh.'

'That's mine.'

Her gaze dropped to the page again before

raising to meet his, a thousand questions visible in the dark depths he'd gladly drown in.

'But—'

'It's a mess, I know.'

Taking it from her, he stared at the document that had spurred him on to get where he was today, the document with a big fat F in the top right-hand corner, the document that had effectively ended his chance of passing high school but had eventually changed his life.

Running his index finger down the page, he stared at the muddle, knowing he could almost recite the thing word for word; he'd looked at it often enough over the years. 'The b's and d's are transposed. Simple words like saw and was are confused. Words are spelled how they sound, like duz for does, pleeze for please, nock for knock, serch for search and jerney for journey. Not pretty, is it?'

Comprehension dawned as her puzzled frown disappeared. 'The lists, your note-taking, the software you wouldn't let me see, that weird shorthand I saw on your desk and this.' She stabbed at the paper. 'You're dyslexic.'

Nodding, he folded it and tossed it onto the table in front of them.

'Diagnosed courtesy of that particular masterpiece. Much too late, mind you, considering I'd failed almost everything at school by then.'

Laying a hand on his arm, she leaned closer, her soft vanilla scent enveloping him in a comforting cloud. 'I have no idea what you went through at school because of it, but look how far you've come in your career. You're at the top of your game and that's great.'

He scanned her face for the slightest hint of pity but all he saw was genuine admiration.

'Thanks. Funnily enough, while I can't spell or read or write real well, apparently I'm highly intuitive and insightful, think in pictures instead of words, have a vivid imagination, think and perceive multi-dimensionally and can use my brain to alter and create perceptions.'

Forcing a chuckle, he laid a hand over hers. 'How's that for a diagnosis?'

Her grip tightened on his arm. 'When did they discover it?'

'After I'd left school. I was throwing out a heap of junk and our neighbour who'd come over to take an old stereo saw this, asked me how I'd coped at school because his nephew was dyslexic too.'

'The teachers never picked it up?'

'The teachers just thought I was a screw-up, along with my folks.'

He could see the pity hovering in her eyes, an apology for what he'd gone through hovering on her lips and he rushed on. 'But, thanks to that guy, I discovered what I was dealing with, sought advice from experts, learned to deal with it, got my high school diploma and didn't look back.'

'That's fantastic. You should be really proud of yourself.'

'I am, but not about how I treated you because of it.'

Her eyebrows shot up. 'Me?'

Nodding, he captured both her hands in his, empowered by the understanding on her face.

'Tony's party, why I acted like a jerk at the end?'

'Uh-huh.'

'It was because of this.'

He jerked his head in the direction of the paper. 'I knew there was something wrong all through school. I didn't learn like the other kids, felt stupid because of it.'

A tiny indentation creased her brow and it took all his willpower not to lean over and kiss it away with his lips.

'We connected that night; why did you walk away?'

Squeezing her hands, he released them, dragged a nervous hand through his hair.

'Until that night, I was doing fine as long as I swaggered around pretending I was cool, making wisecracks rather than knuckling down. It was why I teased you at home, avoided you at school, because I thought someone as smart as you would see right through me.'

He shrugged, knowing his reasoning sounded trite now, feeling every kind of fool. 'That night we clicked? We hadn't seen each other in a few years, I'd always thought you were cute but aloof; yet when I strutted up to you, ready to be rebuffed when I teased, your eyes sparkled. You didn't look away or focus on the buttons on my shirt, you looked at me, really looked at me and, before I knew it, we were talking. Really talking, like I'd never talked to anyone in my life.'

She gnawed at her bottom lip, a thoughtful action that had no right being erotic.

'So it wasn't about my looks?'

Confused, he shook his head. 'Why would you think that?'

With a wry grin, she pointed at her glasses.

'The fact I wore these. And wore my hair in plaits rather than bobbed like the other girls. And had the daggiest wardrobe on the planet.'

'I didn't see any of that.'

Eve's heart swelled with joy as she scanned Bryce's face for the slightest hint he wasn't telling the truth, daring to believe when all she saw was his bright blue eyes gleaming with sincerity.

'Then what did you see?'

Her pulse stuttered and she held her breath as

he reached out, trailing his fingertips over her cheek as if memorising every dip, every curve.

'I saw an amazing girl who loved her brother and her dad, who adored wounded animals, who wanted to be the best she could be by applying herself hard. I saw a cute, intelligent girl who actually looked at me like I had something interesting to say, a girl who could make me laugh with her quick words, a shy girl transforming into an intriguing woman.'

'Yet you still walked.'

He grimaced. 'You left out the part about laughing at you.'

She blinked, the flicker of hurt in her eyes slugging him hard. 'Remember what we were talking about before I almost kissed you?'

Remember? She remembered every tiny detail about that night, despite all attempts to forget.

She nodded. 'Our dreams for the future.'

'That's right. I was so caught up in our conversation, I almost spilled my guts and I couldn't let that happen. At that time, with your brains, you were always going to be successful while I thought I was stupid and didn't know why.'

Her heart flipped, realising what he'd been through, and she reached out to him, covered his lips with her fingers. 'It's okay, you don't have to—'

'I want to; let me finish.' He captured her

hand, lowered it. 'When you were talking about your dreams for the future, I'd never seen anything so beautiful. You glowed, your face was alive and I had to kiss you. Then those jerks interrupted and I had a reality check. In a few hours, I'd let you get closer than anyone and it scared the hell out of me. I couldn't offer you anything, I was a nobody and you were chasing a dream. I had to push you away.'

He shook his head, his smile wry. 'So I laughed along with those guys, pretended what we'd shared meant nothing, and walked away.'

Stunned, she assimilated the truth, silently berating herself for believing the worst all these years, thanks to her own insecurities, focused on the one thing he'd said that she couldn't forget.

'You thought I was cute? I glowed? But I was a geek.'

His hand slid around to cradle her head while he leaned closer, his lips hovering near her ear.

'An adorable geek.'

Her breath caught as he brushed the softest kiss on her cheek, a barely-there movement reminiscent of the flimsiest flutter of butterfly wings against her skin.

She tilted her head to the right ever so slightly, rewarded by a groan as he captured her mouth in a feverish kiss, a hot, raw melding of lips that sent ecstasy spiralling out of control through her.

Shivers of delight ran down her spine as his mouth grazed hers hungrily, repeatedly, his tongue tracing the contours of her lips, dipping into the recesses of her mouth, searching, ravaging, searing a path directly to her soul.

When he kissed her like this, she felt beautiful and treasured and special, rendering her old insecurities irrelevant. When he kissed her like this, she could almost believe that, for one magical moment, they had a chance.

But they didn't. No matter what he'd said, no matter how badly she wanted a relationship, he still wasn't the guy for her. How could he be, when he'd flit off to whichever end of the earth his precious career took him?

He stilled and pulled away, cradling her face in his hands, his eyes shining with passion.

'What's wrong?'

She had to tell him the truth.

It was what tonight was all about but, now the moment had arrived, her gut churned with nerves and her palms grew clammy.

Truth was nice in theory, in the wee small hours of the morning, alone with her thoughts. Putting it into practice with the guy she'd fallen in love with staring at her with tenderness was the pits.

'Don't you want to know why I acted like a crazy person when you dropped by unannounced?'

A soft smile curved his lips. 'Does it matter?'

Oh, yeah. He needed to know why; he needed to know all of it.

'Eve?'

Blinking, she reached up to his hands and disengaged them from her face. She couldn't think, let alone speak with him touching her, no matter how incredible it felt.

'This is the real me.'

He raised an eyebrow, following her hands as she waved them up and down. 'I know.'

'I'm not glamorous. Or elegant. Or super-cool.'

His mouth kicked into a smile. 'Considering some of those sexy suits you wear to work, I beg to differ.'

Her heart sinking, she shook her head. 'Those clothes, the make-up, the blow-dried hair, are all an illusion. A confidence mask I need to step out that door and face the world.'

His smile faded as he absorbed the impact of her words. 'But you're brilliant. And gorgeous. Why would you need any sort of mask?'

Sinking back into the sofa, she covered her face with her hands. How could she explain without sounding like a freak?

'Eve, tell me.'

He gently pried her hands free, his forehead creased with concern.

'This is going to sound ridiculous.'

'Try me.'

He hadn't released her hands and, for a moment, she was grateful. Having him hold her steady, infusing her with solid warmth, was beyond comforting.

Taking a deep breath, she tightened her grip on his hands. 'My new image? The clothes, the make-up, the hair? Courtesy of you.'

He frowned. 'I don't follow.'

'Tony's party was the first night I wore a dress, lipstick, contacts. And you noticed me, treated me like a woman and it felt great.'

'Then I walked. Some guy.'

She hoped her gentle smile went some way to erasing the bitterness lacing his words.

'Actually, whether you walked or not, you did me a favour. The time we spent together? Talking, laughing, flirting? I'd never felt that way before. It felt good, damn good, and I wanted to feel that way all the time. And if wearing that stuff made me feel good, got that kind of attention—' she shrugged sheepishly '—I wanted people to look at me like that all the time. So I undertook major makeovers. Chose a career where people would look at me and think how fabulously glamorous I was...'

She trailed off, feeling suddenly foolish.

'And?'

'The woman I've become is not who I am.

Despite all the trimmings, I'm still an insecure introvert who's terrified of anyone discovering the truth.'

When his frown deepened, she continued, 'I'm a fraud. I hide behind my business and my clothes and my image, dead scared of anyone getting too close.'

'Why?'

He squeezed her hands gently, encouraging, and she knew she had to tell him everything, despite the urge to clam up.

'Because I lose everyone who gets too close.'

There, she'd said it, enunciated her greatest fear and, rather than badger her or belittle her admission, he released her hands to slide an arm around her shoulder, snuggling her into the protective circle.

'Is this about your dad?'

'Mum, Dad, Tony—all of them.'

'Don't forget me. We got close that night and I walked too.'

She focused on the seam of her jeans and a tiny fray, hating the helpless feeling welling, the same feeling that had swamped her after her dad's death and the extent of her loss had really become apparent.

'You to a lesser degree, but you know Mum died when Tony and I were toddlers so that wasn't as hard to take as Dad dying.'

'There's more, isn't there?'

Sighing, she nodded. 'Dad had so many debts, we lost the family home. Tony and I had nothing. And then Tony up and left a few years later.'

He muttered a curse, cuddling her closer. 'And you were totally alone.'

She nodded, remembering the emptiness, the fear, the grief.

'It's why I've shut myself off, why I don't get too close emotionally to anyone. It's not worth the risk, not worth the pain.'

A fragile silence greeted her pronouncement, stretching into uncomfortable, and she risked a glance at his face. What she saw there took her breath away.

Raw vulnerability, totally at odds with his usual confidence.

'What about me?'

'You?'

Tipping up her chin, he stared into her eyes, mesmerising, compelling. 'Am I worth the risk?'

Confusion clouded her brain. Was he asking what she thought he was asking...? Did he want her to take a chance on him emotionally?

Scanning his face for some clue as to his feelings, she plucked at the frayed seam until he stilled her nervous fingers with his hand.

'You're not the only one who shut off from people. I've done my fair share of hiding.'

She scanned his face, surprised at the pain and regret clouding his eyes. 'Hiding from your dyslexia?'

He shook his head, his remorse intensifying. 'I've never had a relationship. Casual dates, plenty, but I never felt truly confident enough to let a woman get close until I was financially successful.'

'Why?'

'Because I've always seen my dyslexia as a flaw. Crazy, I know, because it's readily diagnosed these days and kids get the assistance they need much earlier. But I grew up thinking I was dumb and, when I finally discovered the truth, I still saw it as a defect, a failing. Being financially successful would offset an imperfection like that.'

'Nobody's perfect!'

'I know but, considering my parents' frigid marriage, my lack of close emotional intimacy with anyone, I guess it was as good an excuse as any to never get involved emotionally.'

'Oh.'

Guess that put paid to her hopes for a long and meaningful relationship.

'Until now.'

Her dashed hopes leaped, twirled, did a little jig.

'I asked you a few minutes ago if I was worth

the risk. Maybe this will make it easier for you to answer.'

His gaze locked on hers, sincere and honest and filled with an emotion that snatched air from her lungs. 'I'm in love with you. I want us to have a real relationship, to develop what we've started over this last month.'

His mouth kicked into a heart-warming grin. 'I want us to create fireworks.'

Her heart seized as numbness at his declaration melted into a comforting warm and fuzzy happiness. She wanted to believe him, to take a chance.

But her self-preservation mechanisms were too ingrained, too entrenched. Losing her dad and Tony had hurt, but nothing in comparison to what she'd go through if she opened her heart completely to Bryce and lost the love of her life.

He'd walked away from her once when she'd got too close—he'd said it—so what would stop him doing it again?

Taking a deep breath, hating what she had to do, she slowly slipped out of his embrace. 'I'm sorry, I can't.'

Striding across the room, she propped herself against the marble fireplace, blinking back tears, willing the sobs bubbling from deep within to subside.

'I'm not going anywhere.'

'It's better you do,' she murmured, clenching the mantelpiece so hard her knuckles stood out.

'I mean in the future.'

She jumped as he placed a hand on her shoulder, so wrapped up in her misery she hadn't heard him sneak up on her.

Whirling to face him, she shrugged off his hand, needing to end this now before she broke down completely. 'You will. You'll leave as soon as the next big job offer comes your way. Your work defines you. It's who you are.'

He opened his mouth to respond and she held up a hand.

'You said so yourself. And after learning about your dyslexia tonight, I understand. With every step up the career ladder you take, you triumph over your learning disability, over all those who ever doubted you. I get that. I respect you for it. But I won't hand you my heart, only to have it carved up when you jet off in search of the next big opportunity that comes your way.'

Rather than her words antagonising him, he merely thrust his hands in his pockets and rocked back on his heels, his expression patient.

'Why do you think I told you about my dyslexia?'

That flummoxed her.

Now she came to think about it, he didn't have

to tell her. How he'd treated her as a teenager had no bearing on the here and now.

'I have no idea.'

Sliding his hands out of his pockets, he held them out to her, palm up, as if he had nothing to hide.

'Because I trust you. I've been doing some serious thinking, figuring out why I'm so hung up on work and I've finally worked out that the harder I strive, the easier it is to ignore I have a problem, something I face and fight every day.'

Her resolve weakened but, before she could respond, he ploughed on.

'I told you because I want you to know what you're getting into with me, faults and all. Because I thought we shared something special over this last month. Because I thought you might feel something for me and, if it's half of what I feel for you, it's worth fighting for.'

The tears that had been threatening for the last few minutes spilled over in an angry torrent, splashing against her glasses, blurring her vision.

'Eve, honey.'

He bundled her in his arms before she could resist and, slipping off her glasses and flinging them onto a nearby chair, she buried her face in his chest and let the tears fall in great gushes, drenching his T-shirt, emptying her soul.

She clutched at him while he soothed her,

shushed her, smoothing her hair, her back, gentle soothing strokes that lulled her until she had nothing left to give.

When the last sob subsided, she took a great shuddering breath and pulled away, all too aware of how she must look: blotchy skin, red nose, bloodshot puffy eyes.

Swiping a hand across her eyes, she focused on the damp patch spreading across his chest.

'I must look a fright.'

Tipping her chin up, he said, 'You look like the woman I'm in love with.'

Wrenching out of his grip, she stepped back, the mantelpiece digging into her back.

'I'm not that woman. The last month has been a sham and, after what I've just told you, surely you know I'm not the right woman for you? You're extroverted and outgoing and spontaneous. I'm introverted and shy and private. I'm a homebody, you're a mover and shaker. Stability is everything to me, this place is everything. Your business will always come first—'

'Shh…' He placed a finger against her lips, effectively shutting her up. 'That's another thing I wanted to tell you. I went to Sydney to organise a stand-in for me.'

'Stand-in for what?'

'The Hot Pursuit contract would've had me in Sydney for most of the year.'

'Then what are you doing here?'

'Because my business doesn't always come first. Time to put down some roots and I want to make Melbourne my base.'

'Oh.'

'With you,' he added, in case she hadn't understood that part.

Her resolve wavered. He'd chosen her over his precious business. Some statement—and proof he must really, truly love her.

Could it be this simple? Despite their differences, despite her insecurities?

Gripped by a strange compulsion to prove her point one last time, she flapped her hands around.

'Look at me. Really look at me and tell me I'm the woman you want.'

Stepping into her personal space, he grasped her upper arms.

'Don't you know me well enough by now? Don't you have any idea what I find most attractive about you? This.'

He placed a hand over her heart, his palm burning her, branding her through the thin cotton of her T-shirt. 'Your warmth. Your compassion. Your vitality. Yes, I think you're hot and yes, I love those sexy little suits you wear, but guess what? In all the time we dated, real or otherwise, you were cutest when all ruffled and flustered in that baggy top and cut-off shorts, with your hair looking like a flock of magpies had nested in it.'

She opened her mouth to protest. The guy had to be certifiable if he thought she looked cute when she was at her worst: which was pretty much how she was at home most of the time.

Before she had a chance to say anything, he held his fingers over her mouth.

'I love you now. I'll love you when you're old and grey and wrinkly and toothless. I'll love you when gravity has done its worst. So how do you feel about that? Think you can handle having me around that long?'

Her heart expanded with love—love for this crazy, spontaneous, fun-loving guy who'd swept into her life and made her feel—really feel—for the first time in for ever.

She'd emotionally shut down after her dad died, after Tony left, and now she had this amazing man offering her the world.

What was she waiting for?

The corners of her mouth twitched as she gently pushed away his hand, intertwining her fingers with his. 'You know, I've heard gravity sucks. You sure you want to stick around that long?'

His loud cheer, complete with victory punch in the air, left her in little doubt as to his true feelings.

'I'm sure,' he said, a second before his lips crushed hers in a breath-stealing, toe-curling kiss that left her weak-kneed and trembling and wanting him more than ever.

Smiling against his mouth, she braced her palms against his chest, relishing the rock-hard muscles beneath, eager to explore what she could quite smugly term as hers now.

'Old and wrinkly?'

He nodded, his slow, sexy smile warming her better than the chocolate brownies she'd devoured in a fit of nerves before he'd arrived.

'Yeah, I'll still be around when you're ancient and creased and crinkled all over.'

Laughing, she slid her palms upwards and slung her hands around his neck, toying with the soft hair at his nape.

'Grey and toothless too?'

'Oh, yeah, you can't get rid of me, even when you're a fully fledged member of the blue-rinse brigade and your falsies are in a cup next to mine on the bed stand.'

'How romantic!'

He joined in her laughter, his eyes warm and glowing, radiating a love she'd never dreamed possible while his hands slowly strummed her back, strong and sure and tantalising.

'We're the real deal, Eve.'

'No more deals.'

She stood on tiptoe and pressed a tender, tantalising kiss against his lips. 'Unless you count the one where I intend to make an honest man out of you.'

He groaned and leaned his forehead against hers. 'Let me guess. You want to become a bridal babe.'

Despite his flippancy, her heart clenched with the impact of committing to this man for the rest of her life.

'I do.'

She cupped his cheek and stared into the clear blue eyes she could quite happily spend a lifetime looking into.

Wearing the goofy grin of a guy who'd had all his dreams come true, he picked her up, spun her around until she was dizzy and giggling, finally halting and sliding her down in delicious full frontal contact.

'I guess Eve Gibson has a nice ring to it,' he said, nuzzling her neck until she squealed.

'Is that a proposal?'

Her breath caught as he nipped the sensitive skin above her collarbone, sending shivers of longing racing through her body.

'You bet. How soon do you want to become a bridal babe?'

Her, a bride? Surreal. When she'd devised her crazy plan to not be the last single bridesmaid at Mattie's wedding, little had she known how far she'd go to stay off it permanently!

'Soon, my love, soon. How about we date for a while so you get to see me like this all the time? For now, there's a kitchen full of goodies that need to be eaten and I've heard the way to a man's heart is through his stomach.'

Capturing her hand, he placed it against his heart, where it beat strong and solid beneath her palm.

'My heart's already all yours. For always.'

As his mouth brushed hers in a sweet lingering kiss, Eve had never felt so secure, so cherished, so loved.

Bryce was her present, her future, her dream.

And she had no intention of waking up any time soon.

EPILOGUE

'SWEETIE, the caterers want to know if it's time to serve dessert.'

Eve dragged her starry-eyed gaze away from her husband, talking to AJ on the periphery of the dance floor, and turned to Mattie. 'Sure, tell them to lay everything out on the buffet table, let people help themselves.'

Mattie shook her head. 'I can't believe you did all this.'

Eve shrugged. 'It's what I do.'

'For a job! You should've let someone else organise your wedding.'

'Bryce and I wanted it this way.'

A step back in time, he'd said, a chance to do things right.

She'd been hesitant at first, with so many spectacular venues in Melbourne for a wedding, but the moment they'd stepped into this place, hand in hand, she'd known.

It was meant to be.

The old nightclub on the shores of Albert Park Lake might have undergone renovations and a name change but, as they'd stepped out onto the balcony, memories had bombarded her, and when her fiancé had led her to the rail, enveloped her in his arms and kissed her the way she'd craved all those years ago, she couldn't think of any other place she'd rather get married.

'You're a pair of sentimental fuddy-duddies.' Mattie rolled her eyes, her smile soft. 'Can't wait to see what you do for your tenth anniversary.'

Slipping an arm around her friend's waist, Eve squeezed. 'Whatever it is, you and the other babes will be around to see it.'

Mattie's faux huff lasted all of two seconds. 'If you had to give us a nickname, I suppose we should be thankful we're babes.'

Eve laughed. 'Bryce never should've told you.'

Mattie held up her pinkie, wiggled it. 'You're not the only one who has him wrapped around this. He's no match for all of us.'

'Poor guy.'

'You lovely ladies talking about me?'

Eve sighed and melted against her husband's solid chest as he slid his arms around her from behind.

'All good things.' Mattie winked. 'Now, some bossy events coordinator has given me a job to do, so I better go do it.'

'Thanks.'

As Mattie sashayed away, resplendent in her floor-length amethyst raw silk bridesmaid sheath, Eve turned in the circle of Bryce's arms.

'You've done an amazing job today.'

She tilted her head up, her eyes fluttering closed as Bryce brushed a tender kiss across her lips, an all-too-brief kiss if the tightening of his arms around her waist and the sudden flare of heat between them was any indication.

'It wasn't a job. It was a labour of love.'

'Our love.'

He trailed a fingertip down her cheek, across her jaw, tracing her bottom lip. 'I love you, Mrs Gibson.'

He ducked his head, kissed her again, murmuring against the corner of her mouth, 'And, at the risk of repeating myself for the hundredth time, you look utterly ravishing.'

'What, this old thing?'

She glanced down at her tailor-made empire line gown in rich alabaster satin, her eyes widening even now, after a day of wearing the exquisite wedding gown. For, no matter how many times she saw herself in this stunning dress, she'd never get used to it.

Today, the bridesmaid had become the bride. And she couldn't be happier.

Resting his hand on her hip, Bryce's intense stare travelled down her body and back up, a slow, sensual perusal that left her in little doubt what would happen later when the gown slipped off.

'You know, as gorgeous as you look in this, it wouldn't have mattered what you wore today; you're always beautiful to me.'

Tears stung the back of her eyes, the power of his simple declaration cradling her heart, reinforcing how lucky she'd been to take a chance on this incredible man all these years later.

'So you wouldn't have cared if I'd shown up in a grungy T-shirt, daggy denim shorts and glasses?'

'Not a bit.'

'Bird's nest hair? No make-up? Jewellery-free?'

'Wouldn't matter.'

Laying a hand on his shoulder, she leaned forward, stood on tiptoe to whisper in his ear. 'In nothing at all?'

'Now you're talking.'

His arms tightened around her waist, his fierce hug saying more than words ever could.

Bryce Gibson loved her, whatever she wore, however she looked, the ultimate reassurance for the shy geek girl she'd once been, who'd taken full advantage of her Cinderella moment and morphed into a fully fledged bride.

'Follow me.'

He released her, slipped her hand in his and Eve knew she would follow this man wherever he led for the rest of her life.

They stepped out onto the balcony overhanging the lake, the Melbourne cityscape casting a mauve tinge against the night sky, moved to the furthest corner away from their guests.

She remembered this spot, remembered everything about that fateful night—the night that had ultimately led her here, to this moment, with this man.

Sliding his hands around her waist, Bryce tugged her close. 'We once talked about dreams in this very spot.'

'How could I forget?'

'I just wanted you to know that having you in my life, being married to you, has made mine come true.'

As he lowered his head, his lips warm and firm in a lingering kiss, she melded against him, secure in the knowledge she was finally living her dream too.

FREE ONLINE READ!

One Indian Summer

by Nicola Marsh

Don't miss this short story linked to
Nicola Marsh's novel in
Destination: Summer Weddings!

To read your free online story, just go to:

www.millsandboon.co.uk/oneindiansummer

MILLS & BOON®
are proud to present a new series

Three dramatic and sensual tales of paranormal romance
available every month from June 2010

The excitement begins with a thrilling quartet:

TIME RAIDERS:

Only they can cross the boundaries of time; only they
have the power to save humanity.

The Seeker by Lindsay McKenna

21st May

The Slayer by Cindy Dees

21st May

The Avenger by PC Cast

4th June

The Protector by Merline Lovelace

18th June

millsandboon.co.uk Community

Join Us!

The Community is the perfect place to meet and chat to kindred spirits who love books and reading as much as you do, but it's also the place to:

- **Get the inside scoop from authors about their latest books**
- **Learn how to write a romance book with advice from our editors**
- **Help us to continue publishing the best in women's fiction**
- **Share your thoughts on the books we publish**
- **Befriend other users**

Forums: Interact with each other as well as authors, editors and a whole host of other users worldwide.

Blogs: Every registered community member has their own blog to tell the world what they're up to and what's on their mind.

Book Challenge: We're aiming to read 5,000 books and have joined forces with The Reading Agency in our inaugural Book Challenge.

Profile Page: Showcase yourself and keep a record of your recent community activity.

Social Networking: We've added buttons at the end of every post to share via digg, Facebook, Google, Yahoo, technorati and de.licio.us.

www.millsandboon.co.uk

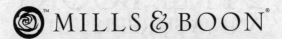

2 FREE BOOKS
AND A SURPRISE GIFT

We would like to take this opportunity to thank you for reading this Mills & Boon® book by offering you the chance to take TWO more specially selected books from the Romance series absolutely FREE! We're also making this offer to introduce you to the benefits of the Mills & Boon® Book Club™—

- **FREE home delivery**
- **FREE gifts and competitions**
- **FREE monthly Newsletter**
- **Exclusive Mills & Boon Book Club offers**
- **Books available before they're in the shops**

Accepting these FREE books and gift places you under no obligation to buy, you may cancel at any time, even after receiving your free shipment. Simply complete your details below and return the entire page to the address below. You don't even need a stamp!

YES Please send me 2 free Romance books and a surprise gift. I understand that unless you hear from me, I will receive 5 superb new stories every month including two 2-in-1 books priced at £4.99 each and a single book priced at £3.19, postage and packing free. I am under no obligation to purchase any books and may cancel my subscription at any time. The free books and gift will be mine to keep in any case.

Ms/Mrs/Miss/Mr _____ Initials _____

Surname _____

Address _____

_____

_____ Postcode _____

E-mail _____

Send this whole page to: Mills & Boon Book Club, Free Book Offer, FREEPOST NAT 10298, Richmond, TW9 1BR.